ALSO BY DIANE JOHNSON

Fiction
Persian Nights
Lying Low
The Shadow Knows
Burning
Loving Hands at Home
Fair Game

Nonfiction
Dashiell Hammett: A Life
Terrorists and Novelists
Lesser Lives

Health and Happiness

Health
and
Happiness

Diane Johnson

Alfred A. Knopf

New York

1990

THIS IS A BORZOI BOOK
PUBLISHED BY ALFRED A. KNOPF, INC.

ISBN 0-394-58717-0
LC 90-53111

Manufactured in the United States of America
First Edition

This book is dedicated to
JOHN MURRAY,
who, however, should not be thought
responsible for my viewpoint,
and to my many other friends who are doctors,
with affection and apologies.

A high moral tone
can hardly be said to conduce
very much either to
one's health or one's happiness.

OSCAR WILDE,
The Importance of Being Earnest

Health and Happiness

1

Alta Buena Hospital occupies one square block in the center of a residential neighborhood, convenient for the rest of the city but inconvenient for its neighbors, with the parking problems it brings, and its fortresslike shape of reinforced concrete casting shadows on neighboring gardens of privet and struggling geranium. Inside, every amenity of a modern interior environment—blond wood, carpets, plants, and skylights—gives an air of a prosperous corporate headquarters, masculine and comfortable, and the female voice over the loudspeaker system, calling for doctors or announcing Code Blue emergencies, speaks in the polite international accent of an airport page, with its reassuring intimations of ordered departures, safe returns.

This voice did something to soothe the apprehensions of Ivy Tarro, a young woman waiting outside the X-Ray Department for the results of a test they had done, dyeing her veins blue and then watching for—they had explained it, but in her fear she had not understood. Her expression, she knew, must be like that of the other people waiting, huddled in their x-ray paper clothes—shame, chagrin, and resignation lending to each countenance an aspect of almost criminal secretiveness that contrasted with the serene assurance you saw in the faces of the nurses and doctors and orderlies and technicians and interns and volunteers hurrying through with their important errands, carrying papers and fluids in glass bottles.

"DR. WATTS. DR. PHILIP WATTS," said the loudspeaker.

Ivy Tarro had never seen her physician, Dr. Evans, before this morning, and already her eyes, like the eyes of a devoted dog—so she felt—scrutinized the door to the X-Ray Department, through which he would walk, in hopes each next person would be he, with news.

2

Dr. Evans was having a minor run-in with the chief attending man, Dr. Philip Watts, a senior professor of medicine, on the issue of getting a private bed for this girl, Ivy Tarro. With private physicians like Evans, Watts could be territorial and uncooperative, preferring to fill the beds with "teaching" cases. Alta Buena Hospital served the prosperous Bay Area community as part of the university medical school, providing excellent private care and also training for interns and residents under the supervision of both full-time professors of medicine and the most reputable practicing physicians. This arrangement was serviceable but cumbersome in that the academic doctors did not always approve of the pragmatism of the community practitioners, and these in turn often became impatient with the abstract and analytic approach of the academics.

Besides serving private patients—people who expected and received the most modern and sophisticated medical care available anywhere, with, also, a certain amount of luxury and comfort—Alta Buena Hospital, for legal and contractual reasons as well as humanitarian ones, took more than its share of the indigent, the poor, elderly, victims and drunks off the street—even people brought in chains by the cops. Though the medical care these poor people received was the same, or better, than the private patients got, they did have to support the inconvenience of interns and residents crowding around their beds, and of hearing their diseases, and their personal habits, discussed.

Had today been yesterday, Evans would have had no problem getting a private bed, but today was December 1, a day of turmoil and changes at the hospital, when all the medical teams and volunteers rotated wards, new interns and residents came to each service, and also a new chief of medicine rotated through—this month, Watts—whose character and habits would set the tone of things until the new year.

Philip Watts was idealistic and demanding. The housestaff of interns and residents had mixed feelings about his months on duty. They admired his diagnostic acumen and his wisdom and humanity, and they enjoyed his lively disagreements with the surgeons, whom he considered a pack of irresponsible butchers. But he was exacting, not least with himself, spending hours far into the night, and though the younger doctors always felt that they learned from him, they also feared his grave look of disappointment at any mistake or omission, his sharp tongue, and his unforgiving attitude to human frailty. He disdained to have a private practice himself, saying that he was uncomfortable taking money from sick people. Fortunately, his wife, Jennifer, had some money.

At this moment, there was one bed left on medical Ward 3F, and Watts wanted to fill it with an elective bronchial biopsy he had told to come in today. But the rules were specific, that a private, paying patient would be given priority, so Watts, after a token grumble, was forced to allot the bed to Bradford Evans's patient.

"But it sounds like the kind of thing you could easily treat at home with indomethacin," he couldn't forbear pointing out.

"In my experience, you better go after these things aggressively, and in the long run the illness is shorter and less dangerous," Evans disagreed, and went down to Admitting to organize it.

3

Loping up to the elevator without looking, Mimi Franklin suddenly saw Dr. Bradford Evans, and as usual they each looked away in deep embarrassment. She thought of Bradford Evans as her particular enemy. They might have been in high school, Mimi thought, from the way, remembering what had passed between them, they couldn't meet each other's eye.

She stared, as if in deep concentration, at the titles on her book cart, and when the up elevator came, flung herself into it, pulling the cart over the toe of a nurse. As coordinator of Volunteer Services, a salaried job, Mimi had a myriad of duties: the book cart, scheduling volunteers to push wheelchairs and read to the blind, editing the auxiliary newsletter, and often filling in for the volunteers themselves—a corps of candy-stripers and retired people of the upper middle class who volunteered to run errands and raise funds, but who often had to cancel or change their days of service.

For no particular reason, running into Bradford ("Buck") Evans like this seemed to Mimi an inauspicious development in a morning that had begun well. She had waked up with a pleasant sense of excitement and possibility, as she had been doing lately, an upward leap of consciousness toward the day ahead, as if she were traveling in a strange country. Though people had told her she would be forlorn when her children went off to college and her nest was empty, she was not. After only a few days, the oddness of the still house had been replaced by a feeling that her life would now open out in some unspecified way. Images, as yet formless, of new possibilities gathered during sleep. She dreamed of love and travel.

Possibility, change, a certain sense of accomplishment when it came to her children, Daniel and Narnia, whom she had raised alone. She thought they had turned out very well, and everyone told her so, too. And now—she was not yet forty—something could happen in her own life. Young enough that she could even have another baby!—though that was certainly not her plan.

And people had recently been telling her how pretty she was looking. She could not see that particular thing herself, because she had always hated her tallness, the length of her neck, pictures of herself like a giraffe peering over the heads of others. But she knew that people treated her like a pretty woman, not a plain one. How disparate, she had often thought, the outer and the inner self, and how importantly the outer one shaped the life you were to live, like it or not. When Narnia's slightly protuberant ears had drawn some kindergarten teasing, Mimi had had them surgically corrected, as promptly and matter-of-factly as she could, so that the ears would never get to be a subject in Narnia's life. She thought of herself as a person who did sensible actions of this kind.

But running into Bradford Evans reminded her that she could be a fool, too, for she realized, as the elevator doors opened again, that in her confusion she had ridden past her stop and returned to 3F, where Bradford Evans was still waiting for the down car, and she was obliged to meet his eye again and feel her face go bright purple. She had never outgrown this curse of blushing like a beet. She pushed the cart out past him, as if she had meant to arrive here all the time.

4

On Ward 3F, the new team of doctors, headed by Philip Watts, was beginning rounds. Mimi saw them walking together, checking on every patient and discussing the treatment. They came past the nurses' station, pausing outside each door, disappearing inside, reappearing with smiles of relief or an alert silence, studying each other's eyes. Sometimes they waited until the doors were closed after them before they spoke. The hot, close rooms gave their cheeks a pinkish, excited cast. Anyone watching them could tell who was getting better, who might die.

Together, a bunch of doctors developed an aura, it always seemed to Mimi, a sort of hum surrounding them, a halo of lordly goodness, though of course she knew she was just projecting it onto them. She had wanted to be a doctor herself.

The new team of doctors ranged in size from the resident, Mark Silver, and Lum Wei-chi, an intern from Beijing, who were the shortest, to another intern, Perry Briggs, a giant young man. Back in their offices, on their coatracks or hung over the backs of their chairs would be a variety of frayed tweed coats or motorcycle jackets or old sweaters, but armored in their uniform white coats, they were beautiful, even the homely Brian Smeed, whom everyone imagined to be chinless beneath his piebald beard. Of them all, the chief, Philip Watts, was most like a television doctor, serious, handsome, idealistic, formal, and irascible. Mimi had also heard him called stubborn or conceited. Since she and Philip Watts were friendly, she had never felt this, but supposed it might be true that he was so used to being right he might have ceased to examine or reproach his own actions. This was a common flaw of doctors.

He was tan from tennis and running, athletic, beginning at forty-five to be gray. "No one, so far as I know, has ever tried to make him," Head Nurse Carmel Hodgkiss had observed. It was she who best kept track of love and sex at Alta Buena. "Not that it couldn't be done."

Nurses were strategic about doctors, speculating on their hobbies and their wives, but doctors filled Mimi, even at her age, with a kind of turmoil. Once when she had gone to bed with . . . one of them, there had been a moment when she sensed, she thought, in his caresses, a certain flutter of alertness, of professional alarm, a certain attention in his fingertips, as if he had felt a lump, and it had frightened her. She had never confided that passage, that impulsive afternoon, to the nurses, especially not to the predatory Carmel Hodgkiss, who would have been interested to hear of frailty and possibility in yet another of the oh-so-married doctors.

5

A kaleidoscope of recollections of this frightening morning was tumbling through Ivy Tarro's mind as she waited, uncertain whether to put her own clothes on again. It was only ten o'clock, it was only an hour ago that it had all begun. She remembered the way the doctor's fingers, prodding her armpit at the edge of her breast, had touched a tender spot that had made her jump.

Looking into her face without seeing it, he had said, "Nothing there that I can feel." That was one thing to be thankful for. He had lifted her heavy, swollen arm and poked again. This was the first time Ivy could remember feeling mortal fear about her own body, had only felt this same *frisson* of panic in the second a stepladder swayed, or when a bus bearing down on her seemed not to see her, or footsteps started up behind her in a dark street.

Surreptitiously her eyes strayed again to her swollen arm, puffed up like a great white sausage. It might have been this way for days. When do you look at your arm, really? She remembered the slight peppermint- or mouthwash-clean smell of the doctor. Now she fastened her eyes on the X-Ray Department door, compelling him with her will to come through it. Doctor wearing bowtie. A sick feeling in her stomach. She remembered her visit to his office, the doctor leaning as close as a lover to feel her armpit from a certain angle, with brow tunneled in concern.

"Venogram," he had said. "We'll have to get a venogram. I'm going to the hospital now anyway. I'll take you over and get you started."

"Right now?"

"Something circulatory. We need to find out what's going on."

She had reached for her blouse, put it on, and begun to button it. There seemed nothing to say. Her mind filled with questions, but she couldn't make herself ask them. She could think of no alternatives to doing as he said. What did she know about her circulation? Yet she had thought that she knew her body, and that it was hers.

"I'll have to call the babysitter," she had said.

And the doctor had pushed a button and said loudly, "Molly, Mrs. Tarro needs to use the phone. I'm taking her over to Alta Buena. Did you come in your car?"

Ivy shook her head. She'd come on the bus. "How long shall I say I'll be?" she asked.

"It could take till noon." Noon!

"I'll drive you," he said. "I want you to take this pill."

In the car, politely, not accustomed to talking about herself and her ailments, she talked to the doctor about the traffic, and parking problems, and the recent election—this last carefully. Doctors are so conservative. BMW. Divorced, she imagined. Portly and pleasant, guarding his secret assessment of her dire condition, soothing her with small talk, not speaking of her arm at all. Then it had seemed that the pill he had given her had already begun to make her feel dizzy, and when she turned her head, the thing she was looking at seemed to lag behind.

"We park here, this is the doctors' parking lot," he had said, and politely, like a man, not like a doctor, like someone on a date, he had come around to open the door for her. As someone would do for someone really ill. Her alien arm lay on her lap and she had avoided looking at it or him. Something was written over the door of the hospital, as over the gates of hell, but in her anxiety she didn't read what it said.

Why should this be happening to her, she was thinking now, crouched in this x-ray cubicle in her paper dress. Why now, in her days of health and happiness, with her new baby, and the return of her body to its strong and slender state?

All at once Dr. Evans was standing before her. "I'm afraid we'll have to keep you," he said.

6

As he led the younger doctors on their rounds from room to room, Philip Watts was thinking that although the month was beginning with even more problems than usual—the clash with Evans, a rumor of cocaine among the interns, an impending crisis in the care of one of the patients, Randall Lincoln—nonetheless he was not as worried about them as he might have been. His detachment was probably due to his accepting another job, as the chairman of a new clinical research unit, to be located in a former VA hospital, under the auspices of Stanford University. This conspicuous career advancement had not yet been publicly announced, but rumor had made it widely known among his colleagues. Making up his mind to do it had cleared up a tormenting ambivalence that had been unsettling both him and Jennifer, and now he felt cheerful and eager to get started. He had been a little uneasy about giving up clinical medicine. After all, he had become a doctor to help people. But the trade-off was that he would have more time to pursue his research interests, and research, of course, ultimately helped a greater number of people. He was interested in the reflex control of blood flow and, together with some marine biologists at Steinhardt Aquariumwas following certain effects of this in diving mother seals. This interdisciplinary study had been stimulating, and he hoped to broaden interdisciplinary approaches to clinical research when he took over at the new place.

And anyway he'd grown ambivalent about patient care, with its disappointing denouements. He was beginning to have an oppressive sense of futility in the face of disease, and to feel disgust at the caprices of fate in awarding sickness or survival with no regard whatever for the moral condition or social value of individuals. He thought of the old saw about the good dying young—Randall Lincoln, for example, stricken with the fatal sickle-cell anemia—and on the other hand the bevies of filthy alcoholic vagrants who lived on and on, some of them admitted to the hospital a hundred times, often taking beds away from the virtuous. Of course Philip knew you weren't supposed to think of the social utility of people, and he did his best not to, but sometimes he couldn't help it.

Philip's hobbies were perfectly orthodox for doctors: tennis and fishing, wine, his garden, art, and the opera. But science was what occupied his thoughts. A vigorous man approaching the height of his powers. The cocaine business intruded only a little on his general mood of self-satisfaction. An earnest first-year resident, Mark Silver—his eyes looking through owlish glasses were large, like a woman's eyes—had come to him before rounds with this moral, or perhaps just administrative, problem. Mark had found out that one or two of the interns had been using coke, and when he had mentioned this to the chief resident, Brian Smeed, Smeed had told him not to worry about it. But Mark was worried about the interns and now about Smeed's judgment too.

This problem had interrupted Philip's thoughts about Randall Lincoln, a cheerful young man of twenty-two whom they had had on the ward before, in crises of his sickle-cell illness, his deformed blood cells trying to push their way through blood vessels too small for them, causing intractable pain. For his courage and resolution, Randall was a general favorite. Despite the sickle cell, he'd put himself through college—the first of his family to do that, and had just finished an M.A. This current attack was the most serious he'd had, and in Philip's opinion, from his deteriorating condition would maybe be the last.

"I asked him if I should report it or what, and he said not to do anything, but I don't know," Mark was saying as they approached Randall's room. "I gather they're not using heavily, but still. What would you do?"

"You mean what will I do, now that you've told me?" said Philip snappishly, for he would rather not have to get involved in something Smeed should deal with. But he put thoughts of it away as he saw Randall's parents standing in the hall outside the door of Room 100.

"He's sinkin' very bad, doctor," Mrs. Lincoln said. "Yesterday he was so bright."

"Yes, I know, Mrs. Lincoln. I saw his test results today."

"Some of the things he say make no sense."

"That could be the medication. But I'm a little worried," Philip said. They had always known—he had always been careful to tell them—that one day Randall would not survive. Some sickle-cell patients could stave death off longer than others, but in the end all died. Randall was large, strong, resolute, intelligent—did that make any difference?

Philip wondered how it would feel to be the mother, the father, and to have created Randall's illness in the bad collusion of their genes. What would you feel, he thought, looking at Mrs. Lincoln's frightened face, giving life to someone and giving them their death right with it? But of course he, as a physician, did that all the time too.

In the room, Randall Lincoln opened his eyes and saw Philip. He barely moved his hand, thumb up. Philip took his hand and held it.

"We're giving you something strong, Randall. Are you in pain?"

"No," he said. The Lincolns stood in the doorway behind Philip, watching the way their son seemed to perk up when Dr. Watts came in. Philip listened to Randall's chest and watched his breathing.

"Oh, thank God, baby," Mrs. Lincoln said.

"I'll let you visit with him, Mrs. Lincoln. I'll talk to you later," Philip said. He didn't like the sinking, comatose way that Randall lay back again, or his groan. Randall wasn't one of those patients—there were many—who exaggerated their attacks to get morphine. He was in real pain, and his morphine was already heavy.

Randall's morphine, interns' cocaine, a question of the action of encapsulated liposomes, an annoying letter from a lawyer who was coming to see him tomorrow, certain problems at home, the need to pick up his car in the shop before five o'clock—should he tell them to replace the stolen hood ornament one more time?—how to prepare Randall's folks, one more time, for the reality that they would, eventually, if not now, lose Randall? These concerns unrolled themselves fleetingly across his mind as they finished rounds and he started down to the doctors' dining room for a cup of coffee, recalculating Randall's dosage of morphine in his mind and finding it correct.

In the hall he noticed the nurse leading someone, presumably Bradford Evans's new patient, the axillary vein thrombosis, into Room 100. She was a young red-haired woman of exceptional beauty. This he noticed in spite of himself—the cloud of red hair, the camellia-like pallor. From this distance he could not see the condition of her arm. But her beauty claimed his notice as a loud noise might, like someone dropping a bottle behind you, or a truck backfiring, the sound impinging on the consciousness of an unwilling man who was thinking about something else.

7

Ivy looked apprehensively around the room, at the bed with its crisp seersucker cover, which the nurse now stripped back, and the blond wood chest with the Formica top, and the various menacing implements for elimination stowed in its niches, and the two television sets positioned high at the ceiling, like surveillance units in a prison, one facing her, the other facing somebody on the other side of a beige curtain hung from a track in the middle of the ceiling, dividing the room. The walls were painted a tasteful pink, not hospital green or anything sordid, but instead fresh and restorative, with no disquieting religious pictures or anything else offensive. Yet she found it terrible.

The nurse took each item of her clothes as she meekly removed them, and hung them in the cupboard, and helped her tie the strings of the hospital nightgown, green, uncomfortably starchy.

"Somebody can bring you one of your own nighties," the nurse said.

"I'm only staying one night," Ivy said.

"Get up into bed. I'm coming right back with your medication," said the nurse.

Ivy climbed into bed. It was only ten-thirty in the morning. At her side, on the Formica nightstand, was a telephone, so she used it to call her babysitter, Petra. Petra said that Delia was asleep.

"I have to stay overnight," Ivy said. "They want to do another test or something. It's nothing serious," she added in as cheerful a voice as she could manage. "Just unforeseen. Are you sure you don't mind keeping her?" Petra reassured her that Delia was always a delight.

She struck the same cheerful note when she called the restaurant to say she wouldn't be coming in to work. "I'm in the hospital!" she said, in a tone of wonderment, as if she were at a happy surprise party for herself. "The most surprising thing! The hospital! No—of course I'm fine."

But then, when she thought of calling anyone among her friends, she hesitated. If she called Emily, she'd have to call Robin. David. Mark. Anabel. Carl. Wasn't it too portentous, too much like sending a black-bordered letter, to call people up and tell them you were in the hospital? It seemed to be asking them to drop things and come see you, and her friends were busy, active people who probably shared her dread of hospitals. And anyway, she'd be out tomorrow. This was just an episode, and it would be stupid to worry or shock people and unsettle their view of life as calm and unsurprising, and remind them of the arbitrariness of fate.

And there was something shameful about being in the hospital—wasn't that it? She didn't want people to know she was in the hospital. The way they would look at you afterward and inquire about your health. The truth, as she faced it, was that she didn't want anyone to know she had anything the matter with her. She didn't want to know it herself.

8

Mimi gathered up an assortment of vases and baskets that had accumulated on Ward 3F and took them down to the Volunteers Office. In time they would have a sort of garage sale of these items. Then she went along to get an early sandwich before a meeting of the fund-raising committee in the afternoon. By some stricture of the professional class system, the nurses and staff did not eat in the doctors' dining room but in a room of their own at the other end of the common cafeteria line that served them both. The volunteers, however, by unexamined custom, ate in the doctors' dining room. Did this imply that they were higher than nurses? Or that doctors were like volunteers, disinterested presences overseeing life and death out of goodness alone? Mimi had wondered about this. She, by some further elaborated convention, though she received a salary, was classified as a volunteer and ate in the doctors' dining room.

The volunteers, however, did not usually sit among the doctors, but alone or among themselves, unless there was only one of each in the room, a doctor and a volunteer, and they happened to know one another. Thus Mimi occasionally ate an early dinner or late lunch, or drank an off-hour cup of coffee with a lone doctor with whom she was friendly. She was popular among the doctors for her pretty smile, soft Virginia accent, and cheerful attention to their utterances, which they felt indicated great common sense and charm.

But she more often sat at an adjacent table, in the position of eavesdropper, and could not help but listen to the odd medical conversations that often shocked her, and behold the huge quantities of caffeine, cholesterol, and fat the senior doctors consumed.

The younger ones ate more healthily. As she helped herself at the salad bar, she watched Perry Briggs, the intern on 3F, build a towering salad on one of the very small plates. He began by cantilevering celery off the sides to serve as a foundation for a giant construction of greens and croutons. As he sat down with the other doctors, flutters of lettuce toppled onto the table where the doctors were eating. Perry was a huge young man, whose faint smell of some sort of sore-muscle liniment came from his violently sportive weekends. He had confided to Mimi that he had entered triathlon events, iron-men events, hundred-mile bike races, and marathons, in the summer before he had begun his internship, to condition himself for the dreaded intern year, legendarily a marathon in itself. It seemed to Mimi he should eat something more substantial than salad. The Chinese intern, Wei-chi Lum, or Lum Wei-chi, as they had finally learned to put it, ate prodigiously, as if permanently in mind of Chinese famine, and besides salad was having a hamburger, beans, and soup.

Mimi sat at one end of a long table where today a radiologist, Dr. Miller, was talking in a loud, easily overheard voice to a group of housestaff about animal experiments. "At Moffitt they're using sheep. Dogs are just too hot a ticket. Luckily the animal-rights people haven't thought of sheep rights yet."

"Cats and monkeys have their partisans," said Mark Silver, earnestly.

"Especially monkeys," Philip Watts remarked, coming up with his cup of coffee. "Those little human faces, those expressions of fear and pain."

Mimi, who admired Philip Watts, wished he could hear how they all sounded, seeming to joke about animal suffering, even though, she knew or wished to believe, they were careful to see that animals did not suffer.

"But the dogs especially, it was dogs that got them up in arms," said Dr. Mason. "The rumors of dognapping. People still have the idea that the pound sells them to us, for us to kill. What do they think the pound does with them?"

Philip Watts said, "When I was an intern, the chief of our service would pay the housestaff two dollars a head for catching cats."

Deeply shocked, Mimi thought of her dog, Warren, and of the sadness of dogs in cages. Had Philip Watts ever entrapped cats? She couldn't believe it. She herself wished experiments could be done on humans, especially on people who caught dogs and sold them for medical research.

After nine years at Alta Buena, Mimi was forced to admit that there were some things about the medical profession she could not admire. A doctor's daughter herself, she knew that doctors were not really full of perfidy or cruelty, and indeed she was always seeing acts of singular kindness and dedication. Perhaps it was only their inappropriate brusqueness, the casual way they took matters of life and death, that bothered her. She would have been a different sort of doctor, she liked to think, compassionate, with plenty of time to listen.

Philip Watts sat down beside her, which pleased her. Mimi particularly admired him. Where others found stiffness and arrogance, she found shyness and reserve, and she felt something kindred, thinking that people reacted to her in much the same way. She always felt she could express to him the reservations she felt about the medical profession as a whole, and when she did, he at least listened. Nurses, she had found, tended to identify with the doctors and became defensive if you said that doctors were callous or abrupt, even though they themselves criticized doctors extensively and in detail, like mothers who won't allow anyone else to criticize their children.

"Tomorrow I'm being deposed," Philip said. Mimi thought of a king, his head rolling, but he was speaking of the Wice Morris lawsuit, something he'd been telling her about from week to week. Dr. Wystan Morris, a surgeon dismissed for alcohol and drug addiction and horrifying accidents in the OR, was suing the hospital, and each of the members of the doctors' committee, for reinstatement, lost wages, vindication, and two million dollars' damages.

"It's such a sad case," Mimi said. "I talked to him one day. Poor old thing. His hands shook horribly—you dreaded to think of him operating on anyone. His . . . illness . . . was so obvious I don't see how he can dare to sue."

"How indeed. I suppose some lawyer got to him," said Philip. "And he has his supporters—all surgeons, of course. I guess they can all easily imagine becoming Parkinsonian drug-addicted alcoholics themselves." He laughed. Though Philip, like other internists, mistrusted surgeons, Mimi thought some of them were quite nice, even dashing. Considering the problems she had had with her former husband, Walter, over the years since their divorce, she could more easily see their objections to lawyers. Walter was a lawyer.

"He should have gotten help," Mimi said. "He was obviously sick—well, they do say alcoholism is an illness. He was so depressed. I was afraid he might—you know—think of suicide."

"Frankly, he should have," Philip said, laughing, then added, more seriously, "I don't have sympathy for a physician who endangers his patients. That's horrible. Wice Morris killed people."

"He should have been made to get treatment," Mimi pointed out. "You could blame the medical establishment for not stepping in sooner."

"Of course we all kill people," Philip said.

This was a point at which it seemed necessary to change the subject, so Mimi said, with her pretty smile, "How are you, Philip?"

"Fine," he said. "Too busy, as usual. This Morris thing and about sixty other things . . ." He had begun to lean intimately toward her, perhaps with some interesting confidence, but at this moment the voice of the hospital page filled the doctors' dining room: "Code Blue. 3F. Code Blue. 3F." Philip listened. He rose, touching Mimi's hand in a friendly but surprising way.

"Excuse me, Mimi, but I'm afraid that's Randall Lincoln. I've just had a feeling . . . I think I'd better go."

Mimi watched him hurry out. She could feel that a flush had made her cheeks hot. Was she really in so strangely susceptible a mood that a brush of the hand of a handsome man could affect her? Of course not—and yet it would be easy enough to think herself a little in love with Philip Watts. Such a bundle of manly qualities! She felt more forcefully her sense of being in a state somehow vulnerable and odd.

She was indulging herself a moment or two in thoughts of Philip —his unaffected, direct manner, an air of sincerity, in part produced by his habit of looking rather too fixedly at the person he was talking to, his romantic good looks and expensive Eastern education: Brown,

Johns Hopkins Medical School. Junior AOA, she was sure. Curiously enough, he came from some western state, Montana or Arizona, and she knew that his father had been a famous professor of medicine before him.

Above all, she admired his excellence as a physician. You couldn't fall in love with someone you didn't admire. This reference to love was trailing unbidden through her mind as Jeffrey Fowler, a surgeon she knew, took the chair that Philip had just occupied.

"Our Philip is rather full of himself, don't you think, now that he's got the Stanford plum?" Jeffrey remarked. "He never has been easy to deal with, but now you can't tell him anything. I hear that Jennifer is none too happy about moving."

"Oh, is it settled? I hadn't heard that," Mimi said.

"It's settled but not official. Heard this one? What're three reasons for using lawyers instead of laboratory animals? Answer: One, there are more of them. Two, they're cheaper. Three, there are things a rat just won't do."

9

In Randall's room, Mrs. Lincoln, anxiously watching her comatose son, became frightened when his breathing slowed. She could remember watching just this way when he was a baby in his crib, awed that he was breathing at all, fearful at each breath, oppressed by his smallness and fragility, and by her own responsibility for this tiny creature. Today Randall appeared large and powerful. If only a miracle could cleanse his blood of this accursed wrong, if the doctors could find out their mistakes and he could rise up out of this bed, smiling again, or if they found some new medicine—that could happen. So he has to get through this crisis. Her mind concentrated in prayer on this. It seemed to her that by looking, watching, sending the message of love, and by concentrating on God's love, she could inspirit him. But, as she watched, she saw his breathing grow more and more shallow, and then seem to stop altogether. She ran screaming for help.

Hearing the operator's voice urgently over the paging system, Mark Silver and Perry Briggs, the intern, who were sitting in the nurses' conference room, and Peter Anderson, an anesthesiologist at the moment walking through the hall outside the ward, leaped to respond. Mark snatched the battered red cart, with its scalpels, vials of adrenaline, electrical stimulators, ECG machines, tubes, and intravenous drugs, and hurtled along to Randall Lincoln's room. The other intern, Lum Wei-chi, ran in. The anesthesiologist was there already.

Mrs. Lincoln, shrinking against the wall, saw the horrible sight of men attacking Randall, pounding on his chest, jamming a tube down his throat and injections into his arm, and hooking him up to a small machine that had appeared from nowhere, and the nurse doing something strange to his feet.

Perry Briggs, notoriously squeamish, had been assigned the job of trying to get a plastic tube into a vein in Randall's arm. As his scalpel penetrated the velvet brown of Randall's skin, and, drawn along the surface, produced a thick, dark, oozing cut, he felt queasy and had to look away. Looking back, he saw that the two sides of the slit had drawn a millimeter apart, with blood welling out between, and with layers of tissue underneath, like a flesh sandwich, each a different color, like striations of rock. Perry thought of the bone that lay deeper, could imagine accidentally striking the bone. He felt a chill sensation of blood leaving his head, rushing to his heart. He had to step into the hall for a few seconds till the faintness passed. Wei-chi put in the cannula.

Now, on the little TV screen of the machine, Mrs. Lincoln could see her son come back from death. A tiny blip began to show in the flat line of his pulse. It struggled to come once more, ebbed, rose again. Mrs. Lincoln understood that this was his life returning.

Perry Briggs could not contain a joyful grin. Mrs. Lincoln began to cry, relieved and upset. "He's coming back," she said again. "What happened to him, doctor?"

"He stopped breathing, Mrs. Lincoln. but he's started again," Perry said. "He's gonna pull through!" It was these moments of joy that made Perry happy he had decided to be a doctor; they outweighed the grisly, sad things a million percent.

Philip Watts, watching from the doorway, checked his impulse to chew them out, so unreflectively did they celebrate Randall's coming back to life. When someone was dying of a fatal illness, the wisdom of reviving him was not so evident. But he was pleased to see that the new Code Blue team had performed well, in no need of his interference, and technically, since a No Code order had not been written on Randall, they were correct in resuscitating him. Saving him to die again. But of course you could always say that, anytime you saved anyone, or drew back, yourself, from the oncoming car, or regained your footing. Saved to die again.

They began preparation to take Randall to intensive care. This was in a general medicine ward, with four intensive-care beds in a special area at the back, a frightening hive of flashing lights, like the ground control of a space mission. Perry and Mark walked behind the orderly and the intensive-care resident, who pushed the bed and machines along the corridor. Ahead, the intensive-care nurses, a team of Filipinas headed by Merci Yezema, waited, speaking in their merry-sounding language, "ding-dong, log-log-long."

Now, the intensive-care resident and Lum Wei-chi adjusted the respirator to a comfortable and supportive pace, and rearranged the tubes. Randall's chest obediently expanded and then contracted, emptying with a whoosh of air that filled a bellows on the machine, its membrane rising and falling like a lung. Mrs. Lincoln stared at it as if she were watching the interior of Randall's body.

To his chest a terminal was taped to monitor the heartbeat. Merci, in her somewhat rough way, snaked a tube up his penis. Another nurse, Edgardo Sanchez, raised an IV bottle higher on its stand, twirling a dial to monitor the dripping of the saline solution into his veins. They all stood for a while, like a spaceship crew, watching the dials. Mrs. Lincoln appeared mesmerized by the fitful blinking of the monitor.

"For God's sake, get that woman out of here," someone snapped at the nurse.

10

With some time before her meeting, Mimi went back up to Ward 3F, where she had left the book cart. The nurses had told her a new patient had been admitted to Room 100, so she paused circumspectly outside the door. If people weren't too sick, they liked a book to settle in with. She knocked, opened the heavy door, and pushed aside the heavy cotton drapery that hung inside. In the far bed, behind another curtain, lay, she knew, a Mrs. Apple, a definite nonreader.

From here you could see only the foot of the nearest bed, the bed of the new patient. Mimi peered apprehensively at the mound of feet under the white covers. You never could know until you were well into the room whether you would find an alert person in the bed, smiling and happy to see you, or someone lying there with thin tubes attached to nose and forearm, fluids sliding along the plastic, eyes fluttered closed. Mimi's heart always leaped with relief to see a smiling patient; she could begin to plan a future for the person. Or her heart sank at the sight of someone really sick. Telling her to come in has been their last act of strength. Too weak to read a book. In this case she would tiptoe out, so as not to reproach the patient with her frailty. She had never got used to seeing a tube attached to a person, couldn't look at the place where it pierced the skin and went horribly in, though various doctors had explained that you have to think of tubes as life-bringing.

The voice of the new patient sounded spirited, so Mimi wasn't prepared for her being attached to a tube. Nor, it seemed, had the patient got used to it; she sat up tensely and made hasty movements of her arms before remembering that she was tethered and checked. She was young and red-haired, with golden freckles on a face of radiant pallor, and dainty fingers, bluishly transparent. Like every patient in the hospital, she looked scared.

"I came to see if you want anything to read?" Mimi asked.

"Oh, thanks," said the young woman, her smile a little tentative.

"I'll push this closer. You can see the titles." She did, and the young woman peered near-sightedly at the book cart.

"What kind of books do you like? Novels? Mysteries? Something deep?"

"Biography," said the young woman. "I guess I like the stories of people triumphing, or even of people broken and disappointed. I like to see how they do." She spoke with a certain deliberate ornate force, despite her frail looks.

"Biography," Mimi repeated, looking at her shelf. "*Emma, Lady Hamilton. Courage and Conviction: The Life of Jane Addams. The Life of Thurgood Marshall*. No, sorry, it's George Marshall. Either way, slim pickings today."

"Never mind," said the young woman. "Never mind. Nothing, thank you. I don't really feel like reading."

"Well," Mimi said, "I can come back tomorrow."

"Oh, God," cried the young woman, "I hope I won't be here tomorrow! That's the point. Why get interested in someone's life only to put it back on the shelf?

"I shouldn't be here at all," she went on, in a puzzled voice. Mimi understood. She sometimes thought the same thing about herself, that she didn't belong in a hospital. She felt there was a danger in being a part of a place people would rather not be in. It could give you an odd, dour perspective, as it did the nurses.

"I feel like it's some mistake," the young woman suddenly said. She looked at Mimi as at a rescuer. She spoke as if she were about to be sucked away in an undertow, or as if her fingers were loosening on a sill high above the city. Mimi inspected her more closely; it was true that she didn't look sick, exactly. A high, indignant pink flush rising under her delicate redhead's skin made her look, on the contrary, healthy. Her eyes, sky blue, were rimmed with extravagant black mascara painted over pale lashes.

She struggled to sit up further, daunted by the tube and by the sight of the suspended drops lined up in it waiting to drip into her arm. "It was just that this morning I happened to look at my two forearms, and I noticed that one was swollen up twice the size of the other. That was all. My arm looked like a boudin blanc! All at once I had this most powerful feeling of death.

"Has that ever happened to you? My stomach crawled, my throat sealed up. It was the most frightening moment of my life; I guess it was the first moment I ever really knew I was going to die. Sometime.

Not even when I was having my baby—there's a moment then, too —do you know? Do you have children? Although, along with the thought of death, you begin to think of ways to get out of it. I thought maybe I wasn't going to die, but I had to know. So I called my OB, and she said I'd better go have it checked right away by an internist and she'd call Dr. Evans but that probably it was nothing."

Mimi felt the spin of dismay in her own veins she always felt at the mention of Bradford Evans. She thought of strokes, cerebral hemorrhages, lumps, all other sudden events that shattered with their unexpected and arbitrary impact. She looked at the young woman's pale forearms, the one swollen and streaked with purple, and the other fastened with a hose, and looked away. "How awful," she agreed.

"He said they'd have to x-ray it, in the hospital. In the outpatient department. He called them while I was sitting there, to be sure they could do it right away. You feel confused and dazzled. All at once I was the center of all this bizarre and frightening attention. Then they looked at the x-ray, and then he said I'd have to stay in the hospital. Nobody seems to realize, you can't just drop everything and go to the hospital. I have a baby at home."

"Oh, they'll have you out of here," Mimi assured her. "Really. They must have felt it was important."

The young woman sighed an anguished sigh. "What about my baby? And I need to feed her."

Was there really a child, perhaps at home alone? "Have you got someone with her?" Mimi asked, imagining a tiny, frightened baby, untended in a crib.

"Well, she's at the sitter's house. The woman who usually watches her. I had made arrangements, of course," said the young woman, sounding offended that Mimi could think she would leave her baby alone.

"There's a social worker here at the hospital," Mimi said, "who can help with arranging child care and such. Do you want me to call her? Is there something I can do?"

"Thank you, everything's okay for the moment. I called again just a few minutes ago. But I just can't believe this is happening."

As she left Room 100, Mimi looked at the name on the chart stuck in the rack outside the door: Ivy Tarro. Of course Ivy Tarro would be there the next day. People always stayed at least two days, usually more.

11

At three, Mimi went to the meeting of the fund-raising committee, an ongoing body concerned at various times with building projects or expanding hospital services, the purchase of cobalt units or CAT scanners or Mammo-mobiles. Now they were hoping for a nuclear magnetic resonance imaging unit and greatly enlarged parking facilities. The hospital, which had a perennial and insatiable appetite for money, or need for money, as it was put, also felt eager to take advantage of the public interest in the terrible new disease AIDS and to repair its own tardiness in foreseeing how this scourge would strain its existing facilities. Millions of dollars would have to be found, and, as the board well knew from earlier efforts, would not be found lying on the ground but would have to be assembled piecemeal from government grants and from personal, painstaking efforts.

In smaller matters of fund raising, the women's auxiliary was left in charge, but the new drive was to be of such magnitude that the male members of the committee—doctors, attorneys, community leaders, and liaison members of the city council—attended in force, throwing into the shade the normal female constituency of a nurses' representative (night nurse Vita Dawson), Mimi as volunteer coordinator, Mrs. MacGregor Bunting (head of the Faculty Wives' Auxiliary), a representative of the Housestaff Wives, Pennyloafers' Auxiliary (teenage afterschool volunteers, candy-stripers, and Home Services workers), and a number of interested doctors' wives.

As Mimi seated herself in the outer ring of the chairs drawn up in a large circle around the table in the Founder's Room, a discussion was already underway, led by Mr. Dolph Dobbs, the well-known banker and head of the S. F. Museum board, a man skilled in fund raising. The subject was individual donations. He had brought with him a printout of names of people known to have given large sums to the arts.

"Of course we realize that arts donors aren't necessarily health donors," he was saying, "but this gives us a target population."

"The problem is, the arts are more chic," said Jennifer Watts, the wife of Dr. Philip Watts. "For one thing, the arts have more parties."

"*We* could have parties," objected Mrs. MacGregor Bunting, wife of the famous neurosurgeon.

"But no one wants to go to parties with doctors," said Jennifer Watts, laughing, and it was by no means clear that she was joking.

"The person in charge of individual donations needs to be a social leader who knows a lot of people, is an experienced fund raiser, and above all, persuasive. I've underlined a few names here. Mary Jane Lindley. Lorraine Waverly, Hanford Swayne. Mary Jane, I know, in particular has been wonderfully effective for the museum. But she has a lot to do. Lorraine occurred to me."

"She's gregarious, she'd call people up. She'd have lunch," Jennifer Watts objected, "but can she close?"

"What about you, Jennifer?" someone suggested, but Jennifer modestly shook her head.

Jennifer Watts was one of the few doctors' wives Mimi knew, though only slightly, through work on these committees. Her pleasant, confident manner had led her to be elected or drafted as the faculty sponsor of the housestaff wives—an organization of the wives of interns and residents, women who depended on each other for companionship in the long years while their husbands were in training.

It seemed natural that younger women would look up to Jennifer. She was a tall, rangy blonde, confident enough of her handsome features to affect a very individual style—no makeup at all, and expensive but simple clothes of light denim or silk. She didn't confine herself to good works—she was a successful sculptor (fiber arts) and a renowned skier. She photographed well, and her picture often appeared in articles about artistic events. Her sculpture was shown at quite a good gallery.

Moreover, she was reported to be perfectly nice, though Mimi found her slightly frightening because of these combined perfections and, perhaps, an awareness of them. Her defect, if any, seemed to Mimi to be a strain of tactlessness, or impatience, as if she didn't know how it was to be a regular, imperfect person, and had little feel for it. Something in her most offhand remarks could seem crushing, as once when she had remarked to Mimi that Mimi was "statuesque." "Mimi, you're so statuesque, you should have been a model," is what she had said. Should have been! What kind of a tense was that to use about someone's life, as if it were over! "Statuesque" was exactly the adjective Mimi's family had always used to encourage her to feel confident about her height—she was six feet tall—and it made her think of statues—huge, clumsy figures in stone.

The cornerstone of the fund-raising drive was to be a gala dinner at Christmas, for which plans were already well underway. Now other aspects of the multipronged effort were being discussed. "Basically I favor leaving the odds and ends to you girls," said Dr. Harling Cooper, representative of the doctors' committee. "I know you know how to organize these things better than we ever could," and passed the discussion on to Mrs. Bunting. Several of the busy doctors took advantage of the transition to hurry out.

"Could we hear a report from the tote-bag and T-shirt committee?" Mrs. Bunting asked. Mrs. Peggy Dworkin suggested updating the logo to reflect the AIDS project. Mrs. Peter Nelson brought up the matter of house tours, which was viewed favorably—"the only hard part is convincing people to clean up their houses, and of course we post monitors and put down plastic runners." Then nurse Vita Dawson, representing the nurses' committee, mentioned that this had been the fund-raising stratagem at her children's nursery school. A beat of awkward silence suggested that, owing to some social distinction, an idea that had been used by nurses might be disqualified for use by doctors.

Mimi's thoughts wandered until she heard her own name being spoken. "What about a cookbook?" the elderly doctor Alf Carter was saying. "The ladies' auxiliary always used to have a cookbook. You could count on everyone to buy one copy at least. Of course I know that's beneath ladies nowadays, to concern themselves with cooking and recipes, but it's too bad."

"We *have* a cookbook," said Dottie Fred. "It's been on sale in the gift shop lo these many years. But I think it's been some years since it's been updated."

"A lot of us fellows are pretty good cooks, too," Dr. Carter continued. "You should ask the doctors for recipes."

"It sounds like Mimi Franklin's department," someone else agreed, bringing Mimi out of her reverie. "Revise the old cookbook, get some new recipes, ask the old contributors to update."

Here Mimi had only to agree. However—perhaps it was owing to the size of the meeting—she began to feel the symptoms of her girlhood stage fright: reddening face, hot palms, and a sort of mute sealing-up of the throat when it came to the matter of actually saying something out loud. She took a deep breath and said, "I could of course." During her awkward, overgrown adolescence she had sometimes been unable to speak a word. "If someone will volunteer to test the recipes, some more expert cook than I am," she managed to add.

"Jennifer, that's you!" cried Dolph Dobbs. "She's a fabulous cook."

Jennifer Watts, smiling modestly, did not deny this.

All at once, in this moment, Mimi felt the disadvantage of not being married. Some sheen of glossy confidence, of protectedness, seemed to surround Jennifer Watts that she herself did not have and could not develop. Even Peggy Dworkin, with her tight gray perm and Eddie Bauer clothes, had it—the air developed by centuries of married women, almost like Scotchgard, something invisible but repellant to stains, while she herself, sitting at the back, not the object of Dolph Dobbs's or anyone's admiration, felt limp and absorbent, like a rag, even though she was as presentable, she supposed, as any of them— any of them except perhaps Jennifer Watts.

This pang was unexpected, because usually Mimi felt the advantages rather than the disadvantages of her life. Her divorce, at such a young age, had been relatively painless, and she had had the pleasure of raising Narnia and Daniel according to her own ideas. Despite years of financial worries she had always had a roof over her head, and had become clever with home repairs, things some man would have done for her but which she had, in fact, quite enjoyed knowing how to do. And she had had the sexual freedom of a man, or so she had always told herself, though when she came to count up the relationships she'd had during the past eighteen years, they didn't come to many.

She had often felt a little sorry for the doctors' wives, women who seemed restless and dependent. The wives seemed, from the perspective of the hospital professionals, like a shadow society of capricious and manipulative goddesses, if "goddesses" was the right word for the group of generally plain, distraught women who turned up from time to time bringing clean shirts or a forgotten airline ticket for their husbands. Though most of the wives were initially nameless, their names would eventually be mentioned in the dust goblins of divorce gossip that scooted through the hospital corridors before some new broom sweeping clean. Mimi, like all the female personnel, was aware that, beside the advantages, there were perils in marrying a doctor.

But now, as suddenly as an accident or stroke, she saw the others seeing her—unmarried, alone, and, compared to Jennifer Watts, not spectacular. Out of nowhere, she felt a stab of envy of Jennifer Watts's flat chest, Jennifer's expensive Italian knit shirt and wonderful shoes of saddle-colored leather, flat, perforated with smart little holes, like a man's, but graceful on Jennifer's long, slender feet. Somehow this getup all at once seemed to symbolize matrimonial privilege.

Mimi reminded herself that it was she who was free, independent, untethered; but it was Jennifer whose filigree scarf seemed to float like Isadora Duncan's, Jennifer who seemed artistic, secure, and free. When Jennifer suddenly got to her feet, apologized for leaving early, and rushed out, Mimi thought she could detect, in the long moment of silence and the faces of the nurses, a perception like her own.

Once on this track, Mimi's mind gathered steam like a train with its brakes failing, carrying an acid load of malice. She felt dislike of the spoiled doctors' wives in their expensive clothes and their dissatisfied faces and their children off in boarding schools, and houses in Marin County with big gardens. But then, as usual, she tried to be fair. How can you say a face is dissatisfied? All of these women were smiling. And—be fair—some of them did art or social work. Of course the really busy ones weren't in this room, except for Jennifer Watts. To be fair, Mimi knew Jennifer must work like a horse to do all the things she got done. And gardens, Mimi knew from her small bed of impatiens and zinnias, were a lot of work. When the top two stories of the orthopedic wing had gone up, giving her garden too much shade for vegetables, she had almost been relieved.

How many doctors' wives had jobs, she wondered, compared to what percentage of regular women? She was ashamed of the petulant way this question presented itself.

They wore wonderful objects gathered on foreign trips—Chinese pendants and turquoise bracelets lined up their suntanned arms, the reward of civility and forbearance in the face of the inconvenient hours their husbands kept, the antics of some of them—you heard of this or that husband disappearing into the linen room with Carmel Hodgkiss. Her mind hurtled along the track of low gossip. If you were married to a doctor you could never ask where he had been or why he was late. The virtuousness of his doings was beyond question!

She hardly knew herself, thinking like this, allowing resentment and jealousy to intrude on her normal mood of peaceful kindness. As the meeting continued, Mimi's fleeting pang retreated, but as she walked home across the parking lot at five-thirty, her thoughts returned to doctors' wives rather than to the subject of fund raising. She was ashamed of herself.

12

At home, Mimi made herself a cup of tea, and tried to put out of her mind her uncharacteristic surge of resentment against doctors' wives and Jennifer Watts. Maybe it had to do with the disconcerting little flutter of the heart she had felt when talking to Philip Watts in the doctors' dining room. She hoped the result of Daniel and Narnia's being away was not to be a new emotional life of inexplicable turbulence involving unsuitable, married doctors. Of course she would like to meet someone suitable. . . .

But no! Wait a minute, she scolded herself. The good part of having an empty nest was that now she could fall in love with unsuitable people right and left if she chose. For the first time since she was twenty, she could permit herself, if she pleased, and if she could remember how it was done, the luxury of a chaotic emotional life.

Mimi was susceptible to men. She liked them. Yet, although she was surrounded by them—doctors, orderlies, patients—she in a way didn't know many. Other women complained of this too—the ones who hadn't given up on men altogether. It was as if, once you were out of college, there were no more occasions the specific intention of which was to introduce you to the opposite sex, and you must just resign yourself to the company of your own. When you were almost forty, the situation was even worse. The alternatives were a set of degrading, impulsive stratagems—singles bars, want ads—that Mimi would not have dreamed of. Despite this, over the fourteen years since her divorce, she had had two or three relationships that had seemed as if they might lead to marriage. But they had not, initially to her relief. She had been rigorous about shielding Narnia and Daniel from the disastrous array of live-in boyfriends and dramas of the heart that many of her divorced women friends had gone in for. Perhaps, she found herself musing now, perhaps she was a little sorry about that?

She drank her tea and read the mail—the usual collection of throwaways, a letter from her father, a postcard from Narnia, and a long legal envelope from a lawyer, which she saved until last because it frightened her. Inadvertent images of peril emanated from the neat embossing of the return address, Michaels, Gilbert and Holmes, Attorneys at Law. She looked again to make sure it was addressed to her: G. M. Franklin. Yes. It was easy to imagine its sinister contents: she had dented someone's car without realizing it, and, having been seen, was being sued or threatened with arrest. Someone, having tripped on her lawn, on, say, those little wire wickets with which she had surrounded a bed of impatiens, was threatening a suit. Or maybe it had coincidentally to do with Wystan Morris, the doctor who was suing the hospital.

Dear Mr. Franklin:
We are authorized by the Board of Alta Buena Hospital, whom we are privileged to represent, to initiate discussions with you on the possibility of the purchase of your property at 3425 Alta Street.

As you doubtless realize, the parking problem in recent years has become one of the most serious facing the hospital. The cornerstone of a projected expansion of our medical facilities includes expanded parking. The projected design calls for a new garage at the corner of Alta and Carter streets. To this end, the board has authorized the purchase of adjacent properties, and a considerable fund-raising effort has ensured that this will be made possible. It goes without saying that we will expect to pay a fair price above market value, to compensate owners for the inconvenience and for their consideration in making possible this desirable improvement in the health-care facilities of this area.

We urge you to let us know when you might find a convenient time for us to meet to discuss this matter personally with you or

your representative. Several of your neighbors have already concluded negotiations, which have proved satisfactory for all.

Mimi was at first so shocked at this that she put the letter down.
Nothing of this had been mentioned at the meeting! No one had
looked at her with guilty calculation. She picked it up again, rereading
with an intimation that it presaged the beginning of something long,
disagreeable, and complicated, and perhaps accounted for the portentous feeling she'd had that morning. After a moment, though, she felt
better.

Looked at another way, although she didn't plan to act on this
letter, and would never dream of so much as acknowledging it, it was
exciting to think of selling this little house, now that the children were
gone—for a large sum, moreover—and moving on to—to what? To
something better, more glamorous or amusing. It was like a novel by
Dickens. You receive a letter from a lawyer promising fortune. Your
life can change, but you have to allow yourself to be swept up in the
narrative possibilities. There is the dangerous aroma of corrupting
allure about a letter from a lawyer promising fortune.

She also realized that the writer of the letter to G. M. Franklin had
not connected her with Mimi the volunteer coordinator. It must be
simply that the administrators or the board had instructed their lawyers to search the county property registry or whatever they did,
ascertain the names of adjacent owners, and write them.

Not a condominium. There was something wrong-sounding in that
idea, as if she were a retired person, or someone just starting out.
Unless it was somewhere awfully pretty, Sausalito or Tiburon, but
that would mean a commute to work. She was used to the luxury of
living within walking distance of the hospital. Resolutely she put real-
estate dreams out of her mind.

But she mused, during her supper, all the same. She had always
wanted to move. This was not the sort of house she liked, not really.
Built in the thirties, small, it had many disadvantages, but it had been
what she and Walter had been able to afford, with the down payment
as a wedding present and a GI loan because of his service in the
Korean War. The house was cozy, it was true, with a nice brick
fireplace and bookcases on either side of it, with glass fronts and
painted latticework on the glass. A wood floor, a small dining room

whose panels had been painted, and which she herself had laboriously stripped, revealing a nice, light-colored redwood she liked. But there was a slight smell of age in the house, of someone old having lived there, which she could never get rid of, and which other people noticed, claiming to smell potpourri or lavender. The bedrooms were small antiseptic rectangles, devoid of any quality of languorousness or erotic repose. They belonged too distinctly to the past, and now the thought of a future including a new house and a handsome lover could beguile her if she pleased.

Mimi's feeling about her past, besides astonishment at how quickly it had flown, was one of embarrassment. When she looked at old photos of herself, dressed in the orthodox costume of the sixties—headband, beads, a toe ring, and an adoring expression, for the photos were always ones in which she herself was incidental—she felt a deep shame. The photos were always of Walter Franklin, her boyfriend and temporary husband, the prominent student leader, protester, activist, and egomaniac, herself looming behind him. Deep shame and mystification. How could she have been someone who had believed not just the things that had turned out to be true, among the political and social beliefs of the period, but all the things, uncritically: free love, mystical drugs, the intrinsic superiority of Indian religions? She had believed every tenet of Walter Franklin.

Walter himself was now a district attorney in a small Connecticut community, and it was she who was the exile, viewed by her family in Virginia, though they loved her of course, as someone who had rather gone to the bad, staying all these years in California, seeming so indifferent to remarriage, and with no regular employment, for they had never grasped that she was paid to volunteer. Though Narnia and Daniel went East in the summers, to visit their grandparents and Walter, and now to college, Mimi went back less and less often.

And yet looking at photos always reminded her that during those crazy, freer days, she had felt more comfortable with her tallness, her long limbs seemed less awkward to her, her fair hair, worn in short curls now, was then long, wildish, and frizzy, with a headband, as if she were a member of a picturesque Amazon tribe. Old photos reminded her that she had meant to turn out an odd, special person, and she wondered how it had happened that she now found herself a regular person, even an ordinary person, not what she had had in mind at all.

She ate quickly, planning to go to her guitar class. She was trying to learn the classical guitar. She would move, she thought, to the kind of place she would never move to. It was good to do something like this at a certain point in life, move someplace that would shock her parents and Narnia—she did not yet think of Daniel as emancipated enough to have views. Someplace much nicer than they thought she thought of herself as deserving. Did this make any sense? Not anything silly like a condominium or singles complex but something elegant and old-fashioned, or else by water, or else a loft, one enormous space somewhere in Emeryville. Many of her friends were artists, even if she wasn't.

She stopped this line of thinking. Of course she wasn't going to move anywhere—there was no reason to, and the idea of being put out of your house for a parking lot was too wicked to think of submitting to, even for the sake of Alta Buena. People could come on the bus or on bicycles, and besides, the hospital ran an efficient and convenient shuttle service for the elderly and people needing assistance.

13

At the end of the day, Philip Watts made signout rounds with the housestaff, glancing with disapproval into Room 100 as they passed by. Here Evans's patient could be seen, sitting up tensely, as if she expected to be dragged away by her IV and was poised to resist. Despite himself, he glanced at her chart, at the nurses' station, and took note of her name, Ivy Tarro, which sounded familiar, and noted that she was on intravenous indomethacin.

They had had to tell the lung biopsy to go home for the moment— it was no way to manage a medical service. You could argue that these banal cases brought in by the LMDs were the kinds of cases the housestaff would see when they got into practice themselves, but in

Philip's opinion, their housestaff years were their only chance to manage serious and peculiar cases, and these should be given priority. Anyway, in his new unit, things were going to be different. Ivy, kind of a pretty name, IV, intravenous. He wondered what the underlying pathology was of her axillary vein thrombosis. Most likely drugs.

He and Jennifer had dinner at the North Beach Bar and Grill. Since their daughter Daphne was not at home—was doing her junior year abroad, in Grenoble—they often ate out. Philip had six oysters and a swordfish steak. Jennifer had Salade d'Artichaux et Prosciutto, and then salmon in puff pastry.

"What's the plural of 'artichoke' in French?" she asked. "This doesn't look right."

"How would I know?" Philip said.

"I think they're thinking of *choux*, the plural of cabbage. That has an 'x.' "

Philip felt, as he sometimes did, the solitude of his dinner, and the slight constraint of Jennifer's manner lately, her formality, now that they had decided he would go to Stanford. He knew she didn't want to move but had decided to be perfect about it. He had promised to explore the possibilities of commuting.

Though they had little to say tonight, they didn't feel like other couples you saw eating in complete silence. His dinners with Jennifer were often full of talk. Now he fell to thinking about the food and about Mr. Dinh, a tiny old Vietnamese man in 107, and of how he'd told the interns to ask Mrs. Dinh to bring in some shrimp rolls or something in lemon grass—something he would like. Probably they hadn't done it. He reminded himself to remind them. Young doctors thought more about heroics than about ordinary things like food and the household worries people had; yet those were often the things that kept them from getting well. He thought of Mr. Dinh's look, feeble and stricken, at the horrible sweet potatoes and gray pot roast the hospital served.

"What is lemon grass?" he asked Jennifer.

"Lemon grass? Some kind of herb? Or vegetable? I don't know exactly what you'd call it."

14

In her room, Ivy Tarro picked wanly at the turkey roll and tried to watch television, but she was still too shocked at finding herself in the hospital to settle down. In a way, the whirling of her mind, its anxious meanderings, reassured her that she was alive. She kept thinking over the day, of how it had begun like any other with the baby waking, breakfast, noticing her arm, the appointment with the doctor, her expectation of going to work in the afternoon and instead being put to bed, with tubes and bottles dripping substances into her veins. She called the babysitter again, and again was reassured. She called Carl Miller, a friend of hers, but she didn't say where she was.

Again and again she went over the events in this strange day, searching for clues. Delia's breakfast, the x-ray, the doctor, and, worst of all, the words: dye contrast, venogram, axilla, Indocin, elevation, drainage, blockage, clot. The monosyllable "clot" was especially chilling, so that her mind balked at it and tried to think of things at home, perversely reassuring, like the bills she had left on the kitchen table—the diaper-service bill, the cable-television bill, PG & E. No doubt it was a law of life that you didn't die with your bills unpaid. She thought about the things in the refrigerator—custard, lamb gravy, that she would have thrown out if she'd known she was going to the hospital.

But surely they wouldn't go green by tomorrow? Surely she'd be home by tomorrow? Had she locked the second lock or just closed the door behind her?

And what would this cost? Of course she had medical insurance—it had paid almost all of the costs of Delia's birth; Blue Cross, reliable, but you were supposed to have told them well in advance that you were going into the hospital. But probably the hospital tells them, in an emergency. Come on, she told herself again, be glad they've found whatever it is. What if I lived in Uganda, or even Mendocino?

She supposed she should turn off the television. It must be disturbing the person on the other side of the curtain, who seemed sicker than she, for the nurses looked in more often, and with a certain grave air. She wished she had accepted a book from the gazellelike woman with the book cart.

Dr. Evans came in, saying nothing in a series of encouraging grunts, and went away. A young doctor had been in, kind of cute. The nurse had offered a sleeping pill, but she refused. Her breasts hurt with milk. She thought of getting up and leaving—what could prevent it? But she was afraid to. The doctor's expression of concern, the contraction of the thick eyebrows, had surely meant something. You couldn't not do what doctors told you or you would certainly die.

All at once Cancer crossed Ivy's mind. Her heart slowed attentively. Why hadn't she thought of this before? It must be a cancer deep inside her someplace, working its way out into her arm, and they weren't telling her. You could see it, though, in the nice nurse's face, and in the compassionate smile of the beautiful book-cart person. It was as if they knew her death was on the way. She felt frozen, blizzards of panic swirling her blood.

Probably her blood was the problem. Probably she had AIDS. She thought of several people she had slept with that might be bi, or use drugs. You *never knew*. She had definitely eaten deadly cancer foods, been x-rayed, bore cancer in her genes, or in her uterus. She'd read about a kind of cancer that comes into your uterus after you've had a baby. There was definitely more to it than just a swollen arm and they weren't telling her.

And if she died, what would happen to Delia? The thought made her gasp. Since Delia's birth, she had been caught once a day, or even more often, with some new and frightening thought, something that had never occurred to her before, like this one, that if she died it would now matter to someone else besides her. If she died—and she had never thought of dying before—her friends and her brother would be sad, of course, but to Delia, who was too little to be sad, it would matter. It would change Delia's life, she would have to be raised by relatives, who did not lead the life she wanted for Delia. Or—each ramification was worse than the last—Delia would be raised by her father. Catastrophe. The thought of motherless Delia brought tears to her eyes. She had to be careful here, and not die. She'd been too happy. Just when something especially wonderful comes into your life, just when you look at the world with satisfaction, thinking how full it is of beauty and interest, just when each day involves something you particularly want to do, you die. And just when her body had gone back to its old shape, after Delia, and was now so full of life and desire. You had to pay for happiness, as everyone had known but her. Tears at the painfulness of this realization rushed down her cheeks and she just let them.

Now the night nurse, a blond woman with an Australian accent, and a name badge that read VITA, came in and began to dismantle the apparatus at the foot of Ivy's bed.

"Your doctor wants to change your medicine, honey. It's in this bottle,"—referring to another of the upside-down bottles attached to a tube that was in turn attached to Ivy's good arm, dripping something into her—"only he wants this to go right in your other arm. I'm going to have to prick you a little." She fitted a pole to the other side of the bed and hung the second bottle on it. Then she lifted Ivy's swollen arm. Ivy watched, wondering at her own passivity—she was usually an alert, involved person. Vita struck with her needle, then again, and then, after a third time, Ivy gasped and shrunk with pain.

"I'm sorry, love," Vita said, "I'm going to have to get the intern to make an incision. I can't find your vein in all that swelling."

Ivy closed her eyes, not wanting to watch the young doctor cut open her arm. She had the idea that her arm would spurt some terrible substance. She thought of once when she had stepped on a tomato worm. She wasn't going to ask what the new medicine was, though she wondered. If it was now the new that slid into her veins, she couldn't tell any difference from the other.

"You call if there's anything," Vita said. "You know the bell's right there," and glided out into the hallway. Desperately, when she couldn't get her thoughts to dwell on anything soothing or reassuring any longer, Ivy called for the sleeping pill.

The night nurse, Vita Dawson, had been surprised to see Dr. Bradford Evans, who didn't usually come in after dinner. He was writing in Ivy Tarro's chart. Vita looked over his shoulder. He was putting Ivy on streptokinase, a large dose for a small woman—she must have horse-sized clots, which must be what was worrying Dr. Evans. Dr. Evans was not a bad-looking man, about fifty, with large shoulders and a roughened sailor's face. Carmel Hodgkiss, coming by with a tray of medicines, gave him a long smile, making Vita wonder if there was something between them.

At nine, Vita made another round, looking in at each patient on her way to the medicine room for the streptokinase. Mrs. Apple was going downhill. The sour odor of sleep had begun to settle reassuringly over all of the patients. She dispensed some sleeping pills, and found some foam leggings for the comatose Randall Lincoln's ankles, which were beginning for some reason to swell, and added the new streptokinase to Tarro's IV. Then she sat down in the nurses' conference room with Mark Silver, the resident, and Lum Wei-chi and Perry Briggs, the interns on duty, to eat her dinner sandwich. She remarked on the change in Tarro's medication.

"She doesn't look too good," Mark Silver said. "Not as good as when she came in."

Perry said, "Why is he using streptokinase?" He was looking it up in the *Merck Manual*. "It's a pretty heavy drug."

15

Midnight. In Room 100, Ivy Tarro had been sleeping. Now she woke with confusion in the dark, thinking she was in a strange place. Then, after a second, she remembered and felt relieved. Although she was in a hospital, she was all right. She even felt hungry, and she wanted to get up to go to the bathroom. But as she moved a wave of dizziness caught her.

And she realized that someone was hiding in the room, not just the other person whose room it was, but someone whose white-clothed legs were visible behind the curtain. Of course she knew that behind the curtain there was another sick person. Sometimes today the sick person had moaned behind the curtain, or the television could be heard, softly, and she had had a sense of its blue light, and had seen nurses walking through with thermometers and food, talking to this roommate. Why was she here with sick people?

And now, in the darkness, someone had entered the room and

walked by her, not paying attention to her, and gone behind the curtain. It must have been that that woke her up. Without raising her head, she followed, with her eyes, legs in white trousers, a noisy apparatus on wheels, the sound of a pump. She was overwhelmed with a sense that it was she who was at risk, she who was in danger because she was awake, seeing something she wasn't meant to see. The penalty for seeing would be death, for death hung about in the room somewhere. She could feel it. The legs stepped this way and that. She shut her eyes, so that she wouldn't seem to see.

She couldn't see what went on behind the curtain, but she could hear. Now she could hear gagging, dental sounds, and terse, alert voices, speaking to each other. Then she heard a weak, tremulous voice—it must be the voice of the person, of the sick, the dying person, the voice of her mirror self on the other side of the curtain. Or was it her own voice?

"Please," it whispered. It was a woman. "Don't tell anyone until morning."

"Shhhh," said a man's voice. "It's going to be all right."

"She's got no pressure at all," said another man's voice.

"Pressors!" someone cried. "Get the dopamine."

"Please," said the voice, more faintly now, "please don't tell," in a tone so sweet, so apologetic, Ivy knew it was not her own. Her heart, as swollen as her arm, seemed to press against her throat, so that she could not cry out. It seemed that she was suffocating but could not cry out, and she shivered in her bed.

For Perry Briggs the horror was that the poor woman was going to die and that she knew it. He was appalled that she should be so conscious, thinking of her family and of how unkind it would be to disturb them, and so frightened to realize that this was the end of her life, here in the unexpected night, so alone except for him and Mark, and what good were they?

Such a living whiteness to her eye, and yet unmistakable to the touch of his fingers, the pulse of blood in her wrist slowing, a certain sound in her breath. Usually, when he heard that sound, he rushed off on an errand, leaving to others whatever came next. Yet he knew he was going to have to be more manly—more physicianly—about this. It was just that until now he had never stood around watching someone die.

Mark and the nurse were making with their tubes a rushing sound of drains, a clatter of metal pans and casters, yet her blood pressure was falling, her blood was falling away from her heart like an ebbtide. Where was it going? Like the last rings of a thrown pebble, it was flattening away to unknown depths. Perry's head felt light with fear. He sat down at the bedside and took the woman's hand.

He thought she smiled in thanks, though her grasp was loose, and her eyes had begun to look funny. He wanted to shake her, or breathe into her. He watched, wouldn't let himself look away, as if he held the end of a thread, until her end dropped, and she died with a sigh.

What should they have done? How could this happen? Already, it seemed to him, her hand felt to be of some other material, like dough or rubber, in thirty seconds no longer like a human hand. This was horrible.

Help me, help me, Ivy, cowering behind the curtain, wanted to cry out but could not. She did not want to take them away from the other, the good, sweet woman on the other side. Oh, save her, she thought. A sob escaped her. They must have heard. She closed her eyes more tightly. She could feel the breath of the curtain as someone rustled it aside to look at her. Through her closed eyelids she felt solemn, appraising eyes.

"Asleep."

"Ah," said the other man. "Well, it's finished anyway. There."

"Oh." A silence.

"Well then."

"I think they were more or less prepared," whispered a nurse as they went by Ivy's bed. "But not expecting it tonight."

"Ordinarily," said Mark Silver to Perry in the hall, "we wouldn't allow a death in a double room. But this happened so fast."

She was old, said Perry to himself, trying not to cry, trying to tell himself comforting thoughts. You had to see death; it was something you had to get behind you. But he hadn't expected that there would be so much bustle and conversation. He hadn't expected that the dying person would be so in on it. "How old was she?"

"Seventy-two," Mark said. "Call the family, will you?"

"No, you. I—I didn't meet them," Perry said.

"There's a daughter."

Don't call them, thought Ivy. She doesn't want you to. She asked you not to! Should she sit up now, and open her eyes, and remind them? But she lay as if unable to move, hiding from them, still hearing the woman's resigned voice. She, Ivy, had a daughter, though she was too little to understand what was happening to Ivy. So if Ivy died they couldn't call Delia, and anyway they didn't even know her phone number, or anything about her. She thought of how it would be if she died in this hospital and no one found out.

Now she realized that though the doctors had all gone they had left the dead person there, on the other side of the curtain. Was she really dead? How cruel to leave her lying there alone. How cruel to leave Ivy lying here alone with someone dead who had been alive watching television yesterday. Ivy had heard her little cough, the tap of a cup on the bed table, and now this clandestine, surreptitious death. She shivered. She didn't feel well.

Death in the room. Ivy could feel his gaze on her too. A choking sensation in her throat became so intense that she was obliged to struggle to sit up a little. She opened her eyes. She stared at the hem of the dividing curtain, expecting death's shoes and pant legs to be visible as he quietly stood over her friend in the other bed. She closed her eyes again, because someone came in and began to do something. In a moment a quiet cortège came through Ivy's half of the room. Through her lashes, pretending to sleep, Ivy could see the shape of the dead body as they wheeled her out. Then a nurse stole in and stood by her own bed. Ivy kept her eyes closed, but she could feel the nurse looking down at her, and then the jab of a needle in her well arm.

16

At seven in the morning the nurses change. The night nurses sleepily wander out into the early morning, toward their Sentras and Accords; the first nurses of the day shifts hang up their sweaters in the nurses' conference room adjoining the nurses' station with its stacks of charts waiting. In their offices, the doctors put on their white coats for morning rounds. Philip Watts's suits have worn-out trousers, while the jackets are still perfect from hanging unworn on the coatrack in his office. Some particular smell arises in the early mornings in the hospital corridor from the disinfectant the janitors wash the floor with each evening. Randall Lincoln's father comes in at eight to spend an hour before he has to be at work. Mrs. Lincoln will come in at nine. Though Randall hasn't regained consciousness since yesterday morning, his eyes at moments flutter open.

In the corridors a rising sound of carts and trays, and the accelerating rush of the elevators, and somewhere the bell of a timer, and raucous noise of an alarm as somebody opens a door labeled RADIOACTIVE. Voices of nurses, sounds of the patients' doors being opened, people being waked. Patients waking up to a relieved sense of being safe and cared for, getting better, or to the recollection that they had forgotten in sleep that they are dying. The sick push themselves stiffly across the cold floors toward the chilly, clean tile bathrooms. Nurses' aides seize these moments to change the sheets. The sheets are stained with blood or feces, sodden with urine, salt solutions, vomit. In the corridors, piles of linen on dollies are pushed along from door to door, and outside certain doors tired watchers stand to stretch and look up and down, worn from a night vigil, or make their way toward the cafeteria. Perry and Mark, tired after the night, go for coffee in the doctors' dining room and prepare for early-morning rounds.

In the mornings, Mimi cut through the parking lot on her way to the hospital. This was the lot kept only for the doctors. The nurses parked elsewhere, in the pay lot. At this hour only the sumptuous cars of the anesthesiologists and surgeons were here, at work since five-thirty.

Mimi had noticed that the brand of car a doctor had went not by his specialty but by his size—Porsches for the short, Mercedes for the tall, a welter of BMWs and Volvos and Alfas for those in between.

Mimi couldn't help but brood about her house being taken for an even bigger parking lot—something of several stories was probably intended—cement labyrinths, reeking of urine, collision, the menace of rape. What an affliction for mankind the automobile had turned out to be, ruining cities, blighting consciousness, the emblem of American foolishness. Of course she wouldn't sell her house so they could build a parking lot.

On the other hand she could picture herself on a redwood deck of an apartment overlooking the water or in a little house in Tiburon. Her emotions contended, ending, as usual, with a self-sacrificing judgment in favor of mankind, against automobiles, and therefore against parking lots. Parking lots should not be allowed to push citizens out of their houses. A vision of hapless humans being toppled by the shining bumpers of numberless cars, lying supine beneath the wheels, a field of flattened houses with cars grazing triumphantly over them. Her blood speeded indignantly. She would stay where she was.

It was early, just seven, but she had a lot to do, with now the extra trouble of the cookbook—organizing the recipes and calling up printers who might be able to rush copies in time for the fund-raising gala. On Tuesday mornings she customarily took the bookcart to OB-GYN, but she had left it on 3F before the meeting yesterday. As she hurried down the corridor to get it, she noticed a handsome young couple standing in front of Room 100, holding a giant and imposing armload of flowers and ornamental weeds. Though this was an unorthodox, even illegal hour for a visit, Mimi was always glad when people had visitors. She worried when patients lay unvisited, and she took extra pains then to press books on them. These visitors were peering uncomfortably into Ivy Tarro's room, directing alarmed glances at each other for an answer to the mystery of Ivy's unconscious or sleeping form, a white mound with its back to them, and a tangle of red hair. These must be friends, and must know if everything was all right with the sick young woman's baby. She asked them if she could help them.

"We know it isn't visiting hours," the man said, "but we can't come in the afternoon or evening." The woman peered at Mimi through

her branches of iris and pussywillow. She looked familiar, but it took
Mimi a second to recognize her as Franni Cedar, the prominent chef,
restaurateur, and food revolutionary, whose weekly television food
show Mimi had sometimes seen.

"She's asleep," said Franni Cedar. "We went in, but she didn't open
her eyes." Her manner was excited and worried.

"Yesterday she seemed concerned about her baby," Mimi said. "Is
the babysitter all right?"

"She takes her baby over to Petra Kelly's," Franni said. "We'll
check. Gee, what's the matter with her, exactly? She said she was
coming in for a test. She looks awful."

"I don't know, exactly," Mimi said. "I'm only a volunteer. You'll
have to ask the doctor, or one of the nurses."

"They said it's a clot," said the man.

"Oh, it's horrible! Poor Ivy!" wailed Franni Cedar. "I saw her on
Sunday afternoon and she was fine!"

"I'm sure she'll be fine," Mimi said. "I'll take those flowers for you,
if you like. Ask the nurse when she'll be waking up." She wanted
them to be sure to come back. They watched a few moments more,
hoping Ivy would stir, but she did not. The visitors moved slowly
off, with anxious sidelong looks into each of the rooms, at each example
of misfortune and pain within.

Something in the heavily indifferent position of Ivy Tarro's head,
awkwardly angled, as if her neck had been broken, stirred Mimi's
fears too. She wondered if she should call someone. But of course the
nurses were watching, and the doctors would soon be in on rounds.
She had the impulse to hurry after the visitors, and find out something
about this young woman, but went instead for a vase, forgetting that
she had yesterday carted away the array of abandoned ugly vases and
chunks of green plastic foam from the nurses' conference room.

Mimi felt an interest in Ivy Tarro beyond the normal, nice human
concern she usually felt for all the patients. Was it because Ivy Tarro
had been so somehow appealing, and because she had talked to Mimi,
confiding her fears? It was interesting to think that she had some
connection with the fashionable food world, though it might only be
that she was Franni Cedar's neighbor, or the nursery-school teacher,
or anything else.

Mimi always got interested in individual patients. She was unable to keep herself from imagining their lives. Her eyes would sting with involuntary tears at the idea of their pain, their courage—their wonderful courage even to remain alive, with a leg like that: so short! all bent over! alone, in a wheelchair, overrun with children, poor—how could people bear their lives, she always wondered, yet they moved through them, buying that blue shirt, carrying that frayed plastic purse, making choices, thinking thoughts, with such a brave appearance of cheer. How could you bear to be a dwarf, or retarded, say, and see life in that frightening, powerless way, things moving past you, never to be grasped at all?

But some patients more than others made her feel too that it could be she inside that ailing form, in the bed. Sometimes something within shone out. But whatever had shone out of Ivy Tarro when Mimi first saw her was now banked or extinguished. She was barely lifelike. For the first time, Mimi felt a stir of real apprehensiveness that Ivy Tarro had a fatal illness.

Mimi stuck her head in the door of Sherry Fine's room, looking for a vase. The surly teenager was awake, watching the "Today" show.

"Did you read the book by Dickens?"

"Sure," Sherry said.

"Did you like it?"

Sherry hesitated, as if, coming from an adult, this sinister, probing question must be examined. Finally she said she'd liked it. *A Tale of Two Cities.*

"I'm only asking so I'll know what kind of thing to bring you next time," Mimi said.

"I haven't quite finished it," Sherry said.

"Time for your pill, Sherry," said the nurse, coming in. "Also, Dr. Mudd is here to talk to you."

Sherry rolled her eyes. The problem with Sherry Fine, Mimi had heard, was that though she was a middle-class child she had been supporting a drug habit by prostitution. She mentioned her parents only infrequently and with rancor, so that the hospital staff was reluctant to discharge her, even if her health had permitted it, until some provision was made for a home for her. Seeing Sherry always made Mimi feel thankful that she had held on to her house, providing a home for Narnia and Daniel. She her supposed priorities had been square, but when you had children, you had no choice. She was thankful too that Narnia and Daniel had been easy children, with ordinary problems. Though they had brought her a good deal of anxiety, this had been more a matter of her own temperament than their behavior, stemming from her own recollections of what it had been like to be a teenager, constantly at risk of traffic death, overdose, pregnancy, and childhood illnesses all at the same time.

Dr. Vivian Mudd was the doctor to whom had fallen the task of thinking about and pronouncing on the ethical implications of medical policies and the dilemmas that seemed to arise daily, mostly to do with whether or not to treat an illness in a person who was going to die of something else. When she had occasionally sat in on ethics rounds, Mimi had heard Dr. Mudd discuss various cases, always with tact and delicacy. Mimi and other volunteers, ministers and mere passersby, were frequently dragooned to provide an audience for the ethics discussions, in the hope, perhaps, that they would somewhere bear witness to the careful thought that went into making difficult decisions of life and death. Also, the doctors were forever anxious about lawsuits, and eager to make their deliberations and decisions as public as possible.

"Our old ethicist—our former ethicist—was a priest," Mimi had heard Mark Silver explain to Lum Wei-chi. "Used to be a priest—then he left the church to get married. They say he used to fool around, before that. He got some woman in trouble, and she came in with an overdose. This was before my time, but Carmel Hodgkiss told me. This was before he became the ethicist."

Dr. Lum had looked baffled. "Did she live?"

"Yes, delivered twins. But he'd fallen in love with another lady by that time, and wanted to marry her, so that's how come he ditched the mother of the twins and left the church and became our ethicist. Now he's at Fordham University as a professor of medical ethics, and Vivian's doing our ethics here."

"Is it not unusual for a woman to be an ethicist?" asked Lum Wei-chi, whose deeply Eastern view of women had struck the others before this.

"Oh, it's the kind of thing women are good at," Mark said. "And this way we don't have to think about it, she just tells us what to do."

"Women are not abstract thinkers. They are pragmatic," objected Dr. Lum.

"Look here, Wei-chi, you can't go around saying that kind of thing, in America," Mark had said.

Lum Wei-chi was nearly thirty, older than the other interns, had had to spend years as a farm worker, on account of the Cultural Revolution, before he could take the test to go to medical school. He lived with his sister somewhere in Chinatown, and planned to go back to China in four years, after his residency, and marry his fiancée. The others marveled that he could be away from her, and his country for so long, but if he missed them, he did not say so, instead presenting a smiling and interested countenance toward whatever the surprising West confronted him with.

He had an appetite for gossip that the others indulged for the pleasure of seeing his delight in the details of routine Western scandal, things so unthinkable in China, he assured them, yet so universal that he understood perfectly. Wei-chi was liked. Behind his continuous, slightly obsequious smile lay indefatigable vigilance, prodigious industry, great intelligence, and humor.

"I believe Chinese women are strong, very strong," said Wei-chi. "My sister is very strong. Of course she is very Americanized. She has been here fourteen years. She become very like American." He sounded wistful. They imagined a gum-chewing teenager with a ghetto blaster, or a computer programmer with a BMW.

The others liked to hear Wei-chi's stories, and he had particular success among Americans with his accounts of the People's Republic of China, especially stories of suffering during the Cultural Revolution. It required no invention to produce these accounts, since anecdotes abounded from his own life, stories of the collective farm far from his home, studying at night for the district medical-school entrance exam. But there were many stories more affecting than his own, especially stories of his brother Yong-gang.

"I am very lucky Chinese person," he often said. "In my country many very intelligent persons cannot continue their studies. For example, my brother, older than me, has tasted the anger and bitterness of this. He was too old to study more when things began to change, after the Cultural Revolution, now he is a bus driver. He lives in one-half of a room, with a blanket down the middle, hung on a rope, another family lives on the other side of the blanket." The Americans would gasp and stare. "Very small room. He would like to marry, but he cannot until he receive a bigger room." Wei-chi was saving as much as he could from his small intern's salary to send to his brother so he could marry.

In fact, the bigness of American rooms sometimes bothered him. When he felt forlorn or wanted to study, he would seek out a small, darkish, homelike space somewhere in the hospital—the file closet off Dr. Watts's office, or the little mop room by the elevators.

17

Ivy woke without knowing she had slept. A faint light from the end of the room showed that morning had come. The death in the night was still in her mind. Now she was alone, and death for the moment had left the room, but almost more terrible than the idea of a corpse in the room was the new idea of the bare bed, sheets stripped off, bare down to the mattress, as if after infection or plague. Like her little brother's bed after he had wet it. To die was a similar biological wickedness, and all trace and memory of you must be aired out.

The idea was still in her mind, powerfully reinforced by the evidence of the night, that she herself had been arbitrarily selected for death, even though she was young. She had thought of death before and never believed in it, but now it was underway, and this hospital was where it was to be enacted, when it came her turn, and this room was where they put you when it was your turn, although her turn would probably not come now, not until night. Or the night after.

She felt much worse than she had yesterday. Her head hurt—it was radiant with heat and pain, and damp beneath her hair. When she tried to lift it, it seemed too heavy on her neck, and then her neck hurt and felt bruised, like a bent stem, or someone's neck who'd been strangled. Trying to follow a thought to its end, she would get lost, could only get as far as wondering why she was there, or about Delia. Then a stir of fear would flatten her back onto the pillow, and then a cloud, a black fog, would confuse her brain with the notion that it didn't matter, and that someone would come to help her, wherever she was. She closed her eyes.

She was barely aware of hands plucking at her arm, lifting it, replacing it on the cover. She could feel the tug of skin where she was attached to a tube. A face smiled over her, and, like an infant, she recognized that it was someone, and she smiled to please it. How long has she been here? Is she getting worse, she wondered, can she be dying already? But it doesn't seem worth asking about. She thought about calling Delia's babysitter, but couldn't seem to think how to do it.

The face was a black face, smiling. "Miz Tarro, think you could eat some breakfast? Some cereal? I'm gonna give you some juice to drink, honey." Ivy, mindful of the nurse's cap, obediently promised to sip some juice, and hands behind her shoulders dragged her up into a sitting position.

She is propped up, leaning against the hard pillow, the round, hard straw thrust between her lips, cold juice sourly trickling down her throat and chin. There is no one in the other bed, behind the curtain. Ivy's eyes open to look at her own arm, which two days ago had been a normal arm. How can it be that an arm, mere appendage, reliable, could betray?

She remembered herself again saying, "There's something wrong—look—it's swollen all up," and remembered the doctor's alarmed face, and the telephone calls. Doctor to doctor: We have a woman here. Her arm. Yes, we can bring her right up. Bring her, send her, catch her. Ivy couldn't remember. Her head was hot and full of pain. Had they led her by the hand, like a child to school? Or written something on a paper? Yes, the doctor's name, and she'd gone in the elevator alone, up two floors, it came back clearly for a moment, then receded, and she tasted the juice.

"That's it, honey, just try to take a little more," the nurse was saying. She took the cup and put a thermometer in Ivy's mouth. In a minute she saw that she was correct, that Mrs. Tarro had a raging fever. She entered the figure on the chart for the resident to see when he checked it.

Now, seeing that Ivy Tarro was awake, Mimi planned to take the weed bouquet in. And maybe Ivy had changed her mind since yesterday about taking something to read. She had noticed that sometimes people who didn't read ordinarily would settle down to the reality of a hospital stay and resign themselves to books. Perhaps they even liked a commitment of time ahead of them. Mimi hadn't come to any conclusion as to whether Mrs. Tarro was a nonreader or a reader. Yesterday the poor girl had seemed too deranged by her new context to enable Mimi to guess. But resignation should have settled upon her by now.

Now, when she saw Mimi, Ivy weakly raised her head. She was worse, Mimi could easily see. Her pale arms, still confined in tubes, lay weakly at her side, as if she'd lost the use of them since yesterday, or as if the tubes were draining off her energy into the bottle that swayed above her. Even her electric hair of frizzy red, which yesterday had stood out from her head in Pre-Raphaelite abundance, now hung in pale, lank strands, and she had smudges under her eyes where the mascara had melted. But, as Mimi approached the bed, leaving her cart in the doorway, Ivy Tarro's eyes opened with frantic vigor.

"You've got to help me," she whispered. Her voice was weak but urgent. "I shouldn't be here. There's nothing wrong with me." Mimi heard something of the tone of a terrified prisoner. But of course nothing makes you stay in a hospital if you aren't sick, Mimi told herself. You aren't a prisoner. Mimi put Mrs. Tarro's panic to normal fear, or medication.

"Can you help me?" Ivy whispered again. "They've made a mistake. Please tell someone I'm here. I'll give you a phone number. I told them I was only going for an x-ray."

"Of course," Mimi began to soothe her. "Your friends were just here. They're talking to the doctor now. Everything will be all right," hearing in her own platitudes of reassurance an unconvincing note. Ivy closed her eyes and turned her head away, making Mimi feel ashamed of being about to say the same irritating things she heard nurses say, the way she sometimes heard herself say to Daniel and Narnia the things her own mother used to say. "You'll be better soon," she heard herself say. "The doctors will help you."

Then, as Ivy Tarro was about to reply, a day nurse came in with a small bottle in her hand, and began to fiddle with the large IV bottle beside Ivy's bed. Mimi withdrew a few steps and prepared to turn away, but the nurse was merely adding something to the mixture that already dripped into Ivy's veins.

"Hold your hands still, girl, you goin' to pull that out," said the nurse, of Ivy's sudden fitful brushing of her cobwebs of crinkly red hair out of her eyes. Now Mimi saw that the nurse was indeed going to give Ivy Tarro some kind of shot, so she stepped quickly back to her cart and pushed it out the doorway, the curtain falling closed behind her.

On an impulse she looked into the nurses' conference room. Here an informal system of collaboration and gossip operated by which the nurses, nurses' aids, volunteers, food people, and orderlies kept each other posted if they noticed that a patient was upset or was taking a turn for the worse. Then the nurse would tell the intern, the intern the resident, the resident the chief resident or private doctor, even, perhaps, ultimately, the head of the service, depending.

Mimi felt she ought to mention to the resident, Mark Silver, who was there reading the charts, that Mrs. Tarro in Room 100 was agitated as well as ill, though she felt a little like a snitch in saying so—there had been something confidential and personal in Ivy Tarro's panic. Mimi had an idea that, if the doctors went in to see if Ivy was upset, she would pretend to be fine, the way she had stopped talking when the nurse had come in. It was as if she had decided to trust only Mimi.

Mimi also knew that the professionals on the ward didn't pay much attention to her medical assessments, because she had a tendency to think people were upset or getting worse when they were fine. They knew it was all a function of her own wish that everyone be well again. She always hoped, in each new hospital case, that the doctor by some clever stroke would find a new combination of tricks or drugs that would happen, this time, to work.

"Yes, I'll look at her," Mark Silver said. "Her temperature is up." Mimi thought him one of the nicest young doctors, perhaps because he was one of the few who took out books. He was not handsome but had an earnest, dimpled smile. He had grown up in the Bronx, or some other borough, and had embarked, he confided to Mimi, on a campaign of self-improvement to do with reading the classics and losing his Bronx accent. He was a second-year medical resident, and, unlike the more research-minded doctors, was drawn to the drama of the intensive care unit and the camaraderie of the nurses' station, if not to one of the nurses. Mark, followed by Perry and Wei-chi, hurried off to check on Ivy Tarro.

18

Philip Watts, getting to the hospital at six-thirty, waited until seven to call Brian Smeed, the chief resident in medicine. "It's about this cocaine business," Philip said. He heard Smeed's tense sigh. He showed up in Philip's office moments later.

"It came to my attention," Philip said. "I wonder what you plan to do."

"I'm inclined to be tolerant," Smeed explained. "I've had a talk with the guy. There was really only one person involved, who might have kind of a problem. A couple of other interns did a couple of lines once. They needed to stay up. I don't think it'll happen again."

"Who's the resident?" Of course Philip understood the various loyalties and proscriptions and considerations of honor that made Smeed ambivalent about answering. But he was also thinking about Wystan Morris, and what substance abuse led to, if nobody stepped in. "I'm sorry," he said, "but I think you'd better tell me, and of course you have to terminate his residency. I'll stand behind that action. Or, if it makes you feel better, suspend him pending discussion with the faculty professional qualifications board and let us take the heat."

"I don't agree with that. I didn't do it because the guy's competent, and it seems gratuitous to ruin his career."

"I can't imagine anything more irresponsible and incompetent and irredeemably final than using drugs, especially on duty," Philip said. "That's flat, that's final, that's an absolute. People's lives, hospital liability—there's all that it says about someone's character, that they could jeopardize their judgment when they have people's lives in their charge—there's too much at stake. It's not even a question of rules.

It's common sense. There don't have to be rules about something as out of bounds as this."

"Jesus, Dr. Watts, that's kind of draconian," Smeed said.

"Whatever," Philip said. "Tell me who it is. He's out of here," and Smeed reluctantly told him.

Next, Philip reviewed the charts, noting the death during the night of Mrs. Apple, and at eight-thirty he met the housestaff for morning rounds. The start of rounds was delayed by the arrival from the Emergency Room of a patient with a drug overdose—coincidentally enough, after the discussion with Smeed, from a cocaine seizure. Judging from the bulk under the white sheet, the patient was a hugely corpulent, raven-haired young man, his face blank and rosy, trailed with tubes in his arm, and nose, overseen by the ER resident, Dave Turner, the cardiology resident, Heather Wu, and a neurologist. At a distance behind them, a delicate golden-skinned, black-haired young woman—perhaps the wife or girlfriend—followed, wet-eyed, gaping with fright to see the ministrations of the doctors. Heather Wu had ascertained that she was from the Philippines, and asked if there were any Filipinos who could speak to her.

It took Turner, Edgardo, the burly male nurse, and an orderly to lift the fat young man into the ICU bed. The Filipino nurse, Merci, talked in Tagalog to the relative as she worked, setting about the business of hooking him up to the life-support systems.

"Apparently they were sniffing some cocaine, in bed, and he had a seizure. It must have been some stuff," Dave Turner told Philip. "This is the second thing we've had like this, this month. There must be some crazy stuff out there." Philip felt a rather unworthy twinge of self-justification.

"She's not the wife, she's the girlfriend," Merci said, speaking of the frightened woman. "She says there's a wife we should call."

"His name is Mr. Rainwater," Heather said to Philip. "Perfecto Rainwater."

"Is he a Filipino? What kind of name is Rainwater? I mean, what does he speak?" Philip asked.

"It's more or less academic," the neurologist said, "since he's completely out of it. His brain's as flat as a roadbed. I think he's an Indian. Native American."

"Welcome to the vegetable garden," somebody said. It was true that the line of the EEG lay as flat as Kansas, except for a tiny hill, a little prairie-dog mound each minute, that told them he was alive. Native American.

"Jesus, it must have been some stuff," Mark Silver agreed.

"Yes, I think he's a Native American," Heather said. "Rainwater? Ask her, will you, Merci, if he's a Native American?" The girlfriend nodded, yes, yes, as if it would help.

Leaving the ICU team to line up Perfecto, Philip went on with his housestaff. They assembled outside the first room, Randall Lincoln's, which he could see was empty, the bed inside neatly made and turned down. He was surprised. "Where's Randall?"

"Down being dialyzed," said Mark. "His numbers turned sour during the night. The potassium increased to 6.5 so we got the kidney people over here at about six this morning."

Philip took in this grave information, and stifled an impulse to rebuke them for not discussing dialysis with him. When the large dose of morphine, given to alleviate the horrible pain of the sickle cells, had stopped Randall's breathing, they had elected to resuscitate him. But whether to subject him to dialysis, an elaborate process to remove the toxins from his blood because his own kidneys had shut down, was a judgment call, since it was by no means clear that he was ever going to regain consciousness, and the fact that he had shown no improvement at all during the twenty-four hours since his crisis made recovery less likely.

One would like to know how much permanent damage had been done to his brain, but this just wasn't possible yet. If he was allowed to slip away in painless renal failure, the worst would now be over, for him and for his poor parents. Instead, they had it all to dread and suffer through soon enough—a few weeks or months at best. Philip decided to write a No Code order, which meant that if Randall's heart or breathing stopped again, no one should try to start it beating. No Code acknowledged that death was death, and that for Randall life was hopeless.

"We are going to have to talk to Mrs. Lincoln about whether, if Randall should arrest again, we should think of a No Code," Philip said to the housestaff. He saw the distressed looks on their faces. "Of course maybe things will be all right for the moment," he added, understanding their emotion. Getting a young housestaff to accept death was one of the hardest things. It was never easy to accept.

"Any extra moments will be cherished by that family," Perry Briggs said. "There's been someone in there with him every minute of the day and night. His mom's been here all night. His brother's there now."

"Yes, it's a nice family," Philip agreed, thinking of the variations of human family they saw crowded around the bedsides, sobbing or dry-eyed, concerned or indifferent, sometimes drunk. There seemed to be some operative principle by which the nicest families had the worst things to bear. And the Lincolns still had Randall's death ahead of them. "We'll discuss it at Morbidity and Mortality Conference. I'm going to write a No Code order."

They walked along past Room 100. In the bed, the private patient of Bradford Evans drooped against the bed pillows, her wrist encircled in tubes, a cutdown in her arm.

"Dr. Watts, at some point we'd like to discuss this patient," said Mark Silver. "Some of us have been wondering why she's on streptokinase, rather than heparin or some other agent, and the diagnosis. Her temperature's elevated, and it looks to me like her arm's infected."

"Has Dr. Evans seen her this morning? Is he here? Could we page Dr. Evans?" Philip asked the nurse. "I don't know what the diagnosis is, I haven't seen the patient." He had noted without concern but with some annoyance that Evans had stipulated that she should be exempted from rounds. And he was surprised that she had been put on a toxic drug like streptokinase. He would have started out, he noted almost automatically, with indomethacin or heparin.

"Dr. Evans hasn't been in yet this morning. He usually gets here about nine-thirty," the nurse noted. "He changed the order to streptokinase last night."

Even from the doorway Philip could see that the patient was febrile. She looked strangely familiar to him; but when she looked at him, flushed but sentient, she showed no sign that she recognized him. He had the idea, almost, that she must resemble someone else; but there was the matter of the familiarity of her name. Whatever it was, it wasn't important. He stepped into the room, followed by his troop of housestaff, and they gathered to gaze down on Ivy.

"I'm Dr. Watts," Philip began. As he was saying this he was surprised, and uncannily dismayed to realize that Bradford Evans had come into the room behind them. He had a guilty sensation of trespassing on Evans's patient, though in fact he wasn't treating this patient and wasn't interfering. But he was in the room, and Evans was notoriously touchy.

"Hello, Brad. I'm just saying hello to Mrs. Tarro. She . . ." It seemed to him that Evans was studying him for signs of disapproval, meddling, or concern.

"I'd be happy if Mrs. Tarro were well enough to socialize," Evans said, crossing to the bed and taking Ivy's wrist. Her eyes regarded him, then Philip, then the others, then Evans again, apathetically. Her eyes were feverishly bright beneath swollen lids. Her lashes were so fair that her eyes looked bare. "Are you feeling better?"

"No," she said, "I feel worse."

"Let me have a look at that arm. Hmmm," said Evans, giving it a painful poke.

"Heparin," Philip blurted, before he could stop himself. "I'd have used heparin."

Evans looked at him, scowling, still clutching her little arm: "Since this is my patient, I'll treat her as I see fit. I'm doing what is best."

"I beg your pardon. I was just thinking aloud," Philip apologized, realizing that he was out of order in criticizing Brad's treatment; she was a private patient, and anyway he hadn't even looked at her chart. He began to back toward the door. "I was thinking of rounds, a discussion. Interesting patient. Perhaps you would present her . . ."

"Out of the question for the moment. She's much too ill," Evans growled, and Philip could see that he wasn't mollified, was irritated by this breach of medical etiquette, this presumptuousness, someone meddling with his private patient, and to make it worse, speaking out in front of her.

"I'm not getting better, am I?" he heard her ask, in a frightened voice.

"This is a stubborn thing, very stubborn," Evans was saying as Philip walked on down the hall. "You aren't getting better. I think I may make your medicine a bit stronger." This said with a heavy note of willfulness.

"The fever could be a reaction to the streptokinase," Evans acknowledged to the housestaff. "That could be the beginning of an urticaria," touching a welt on Ivy's arm. "We'll change the drug to urokinase. It's more expensive but there's less chance of a reaction." The young doctors nodded solemnly, gazing at the tracery of blue beneath the surface of her translucent skin.

"Urokinase—a medicine made from the piss of six thousand GIs." Evans laughed.

Philip was seriously angry at himself for being rude to Evans. He believed it was important that the teaching staff get along with the private physicians, not antagonize them with their more rigorous and academic approach. The rules defining courtesy and cooperation were of course informal, not legislated. They just made sense. You especially didn't embarrass, criticize, or even question a fellow doctor in front of a patient or nurse. For one thing, it was very undermining for the patient if he got the idea that his physician didn't enjoy the perfect respect and confidence of his fellow physicians.

At four that afternoon, he was still brooding on this delicate nuance of physicianly behavior and his own breach of it as he made a slight change in Randall's medication and went along to Morbidity and Mortality Conference, angry at himself and, therefore, with things in general. It was at such a conference as this that a difference in opinion between, say, streptokinase and heparin, should be discussed.

The doctors had gathered in the x-ray reading room, where great radiographs of whitish lungs emitted their eerie light upon the house-staff and local physicians collected there. Philip stood next to Vivian Mudd, the ethicist, and Lum Wei-chi. Dr. Lum bowed slightly. Brian Smeed, the chief resident, was standing behind the table, reading from notes.

"This sixty-year-old white male . . ."

But Philip's mind did not focus on the discussion. He made mental apologies to Evans. He thought of his overhead and volley. He found himself wondering if anyone else in this company was a cocaine user. That seemed such an incredible breach of . . . of everything that he could hardly believe it, yet he believed it. Trying to keep awake, probably. But was it frequent, occasional, a mistake, a problem? There didn't seem to be anything out of order. The company of young doctors were attentive, involved, their expressions absorbed. They weren't sniffling, didn't have red nostrils or hot eyes. They were variously dressed, rumpled or tidy, ties, no ties, beards, clean-shaven, the women in pants or skirts—a paradigm of American social attitudes reflected in the way they dressed. Were the cocaine users the hippies or the yuppies?

Someone asked him a question, interrupting this reverie. Philip answered perfunctorily the half-heard question, and his mind went on with his thoughts, now focused on the neckties. Brian Smeed was wearing a fatigue jacket and jeans, like a student leader from the sixties, strangely displaced in the wrong decade, wearing the same surly look of protest and suspicion they had all worn—himself included, though none of these kids would believe that. Freddie Barlow and Pet Ansel also didn't wear ties and looked sloppy. The women, Heather Wu, Margaret Rose, and Cindy Merrit, were neatly dressed for success, and Cindy did wear a tie. Jerry Purvis and Perry Briggs, both in round granny glasses, wore ties and starched shirts beneath their white coats. These, Philip supposed, were the squares. All the doctors, but especially the women, were festooned with stethoscopes slung around their necks, and beepers, to avoid being taken for nurses.

"May I just say something," Philip heard himself begin, knowing he was going to sound like an asshole, but with a feeling building up in him. "Would it be too much to ask for people to be neatly dressed and wear neckties?"

A murmur, a chorus, of uncomfortable response: yes, no, what's he on about now?

"Dr. Smeed," Philip went fatally on, "would it be too much trouble to be neat? To wash, for Chrissake? I mean, I know you wash, but you should look like you wash." There was a stunned silence, broken only by the hum of the viewing machines. He had spoken to them as if they were a collection of nine-year-olds. The silence was broken by a wild giggle from Wei-chi. For a startled moment, Philip wondered if he had been funny, but of course it was embarrassment that now caused Wei-chi to duck his head in shame.

"I happen to think that the image of the doctor is important," Brian Smeed said, angrily, "and it should be an image people can identify with. I'm against dressing up like God. The white-coat bullshit just makes a class distinction between doctor and patient, and I think that's wrong."

"You might consider it from the patient's standpoint. Would you rather have God taking care of you or someone who looks like, like . . ." The comparisons that came to his mind were too bitter and old-fashioned sounding; he didn't say them. "People have to have confidence in the physician, almost as a first condition." Here he thought of his own thoughtless remark in front of Bradford Evans's patient, tearing down her confidence.

"I would really like to know how patients feel about this," he went on. "Rather, I'd like you to know. I'm fairly sure." Here he thought of Randall Lincoln's parents, and of how soon he must remind them that Randall was going to die. How should you dress to bring that news? Well, surely with dignity? Ivy Tarro. Little Sherry Fine? What, in fact, did they think of white coats?

"Could I go on?" said Smeed. "The pulmonary function studies were . . ."

With an effort, Philip brought his mind back to this topic, but there remained a knot of crossness and self-consciousness, a slight apprehension that he was acting in ways surprising to himself, abrupt and impulsive, with no idea why.

19

As Mimi sat in the doctors' dining room with a cup of tea, Dr. Jeffrey Fowler sat down with her and began to tell her about an experience he had had flying home from an NIH meeting the day before.

"My bad luck to catch that particular flight," he was saying. "Somebody went into cardiac arrest. He was turning blue in his seat. Of course I was the only doctor on the plane."

"Did you help?" Mimi asked, apprehensively.

"Well, yes, but when I was trying to pull him out of his seat—he was kind of wedged in, turning blue—I put my back out."

"Not every doctor would have helped," she said. "Quite often they don't stop at an accident, or when someone is lying there."

"There's a law now," Dr. Fowler said. "They can't sue you if you stop to help. Before, they could, you know, if it didn't work out. It's called the Good Samaritan law."

"How could a person think of that, think of themselves, when a person is lying there in need of help!" Mimi cried.

"You hear some horror stories," Dr. Fowler said. "You stop to help, too late to save the guy's leg or whatever, the guy sues you. These people collect, too."

This made Mimi think of an evening with Bradford Evans. They were walking along after dinner, an early evening, faintly twilight, nine or ten o'clock, not really dark, and he had been speaking of string quartets. Of Bartók. He played the cello. Up ahead, Mimi could see someone lying in the gutter.

In the corner of her eye, in the gutter to the left, someone was lying. Of course one often saw that. People often lay in the gutter in alarming attitudes of sleep or drunkenness, but this form was cast or fallen—something about the twist of limbs, the arms broken-looking, flung outward. He could have been dead but for the staring eyes, staring right at them, or maybe it was a dead stare. But it appeared that Brad didn't see him at all. Yet how could he not have? She had been afraid to speak, afraid to put him on the spot, for which she afterwards despised herself. Looking back on this had confirmed her in her view that things would be impossible with any doctor. They were all alike and it was just better not to get mixed up with them. And yet she had liked him quite a lot.

In fact, she had felt so close to him that evening she had confided some personal matters to him—how she had felt, growing up, at being so tall, though she knew that her feelings of shy awkwardness afflicted adolescents of any size, and her own experiences had been perfectly routine—being endlessly told not to stoop, and that the boys would eventually grow, and that she must not feel that she always had to wear flat shoes.

"But you were always beautiful, I bet," Bradford had said. "I was the smallest boy in my class until the eighth grade, and my voice didn't change till I was sixteen." Yes, she had thought him nice—but how poorly she had understood his character!

"Well," said Mimi, returning her attention to Jeffrey Fowler, "what happened to the man? Did you save him?"

"They made an emergency stop in Pittsburgh and took him to the hospital. He was doing okay. Hey—I have to go. We're locking horns with your precious Phil Watts."

This startled Mimi considerably. Her Philip Watts? Her precious? What would make Jeffrey Fowler say something like that? Did she wear her expressions on her face too plainly, or light up in some obvious way when Philip came in? Did others know something she had not allowed herself to know, or was just beginning to know, about her feelings for Philip? She felt her face grow rosy with dismay.

20

Philip spent the late afternoon disputing with the surgeons about the management of a difficult, complex, and interesting liver case. Then he met the housestaff for signout rounds. Things were unchanged since morning, except that Randall was back from dialysis and Mrs. Tarro was worse. The housestaff wanted to talk about her.

"Dr. Briggs has done the workup," Brian Smeed said. Philip looked at Perry Briggs, the nervous intern, who clutched a folded piece of paper on which he had made notes.

"This twenty-seven-year-old white female was admitted to the hospital by her local M.D.—that's Dr. Evans, in this case—after being seen in his office for a grossly swollen right arm of sudden onset. She gives the story that she doesn't use drugs and is not on any medication."

" 'Gives the story'?" Philip interrupted. "That implies disbelief. Didn't you believe her?"

"Well, yes, but . . ."

"Patients rarely tell 'stories,' " Philip snapped. He believed that doctors did not pay enough attention to what people actually said.

Perry flushed and continued. "Dr. Evans made the diagnosis of a blood clot of unknown origin obstructing the subclavian vein, and this was substantiated by a venogram Monday morning. She was admitted that afternoon and started on indomethacin. Then last night she was switched to streptokinase when she didn't show any improvement with indomethacin, and the dosage of streptokinase was . . ."

"Let's do this tomorrow. I'd really prefer to wait for Dr. Evans," Philip said. "It'd be more appropriate. He can tell us why he ordered streptokinase, now urokinase. Presumably he is expecting to dissolve the clot, which is the effect of those particular agents. Alternatively one might approach the problem with heparin, but no doubt he had his reasons." Here he paused, sensing he was being drawn into a criticism of Bradford Evans. "We can come back to this. Let's look in on Sherry."

Philip was being careful to observe the usual medical decorum. He was as exacting on himself as on the housestaff, for he believed that doctors had to be perfect, and that they could be—not their private characters, perhaps, and not their every decision. He had humanity in perspective, he hoped. But he did believe their motives and their consciences should always bear examination. They should not undermine one another. They should never stay home when they were needed in the middle of the night, and they should go to the library to look something up when there was the slightest question in the mind, something imperfectly remembered. They shouldn't let greed, sex, or family troubles interfere with patient care—drugs went without saying.

A certain discretion ought to be part of the medical character, too. A doctor shouldn't bicker and backbite, or joke about patients, or belittle them behind their backs, though this last lapse was hard to avoid and could be forgiven. There were types of patients he himself couldn't stand—drug addicts, for one. And the very fat. Slightly pitiless of moral weakness in general, he really did pity addiction. It was just that he hated the personality of drug addicts. He found them weasly and manipulative, and something frightened or horrified him about fat people that he couldn't explain; he felt some combination of revulsion and fascination at the rippling folds of pebbly flesh, the dominion of sheer mass, and the misery of desire you saw in their piggy eyes. So he did, he knew, sometimes say something denigrating, out of earshot, to a house officer, about a fat patient or a drug addict, though he was always sorry the moment after.

For the old alcoholics dragged in out of the gutters, with their cirrhosis and their gangrenous fingers and sores and despair, he felt detached sorrow, knowing nothing could ever help them. And equally he pitied and loved, in a way, the suicidal, hysterical young men he often saw, who had swallowed sleeping pills after quarrels with lovers. He didn't like to think of men as being so vulnerable and wretched, and it made him want to shore them up, if only by example—his—calm, in control, magisterial.

21

With one part of her mind, Ivy was aware of the tiptoeing of the doctors past her room, of their looking in on her. But she didn't want to turn or open her eyes. Her head burned and was filled with images from her childhood; it was like being six again, blazing with fever, and her mother was giving her sherbet. It was lemon and pineapple, always the same, the taste strangely present in her delirium. She was afraid of the soft steps of the hospital people, bringing new torments. She heard the doctors stop at her door, heard the one say, "Let's wait for Dr. Evans," and then heard them move away. She didn't care. Indifferently she lay, abandoned. She knew she ought to try to feel a will to live. She was supposed to be a fighter. But still she lay there. She thought of Delia and home, and of Franni and the restaurant, but without interest, as if these were the details of someone else's life.

She had to pee but she couldn't remember what you did. She couldn't remember walking across the room to use the bathroom, or a nurse with a bedpan; yet she must have been peeing, she'd been here now how long? All at once, with a start of panic, she felt a wet trickle on her thigh, and she thought she must have wet herself. She felt warm wetness in her hand, too. Surprised, she opened her palm and saw that it was slickly wet with blood. Blood welling up and exuding droplets, like the hand of a Catholic statue, like the hand of a saint. Stigmata. An unsurprising feature of some unforeseen agony for which she had been selected, she knew not why. She wiped her palm across the white coverlet, smearing it in red. She lay, passive with fever, bloody. Looking at her hand again, she saw drops spring to the surface and slide along the lifeline, the heart line, choking them with blood. She wanted to scream for help, but the impulse was expended by thinking of it, so she laid her head on the pillow again, to gain strength, and closed her eyes again.

The nurse, glancing in, was alarmed at the sight of the bloody coverlet on Tarro's bed, and at the rivulet of blood welling up where the IV went into her arm, blood running down her immobilized arm. She was lying inert, as if she had lost all her blood; the blood trickled into the interstices of her fingers. She didn't seem to notice, didn't seem conscious, and her eyes stared strangely when she opened them, as if in shock. The nurse hastily reassured herself that she hadn't had time to bleed out since anyone looked at her last. She put her head out the door and called into the hallway, where the doctors were involved with a newly admitted pneumocystic pneumonia, behind his isolation door.

"Hey," she called, "this woman is bleeding. Dr. Briggs."

Perry Briggs, as usual startled to hear his name, leaped alertly toward Ivy's room, followed, to his relief, by the rest of the team. The young woman was lying in blood-smeared sheets, as if she had been massacred.

"This makes the point," said Philip Watts, in his calm voice. "Bleeding is one of the risks with streptokinase—the main risk with these drugs." Perry helped the nurse unfasten the IV and stanch the blood that continued to burble from the insertion of the catheter into her arm.

The sight of the cutdown in this beautiful young woman's arm made his stomach turn. The blue tinge of her thin eyelids intensified the odd blue of her pale eyes, with their golden rims of lash. Perry was almost too terrified of patients to be a doctor at all, as Philip had quickly seen. In fact Perry had even hated sticking needles in the practice orange they had begun on. He had been horrified to see the way, with what decision, what relish, the shiny pink fingers of the nurses with their neat fingernails could grasp this instrument of pain and thrust it into the gelid thighlike flesh of the fruit. To him the sensation of the needle piercing even unfeeling citrus brought terrible associations of human muscle; he could almost feel the orange shrink, contract, cry out. Philip had seen before young men too squeamish to be clinicians, but he thought that Perry would probably overcome it.

Ivy Tarro lay like a piece of funerary statuary, pale as stone. Her eyes at one moment opened to look directly, pleadingly, at Perry; otherwise he would have thought she was unconscious.

"Mrs. Tarro! Mrs. Tarro!" Perry said in an urgent, loud voice. "It'll be okay!" He looked anxiously at Philip, to see if this was the truth. Ivy, terrified by the arrival of these doctors and by the gasp she had heard the nurse give, and by the warm feel of her blood, lost consciousness.

Philip Watts, leaning over the bed, picked up the arm, now free of the tubes and bottles, still grossly swollen, as Rosemary Hunt, the nurse, and Perry swaddled the arm in a tight bandage to stop the bleeding from the cut where the tubes had gone in.

"Remember you should be wearing gloves," Philip admonished them. "You don't know about this woman's blood. You must avoid contact with blood." He wasn't wearing gloves. He turned her palm upward. "She's bleeding here too. She must have had a cut here." The blood, like a capped well, ceased its gushing as Perry pressed on the spot and Rosemary slowly wound the bandage around the arm. Philip Watts pulled down the covers and looked at the rest of her body.

Limp limbs sprawling out of short hospital nightgown. Furze of red bush barely visible at her crotch, where the gown hiked up. Philip Watts lifted the hem to look at a rapidly swelling purple hematoma in her groin from which trickled a thin trail of blood. Perry, uncomfortable staring at the private parts of a nearly unconscious young woman averted his eyes, but could not help noticing that her vagina had the slightly ragged lips of a woman who had recently given birth.

"Someone must have drawn blood there," Philip explained. "In this situation, you expect bleeding wherever there's been a break in the blood vessels. Get some pressure on the groin there." The room was filled with the sour odor of blood and the sweetness of the disinfectants. Perry pressed his fingers firmly on the extending purple swelling under her skin, at the margin of the V of pubic hair, and looked discreetly away.

"Her fever may also be from the toxicity of the streptokinase or urokinase," Philip said. "Anyhow stop the drug until the bleeding's under control. I'll take responsibility for doing that. Then check with Dr. Evans in the morning about what he wants to put her on."

The housestaff looked forward to an informative discussion between the two senior physicians, if not an impending clash. Dr. Evans contrasted in every way, temperamentally and intellectually, with Philip Watts. Where Watts was judicious and conservative, Evans was dramatic, forceful, and daring. His strong measures sometimes produced impressive results; sometimes they got a patient into trouble. Philip had a greater trust in the course of nature than Evans had, and was usually content to let it lend a hand; he even had a certain mistrust of medicines and drugs, except for antibiotics, of course, and a few other trusted agents in use for decades. Slightly more people were kept alive under his regime than under Evans's, perhaps, yet it could be argued that Evans's specialty, cardiology, brought him patients who were sicker in the first place.

Interns and residents, always eager to try things out, sometimes chafed under Watts's restraints, especially when he insisted on removing hopeless patients from the intensive care unit or prevented painful tubes from being put down them at the last. In the same circumstances, Evans was usually willing to have another go. A burst of optimism or some manic impulse would compel his pen across the chart, ordaining some extreme but interesting measure. According to Mark Silver, the man had gloomy depressions, "nearly clinical," and people did recall that during the period of his divorce he had taken a vacation of more than two months, unusual for a physician in practice, for whom vacations are money lost; and divorces were expensive.

Evans was about fifty, large, approaching stoutness, but vigorous and active, a good-looking man. He sailed, and according to Brian Smeed, he was famous for the distance he could urinate. If he'd had a few beers, he could be prevailed upon at medical meetings to perform one of his feats, and could hit a target at thirty feet, with the other doctors cheering and yelling. Chad Birkin had also known someone who played the violin in the same amateur weekend string quartet in which Bradford Evans played the cello.

"It's unusual, though, isn't it, for a guy to play the cello?" Mark Silver had commented.

"Mrs. Tarro," Ivy became aware of voices and a doctor leaning over her. Someone continued to press on her down there. Someone began to wash her fingers, sticky with blood. Was this death, then? It came to her to fasten her thoughts, perhaps for the last time, on her baby, Delia, and on the idea of herself as she had been two or three days ago. How long had it been? She had no idea. Nor could she remember Delia's face. All she could remember was some shoes she had bought herself, green snakeskin shoes, but the heels were too high, she couldn't wear them, kept turning her ankles.

Each moment could be the beginning of the process of the end of life. Now she saw that the beginning of her death had been those shoes, evil, green snakeskin, as in some Edenic parable. How her head ached, and made her want to cry, though she was someone who never cried, and thought of herself instead as someone who always laughed and danced in green shoes.

"What are you doing?" she managed to whisper. "What's that?"

"We're giving you some new medicine to control your bleeding," said the face of the doctor, close to hers. "We think this is going to help you."

Ivy indifferently waited to feel the effect of this new fluid, expected it to hit her heart or her stomach with some horrible or lethal sensation, perhaps an icy-cold sensation freezing the limbs. The muscles in her arms and legs stiffened in resistance, waiting for the hit. She thought of mummies, embalmed with fluids dripping into them, wrapped in sheets. Her head began to flame again, as if it had been turned up, and her thoughts almost immediately became less clear under the growing hum. As weak as she was, she tried to smile at the doctor and nurse, so they wouldn't hurt her.

Philip Watts, coming back into the room, saw Ivy Tarro smile at Perry Briggs. There was nothing new in this. He was used to the various patient smiles—the grateful smile, the touching effort at civility that causes someone to smile although in pain; the smile of pain, even, or the smile of relief at coming through. But he was startled to feel that he desired this smile for himself. He was also conscious of a feeling of outrage, medical outrage, at this inexcusable turn of events, a patient getting worse—this poor, pretty young woman who never should have been put on streptokinase in the first place.

22

"What did you do today?" asked Jennifer Watts, as usual, as they sat down to dinner.

"Oh, it was interesting," Philip said, helping himself to a slice of ham. "A standoff with the surgeons, as usual. We had a patient—a labor organizer—a big drinker, and obviously he'd really laid into the stuff for quite a few years. He'd completely destroyed his liver. I wanted Jeffrey Fowler to do a porto-caval shunt, that's a shunt from the portal vein to the inferior vena cava. But the scar tissue was so massive around the liver that when they got in there, they had a hard time dissecting out the inferior vena cava."

"Mmm," said Jennifer, with a certain faraway expression in her eyes as she toyed with her green beans.

"Anyway, they couldn't find the IVC, but they claimed the liver looked normal and that the pressure they measured in the portal vein was normal. I don't see how it could have been, and it must have been hard to measure with all that fibrosis everywhere. So they concluded that the patient must have a splenic vein thrombosis. Well, an obstruction there simply could not account for the presence of the esophageal and gastric varices that the GI people visualized twice, and they decided there was nothing they could do about it."

"Heavens," said Jennifer.

Philip looked at the piece of ham uneaten on his fork. "This is good, Jen. Raisins?"

"Uh-huh," she said. "So then what did they do?"

"Well, they'd come to the wrong conclusion, because when he comes back, he's still bleeding and throwing up blood. He either has to be operated on or else we let him bleed to death—those are the alternatives. Technically he's a candidate for a liver transplant but the surgeons hate to try them on alcoholics because most of them don't stop drinking afterward. So it's no-win. Besides, no one is doing those at our place at the moment. I guess we could transfer him to UCLA. But now the surgeons say they can't do a portal or splenic vein shunt and what they want to do is resect part of the esophagus and oversew the remaining varices. Jeffrey Fowler's been doing these, but the trouble is, all ten of his series so far have died. Also, who's going to pay for all this? He's taking six to twelve units per bleed, that's five thousand dollars per bleed right there, just when our budget's been reduced ten percent anyhow, and . . ."

"Surely they don't want you to think about that?" Jennifer objected, seeming suddenly more attentive.

"It's not a question of thinking about it, it's a question of the hospital being able to afford to transfuse this guy every other day, six to twelve units, indefinitely."

"Well, I just don't think the doctors should have to think about the hospital budget. It's the patient's life they should be thinking about," Jennifer objected.

"Well, of course," Philip agreed. That went without saying.

Philip and Jennifer had taken to making love in a comfortable spoonlike position, like two strangers riding a motorcycle. In this way, while he could nibble at her ear or kiss her neck, they did not look into each other's faces, or speak, knowing, after twenty-one years of marriage, what they would say anyway. "Uhhh," Jennifer would moan, in a remote, dismissive way, as she came, his signal. "Uhhhh," he would say, in his turn, and rest a minute against her warm back until they drew apart and went to sleep. It was nice, they agreed. Often they congratulated themselves on the harmony of their sex life.

23

"Jesus Christ, what went on here last night?" Bradford Evans demanded in the morning, reading the entry on Ivy Tarro's chart, which recounted the bleeding episode. "And her fever's worse! That arm's infected. The surgeons should take a look at it."

"Dr. Watts said the fever was from the toxicity of the streptokinase," Brian Smeed said. The other housestaff fell into an interested silence, awaiting Evans's reply.

"I doubt that very much," Evans said. "Look at the arm. The fever is from infection. That arm's infected. Mrs. Tarro?"

Ivy became aware of his voice. He leaned over her so nearly that her field of vision as she roused herself a little was entirely obscured by his face, which seemed as blurry as a figure on a giant television screen, a great head pronouncing doom. "Mrs. Tarro, your arm isn't responding as we'd hoped to the medicine we've been giving you. I want a surgeon to look at your arm, all right?"

"Anyway," he went on to the housestaff, "the bleeding's stopped, but leave her off the drug for the moment. Brian, would you call Dr. Smithwick or, if he's not available, the chief surgical resident and get him to see whether this vein should be cut out. I'm not going to be in my office this afternoon, so I'll sign out to Phil Watts. But I'll call in to hear what the surgeons say."

This was a good example, Perry thought, of the difference between Dr. Watts and Dr. Evans. Evans would call a surgeon while Watts would do almost anything rather than call one.

24

It was Mimi's bad luck to run into Bradford in the lobby, just outside the gift shop. He was wearing nautical garb of blue blazer, white trousers, and deck shoes.

"Six-pack races," he said, grinning, his face reddening slightly. She supposed her smile might be a little stiff too. She hoped he wouldn't think this was because his mention of sailing had made her think of their afternoon, nearly eight months ago now, which had begun with a plan to go sailing and ended in a motel. She was in fact remembering that, of course, but what had darted through her mind was disapproval at the tactless way doctors wore their sports clothes around the hospital, not altogether blatantly and often surreptitiously. You saw them conceal their gym bags, or slip in and out of their offices in tennis shirts. Mimi tried to smile at him more frankly, and not to look at his shoes.

Mimi's adventure with Bradford Evans still could make her cheeks warm with chagrin. They had been attracted to each other for some time. He would often come down to take books out of the library. In the beginning he had still been married. She'd been aware of that, but had somehow been observing the hospital convention by which this was ignored. They'd talked about marriage in the abstract one afternoon in the nurses' conference room. It was clear that he was unhappy; and she had been rather self-congratulatory about having avoided remarriage for so long. He had said—his words had stayed with her—"There's something to be said for sparing yourself the difficulties in life, but there's something to be said against it, too."

She had always admired his choice of books. He would read a biography of Schumann or the letters of Cézanne. Doctors usually didn't read novels, except for *Of Human Bondage*, *The Citadel*, and *The Andromeda Strain*, but he had read, she remembered, *The Forsythe Saga*, all volumes, and the works of Hemingway.

They had gone to dinner, a few times, and the movies. Then one afternoon he had said, his face slightly averted, "I wonder if you'd like to go sailing some weekend. On my boat . . . we could spend the weekend . . . sail up the Delta . . ."

"Maybe," she had said, hurling herself into life with all its difficulties and, now that he had been so specific, with a rustle of anticipated pleasure somewhere in her abdomen. She felt her face warm up.

"I've always found you so attractive," he said. "I'd hoped that you— you know I'm divorced now?" Mimi had smiled, and they had fixed the date.

She carefully thought over what to pack. If they'd been thirty or known each other better, it would have been clearer, but as it was there was a certain range of possible misunderstandings. Perhaps he was not really suggesting an illicit weekend; perhaps she was just meant to be a weekend guest among others. In any case, she thought, looking at her rather forlorn collection of nighties, nylon garments of indeterminate grayish white or faded rose, she would buy a new nightgown. She had to laugh at her own dithering.

She packed a paperback book, her needlepoint—restful deckside activities—and imagined herself cooking in a nice, clean little galley, and having long understanding talks with Bradford. She realized that she was happily excited about this unexpected and pleasant-sounding weekend, and that it had been a while since she had spent a whole clandestine weekend with a man.

She wore white jeans and tennis shoes, packed sweater and change for dinner, unpacked, reorganized into another, smaller bag—something that could pass for a large purse, spontaneous-looking, informal. She misrepresented her plans to Daniel, then still at home. She'd never been the sort of mother-pal who might have said casually that she was off on a sailing trip with a man.

Unfortunately, at the hour appointed for their meeting, it began to rain. She thought as she walked over to the hospital that she should have brought a poncho, but she didn't go back. Instead, she quickened her steps, and waited in the shelter of the west doorway just as Bradford Evans came out of the door, in white pants and Topsiders. He smiled delightedly to see her.

"Don't get wet," he said, touching her elbow. "I hope this doesn't last. I'll drive around with the car." In a minute he had backed out of a nearby parking space and leaned across to fling the door open so that Mimi could duck inside just as the rain got serious. The car, a dark blue BMW, smelled leathery and new.

"They say it won't last," he said. "There was nothing in the forecast."

"Oh, I hope it doesn't," she said. She had lived in California for twenty-two years, so bad weather had not been among the various trepidations that had crossed her mind. Now she had a picture of herself miserably sick in a smelly hold, while he sat in the teeth of the gale gripping the tiller and sheet.

"How are you?" he said. "Isn't this a great idea? If the weather cooperates."

"Rain seems like an ominous sign," she said, sighing.

At the marina, they could look across the bay through a nearer screen of rain to an aureole of clear pink light around the hills of Tiburon. The air had developed a chill, wet smell.

"Which way does rain move?" she wondered. "Toward us? Away?"

"Moving inland," he said, and his face wore the preoccupied and secretive expression of someone who knows some bad news which he chooses to withhold. On the bay, they could see, a sailboat was struggling toward shore, and others in the distance bowed this way and that like pendulums, their sails luffing in the sudden, changing gusts.

"I suppose we should get aboard," Bradford said. "There's always a million chores." Mimi remembered from her childhood the seesaw feeling of a boat in a storm, and the greasy, close smell of fish and gasoline.

They talked about their childhood boats, and he introduced her to others of the impatient throng hanging around the Yacht Club lounge. Mimi was struck by how many of them looked something like Bradford, fit and slightly square-bodied, their alligator shirts snug across strong middles. Most were accompanied by women—women younger than herself, slender and suntanned, or with rough, seagoing complexions. Her liking for Bradford increased to think that he saw her as fitting into this lithe, sportive set.

Across the bay, the town of Belvedere, so promisingly basking, an hour before, in a mote of sunshine, had succumbed to the widening forces of the wind-driven rain and was now nearly invisible. At last, despairing, Bradford suggested they go somewhere for lunch. As they drove off in the car again, Mimi found herself wishing she had at least seen the boat that was to have borne them up the Delta on their agreeable adventure. The tethered sailboats in their berths, as she looked back at them, pranced like stallions in their stalls—one of them Evans's, impatiently awaiting them.

"Do you like Chinese food?" he asked. Mimi, not wanting to add another negative note to the disappointing beginning, didn't reveal that she didn't. To judge from the faint smiles of recognition—the tiny familiar bows from the black-vested Chinese men in the tiny restaurant, he was known to them, perhaps ate there all the time.

The waiter brought tea and pot stickers; Bradford ordered wine, apologizing that there were no chardonnays. He proposed a toast to fair weather. The rich smell of wonton grease lent a fattening, voluptuous air to what might have seemed, in the atmosphere of Formica and hard green paint, an abstemious lunch. Mimi ate enthusiastically, had forgotten to eat breakfast. The rain continued unabated outside. They gossiped about the hospital, she heard about his children, Cynthia and Joseph, and he heard about Narnia and Daniel.

What they lacked, for the moment, was another subject. The subject was to have been sailing—or sex. In the absence of sailing, and of the pleasant rituals of instruction and learning, and of admiring the natural beauty of the bay and the Golden Gate Bridge, and the receding shore, they still had the hospital and Chinese cooking. But Mimi sensed that they were on the edge of a sort of hole, which might yawn open beneath their feet, leaving them treading on a terrible blankness, or, with good luck could plunge them, via confessions, discussions of their past marriages and the like, into intimacy and friendship.

Thinking about it later, Mimi could not account for the time, or remember the exact words, the warming mood, the continuing rain and neon signs going on along Lombard, a feeling of compulsive glee overcoming their exasperation at the unremitting rain. They left the car parked in front of the Chinese restaurant and splashed across the street. Mimi huddled discreetly under the porte-cochere of the motel while Brad went inside to check in. Laughing up the cement stairs, they fell into each other's arms almost directly.

Mimi remembered thinking that Evans, like other men who are heavier than in their youth, looked somehow better without his clothes, a large, well-muscled man, pleasantly hairy, and an attentive lover, so that all was accomplished, after a few caresses, with mature facility, but eagerly, Mimi too, and the only wrong note was that he had come an instant or two too soon, from her point of view. It had seemed like the sort of first-time misstep that wouldn't happen again, and he apologized and cuddled her affectionately, hoping, she could see, to return to it after an interval. She would encourage this, but not yet, as for the moment she was enjoying the repose, the unfamiliar feeling of being nested in strong, if unfamiliar, male arms. It was here that the medical nature of his touch on her breast for a moment alarmed her.

The interval extended itself. They dozed a few minutes, returned without result to kissing and caresses. Mimi was too unsure of her own attractions to caress him more insistently, for fear of seeming importunate and demanding. Presently Evans got up and peered around the heavy, plastic-lined drape that covered the picture window.

"Red sky at night, sailor's delight," he said, pulling the curtain back so that the red light of the neon signs outside fell on the carpet.

"Is it clearing up?" she wondered.

"No."

Mimi looked covertly at her watch. Seven o'clock, an awkward hour, which in the case of clandestine afternoon lovers would signal the end of the tryst, would be the moment to get up, make another rendezvous, kiss, depart furtively for their separate cars. In the case of strangers spending their first weekend, the course was not so clear. Mimi, holding her stomach in, went into the bathroom. Though she usually hated her long limbs, she thought, looking at herself in the mirror, flushed with sex, that she didn't look too bad.

She splashed her face with cold water and used the toilet. As the flushing sound of the water receded, it seemed to her that she heard the stealthy replacing of the telephone receiver. Without knowing exactly why, this shocked her.

When she came out, Bradford Fvans, now wearing his boxer shorts, was standing by the dresser, by the phone. He had opened a small bottle—a split—of champagne. From where? She looked to see if there was a minibar, but didn't see one. His briefcase was open; perhaps he had brought it? Why a split? Why not a full bottle? Did he plan a whole boating weekend on a split of champagne? These irrelevant and peculiar reflections flashed through her mind unwanted. They sipped the warm champagne.

"I hate to say it," Bradford said presently, sitting next to her on the edge of the bed, "what with the weather, probably I should go back to the hospital. I have this one patient—he's been worrying me. I signed out, but . . ."

Mimi, thinking of the telephone, felt her cheeks flare with shame, with the notion that he was too bored with the prospect of the rest of the night, or with her.

"Of course," she said bravely. "You doctors . . ." she smiled as understandingly as she could. Her years at Alta Buena had taught her the tone of affectionate female resignation that doctors expected from nurses and wives.

"Damnit!" he exclaimed. His tone, to her ears, was patently insincere, so sincere did it sound.

"Maybe it'll be fair tomorrow," he said. "Sunday. Or you could wait here. I mean, while I go into the hospital. Then we'll have dinner. . . ."

"Such bad weather! I think I ought to go home," she said, tactfully giving him an out. "Dannie will worry if he thinks I'm out on the high seas. Well . . ." She hesitated, not good at lies. She had implied to Daniel that she was going to Sonoma by car with a woman friend, and he would not be in the slightest concerned. "And . . ."

She couldn't think of a reason, really, not to wait and go out to dinner, and make love again later, sleep the night in his arms. It was what she really wanted to do, except that they didn't know each other well enough. It seemed so—so shabby, or something. Candlelight dinner on a boat, exciting moments spent lashing things down and throwing lines—these were one thing, and something about a motel was entirely different. She thought of things she had meant to do in the garden this weekend, although of course now, with the rain, she couldn't be doing them anyway. . . . It was really, she thought, that he didn't want her to stay.

"I ought to go," she said again. Clearly that was what he had hoped, although, as she studied his expression, it appeared regretful.

"I didn't mean . . ." he said. "But we'll go sailing tomorrow?"

In the event, it had rained on Sunday too, and Mimi had the whole day to gnash her teeth with chagrin and embarrassment at what she came to think of as Bradford Evans's dismissal. Then, in the days that followed, reviewing the weekend endlessly in her mind, she came more and more to feel that she had been a fool, and the more she felt this, the angrier she felt at Bradford Evans, losing sight of the fact that she had liked him very much. When he asked her to the movies the next weekend, and the next, she'd refused, and refused an invitation or two after that. Eventually, he'd given up asking.

25

Mimi was thinking of this as she unlocked the library, which she held open on Wednesday mornings. She was modestly proud of this library, assembled from ten-cent bookstalls, duplicates from the main library, great-books lists, and bestseller lists. On Wednesdays she mended books and attended to paperwork while nurses, the occasional doctor, and ambulatory patients came to look at the shelves, or people brought in *Reader's Digest* abridgments that Mimi would later throw away. As usual Mark Silver was waiting for her to open, to check out a classic to read while on duty, part of his campaign of self-improvement. "My reputation as a womanizer is very undeserved," he once confided to Mimi. "Basically I'm a serious person," and Mimi had laughed, for she could never have imagined the pudgy, garrulous Mark as a womanizer. Today he took *Moby-Dick*.

An exhausted-looking black woman in slacks came in to look at the shelf of inspirational works. The slowness of her movements and drawn skin were things Mimi often saw when people had been up all night.

"They told me I could come down, get something to pass the time," she said. "I sure have been spending a lot of time here."

"It can seem long," Mimi agreed. She, like others at the hospital, had mastered a stock of noncommittal but sympathetic-sounding phrases with which to converse with the tired, anguished people waiting around. She could imagine how horrible and long and unendurable it must be.

"My son's in intensive care," the woman said.

"I'm sorry," Mimi said. "I hope . . ."

"I think he definitely better today," the woman said, smiling. "They say his kidney's not workin' yet, but he definitely woke up a time or two and looked at me, and I know he knows me. It's a slow-goin' thing."

"Oh, I know," said Mimi, who in fact had never watched at the bedside of a sick loved one, and always marveled at the cheerfulness and courage of people who were called to do it. How could they be so brave? She was sure that when the time came, when her own father or Aunt Faith was sick—the thought of Daniel or Narnia could not be borne—she herself would not be brave.

"Randall had a learning problem when he first started school," remarked the woman after a while. Only now did Mimi realize that this was Randall Lincoln's mother. "We thought he wouldn't ever learn to read. But he done. He had special help."

"That is needed, sometimes, to get a kid started," Mimi agreed.

"He was bright. We all knowed he was bright. I'm not sure the school know that, but we did. He was bright from the start. The school sent this young woman around to work with Randall after school. Either that or put him in the dumb class, but we didn't want that, for fear he'd get the idea he was dumb."

"No, you don't want that," said Mimi.

"She said to us, 'You don't have no clock. How do you expect him to read and you don't have no clock? Well, I had a watch, my husband had a watch. We knowed what time it was. I never did see what that clock had to do with it."

"Just some theory she had," Mimi said.

"Anyway, he got a scholarship to college, and I always did wish that young woman would hear that."

"You must be proud of him," said Mimi.

The rest of Mimi's afternoon was quiet enough. At four she locked up and prepared to go up to 3F to man the nurses' station while the desk nurse went to a meeting. As she walked by the door to the gift shop, she was stopped by the mention of her name, people talking out of sight in the adjacent Volunteers Office.

"Now that the ability to read is no longer current, the obvious thing would be to close the library, and extend the Volunteers' Office in there." This sounded like Jennifer Watts's voice. "Of course, poor Mimi—she's wrapped up in the library; it'd be hard on her."

"Oh, we could find something else for Mimi," said someone, probably Dottie Fred, the assistant hospital administrator. Mimi paused, reluctant to pass the open doorway, which might embarrass Jennifer and Dottie Fred with the idea that she had heard them. And yet they hadn't said anything rude or denigrating. Why was her heart pounding with extra force, as if she'd been caught doing something bad? She waited a few more moments in the hall, hearing the sympathetic words "poor Mimi—she's wrapped up in the library" as a sting and a reproach.

26

Philip Watts was late for his afternoon deposition session with the attorney for Wystan Morris, the surgeon who was suing for reinstatement after his hospital privileges had been rescinded by the board. Hospital officials had noted an untoward number of deaths among his patients, he had been sued for malpractice seven times, and occasionally he seemed drunk. Now the lawyer, in a side-vented blue suit, annoyed to have been kept waiting by a doctor, was pacing officiously in front of Philip's office, practicing his courtroom air of contempt and hostility. Inside Philip's office, he spread out papers from his briefcase, and reminded Philip that depositions were as legally binding as courtroom oaths.

"Describe briefly the procedure by which a hospital rescinds the privileges of a staff doctor," he asked, turning on his tape recorder.

"Well, first, attempts are made to talk to the doctor," Philip said. That had been his unpleasant task, at the time. "There's a committee, very informal, the 'three wise men,' a secret committee of reliable people to whom things can be told, who supposedly have good judgment, and if there's a doctor who has a problem, one of the wise men goes and talks to him. Tries to help, or suggests he get treatment, something like that."

"Secret committee," said the lawyer with satisfaction.

"Then, if the problem persists, a full board meets, reviews the evidence, and makes a decision."

"What sort of evidence?"

"Evidence of errors in judgment, or evidence of substance abuse, lawsuits, complaints, whatever."

"Surely errors in judgment are a matter of opinion? Of judgment?"

"Well, usually you can judge from the results," Philip said.

"And how do you develop evidence of substance abuse?"

Philip sighed, seeing that he was in for a disagreeable afternoon, and, eventually, if it was he who had to be the hospital spokesman, a disagreeable day in court. The fellow smirked at everything he said, and jotted things on his yellow legal pad, punctuating them with, as Philip could tell from the emphatic downward strokes of his pencil, exclamation points. He himself had seen several of Morris's botched cases. People who had died who didn't need to die.

Of course this bastard seemed not at all interested in what Morris had actually done. The Wice Morris stories were legion—had begun with rumors of little things that had astonished the nurses or residents in the operating room—chances taken, long moments of inattention or stupefaction, laughing when a slashed artery spurted gallons of blood. Philip had himself seen him nodding off in the late afternoons in the doctors' dining room. Eventually they heard he had been arrested for drunk driving.

Then came poorly prepared operations on people who couldn't survive them. He'd taken out a right, functioning kidney instead of a damaged left one. Once or twice the residents had refused to assist, producing high dramas of insubordination. But the thing had been gradual, and too much time had passed, Philip had to admit, before someone—himself, as it happened—had decided to take action. By that time several lawsuits were pending, a few people dead. Philip couldn't even imagine how such things could happen, but they had.

"Nobody feels worse about it than I do," Morris had said, with a smirk of camaraderie, when reproached. "But hell, Phil, which of us doesn't have a bad day? That's the hell of our business—we all have to live with our mistakes."

In the doctors' dining room, everyone had agreed that Morris was in bad shape, but the doctors had been divided about whether to unite behind him or repudiate him. "If we acknowledge that he's been at fault, the lawyers are going to own the hospital," Jeffrey Fowler had said. "Let's just send him to dry out somewhere." In the end, when Morris resisted the counsel of the three wise men, the hospital administrators had insisted that the doctors' board rescind his hospital privileges. Philip patiently recounted the horror stories, omitting, of course, Jeffrey Fowler's point of view.

27

As she sat at the nurses' station, prepared to give information to visitors, Mimi thought about Jennifer Watts's remark and the oddness of people thinking she was wrapped up in the library, as though she gave it some unnatural amount of attention. She gave it, she thought, the same competent attention she tried to give all aspects of her job. There was in a way something slightly shaming about being too wrapped up in things, as if the rest of your life were defective. A visitor, a middle-aged woman in a pink jogging suit, broke in on her thoughts by asking for Ivy Tarro.

"I looked in her room and she's not there," she said.

"We'll have to ask a nurse," Mimi said. "Her name is still here on the list, but the lists aren't always up to the minute." She felt a stir of hope that Ivy might have suddenly got well and gone home.

"I babysit her little girl," the woman said. "I thought she was going to be home yesterday, and now today I didn't hear from her, and no one answered in her room, so I thought I'd better come over. Poor little Delia really misses her. Luckily she takes a bottle all right, and I don't suppose she has any sense of time."

"How old is Delia?" Mimi asked.

"Four months."

"Well, let me find where Mrs. Tarro is," Mimi said. She looked into the nurses' lounge and asked Merci Yezema, who guiltily put down her cigarette and said she thought that Tarro was down in x-ray. "They may take her to the surgical service afterward," she said.

"Transferred to the surgical ward," Mimi explained to the baby-sitter. She felt an unexpected regret. It often happened that patients were transferred, and since she, on her various errands, went into all the wards, it was often she who brought back word to the doctors and nurses on 3F of the interesting or likable ones.

At five-thirty, Philip came back to the ward to make signout rounds, residents falling in behind him like ducklings, clutching their clipboards, minds full of numbers. In the intensive care unit, the rhythmic sucking, gasping, sighing, aspirating, pumping wheezes of all the machines gave the sound of being on a huge ship. There were two new patients in the ICU—an elderly Oriental cardiac patient with no lung function, Dr. Kim, and an old alcoholic brought in from the park with heart failure. This meant that all the 3F ICU beds were filled.

Mr. Lincoln dozed on a chair outside Randall's room, and Mrs. Lincoln, arms wrapped around herself as if she were cold, edged nearer the doctors to watch their examination. Randall had regained neither consciousness nor kidney function.

"Mrs. Lincoln, you understand Randall's condition is very bad. You have to prepare yourself for the possibility he's not going to wake up," Philip said, it seemed to him for the eightieth time.

"He waked up today, doctor! He looked at me and smiled. I'm sure he hear when we talk to him."

"We don't find on the EEG any evidence of that, I'm afraid. I'm afraid he doesn't hear."

"He's not in pain now, and that's one good thing," Mrs. Lincoln said. "He hurt so bad when the attack come on."

"It's true, he's not in pain now," Philip agreed.

Neither was Perfecto Rainwater in pain. In Perfecto's room he turned up one of Perfecto's eyelids. The pupil of the eye was fixed, as it had been earlier, and did not respond to Philip's little flashlight. The neurologist had also seen him, and entered a big zero on the chart.

Near his bed, two tiny women, his wife and girlfriend, sat leafing through the old *Reader's Digests* on the table. Their shining blue-black hair seemed to have been done by the same beauty parlor. These two women had produced a situation of great drama. The wife had insisted that the other, the girlfriend who had been with him during the cocaine incident, be refused admittance to the waiting room, and had made a quite surprising scene. By what process the two women had become reconciled and now sat side by side no one except Merci Yezema knew, for it was Merci alone who talked to them, in Tagalog. Perfecto had met them both while a serviceman in Manila, had imported them, and now abandoned them. Had Perfecto learned Tagalog?

Philip was worried that Dr. Kim might be getting pneumonia. "When I was in medical school," Philip told the residents, "there were plenty of old professors around who could remember the days before antibiotics. Antibiotics are almost the only real medical breakthrough this century." He noticed the restive look the residents usually wore when he began one of these reminiscences, all except Wei-chi, who listened attentively to them, as if memorizing them. In his housestaff days, Philip too had been eager for accounts by people who had seen the great Sir William Osler, or Thomas Lewis, or who told about studying in Vienna when that had been the great center. "We'll start Dr. Kim on antibiotics. You can imagine what treating pneumonia was like before antibiotics. Nursing was all-important, the sponging with alcohol to bring the fever down. There was the idea of the crisis, and the fever 'breaking.' "

The young doctors looked relieved not to have lived in those benighted days. "His Po$_2$ was 50, while breathing two liters of nasal cannulas, so we upped it to four but he may need to be intubated," Mark Silver said, bent on going on with his report.

"When someone was likely to linger painfully, they used to put them in a certain corridor on the way to X-Ray, this was at the old Mass. General—this corridor was cold and open, and they'd get pneumonia. We called pneumonia the old man's friend," said Philip. "Nowadays, the old man gets days of torture with a tube down his gullet, and his family gets a bill for thousands. Which is the better way to die?"

"I didn't go into medicine to kill people," remarked Brian Smeed.

The big Australian nurse, Vita Dawson, was reading at the nurses' station, and though it was only six, the janitors were washing the hallways already. On the ward the doctors looked in on Mrs. Ames, lung cancer, a plucky seventy-year-old with a gravelly smoker's voice, in a frilly nightgown, hair newly done.

"I'm going to beat it, doc," she said. Her husband, suit and tie, soldierly white mustache, jumped up to shake his hand, grinning.

"This girl is brave," he said. "She's got a lot of guts."

"Well, that has a lot to do with it," Philip agreed, but was thinking of her x-ray—unresectable primary and probable right lower-lobe metastases.

"You're a doll," said Mrs. Ames.

Then they looked into Ivy Tarro's room. Her bed, neatly turned down, was empty. Philip stepped back out the door to verify the room number; he glanced at the bathroom. The bathroom door stood open, no one inside. He felt a sudden, uncharacteristic panic.

"Where's Mrs. Tarro?"

"She went down for another venogram," Mark told him. "They took her to X-Ray about two, but she's not back yet."

"Who ordered the venogram?" Philip asked.

"I did," Brian Smeed said. "Dr. Evans told me to get a surgery consult, and the surgeons wanted a venogram."

"Dr. Evans signed out to me," Philip said. "You should have checked with me. A venogram is not a benign procedure."

Abruptly leaving his entourage, Philip hurried down to X-Ray. A venogram involved a toxic radio-opaque dye, and could be dangerous when a patient was already bleeding. Worse than that, almost, was the breach in chain of command. Philip was punctilious, considered it important that each doctor, at each niche in an elaborate hierarchy, not neglect his duties on the one hand but also not overstep them. It was the patients who suffered either way. Smeed had not been warranted to authorize this venogram. Philip pictured the pale little arm further distended with poison dye, could picture her frightened and puzzled face.

In X-Ray, a couple of cowed patients in green gowns waited, knees protruding into the common sitting area. The nurse just coming in hadn't seen a Mrs. Tarro having a venogram. Al Finkley, the radiologist on call that afternoon, came out from the back, dressed to go home, and told Philip that a young woman with a subclavian vein obstruction had been taken directly to Special Procedures after she arrived.

Philip, now bent on rescue, walked through the general x-ray room. In the first Special Procedures room, a small form lay on a bierlike table, which was being raised, with an otherworldly hum, toward the scanning eye of a cranelike monster above her.

"Hold it," he called to the technician hidden somewhere behind lead, like a projectionist out of view. He approached the table. But it was a tiny old woman, who stared in silent fear at Philip's glaring face above her.

In the next room, a nurse was painting someone's leg blue, with dye out of a big bucket, and another person lay on a gurney in the corner, but neither was Mrs. Tarro.

"Look here, did you have a venogram in an arm? Young red-haired woman?"

"No, but I just came on," the nurse said. "I haven't read the registration docket. Try the other room." But the other Special Procedures room was empty too.

"Who's on call?"

"Dr. Field. He's back there."

Philip knew Bill Field, the president of the hospital Gourmet Wine and Food Society. Field was just hanging up his suit coat. His white coat hung on a chair nearby.

"Bill, I'm looking for one of our patients. She came down for a venogram, but she's not here and not back on the ward," Philip said, hearing the rising note of fright in his voice, like the parent of a lost child.

Bill Field stared like a campaign general through the x-ray-opaque glass of his sanctum toward the battlefield of x-ray rooms. "Hell, Phil, we don't have her here," he said. "I looked things over when I came on."

"*Did* you have her?"

"No idea," Field said. He went with Philip to the reception desk, and together they studied the manifest of procedures performed that afternoon.

"Oh, shit," Philip said, seeing for himself that the girl had been taken to surgery. He leaped into the elevator, which had briefly alighted so that the janitor could collect a trash barrel, and took it to A floor without thanking Bill Field.

He was automatically braced for dispute. Jurisdictional quarrels with surgeons were especially common and infuriating. What little judgment surgeons had, it seemed to him, was never exercised if there was any prospect of cutting, however moribund the patient, and the wishes of the physician however opposed. Surgeons had no common sense, were quite capable of any kind of misconceived and renegade intervention. He could believe that somebody had had the idea of resecting her axillary vein. Certainly without clearing it with him, presumably without clearing it with Evans. But that they could have stolen Mrs. Tarro, on his, the medical chief's, own watch defied belief. Yet he believed it.

"A young woman just down from X-Ray," he demanded at the

operating room desk. The nurse gestured toward the thick, cafeteria-like swinging doors behind her.

"They took her in about ten minutes ago, Dr. Watts," she said. "The poor thing was really panicked. Are you her internist? We had to restrain her a little. She was trying to climb off the gurney. One of those people who are sure they're going to die under the knife." She smiled at the silliness of patients, their lack of faith. "Anyway," she went on, "until a few minutes ago they were waiting for the anesthesiologist."

Philip hesitated a second or two. A venogram was bad enough. An operation could be catastrophic. It seemed melodramatic to burst, unscrubbed, into the OR. But he did.

The operating theater held the expected scene of green-garbed surgeons huddled together over an inert form. One undraped breast, surprisingly ample for a delicate-looking woman, had been painted with a greenish tincture, with dotted lines in purple drawn at the axillary insertion. At first glance it seemed they could be planning a mastectomy. Legends of surgical error hummed in his ears, drowning his own loud shouts of "Stop! Stop!"

Cool glances of surprise, of polite inquiry, over the green masks. Knives uplifted.

"What are you doing?" Philip struggled for a calm, collegial tone. The operating-room nurse instinctively grabbed Mrs. Tarro's wrist and read the name bracelet.

"This vein?" said one surgeon behind his mask, probably the chief resident in vascular surgery. Philip couldn't remember his name.

"I don't want you to touch that vein," Philip said. "I don't know how she got down here. This is really unacceptable. You can't just take a medical patient to surgery without clearing that with us. Surgery is not warranted here. How did this happen?" He knew he was starting to rant. He subsided.

"Brian Smeed asked for a surgical consult."

"Consult!" Philip screamed. "It looks to me like you're operating here. That is a decision *we* make, when we hear your opinion."

"This vein's infected, she's febrile, she hasn't responded to the antibiotic, it needs to come out," said the resident in an injured but emphatic voice.

"Oh, Jesus Christ, this is not even my patient," Philip said. "Take her back upstairs and I'll get in touch with her internist. But she's not infected. The fever's from the drug, streptokinase."

The surgeons still stood, as if mesmerized, unrecognizable behind green masks. One took a step toward Philip, and Philip, surprising himself, raised his fist. The man stepped back again. "Take her out," Philip said. Still they didn't move. He repeated this order. Again, a long moment, full of a curious potentiality for violence, extended in silence. Finally, the nurse pushed her instrument cart away from the table and raised the light.

The anesthesiologist had already begun folding his tubing. "I'll bill this as a completed procedure," he said, "okay?"

"Yes, okay," Philip snapped. The surgeons gazed, it seemed regretfully, at the smooth, exposed flesh. Philip came further into the operating room. The strong lights were hot on the top of his head as he peered at Ivy Tarro. Her face, even with the calm of anesthesia, bore traces of anguish. He thought he could discern a tear stain, a dampness at the hairline where her head was wrapped in a bandage of sterile cloth. He was moved in a way he was at a loss to put a name to. Relief and success were surely part of it—he had frustrated the surgeons and rescued the young woman. The idea of her green, vulnerable breast made him catch his breath. He had a strong impulse to pick her up and carry her in his arms to safety, like a fireman. Sudden sensations growled in his middle. He was dazed, even. Had he remembered to have lunch?

He hurried back to Ward 3F. Wei-chi, the intern on call, was reading in the nurses' conference room.

"Dr. Lum, will you go down to the recovery room and stay with Mrs. Tarro, that's our patient with the blood clot, and bring her back up here when she wakes up?"

Wei-chi stood with an embarrassed expression, putting down his magazine, which Philip saw was some kind of Chinese girlie magazine, with a brightly dressed, smiling woman on the cover, wearing a spangled dragon crown.

"Somebody left here," Wei-chi mumbled, scurrying away.

Still agitated by his confrontation and by the narrowness of the young woman's escape from the knife, Philip slammed the door of his office shut. It seemed an unfamiliar and unwelcome place. He wanted to get out of the hospital.

He hated this queasy feeling of excitement, of danger, even. He kept seeing mingled images of the girl's green breast, her unconscious face, and the bright, beckoning, erotic smile of the spangled girl on Wei-chi's magazine, and he was conscious of a sort of hypertensive pounding of excess visceral blood, as if he'd almost hit someone with his car.

28

As Mimi ate her supper, her phone rang, and a man's voice asked if Mr. Franklin was home. Mimi, with the single woman's reflex prudence, implied vaguely that he was not handy to the phone, and asked if she could take a message. The caller identified himself as Mr. Tabor from Alta Buena Hospital.

"We sent Mr. Franklin a letter a few days ago. I'm calling to set up an appointment with him."

"I'm G. M. Franklin," Mimi admitted, supposing she couldn't indefinitely conceal this fact.

"You are? Did you get a letter we sent you a few days ago?"

"Yes," Mimi said. A silence. She was driven on. "But I haven't really had a chance to give it much thought. I'm not inclined . . . at the moment I'd say I'm not really interested, I . . ."

"We'd like to talk to you, when it's convenient. Do you live on the premises there at Number 29? Then of course you know Alta Buena Hospital."

"I'm often at Alta Buena. I work there," Mimi said, rather irritated to be unknown to this hospital functionary. She knew who *he* was.

"Then we could perhaps meet at the hospital, at your convenience," the man said smoothly, "or if you prefer, at your home," sounding like a funeral director, in a voice of reassuring mellifluousness.

"I'm there every day," Mimi said, stiffly. "Whenever you like," hoping that the vagueness of this arrangement would keep it at bay.

"Tomorrow?" he said. "Anytime tomorrow."

"Not tomorrow," Mimi said. "I have meetings, and . . ."

"The day after?"

"Look, Mr.—um—well—we both know that I'm not selling my house." Was she not, then? Hearing these words come out with a vehemence that must reflect her inner wishes made the matter more certain in her conscious mind. And she was sure she didn't want to talk to this awful man.

"I think when I explain to you your position," he said, in an ugly voice.

"It would just be wasting both our time," Mimi said, and when he made no reply, after a second she hung up. It was the rudest thing she had ever done.

She went on as she had been planning to her yoga class and then to the movies with a friend, Lorine Bates. The movie proved to be monotonously violent, filled with endless car chases, during which Mimi's mind wandered more than once to the words, overheard that afternoon, "Poor Mimi, she's wrapped up in the library." They returned to her with dawning force, as a form of shame. Was she a pitiable person, wrapped up in useful but far from vital charity, foolishly devoted to her harmless, low-paid service job? Is that how successful women like Jennifer Watts perceived her? Did men think of her as someone whose most interesting activity was pushing a book cart? Was this her most interesting activity? And was there anything the matter with that? Wasn't it more than some people had? Was it enough? If her life was incomplete, what was lacking? A relationship with a man, obviously—but was that so important? Did she want to be someone who thought her life was incomplete without a man? Didn't she really think this herself? She felt returning upon her the same feeling of irritable panic she had felt at the fund-raising meeting, and again when she had read the letter about selling her house.

She wasn't often given to introspective flights of this kind, but the darkness of the theater and the strains of Beethoven, punctuated by horrendous metallic crashing noises, compelled this train of thought. Sell your house and get out was one track. But clattering along it, even in her mind, filled her with dismay. Was she not happy the way she was, in the little house she had worked so hard on, helping people at Alta Buena? Was that so bad?

———

In the recovery room, sitting in the metal chair at Ivy Tarro's bedside, Wei-chi found himself wishing he had brought something to study— the *Merck Manual*, or at least a list of English words. She would be a while waking up, he thought, so still was she, so thickly anesthetized. With acupuncture she would be smiling now, awake and fresh. Resection of a subclavian vein, very suitable procedure for acupuncture anesthesia.

He was preoccupied, thinking of a quarrel he had just had with his sister. "Goddamn, Wei-chi, I gonna tell you something," she had said, narrowing her eyes at him, spreading her fingers on the oilcloth table cover. Wei-chi had looked up from his bowl to see her malevolent gaze. He pressed the bowl to his chin again and began to eat his rice with the appearance of concentration.

"You Goddamn," she said. "I know you keep money. You say you so poor. You give me some money here, that's final."

"Yan," he had tried to soothe her. It was his view that she didn't need money. It was the family in China that needed money. She lived an American life, with breakfast cereal, green tea, and stereo.

"I telling you last time," she had said. Had she meant it? Why was she so irritable, and so uninterested in the fate of their brother and two other sisters? But Yan was the youngest sister, and did not seem like the others. She hardly knew China, didn't understand it, and Wei-chi didn't understand her.

Now he became aware of a silence unnatural in a hospital, as if the walls of this room were padded. The usual noises of rolling carts and clanging metal beds and amplified voices did not penetrate here. From time to time the recovery-room nurse would look in, and, reassured to see a doctor there, would leave again. After two hours, Mrs. Tarro had still not moved or waked.

Nine o'clock. Three hours. With growing alarm, Wei-chi lifted her left arm. He didn't like the repellent limpness, the slight chill of her skin. When he let go of the arm, it dropped like a stone to her side. He thought of old grandfathers in China, thought of their leaden hands and twisted mouths. Physicianly instinct told him what had happened here: stroke. Yet was this not very strange? He hurried to the telephone and called 3F.

Rushing down, Mark Silver and Brian Smeed agreed it looked like some kind of stroke, some bleeding into the brain. Her left side, they ascertained, was paralyzed, her eyes stared unseeing when they stretched back her lids. She lifted her right hand weakly as if to push them away, but it was reflex; she was unconscious.

The residents were stunned. She appeared to have sunk into a coma as impenetrable as Perfecto's or Randall's. Wei-chi, as if personally responsible, wrung his hands, saying, "She needs ICU bed," again and again. "I thought she not waking up right."

Without understanding what could have gone wrong, the chief resident, Brian Smeed, agreed that she needed a respiratory unit and some lines until her vital signs were stable. He got on the phone to Bradford Evans.

All six of the medical ICU beds were full already. Mark Silver rushed up to Ward 3F to try to call around for a bed somewhere else, maybe cardiology, or the surgery ICU, since, after all, this was in a way their doing. But both the surgery and cardiac units were full, and the cardiology resident, Heather Wu, pointed out that Dr. Kim, whom they had taken on 3F, was actually a cardiac patient, so full were they on cardiology. The question became whether they could move one of their own patients out of intensive care and onto the general ward to make room for Ivy.

"I think we can take Mr. Rainwater Perfecto off life support," Wei-chi said.

"Yeah, I agree," Mark Silver said. "He's breathing on his own, and anyway it's not going to matter." It was fairly clear that Perfecto was never going to wake up. "For that matter, we could take Randall off; he can breathe on his own. Anyway, she may not need this very long. This could just be some kind of reaction to the anesthesia. She didn't seem that sick. I mean, there's no underlying pathology to explain this episode."

Bradford Evans, when his answering service was able to reach him, was dismayed, cursed on the phone, and said he'd be right in.

"I'll call Dr. Watts," Mark said, "and ask him if we can move someone, and who it should be."

Philip was eating at home with Jennifer. If she could be said to be eating—picking at a strange green mound on her plate.

"Spinach. I'm supposed to be doing extra iron and zinc," she said, with a mischievous and rather embarrassed smile.

"Why?" Philip asked.

"If you promise not to laugh—iridology. Marian Hempel's art teacher's wife is an iridologist, and she wanted to practice, so Marian and I had our irises done."

"Your irises?"

Jennifer leaned toward him and widened her eyes. "Do you see the various shapes and colors in the iris? Apparently they tell a lot about your general state of health, vitamin deficiencies, things like that." Her eyes a healthy lion color with dark specks. He had always admired them. She peered, inviting him to penetrate the secrets of her physiology.

"It is true that you can tell certain things from the eyes," he conceded. "High blood pressure, for instance."

"She felt I should do without animal protein and wheat flour." Jennifer laughed. "Why not? And do a lot of E."

Philip heard his beeper, which he'd left in the kitchen. At the kitchen phone, he listened to Mark's account of the crisis with Ivy Tarro. He struggled for a detached and professional reaction, but dismay made his voice catch.

"We're putting her in the ICU, but to put her in, we've got to move somebody, and we thought Dr. Kim, the new patient from cardiology, or Randall or Perfecto—they're all three breathing on their own and relatively stable. Which one?"

"Perfecto," Philip said, almost automatically. This response was instinctive, based, to be sure, on decades of making such decisions. But a second's further reflection confirmed it. Perfecto—so large, fat, and vegetative. The alert Dr. Kim had more to gain from remaining in intensive care.

Philip was used to this unpleasant feature of being the attending physician, the duty of triage. If his residents were right that Mrs. Tarro, basically not a very sick young woman, had suffered a crisis from which she could, he hoped to God, be saved by intensive care, then someone doomed anyway would have to be moved. Such situations were often before them, and the basis of choice was fairly simple to defend. Perfecto's coma was probably irreversible. The matter with Randall was less clear. Randall might one day wake up—his mother claimed he did wake up from time to time. But his kidneys were probably irreversibly damaged and he would required dialysis every other day, a four-hour procedure gratuitously performed at great expense on his unconscious form, ridding it of its toxins but not of its underlying, fatal illness.

"That's what we thought too, Perfecto," Mark said. "His brain's fried but his breathing's fine."

Philip was shocked that this had happened to Ivy Tarro. He'd been concerned that she couldn't support an operation, but he had regarded her underlying health as stable. He asked Mark to check with the anesthesiologists to see what anesthesia had been used, and did not reiterate his fears about the effect of the drugs urokinase and streptokinase. "I'll come in," he said. "Meantime get a scan."

"Finish your dinner," Mark reassured him. "We got Dr. Evans, and he's on his way in."

Of course, Philip went on thinking as he sat down again at the table, they might be in the presence of some deeply sinister pathology, the first manifestation of which had been the swollen arm, which was only now declaring itself, and against which the wicked drug streptokinase had been futile, or even had exacerbated the underlying process. But he racked his brain for an explanation for what it could be, and tried to curtail the unnatural anxiety that he felt.

"Do we know someone named Ivy Tarro?" he asked Jennifer.

"In a way. She's the maître d' at Franni's. The maîtresse d', I suppose one says. We've often seen her. She's a kind of a personage on the trendy food circuit."

That was it, of course. The smiling, trim young woman with a notebook in her hand, peering near-sightedly into it, leading you to the table with pleasantries about the menu, and a confidential manner that made you feel she had found you a place to sit because you were you, or rather, because you were Jennifer, as it was Jennifer who knew, and was known on, the local restaurant scene.

"She's in our ICU," Philip said. "She's been on the ward for a couple of days, but I never could remember where I knew her, and that's the resident saying she's gone sour." His stomach crawled as he said this.

"How awful," Jennifer said, "a girl in her twenties?"

"Twenty-seven."

"Drugs?"

"No. And now it looks like she's had a stroke."

"My God," said Jennifer sympathetically.

Philip, fearing that his distress would somehow show, revealing to Jennifer the inappropriate excess of emotion he was feeling, said nothing more, but he was tormented by thoughts of the green breast, the tear-stained cheek, and the way her hair had curled damply at her hairline.

On the ward, Merci Yezema began to unfasten Perfecto from his respirator. For the other waiting families, it was a relief from the torpid watching hours to see some action, some change in the status of someone, but for Perfecto's wife and girlfriend, it was terrifying to see their loved one—still so large, rosy, and doughy—being detached from life support. They clung together.

Brian Smeed took them into the corner of the lounge to sit them down and explain that they were moving him into a more comfortable room because they no longer expected him to be helped by those artificial machines.

"Sometimes mother nature should be given a chance," he said. "Sometimes the body gets dependent on the machines. That weakens it. Sometimes people do better on their own." They stared at him. Merci Yezema, leaning in at the door, translated his words. Their worried eyes turned to her.

"Mr. Rainwater will be in the general ward, right back there. He'll still be getting the same excellent care," said Brian to Merci, who repeated it in Tagalog. He sighed.

The women understood that the doctors were giving up. They felt in their purses for damp wads of Kleenex. They sniffled and did not stir. Brian touched their shoulders and left them sitting there. Presently they came and watched as Perfecto was slowly trundled off to the ward, breathing reliably, and they followed after him as after a bier.

Ernesto, the nurses' aide, stripped the bed and expertly replaced the sheets. He and Perry Briggs brought Ivy up from recovery on a gurney, and when the room was ready lifted her into the bed.

"I knew Dr. Watts would decide to move Perfecto," Ernesto remarked. "He's got a thing against fat people."

"Jesus," said Perry, watching Ivy. "She seemed a lot better this morning." Though he had studied, in physiology, the processes by which the body refused, shut down, closed off, stopped, they still puzzled him. What, he had often asked himself, was life actually? Was it now leaving this young woman? Why? He didn't understand. "It seems like people come in here perfectly healthy and we manage to kill them."

"I think she's going to wake up," said Bradford Evans after his examination. But he looked grim. "You can't ever really tell with something like this. Well—we'll get a CAT scan. Perry, put a catheter in. We'll see about a feeding tube later."

Merci Yezema, seeing Perry stare morosely between Ivy's legs, looking for the—it seemed to him—unbelievably tiny hole through which women have to try to pee, took the catheter from him and expertly inserted it into the urethra, and arranged the plastic tubing and bag around the foot of the bed.

29

Philip hurried to the hospital in the morning just after six and went directly to the intensive care unit. Since this unit came under the jurisdiction of his team, looking in on Ivy Tarro was no longer a violation of protocol, and he was expected to get involved in her care. But he dreaded the sight of what he knew he would find, someone formerly lovely and vital, now stroked out and machinelike, unrecognizably swathed in foam bandages and flexible hoses. The CT scan showed a hemmorhage in the right parietal area, with swelling.

"Leave the endotracheal tube in to protect her airway," he said. "I think she's going to wake up before too long." This was said with more hope than conviction. Everything where this girl was concerned had gone wrong so far. But it was easier to deal effectively with this crisis than with his own feelings of rage and dismay.

Philip told himself that the start of emotion he had felt for the inert and increasingly frail young woman—patient—an inert shape in a hospital bed—was just normal humanitarian anguish at seeing so many medical mishaps befall someone so young and vital. At the same time, he knew this was not the entire explanation. He believed that emotions, in general, did not repay investigation—motives either—psychiatric opinion to the contrary notwithstanding. But he could just bear to look within himself and recognize, and forgive, that he found her beautiful. He was attracted to her, or had been, and then she had been stricken in this unexpected, sad way, and taken from him as surely as is the glimpsed face of someone in a car or train, or an actress on film, mere celluloid capable of generating in the viewer, through some need of his own, a dream of ideal beauty—a quite disproportionate response.

Will she die? Now she was attached to four machines, each monitoring and directing the delicate organism that had formerly, it had seemed, been healthy and strong. The machines extrapolated the faint, reluctant coursing of her blood, the inertia of her heart, the sullen intractability of her lungs from the faint, wavering lines on screens and rolls of paper being watched, read, and wondered at. Might she die?

Once she was hooked into the life-support system, the prospect of immediate death was diminished, but the anxiety they all felt, and the underlying questions, remained, about why she had suffered a stroke and what the outcome would be. People talked in the presence of her still form in abashed, low tones.

A romantic ache. Philip was conscious of an ache of unhappiness and an obsessive need to peer into her cubicle each time he came into the ICU—nearly hourly.

He was anxious that the housestaff take a lesson from this whole horrible episode—a young, beautiful woman left impaired, maybe permanently, by reckless administration of dangerous drugs, and he awaited the chance to bring it up at the M & M conference scheduled for Friday.

At first there was no consensus about what could have caused Mrs. Tarro's stroke.

"Vascular accident," the anesthesiology resident thought.

"She was afraid of surgery. She was very upset. She tell me when I take her down to surgery," Wei-chi said.

"I think it's a reaction to the anesthesia," Mark Silver said. "Halothane. Her blood could have dropped."

"It's hard to see, with all the streptokinase in her, how her blood could clot at all," Philip Watts had remarked.

Bradford Evans believed the stroke to have been caused by her underlying condition, which he maintained could not have been predicted from the results of the manifold lab tests they had taken when she was admitted: SMAC panel, urinalysis, CDC, and electrolytes. Now he ordered a CAT scan. Before the results, all they could know was that for some reason blood had seeped into her brain, and she had had a stroke, just like an old person.

Philip studied the reports. The CAT scan showed a small hemorrhage in the left parietal area, no shift or edema, no communication with the ventricles. Such a hemorrhage would be connected to the drug streptokinase, which was designed to thin blood and take away clots, and which had caused an earlier episode of bleeding. He was sure. Even before the planned discussion, factions arose. The streptokinase, or Bradford Evans, faction, covertly directed by Brian Smeed, and the Philip Watts, or heparin faction, discussed, when Philip and Evans weren't around, the relative merits of the two drugs, the relative judgment of the two senior physicians, the two drugs, whether or not surgery should have been performed, and the probable etiology of Mrs. Tarro's subsequent collapse. Such medical gossip encircled most patients whose courses had not gone smoothly, and above all when differences of medical opinion had arisen. Like a lottery, like a quiz show, Ivy Tarro's condition lent interest to the long hours of waiting around. It was something both to learn from and to lighten the tension of death and sorrow, the matters in which they were trading.

"Dr. Watts thinks it was the streptokinase that did it," Rosemary Hunt told Mimi. "Dr. Evans did give her a big dose."

"That wouldn't surprise me," Mimi said severely. "He spends too much time on his sailboat," an association of ideas that Rosemary did not quite follow.

Mimi, who had recognized Ivy's friend Franni Cedar, was able to help the social-service personnel know whom to notify about Ivy Tarro's grave condition. Franni Cedar had told them about a brother in Rochester, New York, and rushed in herself, immediately upon hearing of Ivy's stroke, with two other people, and another of the enormous and fanciful bouquets, this of yellow tulips, oddly out of season, and mistletoe.

"Hello," Mimi said, heading them off outside Room 100. "I'm afraid Mrs. Tarro has been moved to intensive care. As the social worker probably told you . . ."

"She's going to die, isn't that what you're telling us?" cried Franni Cedar. "Ivy's going to die? From an operation? I talked to her yesterday and she didn't even mention an operation."

"You should talk to Dr. Watts," Mimi said, as soothingly as she could. "Yesterday she took a turn for the worse, and they felt they had to do some surgical procedure. Dr. Watts can give you the details. I believe they're saying 'vascular accident.' "

"Oh, my God," Franni Cedar said to one of the men with her, "that bag lady that came into the restaurant and told our fortunes? She told Ivy that a great, definitive change was coming into her life. Remember? That was Saturday, or Friday. And at the time we thought she meant Delia, naturally. We wondered how she could have known about Delia. Remember?"

"I don't think I was there," he said.

In the afternoon after signout rounds, in the nurses' conference room, Vita Dawson was conscious of having caused a profound, shocked silence as she spoke. After she had said it, no one in the room replied. After an endless moment, two of the interns leaped up and strode busily out. Someone put the microwave on, someone turned the television on, chairs scraped, faces were averted.

"All I said was I thought if she came out of this she should bloody sue," Vita said.

"I don't know," Heather Wu, the cardiology resident, said at Ivy's bedside to Mark Silver. They were talking of Wei-chi's desolation about Ivy's condition. He was seen peering at her a dozen times. "I admit it's cute the way he hovers over Mrs. Tarro. I think he thinks he's responsible for her because he was put in charge in the recovery room. It's a Chinese idea. If you rescue somebody, you have to keep looking after them. They remain your responsibility."

"In that case, how would a Chinese dare become a doctor? Every patient would become his lifelong responsibility."

"I don't personally believe it, it's just the tradition," Heather said, turning snappish the way she always did when the others tried to make her responsible for Chinese thought. "I just don't like these mainland types. I know you're supposed to admire them, the way they're willing to live inside a packing crate just to get knowledge, and all that suffering they went through during the Cultural Revolution. But I don't know—have you ever had Wei-chi to dinner? He eats everything in sight. Personally, I think he's kind of got a thing for her."

"As scientists, the Chinese are amazing," said Mark. "They stand up in their Mao jackets, so meekly, would humbly like to present report of unworthy experiment practiced with extract of tiny flower up in mountains in China. Velly old ancient idea had by ancestors. After trying it on one million patients, we find that the T-lymphocyte helper cells are stimulated by the beta-blocking reagent. . . . it's like they've gone from zero to sixty in two seconds."

"Do you think Wei-chi will go back to China?" Perry Briggs wondered. "Will he try to stay here?"

"He's supposed to be engaged to someone in China," Heather Wu sniffed.

The doctors visited Perfecto Rainwater on signout rounds. In his new bed on the general ward, he lay as placid as a walrus, as dormant as a bear, as inert as a rock or log. He breathed. A catheter drained off urine from his bladder; his bowels moved—into a pan thrust beneath his buttocks if the nurses had guessed right, or else in the bed. Each nurse, on her rounds, listening to his heart, found it beating strongly and steadily. His pulse and temperature were normal. Only his brain refused to animate the electrodes fastened to his temples. A straight, straight line lay across the bluish screen of his monitor. Mrs. Rainwater and the girlfriend abbreviated somewhat their hours of watching, but Mimi still brought them books and magazines as they sat on the Naugahyde sofas of the day lounge, eyes staring with lack of sleep and suppressed animosity. Mimi saw that neither was willing to leave the other woman to watch alone.

Randall Lincoln's younger brother, people guessed, had just joined the army, for his hair was now shorn military short and he wore those distinctive heavy shoes. Some nights he persuaded his mother to go home, and then he slept in a sleeping bag on the floor near Randall's bed—against the rules, but they let him. The wheeze and whine of Randall's machines didn't seem to disturb him.

This afternoon, Perry was presenting a new case on signout rounds. "This seventy-year-old white male with severe chronic cardiac insufficiency was transferred from Mount St. Pity when he assaulted the intern there with a weapon."

The man in question lay glaring with baleful eyes, his mouth stopped with tubes. His knife or gun or whatever it was had been taken by the police. Philip and the resident housestaff crowded closer and peered down at the miserable man, who gazed back at them with defiance.

"He has chronic heart failure and lives alone but does well with home oxygen," Perry intoned from his notes. "This is his fourth admission. Uh—his record says he asked not to be intubated if he came in again."

"He didn't want the endotracheal tube?" Philip asked, looking at the patient. The man, named Holmes, blinked in assent. The business of the breathing tube was of special concern to Philip. These tubes were uncannily painful and distressing to people, and sometimes people who knew they were going to die soon preferred to die sooner rather than have one; they didn't want to suffer again with the hideous, strangling tube or futile, painful operations and would rather just die. But the interns and residents in the emergency room would often forget to look at the list of names of people who had asked that, the next time they were found unconscious and near death, no tube be put down. "Did you look at the list?" Philip asked.

"I couldn't just stand there and let him die," Perry protested.

"But that's your job!" said Philip. "Sometimes," he added, more gently. "Often. Of course it's tempting to try to do something heroic, and usually you can prolong life by a day, or two or three, or even a few months by using some drug, or ordering some procedure. And these are usually miserable months for the patient, and expensive and anguishing for the family. Is that humane? Sometimes it takes more humanity and courage to let nature take its course. No one likes to have a death on his watch, and, sure, you may have afterthoughts and worries. You may suffer tormenting second guesses. Could he have been saved? What if I'd tried thus and such? But these torments are in your job description too. You don't have the luxury of indulging your curiosity if in doing so you make someone suffer. Remember that you should never cause suffering."

Despite the passion in his voice, and his rather satisfactory impression of having been eloquent, the interns and residents looked unconvinced. In the firmness of their jaws he saw that they were bent on combating nature, and defeating it, not giving in to it, and if people suffered, well, that was how it was.

"This girl was admitted only four days ago," said Rosemary Hunt to Edgardo, the other nurse, before the doctors got to Ivy's room on their rounds. She lifted each of Ivy's arms to wash them, pulling up the pink cotton gown to wash her breasts and belly, and between her thighs. "She looked fine when she come in here. You never know, do you? If I was to wake up some morning blind as a bat, it wouldn't surprise me none, or I found I couldn't speak, or maybe walk. Nothing does surprise me, but it do surprise me that this girl has gone down like this."

The doctors came in and stood, solemnly regarding the inhalations and exhalations of her chest. Dr. Watts touched her wrist and looked at his watch.

"Has Dr. Evans been in this afternoon?" he asked.

"He said there was nothing to do now but wait," Perry said.

"We can give her a T-piece trial to see if we can take her off the respirator. If she's breathing all right, we can get this tube out. I'd like to put her back in a room, but check with Evans before you do anything."

"Help me with her gown," he said to Rosemary. She hesitated over whether to shift her and untie it at the back or pull it up. "Never mind," he said, suddenly conscious of the group of residents ready to peer at Ivy's breasts, and fumbled with the sleeve instead, and pressed his fingers into her armpit.

Here he felt the resistant vein, like a strand of heavy cord, and the firmness of the edge of her breast. He hoped the others could not see on his face the emotion, the desire so inappropriately strong, that he was feeling.

30

After work, as she came out of the hospital with her carryall full of recipes, Mimi was attracted by a violent display of purple fuchsia and cineraria on the lesbian commune flower stand by the front entrance. She stood looking for a long time at the vases and colors, thinking it would be nice to take Ivy Tarro something. She chose some tiny pink rosebuds and baby's breath. She didn't usually take flowers to the patients—maybe she had this impulse because she hadn't succeeded in finding Ivy a book that was right, and now maybe Ivy would never read anything ever again.

She went back up to the ICU station. Nurse Rosemary Hunt took the flowers and put them on the nurses' stand where the other patients could see them also, if any were to come to. On the window sill already were the huge floral arrangement from Franni Cedar, some gladioli, daisies in a glass, a little Christmas tree trimmed with paper ribbon and Styrofoam balls—the first reminder of the season to have appeared. It was possible to tell the length of a person's hospital stay by the flowers—by the second week, the flourishes of lilies and long-stemmed roses subsided, and only the pot plants, falling out of bloom, remained, until they too pointedly reminded of transience and death, and the nurses discreetly removed them. Now, Mimi was happy— she could not have said why—that the rosebuds were the prettiest flowers in the room.

Jennifer was going to one of her art things he hadn't wanted to go to, and Philip was faced with the prospect of dinner alone, which in his upset, strange frame of mind seemed horrible. So he was glad to run into Mimi, carrying a bouquet. She was attractive and sympathetic, and as involved as he with the drama of Ivy Tarro.

"Would you like a bite of dinner?" he asked. "Somewhere near here? I'm coming back after dinner."

"Sure," said Mimi, surprised. Philip and she saw a lot of each other, but seldom outside the hospital, and then only at public things.

"Where shall we go?" he asked, evidently used to leaving such decisions to women.

"Let's go to Franni's," Mimi said. "That's where Ivy Tarro works. It's early enough so that we can probably get in, and anyway, this week we probably have a little pull there."

Franni's Restaurant was decorated in the best California-food-movement style, with redwood paneling, mirrors, ferns, posters, a pizza oven, and Breuer chairs. And, though it was only six-thirty, a crowd. Mimi felt that she and Philip, in their plain working clothes, looked a bit dowdy next to the expensive leather jackets and designer sunglasses. But they attracted attention—her height, Philip's good looks. People looked twice at them. It was not unpleasant, the sensation of being a couple with Philip.

They gossiped lightly about the hospital, the fund-raising drive, the cookbook project, their children. Mimi's daughter, Narnia, and Philip's daughter, Daphne, had known each other briefly in elementary school, before they went to different junior high schools.

Mimi told Philip about the phone call and letter she'd gotten from the hospital, wanting her to sell her house. "I'm afraid I dismissed the idea out of hand. It's hard to decide, just like that, to do something you never ever thought of doing. I'd never thought of selling my house. Of course, if I could find something better . . ."

"There must be a lot of things on the market. Have you looked? Lots of neighborhoods would be more pleasant than living in the shadow of Alta Buena, I would think." Mimi could tell that he really had no idea and had never read a real estate ad. He lived comfortably in a beautiful Victorian house in Presidio Heights.

"The house where I brought up Narnia and Daniel! I wonder what they would say if I sold it? But I have a feeling there's a huge gap between the houses I really like and what I could afford."

"We're moving, I suppose you've heard," Philip said. "I'm looking forward to it. Do you think there's such a thing as an instinct, a drive, toward changes and upheaval? As a way of staying alive, maybe?"

"I believe there is at your time of life, Philip." Mimi laughed. "A well-known thing in men." This remark was uttered quite spontaneously, but with more familiarity than she was used to with Philip. She was relieved to see that he accepted the note of intimacy and allowed her to tease him.

He laughed too. "It's almost time for me to take up golf and chase young women."

It did not escape her, or him either, as he said this, that he was having dinner with a pretty woman not his wife. They smiled at each other. Mimi's heart sped and spun. Philip, so attractive. Did she have compunctions about adultery, she asked herself? Not really.

Franni Cedar herself, in a tall chef's hat, was working her way through the restaurant, greeting the diners. When she saw Mimi and Philip, she rushed over and sat down.

"How is she tonight?" she asked. "Everyone is so upset. I talked to her brother. He's planning to come out."

"I don't think she's in mortal danger," Philip said. "I think the resident explained that to her brother. If any decisions need to be made for her, of course we'll get back in touch with him."

Franni Cedar sighed, her cheerful, high-colored face subdued by reflections about mortality, reflections so unsuited to the mood of the restaurant, where all was appetite and sensual pleasure. "Do you think it was anything she did?" she asked. "Ivy's my dearest friend, we go back to the beginning of the restaurant. She's almost one of the founders, and she *is* one of the co-owners, you know. But Ivy has, had, has a kind of wild side, not bad or anything, but reckless, and she'd stay up all the time—neglecting her health, I'm trying to say, though during her pregnancy she was perfect, she wouldn't even have so much as a sip of wine. Could it be cholesterol? Naturally I thought of that. Ivy would eat pâté, or bacon, eggs nonstop, that's what I mean. Reckless."

"The problem was in her veins, not her arteries," Philip said.

Franni looked uncertain of the difference. "She's not going to die, is she?"

"I don't think so," Philip said. "The question is more how will she recover? Will she recover her speech, for example, will she be able to walk?"

The idea of an Ivy paralyzed, speechless, reduced to a shell, had not occurred to Franni Cedar, or to Mimi. Tears stood in Franni's eyes. "Oh, my God. It's easier to imagine Ivy dead than living like that," she said.

She continued on her rounds, sending them brandy on the house to drink with their decaf. Philip, since the mention of Ivy Tarro, had fallen into a pensive, gloomier mood, and knocked the brandy back like a cowboy in a film. Mimi found herself trying to recapture the charming rapport of their earlier moment. "There never is any way to think about people's misfortunes, is there?" she said. "One would almost prefer that people did bring things on themselves. So that the things that happened to them would be their fault."

"That's true of most of the patients we have," Philip said. "It *is* their fault. They smoke or do drugs or overeat. And that does make you marginally less sorry for them. A little less sorry, but all the sorrier for—what?—the pain of existence, that makes people need to do the things that kill them. I don't know. Did you ever smoke?"

"Well, grass, in my hippie college days," Mimi said. She saw that this connected with something he was thinking, or caught his interest, seeing her as another kind of person, a chick, smoking grass. The idea of a younger Mimi reminding him that the same person still lay within her. A reckless person with no compunctions about adultery. She could feel her own tangled-up feelings, with no time to sort them out.

Outside, crossing the street to the parking lot, he caught her hand protectively, as if she were a child. People never did that; she was too tall to need leading across the street. In the hospital parking lot, when they got out and Mimi turned toward her house, Philip kissed her on the cheek, but with attention, an expression of concentration as he looked into her eyes, his hand on her shoulder firm, even proprietary.

She walked home, suffused with amazement. She saw what she had not seen before, that the sympathy and affection between her and Philip were not just her imagination or wish but something objectively true, and true for Philip too. He liked her, was attracted to her. Their calm friendship, which had gone no further than the brush of hands but seemed now as if it could go further.

Could it ever go further? Usually Mimi's practical side put a check on her erotic imagination, but now she let it out a little, to course along. She could imagine a meeting—a clandestine lunch in a Chinese restaurant—no, not a Chinese restaurant, a French restaurant. She remembered the words of Carmel Hodgkiss: "No one had ever tried to make him. Not that it couldn't be done, but where would you start?"

Of course she wouldn't try to seduce Philip—what idiotic thoughts. Here she was, the colleague of Jennifer Watts, and a person with principles to boot. But suppose, for the sake of this line of thought, Jennifer were not around. Dead or divorced. Sorry, Jennifer, but this is only a game, thinking this way. Maybe she ought to dress up a little. She ought to try to be alone with Philip, just to see what would happen.

Once she had allowed herself to think of love and Philip in these concrete terms, Mimi could not control her thoughts. She just couldn't help having very graphic fantasies about being in bed with Philip, being the next Mrs. Philip Watts, even, her housing problems solved, and all she could tell herself in the way of stern common sense couldn't prevent the idea from popping again and again into her mind.

31

Harvey Mason filled in for Philip at morning rounds on Friday while Philip drove down to Sunnyvale to look again at the facilities of the envisioned institute for clinical research. It was to be installed in a VA hospital the government was pulling out of, and would combine the leftover VA staff with some Stanford University faculty under the auspices of the new director—that would be Philip—with funding both from the federal government and Stanford. One attraction of this new job for Philip, in some moods, was the freedom from the regular hospital routine. This would be his own department, the facilities were excellent, and the prestige considerable, accruing as it always did to those with money and space at their command. But the complicated funding procedures, and the prospect of an infinity of grant writing and personnel decisions, were disadvantages, as was the necessity of having to move.

Today he had a long talk with the Stanford dean, Matt Norman, and together they visited some of the laboratories. His impressions of the Stanford faculty had been favorable, of the VA staff less so. Without a director for some time, the work there had become haphazard. He observed privately to the dean that as incoming director he planned to get rid of some dead wood.

"It sounds harsh, but there's no point in beating around the bush: I'll want to let at least eleven of these people go."

"That's one of the things we looked for in our new man," the dean confided. "Someone who in addition to being a fine scientist and a talented clinician can wield an axe." Meant as a compliment, this disconcerted Philip a little. He didn't quite like to think he had a reputation as a hatchet man; he thought of himself as mild and collegial.

After an elegant lunch in Matt Norman's club with several of the senior faculty, Philip drove back to San Francisco, timing the drive—too long for a comfortable commute. He was bemused by the paradoxical disappointment of getting what you want. Reviewing the drawbacks—the time to be spent on administrative matters, and doing less hands-on patient care—tarnished a little his pleasure at seeing the splendid laboratories and viewing the exciting projects. But the new job had the virtue of being new, and of promising to relieve him of the exasperations of Alta Buena, some of which descended on him full force when he got back.

First, Perfecto Rainwater's family was demanding that his Native American practitioner be allowed to come and treat him. Philip gave permission, but ran it by Tabor, the hospital administrator, anyway.

"You mean Indian medicine men? Out of the question," Tabor said on the phone.

"It's a matter of religion, I think," said Philip. "We allow other people their religious rites, why not this? Anyhow, I gave permission already." Seconds after they had hung up, his phone rang again and he recognized the incoherent bellows of the chief of surgery, MacGregor (Mack the Knife) Bunting.

"See heah, see heah, Watts, this will not do. You sons of bitches theah think you can innerfeah in the—right in the Goddamned OR. What do you mean, comin' in theah and takin' that patient right off the table?"

"Yesterday? You're talking about Mrs. Tarro? Your boys took her in without our authorization, for one thing."

"The hell, the hell they did. I looked at the order mahself. Your chief resident signed it. But that's not the point . . ."

"The point is that we didn't think she could support the procedure, Mack—her vascular system—and in fact she stroked in the recovery room. But besides that, I'm not having these kidnappings by your crazed, knife-happy residents."

In the course of many confrontations with Mack the Knife Bunting, their rhetoric had escalated considerably, Philip noticed as he said this. They were close to saying what they really thought.

"I'll tell you what, Philip, I've had it, I'm gonna ask for a review of this. A full staff hearing. In my opinion surgery and medicine need to get some things straight, and I have to say, I hold you personally responsible for a lot of this."

"Well, I hold you . . ." Philip was beginning, then stopped, interrupted by the sense of someone's presence in the open doorway of his office. A small Oriental woman, perhaps some relative of Dr. Kim. But instead of the smile of polite diffidence he was used to seeing from the families of Oriental patients, this woman was scowling fiercely, her eyes lit up like a dragon's eyes. A couple of tiny, china-doll children and a baby in a stroller watched from behind her.

"Fine. I have to go, Mack, let's get some of these procedures reviewed. I couldn't agree more."

"Yes?" he said to the woman.

"You Dr. Watts, you the head doctor here?"

"I'm the attending this month," Philip said.

"Lum Wei-chi doctor here?"

"Yes."

"Yes. I come to say he can't stay at my house no more. You pay him, he steals the money and puts it in the bank. Why should I let him stay my house free? You give a house to other doctors." She came closer to Philip's desk. He rose.

"Please sit down, Mrs. . . ."

"I am the sister of Lum Wei-chi. He has been living at my house. How much you pay him here?"

"Well," said Philip, not wanting to betray Wei-chi in some unknown way, and also not knowing what interns made now. "Not very much."

"He tell me he don't get nothing. Now I find out he put that money in the bank."

"It can't be a large sum," Philip said, backing a little from the violent waving of the woman's finger.

"I bring his stuff," she said, turning back into the hall to seize the handle of a blue nylon sack on wheels, which she now rolled toward him. "He can't stay with me no more. You take him. I know you give doctors a house here."

"I'll talk to him," Philip said. "Perhaps he hasn't understood your feelings." He didn't understand them himself, but fell silent before the force of her anger. A shirtsleeve dangled beneath the flap of one side pouch of the sack. Abruptly, Wei-chi's sister turned and pushed the stroller off down the hall. Philip wheeled the bundle out of the way into the corner of his office and wondered what on earth Wei-chi could have done. Poor Wei-chi, model of civility and rectitude. Poor devil! His sister was certainly furious, but perhaps it was only that he was one body too many in a crowded household. But what to do with him now? So far as he knew, the interns' quarters consisted of a few sleeping cots, not so much as a bureau drawer, and were hardly fit to live in full time.

Next, in the doctors' dining room for a ten-minute break, he was waylaid by Mrs. Maline, the sickle-cell coordinator. He couldn't at first remember her name, but stopped politely when she asked if she could have a word. The extreme opalescence of her spectacles obscured the expression of her eyes. He sat down opposite her, with his coffee.

"I'm Shirley Maline, one of the Sickle-Cell people? I wanted to have a word with you about Randall Lincoln." Philip nodded again. "You know he's on dialysis?" she said.

"Yes, I know, of course."

"Well, the Federal Kidney Program could pay for his dialysis, but we can't come to an agreement with the kidney people there—that's Jim Hernandez—you know him?

"Well, Jim Hernandez says Sickle-Cell Anemia should be picking up this cost, and I just don't agree. We can get most of Randall's other costs, but the dialysis is separate. For one thing, there's the question of authorization. You're the doctor of record and you didn't authorize this putting him on dialysis." Her expression challenged him to deny this. "These people think they can lay on just any procedure and send us the bill. We've got to prioritize our costs, and Randall Lincoln could wipe out our budget for the year. So to begin with, we have to take the position, we don't pay for what the doctor of record didn't authorize."

In the rising tone of her voice Philip could hear echoes of the animated discussions she must have had with Jim Hernandez.

"Technically I didn't authorize the dialysis because the resident did; the patient was started on dialysis when I wasn't around. That doesn't mean we didn't approve it," he said, deciding not to tell her that he probably would not have started Randall on dialysis.

"What's the long term on Randall?" Mrs. Maline asked.

"Well, you know the long term, Mrs. Maline. I thought his illness was terminal this time. This might have been it. He arrested and was resuscitated, but hasn't regained consciousness, and his kidneys have quit."

"Is he going to come back to a meaningful life for the time he's got left? Is he going to wake up at all?"

"Is that a criterion for spending your funds?"

"Of course not. We're there for people all the way."

"I don't think he's going to wake up," Philip said. "The neurologists don't think so either. On the other hand, dialysis could keep him alive indefinitely. In fact, I'm wondering if dialysis doesn't in some way protect against sickling. The dialysis may be prolonging his life, but life in a coma."

"See, I just don't think we should have to pick up the tab for that. We've only got so much money," said Mrs. Maline. "I'd appreciate it if you could discuss this with Jim Hernandez."

Philip nodded, venturing a sip of his coffee, from which the tantalizing curl of steam had departed.

32

Mimi, with the help of Meg Swanson, the volunteer secretary, had put out a duplicated call for recipes, one request to each doctor and to each doctor's wife. They had included the instruction to respond quickly, in the hope of finishing the revision in time to sell copies at the fund-raising gala. In the meantime, the editorial committee, composed of Mimi, Mrs. Rank Briscoe, wife of the eminent thoracic surgeon, and Jennifer Watts, was meeting to review the recipes in the existing book. They would analyze the general categories of hors d'oeuvres, meat, poultry, fish, casseroles, salads, soups, and desserts, and then Mimi would collate all the recipes and find out if they were short of soups or casseroles, or had too many examples of salmon mousse.

Reading over the recipes, Mimi knew at once that the old recipes were all wrong. Narnia had gone through a vegetarian phase, and Daniel ate nothing but cereal and hamburgers, so she'd done little fancy cooking for years, but she could tell that these recipes seemed faintly dated. Many contained certain ingredients, like canned mushroom soup, that certainly had been in vogue when she was first married, twenty years ago, and which she had forgotten about in the meantime. She pointed out one or two recipes to Jennifer.

"A litany of death." Jennifer laughed as she read. "Beef Stroganoff, with sour cream, canned mushroom soup, and ketchup! Who on earth sent such a thing? Oh. Mrs. Madding Cramer." They exchanged doleful grimaces, for the revered Mrs. Cramer, wife of the retired dean, had been one of the most enthusiastic backers of the old cookbook, a solid money maker lo these ten years. Moreover, she'd volunteered to do some of the typing on the present version.

"Lord, listen to this," Jennifer plunged further into the manuscripts, reading aloud from the preface—by Dr. MacGregor Bunting, the most prominent doctor on the staff. " 'All hail the culinary virtues represented here. . . . But it behooves us, physicians that we are, to add a cautionary note. Lean meat and vegetables will keep us trim and healthy. The sinful pleasures of carbohydrates must be left to the young. She who would preserve her comely figure—or that of her husband—should avert her eyes from the sight of potatoes and spaghetti. Entertain no thought of chocolate cake. But daily prudence can earn rewards. A section on dessert has not been omitted. . . .' " Here Jennifer Watts began to make a funny combination sound of laughter and indignation, and shook her head. "We'll have to ask him if we can change a few words. You do it, Mimi."

"Me!" protested Mimi. "Oh, dear," thinking of the lofty Dr. Bunting, world-famous neurosurgeon and chairman of surgery, who had the air of never having changed a word in his life.

"He'll listen to you, Mimi, you're so pretty, and me—I'm just an internist's wife." Jennifer laughed, gathering her purse and papers, as usual running late.

Mimi saw that the cookbook must all be changed, and yet, when she thought of those nice women thoughtfully writing out their favorite recipes, and their husbands' favorites, it made her feel unaccountably gloomy, sad to think of the futility of female effort and about how people grow older and out of date. Presumably the recipes they would receive from the younger women would be more fashionably full of complex carbohydrates and red-pepper purées.

She went along to the doctors' dining room and was just sitting down with Philip when the room was struck silent, people frozen, cups midway to lips, as if it were Pompeii. Wystan Morris had suddenly appeared. He had walked into the room, with an expression half insouciant, half abashed, something in his milky eyes and deeply empurpled cheeks making him look broken and defenseless despite a measurable improvement in the confidence with which he carried himself. He walked briskly and with authority, and he'd lost weight.

"Been to Betty Ford," Mark Silver whispered, and this information traveled to each of the several tables.

"How ya doin', how ya doin'?" he was saying to the doctors at the table just inside the door, shaking hands all around. The surgeons seemed glad to see him. Even Philip, for all that he bore against this unconscionable killer, was glad to see him back on his feet. Morris, despite his bulk, had a high, thin voice, like an old recording. He got a cup of coffee from the dispenser and was making his way to Philip's table.

"Nice to see you fellows, I just thought I'd have a look in. Old habits die hard. Well, ha ha, I shouldn't say that. I've kicked some of my old habits, I mean the habit of stopping in."

Jeffrey Fowler, who like the other surgeons had been generally on Morris's side, against the internists and against the statistics that showed an unusual number of fatalities under his knife, stood and clasped Morris's hand. "Sit down, old buddy," he said. "You're looking great."

"Well, it's a long road back," Morris said. "If only I could undo it all. But you can't, all you can do is make amends, thank the Lord."

It struck Philip as inappropriate of Morris to come have a cup of coffee with the people he was suing, let alone talk about the Lord, but all the same he shook Morris's hand, and explained politely that he was rushing back to the ward. This he did, leaving Morris with Mimi and Jeffrey.

"People have been great, just great," Morris said. "I guess people understand how the strains, the pressures on a surgeon build up over the years." As he seemed to be preparing a monologue, Jeffrey Fowler leaped up, apologized, clapped Wice Morris warmly on the shoulder, and left. Mimi would have liked to leave too, but feared it would look too pointed a mass desertion. Instead, she smiled encouragingly. His voice still had a roughened, whiskey, cigarette rasp.

"It's the kind of damnable thing that creeps up on you," he continued. "It's an allergy, of course. In my case."

Mimi, not sure to what substance or allergy he was alluding, continued to smile, embarrassed at his confidential manner, which seemed to tell others that they were fast friends. They drew surprised looks from newcomers to the doctors' dining room.

"It got so bad, I'd have to have a little gin before operating," Morris confided, even proudly. Mimi knew that confession came easy to reformed drinkers, was something they learned in their therapy.

"Not that I wasn't capable of operating. I thank God I never let it get that bad." Mimi had heard the tales of deaths, strange sepses, forgotten sponges. "But I was taking a little gin to steady the hand. The hand would shake from the pills, the gin would steady the hand, the pills and gin together would make me incredibly sleepy. I never could shake that feeling of sleepiness—after the operation, of course, or I'd get the resident to close, if I felt I wasn't going to make it

through. The worst was when I couldn't remember what I was supposed to do."

Mimi had heard stories about how Wystan Morris in the operating
room would say, pretending to joke, "Now we're taking out that
kidney, right?" and all present would scream, "Appendix, appendix."
In this crafty way he would ascertain just what he was in there for.

"It must have been awful for you," Mimi agreed.

"Thank God I realized in time what a danger I was to myself and
others. When I think how I drove in that condition, I break out in a
sweat—I even drove my *family*," he said.

Morbidity and Mortality Conference was held each Friday in the large
x-ray reading room on the second floor. A big room was necessary
because these conferences were well attended. Interns and residents
from other hospitals besides Alta Buena liked to come, for the Alta
Buena cases were usually peculiar and complicated. Whoever was
acting as chief of service acted as moderator. The discussion, since it
was held for the purpose of instruction, was conducted along the line
of a quiz show, and pizza was served.

As the second-year resident in charge, it was Mark Silver who was
to present Tarro. Most of the audience had not heard of the case, so
Mark reviewed her admission with a swollen arm, the drugs, the fever.
Philip found himself listening with as much attention as if it were
brand new, as if in some phrase of Mark's a clue would be found to
her condition.

". . . seen by her private physician—that's Dr. Evans, who's here
today—and a diagnosis of subclavian vein thrombosis of unknown
etiology. Her lab findings were: hemoglobin 13, hematocrit 39, WBC
11,500 with 78 percent polys and 5 percent bands. Urine normal
showed only a few white blood cells; lytes and SMAC 20 were
normal."

Now the radiology resident showed a chest film on the radiant
screen, and pointed out its normality, and then the venogram showing
the axillary clot.

"The patient was started on indomethacin, and when she did not
respond, the medication was changed to streptokinase. Then, she
developed fever, so streptokinase was changed to urokinase."

"Let's stop it here for the moment," Philip said. It was now the practice to call on members of the audience for opinions and guesses. "Heather Wu—have you any comments? How would you have treated this patient?"

"I shouldn't comment, because I know something about it," Heather said, looking at Wei-chi.

"Okay, Lacey Tanaka." Lacey, the perfect resident, could always be counted on to give the perfect answer.

"I think I would have started her out on heparin," Lacey said. Philip inwardly smiled.

"Why is that? Explain."

"Well, that's the drug of choice in a mild venous thrombosis. Cheap, relatively free from side effects, easy to use."

"Would you use fibrinolytic agents like streptokinase?"

"Not in this situation."

"Explain, why not?"

"Well—in this situation—those are usually used for severe venous thrombosis of the legs or pelvis, where you have marked evidence of venous obstruction, and if there's fear of permanent damage to the venous valves, but I gather that wasn't the case here. And that nearly always happens in the lower limbs; this was in the woman's arm."

Philip asked Fred Barlow, an ER resident, "Do you agree?"

"The fibrinolytic agents are sometimes used to treat patients who have documented pulmonary embolism or who are in shock or are hemodynamically unstable," he said, contentiously. "But I might use them on this woman. I gather she was in underlying good health. They work quickly and would prevent permanent damage to the venous valves."

"Those are the issues, certainly," said Philip. "Okay. Dr. Lum, tell us what's happened."

"She develop fever, then she begin to bleed, so we stop the uro-kinase, and the surgeons were going to resect vein, then she suffer a hemorrhagic stroke with left-side paralysis and coma. She still in coma but seems to be regaining function on her left side." The audience rustled with surprise and interest. Philip called for the CAT scan to be shown.

"Now I'll ask the private physician, Dr. Evans, to comment on why he chose the fibrinolytic agent instead of the other options and on the result."

"Well, Dr. Barlow touched on the reasons," Bradford Evans said, evidently perfectly at ease. "When she was initially unresponsive to indomethacin, I felt that a rapidly acting agent was preferable, to blast that clot out of there and get the poor girl out of the hospital. Here is a single, working mother with a young baby at home—those are the things we physicians out here in the trenches have to think about, you know. In the ivory tower here, it's all very well to talk about going slow and elaborate workups. More and more, in practice, it's hospital costs we have to keep in mind in the choice of treatment."

Philip, as moderator, was barred from moralizing, but he trusted the whole point about fibrinolytic agents had been made clearly enough to teach the housestaff the lesson to be learned.

"How do you explain the stroke? She'll end up staying much longer than should have been necessary."

"That was unforeseeable, and no reason to think it was from the streptokinase. Remember, we still don't know why she had that clot in the first place," said Bradford Evans, with his engaging grin. At this, it seemed to Philip that Evans might be getting the last word after all. The right and wrong of the case was so evident, and Evans was so unconscious of error that Philip didn't trust himself, in his exasperation, to say anything more.

At the end of the day, Philip took Wei-chi aside and described, as matter-of-factly as possible, the visit of his sister. "But we'll put you up at our house a night or two. When the services change, after New Year's, you can probably stay in the residents' rooms."

"Oh, I couldn't inconvenience—I should so regret . . ." continued the stricken Wei-chi, eyeing the sack of his belongings on its peculiar wheels.

"It's okay, really. Absolutely," Philip assured him. At seven, when he was ready to go home, he took Wei-chi's arm, and himself began to wheel the thing toward the elevator. Wei-chi, as if unwilling to deal with this humiliating apparatus, silently followed.

Jennifer was surprised but not ruffled, was used to Philip's circle of visiting firemen from the NIH, or England, or Canada, or France, or Duke, or Boston. He had never before brought home a homeless housestaffer, but what was the difference? She pleasantly showed Wei-chi to the guest room—large, handsomely furnished in family antiques—and explained what they usually did about breakfast. Her smile was vague, a smile that Philip recognized meant she may not have yet focused on the reality of some new, Chinese person underfoot. Or else she truly didn't mind having him.

33

In the intensive care unit, the hours, a day, two days stretch along. Nurses, doctors, aids, orderlies, slip in and out, speaking to her. She can hear, or her mind imagines. It seems to her in her coma that they invade her with their words. Sometimes it seems to her that they whisper strange questions: "Are your periods regular?" they seem to say. Is it one doctor or all doctors who say, "Let me check your breasts, let me touch you." Is she dreaming this or is it true?

If her eyes could fly open, would there be a doctor in the room? Yet she cannot open her eyes. It seems to her that a deep male voice says, "Tell us what is going on inside your body. You can tell what we cannot. We can see but you cannot. You can tell but only we can see.

"In your body there are processes, divisions, secretions, stirrings, tides. You are a creature of the moon and oceans. We know how you are like the fishes in the sea. Your blood is like the dinosaur's blood. The agent dripping into your blood is made from the piss of six thousand GIs."

All that as in a dream, and then, in an instant, awareness, a hot pain, as if someone had put a fist down her throat, or was pouring hot, oily poison into her. She opened her eyes. She was in the hospital. She did not recognize the room, or remember what had happened.

Gradually she got a sense of the distant parts of her body; she could tell that something was jammed down her throat and that her arms were pinned down, imprisoning her. Her feet seemed to be attached to her legs, but one of them, and the leg, ached numbly, and her head ached. Slowly, she took stock. Worst was the dreadful choking, and a feeling of nausea pressing upward against the obstruction in her throat. Yet she was not frightened. She did not think of complaining against this new condition, but only of getting to understand a new reality.

Someone near her said, "She's waking up. But she'll still need to be intubated."

Ivy directed her mind to remember, and now could remember being taken for an operation, and the hands pushing her down, and the sounds of her own screams.

She fell back into sleep, and dreamed she was swimming, until the current became too strong for her, and as she was being washed away, she was saved by grabbing onto two colossal legs standing in the water, the huge legs of a giant, its head invisible far above. From the shore behind her she could hear her baby shrieking as if she were being bayoneted.

She did not know how much time had passed before she woke again. She was pulling against the thing that was tethering her right wrist. She could not feel her other arm.

"Come on, honey, can you move yo foot?" said a woman's voice, but she couldn't see who it was. Then, by swiveling her eyes to one side, she could see a nurse, her face and voice familiar, and an Oriental doctor. She pulled harder at the strap, almost reassured by the pain in her wrist, connecting her to the world.

All at once she thought it was her breasts, thought about how it was said you wake up like this when they have cut your breasts off. You can tell they've cut them off by the bandages wrapped around you, and by the look of compassion and concern, as on this doctor's face now, a look that says, We are sorry you are mutilated, damaged. Horror made her gag. But she was not here because of her breasts. She remembered. Her arm.

Another voice said, "Let's see how much mobility she has."

And another said, "I think we can put her in a room."

She must have closed her eyes again, but she could feel people lift and carry her, wheels rumbled under her, as in a tumbril, and when she again came to herself, her hearing and her mind were clearer. She thought of Delia. Outside, away somewhere, she heard a man's familiar voice saying, in a teacherly tone, "When someone is afraid of an operation, you have to believe them. You can't take a chance. You should never send them to surgery in that mood, because they might actually die of fright. They die of irrational fear or the fear originates from their inner sense of a condition they can't describe and you have no way of knowing about. Sometimes people have a sense that it's time for them to die, that's all. Or it can be a matter of will; it's as if they will themselves to die. I've seen it too often. If they have a feeling, respect it. That was part of the reason we brought Mrs. Tarro back without surgery. She was afraid of dying, so she might have died. I pay attention to people who have intimations of death."

"But what if they need the operation?"

"That's a tough call. Luckily they often don't. You have to protect them from the surgeons, because surgeons don't pay attention. I stopped the operation for other reasons too. It would have been an unnecessary procedure, number one, and, two, her physician hadn't authorized it. Neither had I. He had signed out to me."

Hearing this, Ivy stopped breathing, the better to listen. Her situation was becoming clearer. She had been near death and had been saved. She was still the protagonist in a struggle between the forces of life and death, contending for her, and life for the moment had won. But dread told her the issue wasn't finally decided. She looked wildly around for a person, a hand, but the room was empty.

Only now did she realize that she couldn't move her left side. She was conscious of her arm's weight, and of a painful numbness in her wrist and shoulder. Her attention, like a scanner, traveled to her calf and ankle. When she stirred, her right leg moved, the other could not. For the first moment, this was more strange than frightening. The clearness of her mind, after the muddle of days, was itself so like coming back to life that she could not for a moment realize that life was qualified by this new handicap.

The leg didn't move, didn't respond to the explicit direction of her mind; neither did her arm. She felt she was half made of lead, or half metamorphosed as by some pursuing god, like those statues of the nymph Daphne, with trees sprouting from their fingertips, an image she had once thought so harmlessly pastoral, now it revealed its horror—the allegiance of the body to the vegetable world, the dominion of the mind only provisional and temporary. She was half vegetable. With her vigorous self she turned, thrashed, tried to sit up a little and think what to do.

She had a sense of being outside time. She had to know about Delia. The telephone lay beyond reach across the room, impossibly remote, as on a distant shore. She would have to get up. She felt strong, and hitched herself up on her elbow. She felt funny, but strong enough, and, needing to believe she was strong, she thrashed with all her force over the edge of the bed toward a pair of paper slippers on the floor. Then as she felt the cold floor under her toes, she fell thunderously, and found herself sitting on the floor with a tearing pain in her throat and a bitter pain in her tailbone where she had smacked it on the metal of the bed. Her own scream rang in her ears.

She didn't at first understand that her leg had buckled. Her arm lay limply at her side. She carefully felt for the rail of the bed and grasped it with her strong arm, but she couldn't move. She smelled strange to herself, sweaty and peculiar. Sweat poured down her side and down her temples.

Now she saw that beyond the curtain that hung on the other side of the room, a tiny woman, agelessly old, was watching her.

"I've pushed the button," the old woman said. "I've called them," and in seconds, nurses rushed in, exclaiming, shouting, their reproaches and self-reproaches. The handsome doctor, Dr. Watts, came in with the nurses. "God damn it, where were you people?" he snapped at the nurses. "Mrs. Tarro," he said, gathering her up, "what happened? Can you speak?"

She hadn't tried to speak. She shook her head slightly, no, and closed her eyes. He took her hand, which lay limply in his.

"Push on my hand," he said, and felt a feeble movement.

"How did she fall?" he asked Merci in a censorious voice. "Why weren't there any nurses here? Jesus Christ, this isn't Manila." He helped Merci lift Ivy back into bed, and Rosemary Hunt came in to tuck the bedclothes around her.

Philip called for Wei-chi and Perry to examine her and make sure she hadn't hurt herself. At this moment Edgardo came carrying Ivy's clothes from the ICU closet. Philip paused, feeling an interest he could not help in the strands of pink and blue glass beads, an Indian gauze scarf, blue, slightly crumpled and old, a roughly knit sweater in shades of pink and blue. He imagined her wearing the sweater, with the scarf wrapped around her hair. He looked at her again as she lay in the hospital bed, eyes closed. Her lower lip was swollen where the breathing tube had pressed against it. He was aware of wanting to press his lips against the swelling. He hurried out of the room, with another harsh remark to Merci Yezema.

The word spread quickly that Ivy Tarro had regained consciousness. She lay, unmoving, eyes open, hearing and wondering. She couldn't speak.

"Hey there!" said the gaggle of doctors to Ivy later, on their rounds, smiling broadly, delighted to see that she was conscious. Ivy felt tears of love to see their smiling faces. "That's a girl," they said, and she smiled back, despite her hurting spine, despite her shock and her unmoving limbs. She could feel that her smile wasn't right; it felt as if she had been to the dentist. Her cheek hung strangely, and felt thick. The doctors poked and pulled her stonelike arm and leg. But she felt happy. She was not frightened. It did not occur to her to complain.

In the afternoon, Dr. Evans came, and poked and prodded her limbs. She could feel his hand on her foot, drawing a line on the sole of her foot, but the sensation was faint, as though she were wearing a thick sock.

"You've had what we call a vascular accident. Some bleeding into your brain has blotted out the center that controls movement," he said. "This is serious, but we don't expect it to be permanent. I think you're going to go waltzing real soon. We'll be needing to do some tests to help us understand what's going on, okay?"

Ivy could tell he was speaking to her in an extra loud voice, as if she were deaf, but her hearing was sharp, even painful, as if words were vibrating dentist drills on her eardrums. She could smell his shaving lotion. She tried to read his broad, smiling face. She directed relief and gratitude and love at him, for paying attention to her like this, and speaking so kindly. She felt, again, her smile stretch, involuntary and beseeching.

When Philip came by Randall Lincoln's bed on afternoon rounds, he found Mrs. Lincoln reading aloud to his corpselike form. His eyes were slightly open, showing little moons of sightless white. The mouth was slack, and there was a gurgling in his throat that the nurses should check. Near him, the dialysis machine, attached to an artificial shunt in his wrist, made a low, washing-machine sound.

"I don't think he can hear you, Mrs. Lincoln," Philip said.

"I think he can, doctor. I read it." She showed him a book, from the hospital library, and a passage telling how people in a coma can hear nonetheless. As they lie there, they can hear people say things. Philip thought of Mrs. Tarro hearing him criticize the streptokinase, or Perfecto hearing Mrs. Rainwater saying to his girlfriend, "He never was any good." It was an unnerving idea, that people could hear in coma, and of course it couldn't be true.

"Well, I hope you're right," he said.

"I believe it helps him to hear something interesting," she said. "That keeps his brain going, and that helps him overall. My voice going into his brain, it's a human contact, it probably don't matter too much if it's a good book, but in case it do . . ."

How much better, Philip thought, if she would just get resigned to Randall's fate. But he admired her, and something always touched him about these displays of human constancy.

The doctors' parking and advisory committee was meeting at one table in a corner of the doctors' dining room—fourteen senior doctors in white or green, stethoscopes dangling, some wearing caps of green and gauze, all with coffee. They had settled to hear Rank Briscoe, the chairman, talk about discouraging obstacles that were shaping up in front of plans for the parking structure. There were signs of resistance from the neighborhood, and even one of their own volunteers, Mrs. Franklin, who happened to hold a key parcel, was refusing to discuss selling. "You'd think one of our own people would be more understanding. It isn't as if we aren't prepared to pay a fair price."

"For that matter," said Dr. Harvey Mason, the gastroenterologist, "who'd want to live next door to a hospital? The ambulances, the traffic—you'd think she'd be delighted to sell and get out."

"Tabor thinks that someone is advising her," said Rank Briscoe. "These people have us over a barrel, and they know they can stick it to us."

"Have you heard this one?" asked Jeffrey Fowler. "What's black and tan and looks good on a lawyer? A Doberman."

"It seems rather hypocritical of her, to play the selfless volunteer by day, and profiteer at the same time," someone said of Mimi.

"*Paid* volunteer," Harvey Mason reminded them. "She's technically an employee." Philip, who was not a member of the parking committee, and was seated at an adjacent table, could not forbear pointing out that people get attached to their houses.

"Mimi Franklin is a lovely woman. A lovely woman," added Bradford Evans vigorously. The others fell silent in surprise, startled that Watts and Evans seemed to be agreeing on something. And what was more surprising was that Buck Evans was one of the principal investors in the parking corporation, if not the principal investor, and hence had most to lose if the corporation had to pay a high price for the adjoining properties.

"She's probably not being unreasonable, she probably just needs time to think it over," Evans went on.

"Excuse me," Brian Smeed, the chief resident, said, coming up to the other doctors. He seemed uncharacteristically excited. "I'm sorry to interrupt. Um—the nurses on the three medical wards have just walked off the job. I've got the housestaff filling in, but . . ." The other doctors stared.

"Why on earth?" Philip asked, rising. "Isn't it rather sudden? What's the matter?"

"Apparently; I—well—they say it was because of an ethnic slur. By you." A slight tincture of satisfaction in Smeed's voice was perhaps only audible to Philip himself.

Jennifer brought the dishes to the table: veal piccata, dressed with lemon, baked potatoes, and salad. She served Philip and Wei-chi all the veal, and forked a leaf or two of lettuce and a small potato onto her own plate. Philip, used to her strategies for keeping thin, didn't pay much attention, but Wei-chi looked with concerned disappointment at her abstemiousness.

"I've decided to give up meat," she explained.

"Really? Some meat's all right, Jen. Fish. Veal's low-fat," Philip assured her.

"I haven't decided about fish," she said. "Maybe I'll eat fish. But not veal. Do you know how they raise veal? In blackness. In dark sheds, to keep their meat white. They get no exercise, never get to roam or eat grass. No, I'm giving up meat for moral reasons."

Wei-chi, accustomed to the peculiar scruples Westerners were always developing against such delicious food as sea slug or bat, saw nothing unusual in Mrs. Watts's pronouncement. It seemed to amuse Dr. Watts. "You're probably right," he said. He said that though he was not inclined himself to give up meat for moral reasons he had certainly cut down his consumption of beef.

"It raises the question of whether one ought to cook it and serve it," Jennifer continued. "Don't laugh. I'm only half serious, you know. But of course, that's half serious. I know these are silly food fads. But I've begun to feel that the food we eat is disgusting, probably poisoning us, and that we have to take charge of it. There's really a lot of evidence. Of course I know that doctors don't believe it, but that's just because you haven't been trained to think about nutrition."

"I like to think I'm capable of conclusions that don't arise from my medical school training," Philip said. "Besides, I can always get a steak at a restaurant if I crave one," he added more genially. "If it makes you feel compromised. But I would like fish or some kind of protein."

"Fish, all right," Jennifer agreed.

"I don't get much lunch, you know," he reminded her.

"I know. The food's unspeakable at Alta Buena," Jennifer said. "How is Ivy Tarro?"

"Her arm's not responding. She's getting back some function on her left side. In my opinion, the whole thing is entirely owing to the wrong drug in the first place." He went on to describe the contretemps between himself and Bradford Evans, Evans's general tendency toward dramatic drugs, his own sense of foreboding in this case.

"Why didn't you do something?" Jennifer said. "How could you let them give her the wrong drug?"

This irritated Philip. Jennifer seldom showed much understanding of the simple protocol without which things would fall into chaos in a hospital. Somebody had to be in charge of every case; and if everybody second-guessed everybody all the time, and countermanded other people's orders, in the interstices people would die.

"I just don't understand that," Jennifer objected. "You know she was getting the wrong medicine and you just allowed it?"

"Well, it's you who don't understand," he said, and they let the matter drop, with a slight tinge of ill will, Jennifer glancing at him from time to time as if he were a cruel, unreliable person.

34

Ivy was strangely content. She had become a patient. Lying in bed, as on a cloud in space, her thoughts could spin above the people down below. She lay, submissive to the hands that came to turn her over, wash, bend, and pull her limbs, and to the voices assuring her that she would walk and talk. Soon! they said brightly. When no one was around, she tried to speak. A gagging low sound would percolate in her throat, a sound so inhuman that it frightened the other woman in her room, Mrs. Tate, who called the nurse the first time she heard it.

"Pushed the panic button," Mrs. Tate said.

Panic when she thought of walking. Soon she would have to try to walk across the room, with her numb log leg, her thick arm hanging, reminding her she was no longer light and beautiful and couldn't dance out of there. Years ahead, all by herself, day after day, alone in her kitchen or creeping to the baby's room, with no one to see her or feel sorry for her or to encourage her, she'd stump along, a half person, because of some message from God or bad luck in a lottery or mean gene or personal sin or mistake of an unknown enemy or council of fates deciding to test her, or an environmental factor like some insecticide or poison dumped under her apartment, or radon gas, or rays, a microwave or the TV, or a radium dial or a wrong prescription or a crazy person putting something in her aspirin bottle. Now asleep, now awake, now content, now full of rage, she dreamed away the afternoons.

The doctors touched her, rearranged the covers, spoke to her. When they left after their rounds, she would lie there, reassured, thinking of home or Delia, or even of breakfast. Two of the doctors were handsome. She could imagine them—the notion sometimes trailed into her mind—could imagine them doing other things to her. One at a time, while the other guarded the door.

On the wards, the orderlies and interns were emptying bedpans. Vita Dawson explained to Mimi about the nurses' strike, begun by the Filipinas, following Philip Watts's harsh words to Merci. Mimi was surprised at the sisterly emotion of indignation she herself felt, even though she knew that Philip was not as discourteous to nurses as many of the doctors were. Dr. Bunting, it was said, had once thrown a tray of implements at a nurse. She couldn't forbear bringing the strike up when she saw Philip in the doctors' dining room.

"So you'll say you're sorry and that will be that?"

"Unless they've tacked on a few demands, which they probably have," Philip said.

"I'm sorry, but I just find it all very irritating," Mimi said. Why did she, she wondered?

"Oh, I know I shouldn't have spoken in that harsh tone. I know they're sensitive," Philip agreed.

"I mean, it's irritating the way doctors can say any old insulting thing to nurses and then imagine all they have to do is apologize. They don't see that they've revealed their real contempt, and the way they take these hardworking women for granted. There's no way you can take that back, because it's true."

"My word, you sound like Jennifer!" said Philip mildly. "I have great respect for nurses. I believe they're the most important part of the medical team. The hospital literally couldn't run without nurses, we all know that."

"Well, it's running now, isn't it? The interns are emptying the bedpans. It's just that they usually don't have to."

Philip was taken aback by the unexpected feminism of Mimi's tone and sentiments. What was eating Mimi?

"And you could say the same for the volunteers," she went on. "Dozens of hardworking women, unpaid, the hospital couldn't even run without them, and are they ever acknowledged or given any kind of status? No, the doctors just tell them to get out of the way once in a while, or bark commands as if they were nurses. Without all the things that volunteers do, the hospital would have to hire more nurses, right? The volunteers are unpaid, and the nurses are underpaid, and you know why? Because they're women." Mimi looked quite rosy and fierce, a lovely woman, it was true, especially when exercised like this.

"Some of the nurses are men, and some of the doctors are women," Philip said, wondering what was really bothering her. After all, she had a quite high status at the hospital, though probably her salary was low.

"That doesn't alter the underlying injustice," she said.

Then, of course, she saw that she was resentful on her own behalf, of the way men, and hospitals, cared nothing for the feelings of women and put them out of their houses without compunction.

"I was hoping to catch you," said Mr. Tabor to Mimi, who was turning in her tray. Tabor smoothly took the tray and carried it to the return window for her. "There's something that might interest you about the planned parking facility. From an investment standpoint. If you have a moment to stop into my office this afternoon, I can show you the numbers. Are you having coffee? Basically, it's an investment I think might interest you."

And Mimi did feel a stir of interest, despite herself, at the idea of something directed and purposeful like an investment, to resolve the confusion she had been thrust into. Though she knew that investments proposed to single women must be resisted on principle, she supposed, coming from the hospital administrator, this one must be legitimate at least, and was no doubt connected to her house situation.

"It won't hurt to listen," she said, smiling. He ceremoniously drew her a cup of coffee from the dispenser and departed. "See you later, then."

Mimi sat down with Bill Field to drink her coffee. She had been relieved not to find herself a complete pariah among the doctors. She had been conscious of a chill for several days at the doctors' table, and she knew it must be about the parking lot. She had to stifle an impulse to explain herself to them—"I need to figure out what to do with myself, that's all."

"The hospital, of course, is a nonprofit corporation," said Mr. Tabor to Mimi later, in his office, unrolling his charts. "Therefore, it doesn't get involved in certain aspects of the hospital program—with the laundry, for example, or the parking—it contracts these out. Basically the hospital will enter into a contract with outside contractors for building and running the parking facility.

"A group of investors puts up the money—it's a fabulous investment opportunity. Assuming a net profit from your property, after you've repurchased a living unit, the investment group is prepared to offer you discounted shares in the parking-facility enterprise.

"It seemed to us, with your long-term commitment to Alta Buena, you would see the attractiveness of this as an investment, while at the same time, along with other people who have faith in the future of Alta Buena, you would appreciate the opportunity to—invest in something you believe in."

"The other investors?" asked Mimi.

"Well, the doctors, of course. Who would have more faith in the future of Alta Buena than they would?"

"No, well, I see that," Mimi said.

"There's something else," he added. "To put it bluntly, Mrs. Franklin, there is every reason to think a condemnation proceeding would be resolved in the hospital's favor. This is a public facility. The issue is the public good. You do understand that society can act, in some circumstances, collectively in its own interests? Just as if the city were going to build a road through your yard. It could condemn your property and give you a price, which it would decide on. Not always as fair a price as could be arrived at if you negotiated." As he said all this, he did not look directly at Mimi, as if he were slightly ashamed of this tactic. Nonetheless, he was saying what he was saying.

As she walked home, she felt energized by indignation. Although it was prepared to pay something, Alta Buena was basically prepared to put her out of her house without adequate compensation! And Philip Watts was the most obtuse man she had ever met!

"I had the most exasperating thing happen today," Jennifer said to Philip as they sat down to dinner. "I was meeting Francine Darrow and Dolph Dobbs and Martin for a late lunch before the board meeting, at around two—this was in North Beach, at Tony's, and the maître d' said, 'I'm sorry but we don't seat ladies unaccompanied!' At that hour and in this day and age! The implication was that we were prostitutes! And by law don't they have to seat anyone, even if we were?"

"I don't see that it follows that they thought you were prostitutes. Why would they—well-dressed, respectable women?" He courteously did not add that she and Francine were also both a little old to be taken for prostitutes; of course they were both very good-looking.

"Then why wouldn't they seat ladies unaccompanied? Francine and I were furious, and when Dolph and Martin came, we told them. We wanted to leave, naturally, and they couldn't understand what we were on about."

"But you got seated, didn't you?"

"Look—suppose you were meeting two, I don't know, black colleagues and the restaurant wouldn't seat them, wouldn't you leave? Two black teammates or whatever?"

"Of course. That happened once, in high school."

"Well, why wouldn't you defend a woman in the same way?"

"I suppose I would, now that you mention it," Philip said, not sounding very convinced. He added, "It's awfully hard to get into Tony's as it is. I suppose Dobbs was thinking of that." He took note of Jennifer's hiss of exasperation.

In the light of the nurses', and Mimi Franklin's outburst today, this experience of Jennifer's made Philip reflect that although he had been brought up to feel fair-mindedly that women were just like men, they actually were very odd.

35

A committee of the nurses, which did not after all include Merci, had accepted Philip's apology with an apology of their own: Philip was not the worst offender; it had been the culmination of a number of episodes, a feeling building up. It seemed from the glances they exchanged that there had been differences among themselves—nurses who thought they should continue, nurses who thought the thing should be discussed with all the doctors, nurses who personally had nothing to object to. Philip forbore to assail their shaky consensus with any complaint of his own, just made his excuses—he'd been upset, finding the patient on the floor—and accepted their assurances that he was usually consideration itself. He left them arguing among themselves. To him this was neither the most nor the least of certain odd things that had started to happen to him, and he felt he had to stay relaxed, as if he were about to perform one of those physical tricks of gymnastics or ski jumping, where tensions and self-consciousness would bring you down with a crash.

"Today," a strange, cruel-looking woman with dyed yellow hair and glasses on a string said to Ivy, "today the doctors want you to try to begin walking." At this she left Ivy's room and came back with a chrome cage, like an old-fashioned hoop skirt, with little rubber-tipped chicken feet. She stood it in the corner. Edgardo, the male nurse, appeared behind her, with strong arms under her arms to lift her onto her feet. The woman and Edgardo put her in the cage. In this contraption, Ivy could step—one step, then two. At first it wasn't so bad. But it was like walking when your foot has gone to sleep. Her leg felt like a frozen bottle that had burst. The thick icy sludge in her ankle made her crumple. Arms steadied her. Ivy had seen these devices. You saw very old people in them, accompanied by bored-looking Hispanics in white uniforms, creeping along the San Francisco sidewalks.

"That's a girl," said Edgardo and the physical therapist, making her try again.

But I'm never leaving this room while I have to be in this thing, Ivy thought to herself. She clumped around and around the room, around and around, her heart raging.

"That's good, dear. Go, girl," said her roommate, Mrs. Tate, a tiny old woman who could not stir, was attached by too many cords and tubes to her bed. Where her hair had been, she wore an old-fashioned frilly crocheted cap, but Ivy had seen the nurses washing her downy bare scalp. Ivy could not reply to Mrs. Tate's encouragement. When she tried to speak, her tongue didn't feel right and she hated the raspy, queer shape of her words. But she smiled her thanks.

Sometimes, weak and tired, Ivy would abandon her struggle with her walking cage and sit in the chair and listen to Mrs. Tate's stories. She understood that Mrs. Tate was dying, but it didn't seem sad. A spark burned in every one of Mrs. Tate's cells, some spark of spirit or experience. She would be alive right up until she died, and maybe after. Ivy studied her. A profile in courage, and Ivy feared her, in a way, for making clear how close the stages were of life to death. She had an image of a candle flickering in the draft in an open window. She herself was a mere candle. Delia was a mere candle.

Mrs. Tate did not trust or believe in the medical profession. She had been treated in a clinic in Tijuana.

"The Santé clinic. They use lemon juice. They give you the lemon juice IV. This acidifies the viruses. The viruses can't live in an acid environment. Cancer is caused by viruses in ninety percent of the cases. I knew a woman who had the other kind, the alkaline cancer. Then they give you a yogurt diet, with iodine.

"The medical establishment doesn't want this known, of course. Think what would happen to the medical industry, the drug industry, the hospital industry, if the acid-alkaline thing were generally known. The thing would collapse. Oh, it's a little more complicated than I'm making it sound; you have to know what you're doing. They monitor your blood, you get vitamins, because the lemon kills certain vitamins. And they monitor the Candida albicans. That causes much more human illness than people realize. I think they're starting to understand that.

"I say nothing to these doctors here. They don't like it if you've gone to Tijuana. It's a challenge to their authority. Sometimes they refuse to treat you if they find out you've been to Tijuana. My doctor here doesn't know. Dr. Watts. But I'm taking the drugs, I'm taking the vitamins." She took out a bottle from her bedstand, filled with large green capsules. Ivy admired them. They seemed to radiate health-giving properties.

"You have to fast for six days, with nothing but lemon juice and molasses. This cleans you out, before the treatment begins. I recommend that for anyone, sick or not. Lemon juice and molasses."

Here she had to stop, choked by sputum, stifled by wheezes rising in her throat. Her skinny, concave chest seemed to contract like bellows, and her huge tongue thrust itself between her lips at every cough. She lifted her transparent arm an inch off the coverlet, trying to cover her mouth, but could lift it no higher. Ivy would have liked to help. She didn't like to stare, but she did.

At this moment, the nice nurse Rosemary looked in, and then, soon after, Dr. Watts came in. Ivy was aware of how Dr. Watts made her blood warm. Usually he had a train of younger doctors behind him, but now he was alone. Mrs. Tate seemed to cringe when she saw him, and tightly closed her mouth.

"I've ordered some new medicine for you, Mrs. Tate. I'm here to lecture you on taking it faithfully, even though it tastes pretty ghastly. It's just one of those things we haven't found a better way to administer than just to have you swallow it. Think you can do this?"

"You're the doctor," said Mrs. Tate.

"I'm going to watch you take it the first time," he said, nodding to Rosemary, who began to pour a gooey syrup into a spoon, like a nanny in a nursery. "To see how tough you are." He took the spoon from Rosemary and waved it like a hypnotist before Mrs. Tate's face.

Mrs. Tate drew a breath and held it, with a wild, conspiratorial look of desperation at Ivy, as if to say she knew this man was trying to kill her. Dr. Watts was steady-handed, and thrust the spoon at the old woman's mouth.

The huge, dark tongue came out, and he laid the spoon on it, and tipped it. Being a doctor, Ivy saw, was something like motherhood, though she hadn't been a mother long enough to know in what other ways this might be true. A look of disgust passed over Mrs. Tate's face, and a ripple in her esophagus moved the parts of her skinny neck up and down. Then she smiled. Dr. Watts patted and congratulated her. Ivy yearned to please him too.

He leaned over her in her chair, as he left. "How are you, Mrs. Tarro? I see they've got you walking. That's good. How's the speech?"

"Fine," she croaked. "Thank you."

He took her hand. "Good," he said. "Squeeze my hand." She squeezed his hand. "That's good," he said, "very good."

———

Fine, thank you? thought Ivy, watching as he left. Couldn't she have thought of three better words than that? And wasn't it stupid to say you are fine when you are lying half-paralyzed in a hospital, when a week ago you really were fine?

But of course compared to Mrs. Tate she is fine. She thinks of that. How can you say you are other than fine when Mrs. Tate is lying there dying with her bones sticking out of her skin? How can you say you are other than fine when a handsome man asks you? Out of politeness to other people, you must say you are fine, you must not bore them with your symptoms, you must not go on about yourself.

She knew these were stupid and inappropriate considerations, but she'd never been sick before, had only been to parties, so to speak, so that was the behavior she knew—don't talk about yourself, ask him about himself. Now I'm learning hospital. She had the impulse, in her slurred voice, to try saying, "Why me?" but instead, falteringly, she said aloud to Mrs. Tate, "Why not me?" Who was she to claim exemption from bad luck? She had to admit, why not me?

Mimi was reassured that lots of flowers had begun to arrive for Ivy, as if she had been incognito before, and only now was officially in the hospital, as if people had imagined she was only to be in for a moment, and now accepted that she'd be in for weeks. Now that impressive and poetic bouquets and potted plants began to appear, revealing tasteful or well-off friends, Ivy seemed better protected but more mysterious than before. Mimi found herself watching for Ivy Tarro's flowers rather jealously. Ivy read the cards on all the flowers. She thanked Mimi for the rosebuds. "So beautiful!" she tried saying, her words funny and slow. She wanted to say that she'd noticed that sometimes rosebuds don't open all the way, just shrivel into peas, but Mimi's had blossomed. But she couldn't say "shrivel."

"What are you looking for," the real estate lady had asked Mimi. "I don't know exactly," Mimi had said. "I guess I need to know how much my house is worth, and what I could find in the same price range."

"May I just bring a few of my colleagues?" the real estate lady had said, with a certain reservation in her voice that made Mimi's heart sink. These people were now swarming over her house—six or seven women, uniformly blond and well dressed in suits, and one man. They carried notebooks and gave her friendly smiles that did not disguise the appraising nature of their visit. Mimi, as if cursed with a malign gift, could read their denigrating thoughts. Only one bathroom, they thought. That maroon tile is very thirties.

I didn't really choose that bedspread, Mimi found herself wanting to say. It just happens to be the bedspread I have. In the corner of the window sash, she could see, if they did not, a smudge of mildew where she hadn't been aware of a leak. Like termites, the real estate agents lit, swarmed, and departed, leaving Mimi alone with Mrs. Thorn, the woman to whom she had first spoken.

"They'll work up the comps," she said. "We'll let you know. Meantime, there are one or two things I could show you this afternoon."

These things, as Mimi had feared, were unspeakable. There was indeed a gap between what she would like and what was roughly equivalent in value to her own house—in other words, what she would like was not the same as what she was used to. The tormenting paradox was that she saw she would not be happy in something no better than she lived in already. She was not prepared to move into this horrible little house that she was shown, in a foggy part of town, or into a condominium with textured sheetrock walls and bleak stairwells. Didn't your house say everything about you? Did a humble house infect you with its smallness and docility? Did it retain you and constrain you in the life of a slave?

And yet these were worth what her house was worth. In the real estate mind they were the same. She thought, while knowing there was no mistake—while knowing that others found her house musty and small—that there must be some mistake. Real redwood and glassed-in bookshelves counted for nothing! But, she was sorry to find, she was not able to feel a defensive, renewed affection for her own house, either. The devaluation of it by others simply increased her discontent. They knew what she had always known.

"I thought my house would have gone up in value," she said forlornly to Mrs. Thorn.

"Of course it has," she said, "but so has everything else." In the days after Mrs. Thorn's visit, Mimi's house panic grew. Would she be well advised to sell and get out? What was the relation between people and their houses? Why were people always saying, "Get out of my space" or "I need space." She would become—her thoughts became momentarily wild—a bag person, a shopping-cart woman, and install herself with the other bag ladies in front of the entrance of Alta Buena!

How had these women lost their happiness? By unwise real estate transactions? Could you get happiness from a house, a job, a man? Had she blighted her chance of happiness by speaking so strongly to Philip Watts about the nurses? What was happiness anyway? Could you pursue it, or did you merely have it within you, like a virus that could pop out at any moment or lie dormant? She had had it, she knew, while she led the plain life of Daniel and Narnia's hardworking mother, coordinator of Volunteer Services. Why had it all at once deserted her, like a bird that has flown the coop? You think you have it, and then one morning the cage door is open, it is gone. You heard people talk of finding happiness, but you never heard them talk about how it can be lost.

Philip, stopping to look at the charts at the nurses' station, could see an animated group, including Wei-chi and Perry Briggs, going into the room of Tarro and Tate along with several visitors. On his way back to his office he glanced in, perhaps to protect Mrs. Tate from too much excitement, and could see Ivy Tarro, sitting in the chair, rapturously clasping a pink-wrapped infant, while the others gathered around smiling, and Wei-chi was actually making a clucking noise as he peeked into the folds. Though this was a happy occasion, uniting the poor young woman, after all she'd been through, with her baby, still he found this reference to her outside life disconcerting. It was like seeing people for the first time in their street clothes. Sometimes you didn't recognize them, and they always looked healthier than when wearing their sick costumes of gowns or pajamas. Mrs. Tarro's expression of delight, her normal radiance, made her look like a madonna.

He was glad Wei-chi and Perry were in on Ivy's reunion with her baby. It was good for the housestaff to realize that patients have outside lives and responsibilities, and it was nice for them to witness a happy scene, since so much of what they saw was tears and death. He knew that the hospital social workers had checked to see that Mrs. Tarro's baby was being taken care of after her stay had been so unexpectedly lengthened. A hardship, he supposed, for a young mother to leave her baby for—what was it?—nearly two weeks now?

Later, when the party of visitors came by his office on their way to the elevators, despite himself he got up and strolled along behind them. Why? As he approached, the elevators opened, and they stepped in, turning toward him to face the elevator doors, and in an instant the doors closed on them, leaving him with only a fleeting impression of the baby: black.

Not exactly black, but dark, dusky, with tight little curls showing under a pink bonnet. Not a child who would be described as white. The child waved a tiny fist, as though acknowledging his surprise. A cute little baby, but black. *And* black, he meant. Adopted?

Rape involuntarily crossed his mind. Had Ivy been a rape victim? Then he felt ashamed that this racist idea had even darted into his head. Along with fleeting thoughts about how some white women preferred black lovers. But of course, for all he knew, Ivy's husband was a well-known black professor or musician, unfortunately away during this illness. A folksinger or rock star, an immensely rich boxer. How mysterious she was. The duskiness of her baby symbolized ideas, values, experiences of which he knew nothing. It was disturbing and exciting. He longed just to talk to her sometime.

"What in God's name is wrong with the bread?" Philip asked Jennifer, biting into the stiff, stale substance on his plate. He noticed that Wei-chi was also looking at it with a certain apprehensiveness.

"It's 'naturally leavened,' " Jennifer said, laughing. "It does take some getting used to."

Philip put it to one side without comment, too polite to continue to criticize the food, especially in front of a guest.

"Our bakery has been persuaded by a theory that it may be yeast that causes cancer, and all of this candidiasis going around," Jennifer explained. "Yeast infections. There's a theory that they're caused by commercial yeast."

"As opposed to what?" Philip wondered.

"As opposed to natural leavening. Lactobacillus. Something called phytin is eliminated, and—I don't remember the technical details, naturally. The bakery passes out a brochure with your first loaf. The point is natural fermentation versus commercial yeast."

"That's like refusing to take commercial penicillin," Philip said, laughing.

"You don't have to eat it," Jennifer said, with a certain asperity. An expression of anxiety was apparent on Wei-chi's face: to eat it or not to eat it? Which of his hosts to offend? He picked it up and put it down. Philip watched Jennifer, thinking it rather mean of her not to say something to resolve his dilemma. Finally, Wei-chi ate it, strong white teeth crunching with every appearance of relish. Philip, with a rebellious feeling, left his.

36

"Did you see Ivy's baby?" asked Carmel Hodgkiss, the head nurse, unwrapping her sandwich in the nurses' conference room. The sleeping Perry Briggs stirred on the sofa. The others dropped their voices.

"It was very ugly," said Wei-chi, vehemently. "I don't know how she all the time wanting to see it."

"Ugly? I don't know," Rosemary Hunt disagreed. "The ugly ones are the ones that get the dark skin but then the yellow, kinky hair. They don't ever look quite right to me. Her baby is cute."

"Yellow hair is generally ugly," Wei-chi agreed, not quite sincerely. He believed it looked all right on Westerners, but was aware that they believed that Chinese admired it. He wished to refute this. Mrs. Tarro, so generally pretty, he thought, and with a small nose, had hair of a terrible, even unlucky color.

Each day a little strength returned, a syllable returned. Philip saw her in the day lounge with Perry Briggs. This caused him a certain undefined pang that he felt, also, when she walked in the hall on the arm of Bradford Evans. He saw this more than once. At other times, thoughts of her drifted across his mind, not coherently, in the middle of a drug calculation or clinical impression as someone's heartbeat under his fingers, or as the slight swelling of a spleen redirected his thoughts. He looked in on her at plausible intervals. Sometimes she would be lying there, just gazing, the way really ill people do, but if she was feeling all right, she might be found doing odd things—polishing shoes, for instance. She had collected a heap of assorted shoes—white nurses' shoes, some pretty little pumps—perhaps those were hers—a pair of man's shoes. Whose?

He felt himself stricken after these encounters with Ivy. Sometimes he would pace around his office with a queasy feeling of excitement, sometimes his head ached. He would think about it from the beginning: how he had happened to look in her room, hoping to see her improving, how he had once seen her sleeping, a vision of pallor and golden-red hair, and when he had examined her, her rather bitten fingernails, and the rescue from the operating room, the tear stains on her cheeks. But he could not understand how all this added up to a feeling of infatuation, of desire. What he really wanted was to fuck her.

Mimi saw Ivy Tarro walking in the hall, being helped to walk by Bradford Evans, though she was sure she had seen Ivy walk perfectly well by herself that same morning. Ivy was looking up with luminous face into his face, her hair brushed into a copper cloud, and Evans was looking down on her like a pleased father taking her down the aisle, or a rich sugar daddy. These images of masculine protection were especially apt to occur to Mimi these days, she knew, because of her property problems. Bradford Evans was, after all, Ivy's doctor, and it was natural that he be pleased with the progress she was making. All the same, these attentions to Ivy Tarro confirmed Mimi's view of Bradford's light character. She felt a wave of irritation at Ivy, even though she of course liked Ivy a lot.

Everyone, it seemed, was interested in Ivy's progress. She had an effect like heat. Perhaps it was because of her flamelike hair. Rosemary Hunt believed that Perry was in love with her, and they all thought it was cute how Wei-chi hung around. Both Watts and Evans made rounds to see her twice a day. Mark Silver said that he thought Bradford Evans's frequent visits were to avert the terrible lawsuit that Ivy might justifiably visit on him, and Watts, of course, was the attending man. It was his duty to see her.

It was clear to Mimi that Ivy was not a great reader. At first she had taken Mimi's suggestion of a biography of Rebecca West, but it continued to lie on the bureau where Mimi had left it. On her next visit, Mimi took it back, tactfully inventing a story about someone else wanting it, and suggested some other titles. Finally Ivy accepted a book about rain forests.

"I'm not really in the mood for anything human," she apologized. "There's too much human drama around here. Just some restful trees, and snakes gliding up them, that's perfect."

But on her painful-looking walks, up and down the corridor, stopping to hold on to a doorknob or wall, she concerned herself with people. She got to know Mrs. Lincoln, smiled encouragingly at Mrs. Kim, the Vietnamese lady who waited by the bedside of her tiny husband, Dr. Kim; she joked with Mr. Gibson and the new drug overdose, Davey, and with the nurses Vita and Rosemary. Sometimes she simply stood in her room, too restless to sit, too weak to walk, holding on to a chair back as she listened to Mrs. Tate's opinions.

"Randall Lincoln is the saddest story I've ever heard," Ivy told Mimi. "That family placed all their hope in him. Did you know I went to high school with Randall? His mother says it will take a medical miracle now."

"Oh, I know," said Mimi. "You have to get so hard-hearted in a hospital to bear all the sad stories." But of course she never had.

In a way, Ivy loved the hospital. She loved the doctors, loved the delicacy with which they poked and listened for the rhythm of the blood. She loved all doctors, even the ones who were obviously jerks. Mark Silver was probably a jerk, and Brian Smeed perhaps. Before this, when she'd had Delia, she'd loved her OB, Dr. Barrow, who, it had turned out, had been out of town when she went into labor, and a woman doctor had delivered Delia, and then Ivy had loved her too, so it wasn't just a sexual thing. Maybe not a sexual thing at all!

But desire did play a part in the interest she felt, watching the doctors on their rounds and at their work. She could see them congregated in the nurses' place behind the nurses' station, heating things in the microwave. She wanted to but never could hear what they were saying. She desired their secret exchanges of knowledge, things they knew about who would die, who would live. She would walk slowly between the day room and her room, pretending to be practicing her walking, but she was watching doctors.

Her real life, her life outside the hospital, seemed more and more remote to her, seemed to lie beyond her recollection or the reach of her strength. When Franni or one of the others from the restaurant came to see her, and told about something new with polenta, or problems with the lease, these seemed the distant concerns of strangers. Even Delia, though Ivy's heart stirred maternally whenever Petra brought her in, even Delia between times seemed an abstraction, the symbol of a new life phase she had hardly got used to, until everything had changed and her blood and her limbs had given out. Her various suitors, former lovers, male friends, seemed especially alien, boyish, and unfocused. Her interest was doctors.

"I owe a lot to Dr. Evans," she told Philip once. "What if he hadn't happened to be in his office the day my arm swelled, or what if I'd lived deep in the country?" Her speech had improved, but she still spoke slowly. Philip waited for her to say the whole sentence, like waiting for a stutterer.

"It's hard to know what might have happened," said Philip, keeping his reservations to himself, thinking she might have been a hell of a lot better off. It had not yet occurred to her to blame anyone, anything for her illness. She had the radiant fatalism of someone marked by destiny.

It occurred to Mimi to ask Ivy if she would look over the recipes for the cookbook. It would be a help and would help Ivy pass the time. As she handed over the little bundle of newly submitted recipes, she asked Ivy how she had become involved in food. Ivy told her, in her slow speech.

"I can't really cook," Ivy said, "I majored in nutrition in college, because I just thought food was interesting—the action of the carbohydrates, the reaction of the protein, and the idea of food in the world interested me—the physiology of food, and the way it makes people happy and healthy, or unhappy and unhealthy." Then she had done an internship at Chez Alice, at the height of the food revolution and was swept into it. "All my friends became chefs, or opened restaurants, or began growing *frisée*, and then Franni got so famous. But all I turned out to have was an unsuspected talent for programming diners in my mind. I can't boil an egg, but I can tell how long people will take to eat, and where they should sit. It's like an idiot savant kind of thing that not everybody can do, but what good is it really? So I happen to be a hostess in a restaurant, but I could equally be a taxi dispatcher."

"Did you grow up in California?" Mimi asked.

"Uh huh, right here. I went to Lowell High School. Randall Lincoln was a couple of years behind me."

Mimi wanted to ask if she was married, and about the history of her baby, but she had never been comfortable asking questions as personal as that. Ivy didn't mention a husband, and only rarely spoke of her baby. But it was usual, after a week or two of hospital stay, for people to stop talking about the world outside.

Mrs. Lincoln had been delighted beyond measure to find someone who knew Randall, and who had an idea of him beyond this inert and unwelcome form in the ICU. Ivy had remembered that Randall played basketball, and had got a scholarship, and had been the treasurer of the junior class.

"He wouldn't remember me at all," Ivy said. "I was definitely a mouse. No one would remember me at all in high school."

"Absolutely," Ivy agreed with Mrs. Lincoln's theories. "I do believe you can hear while in a coma. I was in a coma for three days, and I think I do remember things that people said." She grasped for a fleeting memory of voices. A woman's voice saying, "It's a crime," and—was this possible?—a man's voice saying, "Nice tits."

That, surely, was not possible. Doctors were always so polite. Maybe someone cleaning the room? But then—how horrifying to think she had been exposed to the view of someone just in there cleaning the room. Probably what you heard in a coma was the voice of your own unconscious, expressing its fears or its desires.

"Anyway, I can tell he hear, he look this way sometime, and once he give me a sign with his hand, like 'keep on,' " Mrs. Lincoln said.

"I've remembered where I saw you," Philip Watts said to Ivy one day in the day lounge. "In the restaurant. Actually, my wife knew your name." Immediately, he wished he hadn't mentioned his wife. Not that he meant to conceal the fact that he had a wife, why should he? She smiled.

"The food in your hospital is not very good," she said. "I mean, I'm not one of these messiahs of good food—I guess the food in a hospital ought to be a little plain so people will want to get better and move on. But, really, lunch was so awful—I wish I could just visit the kitchen, or talk to the chef."

" 'Chef' might be dignifying it," Philip said. "Dieticians."

"Dietician! What a terrible word," Ivy laughed. "It makes you think of two terrible things, diets and morticians."

"How are you feeling today?" He hadn't meant this to be a medical visit, especially, just a friendly one. Almost automatically, Philip took her wrist, and, glancing at his watch, confirmed that her pulse was rapid.

"Fine," she said. She took her wrist away and smiled. "It's not fair—you can tell how you make me feel."

There seemed a long moment. The astonished Philip felt his own pulse start a little.

"Do you say that to all the doctors?" he asked.

"No, I don't," she said, looking at him a certain way she hadn't looked at him before. He found himself remembering how her friend Franni had said she had a reckless, wild side.

After this conversation, Dr. Watts did not take her wrist or touch her again. Despite her wish, which hung in the air, his too—a sort of sizzle of intention they both could feel—that he should put his fingers on her wrist or touch her cheek as if to see if she had fever, he did not.

More and more, over the long days, her thoughts dwelling on doctors had come to focus on Dr. Watts. More on Dr. Watts than on Dr. Evans. She found herself imagining herself doing things to him—unzipping his pants and reaching inside, all the while he was trying to keep his mind on what he was saying, talking as he did each day to the string of other doctors. Somehow they couldn't see what she was doing. . . .

Sometimes panic overtook and ruined this line of imagining. Stop! Isn't this what madwomen do in asylums—reach for the crotches of doctors? Sometimes she thought she was getting better, but other times she realized she was a cripple now, and she was going mad. She realized these were the sickly sexual fantasies of the morbidly, terminally ill.

37

Ivy Tarro had read over the recipes for the auxiliary's cookbook, and returned them to Mimi with a smile that suggested that Mimi had been right in her reservations about them. "There's nothing really wrong that I could see," Ivy said. "You should probably have more about vegetables." Mimi had eliminated Dr. Bunting's warnings about carbohydrates and put the manuscript into the hospital interoffice mail rather than confront him, explaining that time was of the essence and that they were rushing into print. It remained to make the final selection of recipes—for this she had asked for help from Jennifer Watts too—and rush things over to the printer, who had kindly offered to donate the paper and labor, and would have the copies in a week, in time to be sold at the gala fund-raising dinner. Meantime, she took the manuscript to a final meeting of the gala subcommittee.

The meeting turned unexpectedly acrimonious, first on the matter of the gala, and then, unexpectedly, about the cookbook too. The influential and very rich Jane and Fulton Tenier had agreed to host the fund-raising dinner at their splendid house. Though they were often abroad, it turned out they would be in San Francisco on that evening, were interested in health, and said, when approached by

Mr. Dolph Dobbs, that they would be happy to get behind the hospital drive, though Jane Tenier had confided to Jennifer Watts that hospitals were not really her kind of thing ordinarily—she preferred the arts— and this should be thought of as a one-shot response to the all-out effort that was beginning to draw considerable publicity and support for Alta Buena.

"I understand perfectly," Jennifer had said.

Though the dinner was already planned in most details—each course and the service to be donated by a famous local restaurant— and was heavily subscribed, certain things were still lacking—notably a theme that the newspapers could easily grasp and write up. The hospital had several target areas—the AIDS follow-up clinic, parking-lot expansion, equipment, new labs—but all of these, except for the AIDS clinic, were conceded to be a little abstract, impersonal, and removed from the human things that moved people most. So it was decided that the publicity office should begin to present and highlight some of the most sympathetic and impressive success stories of patient care at Alta Buena. Also, perhaps, some individual could be chosen to symbolize the whole human effort, the raison d'être behind any hospital, in case there were people—this was brought up in the meet-ing—who wouldn't like to give their money to parking, or even for AIDS research, but would give to buy wheelchairs or books for the library, or a cobalt unit, or Christmas cheer for hopelessly ill children. "People like to associate the money with a face," Dolph Dobbs had explained. "We need a poster baby."

"I really think that to use a child for publicity is a cliché, and in questionable taste," Jennifer Watts said.

"How about a well baby? Someone premature who was saved. The whole happy family," someone said.

"The mother of a young family, who was saved. From cancer," said Mrs. Rank Briscoe.

"A chronic case. Bravery. Someone helped to live with chronic pain," Mimi suggested.

"Rehabilitation. Someone who walks when they thought they never would."

"Too March of Dimes. How about an old person living a full life after he'd been consigned to—you know, an outreach thing."

"AIDS caring."

"No!" cried several ladies at once.

"Well, who are the wonder patients at the moment?" Jennifer Watts asked, with her habitual impatience. "What's the matter with reality? Let's find out who's out there."

"I see you are as usual determined to leave surgery out of it," said Dollie Briscoe. Surprised at her angry tone, her colleagues waited for her to explain.

"Not one of those suggestions has anything to do with surgery. Just as you're leaving surgical recipes out of the cookbook. There's not one recipe in there from a surgeon or a surgeon's wife." Her husband, Rank, was second only to Dr. MacGregor Bunting in the Department of Surgery and in national prestige.

"That can't be true," objected Mimi.

"And what would you expect, considering the editorial staff," Dollie said, glaring at Jennifer Watts.

"I admit I took out the more repulsive recipes," said Jennifer crisply. "And the duplicates. But it never occurred to me that all the repulsive recipes could be from surgeons or their wives." With her sly smile.

"Naturally we want every department to be represented," Mimi said, as soothingly as she could. Clearly she would have to spend the evening going over the manuscript again, balancing pathologists with orthopedists and so on. She regretted having accepted the editor's job.

"I can't go to a movie tonight," she told her friend Hannah Barton. "I'll be up all night as it is, doing a really thankless task."

"I think you spend too much time on Alta Buena," Hannah said. "What has Alta Buena done for you?"

Philip Watts had explained Randall's illness to Ivy one day in the day room. It was interesting about Randall, Ivy thought. Tragic but interesting, that his cells were the wrong shape to travel through his blood vessels, so that they must battle to wedge their way through capillaries too small for them, the process causing unbearable pain. It was interesting but unfair that this, along with racism and economic disadvantages, could only happen to you if you were black. Ivy read an informative pamphlet Mrs. Lincoln had. She had asked Mimi for a book on sickle-cell anemia, but Mimi had apologized that she didn't keep medical books.

"Too scary. They frighten people," she said. "I have some health pamphlets, though."

Ivy took "Lower Your Cholesterol" and "Diabetes and You."

Ivy eavesdropped in the halls, listened in when she could on nurses and on doctors' rounds, was drawn into the drama and the new vocabulary. She told herself, If you are sick, you'd better understand as much as you can.

One intern, Perry Briggs, would tell her what was going on, though the older ones, like Dr. Watts, or like Dr. Evans himself, would often resort to mysterious aggregations of capital letters. His CPK was QNS, down, they would reply, or else could be discreetly silent, loftily refusing to gossip about someone's medical condition. Dr. Evans also used irritating euphemisms about her own condition, as if it were too crude and pointed to say straight out, perhaps even bad for her. "We just aren't sure about the precipitating event," he would say. "Your body just acted up on you."

"But why?" Ivy would say. "What's the name of my condition? There has to be a reason."

After midnight, Fred, the janitor on the third floor, came around to gather the plastic liners from the bins and bundle up the stained, the deadly, puss-sodden, blood-smeared wads, and all the thin rubber—the dozens of gloves rolled into little condoms stripped of hands—a thousand, five thousand gloves? And needles,. swabs, gauze, things to soak up, to smear, to stain. People might think all this disgusting, but Ivy found it fascinating to think what was in Ferd's bin. Gross but fascinating.

Some nights she would not take the sleeping pill, but lie awake thinking about her own body. This was the worst of what had happened to her, that once she knew her body could act up on her, how could she ever trust it again? Now she'd be obliged forever to listen to its complaints, like those of a boring companion on an endless journey.

Or its desires. She often thought about Philip Watts. What would he look like not in his white coat? Imagine if she were lying here in the dark—Mrs. Tate is not here—and the door opens, and in the dim light she sees it's him. He closes the door behind him. In this version there's a lock on the door; he locks it. Walks slowly toward her, untying his tie. No, as he sits on the edge of the bed, she reaches up and unties his tie. No, get serious. She unzips his pants and buries her face in his lap. Or he is listening to her chest, then he puts down the stethoscope and takes her nipple in his mouth. Then . . .

38

Vivian Mudd, the hospital ethicist, had convened a meeting in her office with the idea of resolving some of the issues surrounding the case of Randall Lincoln. Philip greeted the Sickle Cell Anemia woman; Jim Hernandez, the federal kidney coordinator; a new woman who was introduced as the Lincolns' minister, the Reverend Bessie Turner; Brian Smeed, the chief resident; Randall's aunt; and Tabor, the hospital administrator. Philip reviewed the clinical situation: Randall, in the course of an episode of sickling, had suffered cardiac arrest.

"Some say from getting too much medication," put in the minister. Philip wondered what lawsuit this portended.

"He was resuscitated, but he has not regained consciousness, and has lost all kidney function," he continued. "In the expectation that he would regain consciousness, he was put on dialysis. However, it's now been twenty days, and he remains in a coma with no visible signs of recovery. Even if he had regained consciousness, he still has sickle-cell anemia with all its complications and fatal outcome. The issues now are whether to continue dialysis, and whether to resuscitate."

"If you don't dialyze, he would pass away, is that right?" asked the minister.

"Painlessly and naturally. The family are opposed to discontinuing dialysis, but I think that is because they haven't accepted the reality of his fatal illness. Also, even if he regained consciousness, he wouldn't be Randall. In all likelihood, his brain has been severely damaged. There is no possibility, even in the extremely unlikely case that he might regain consciousness and be sentient, that he could ever return to normal life, and he would always be on dialysis. Needless to say, at the moment, if he were to arrest again—if his heart were to stop again—the order is a No Code. That is, he would not be resuscitated. But in fact he seems fairly stable. We don't know the effect of chronic dialysis on his blood condition. It may be helping his sickle-cell anemia, but that could only be temporary.

"I worry about his parents. They're very unrealistic. They want us to resuscitate if he should arrest again. I think they expect him to get well, and I can't seem to make them understand what his real future is."

"Well, I agree with you, doctor," the Reverend Bessie Turner suddenly said. "I hate to see them breakin' they heart. Sometimes it's God's will. I don't mean they goin' against God's will, it's just that they don't believe He's callin' Randall yet. But I believe so. I've seen the sickle cell before, and it's ugly, it is the devil. But what I say is, What has Randall's life been for? I just pray let him do some good for something or for somebody, some other life let it be better because Randall was alive, then I think his mother could let him go. It would be easier if she could see in her heart that his struggles, and the whole of they struggles, was not for nothing."

"Plus the cost to the taxpayer," said Dick Ramirez, "not that we can put a cost on human life, but it isn't a case of life or death here, it's a case of death—when and how much."

"And from what," added the Sickle Cell woman. "It's our position that he is a kidney patient now, and these costs should be borne by the feds. Well, you know our position."

"I take it everybody agrees with the decision No Code on Randall?" Philip asked. "As for withholding dialysis, that couldn't be done without the permission of the parents." Finally, they all agreed that nothing, really, could be done for or to Randall unless his heart stopped of its own accord, and they might have to dialyze him forever.

After the meeting, Tabor drew Philip aside. His face was flushed and angry. "Phil, you doctors have to review the No Code policy. If Lincoln had been a No Code, this wouldn't have happened. And about these Indians—what the hell were you thinking of? We've got enough liability problems." He sighed as if never were man so beleaguered. For an instant Philip had no idea what Indians he was talking about.

Philip went over Randall's situation one more time with Mrs. Lincoln, with the Reverend Turner along. Mrs. Lincoln was as usual polite, attentive, grave. Philip spoke in as kindly a tone as he could, given that he had really become impatient with her intransigent fidelity. "For every day he passes in the coma, Mrs. Lincoln, the more likely it is that he won't come out of it. The medical bills—the dialysis alone is thousands a week."

"It's not appropriate to speak of that, doctor," Mrs. Lincoln said. Philip knew that, of course. "We don't care about money. We have a house, and we're prepared to sell it. Money don't mean nothing here."

"All I'm saying, Mrs. Lincoln, is that at the meeting we discussed how if Randall's heart were to stop again, we'd have to question the wisdom of bringing him back to suffer longer. At some point, this tragedy . . ."

"You said he wasn't suffering!" Mrs. Lincoln's voice rose sharply, and the Reverend Bessie clamped a husky arm around her shoulder. "You said he doesn't feel anything!"

"No, that's true, he's not suffering," Philip agreed.

"Well, thank God for that. I believe in God, Dr. Watts."

"But he's not living, either. He is in an irreversible coma with no kidney function," Philip said, yet again, as plainly as he could.

The No Code issue came up again later in the afternoon when the Vietnamese-speaking nurse in Day Care had a moment free to talk to Mrs. Kim, wife of the heart patient Dr. Kim. Wei-chi had been able to communicate with her a little, through some Chinese dialect that neither spoke well, and Philip had wished to be sure that she really understood that if her husband's heart were to stop—his damaged heart or nearly nonexistent lungs—they would not use artificial means to prolong his painful struggle a few more days or weeks. Philip had written the No Code order.

At this news, Mrs. Kim had smiled and beamed with such bright attention, such desire to please and to agree, that he had been disconcerted. Of course, he had no notion, he recognized, what she really understood or felt. He made a note to discuss it with one of the Kim daughters who spoke English and was said to be a resident in hematology at Stanford.

As usual, a No Code order elicited lively discussion from the residents. Someone could always think of a last-ditch maneuver, a heart stimulant, a drug to support the blood pressure. These vigorous young people did not want to think about death.

Philip felt tired as he drove home, and mildly depressed. It was his customary feeling during his months on the wards. Of course it upset him when people couldn't be saved, or were diagnosed with fatal diseases—it would anyone—but it also upset him when the young housestaff wanted to use strenuous and painful measures in hopeless cases. And then it depressed him that there were so many hopeless cases, that no absolute progress had been made in curing anything at all since he'd been in medical school. Nothing much since antibiotics, when you really faced it, that and one or two rare cancers—Hodgkins and leukemia, sometimes.

His job, it seemed to him, was just one of making futile but difficult decisions and trying to reassure, often hypocritically, as in the case of Mrs. Ames, or prepare people who refused to be prepared, like Mrs. Lincoln. Only once in a while could you think of something unexpected that would pull someone through. And as often as not this involved saving someone from the mistakes of his family doctor. As in the case of Mrs. Tarro.

Maybe an office practice would have produced a more rewarding proportion of saves and cures, as well as make more money. In the hospital, things were by definition already grave.

"You're having a midlife crisis," Mimi Franklin had said. But what, exactly, was the midlife crisis?

Philip and Jennifer had dinner at Sukiyama, the sushi restaurant on Fillmore. Jennifer picked at her scallop sashimi. "I haven't decided what to do about shellfish," she said. "I can't believe they actually suffer. What was your day like?"

But it seemed somehow too much trouble to tell her. He didn't want to hear it again. They ate in a rather morose silence, like a quarreling couple.

In the long evenings, between dinner at five-thirty and sleep at nine, when the nurses would look menacing if you were still awake, and

Mrs. Tate would be drugged again and her bed cranked down flat, and someone would ask Ivy if she'd like to take something to help her sleep, Ivy would read to Perfecto or Randall, or talk to Mrs. Lincoln, or watch by Randall's bed and give the poor woman a chance to get up and stretch her legs.

"You walkin' better. You don't hardly limp," Mrs. Lincoln said tonight as Ivy came in. Next to Randall, Ivy felt almost ashamed of walking. Even her arm, which was now but barely swollen, looked almost in rude health next to the fragile arm of Randall. But she did limp. Her foot dragged and ached, and she was obliged to use this crutch.

"You know something," she told Mrs. Lincoln, "if your one leg doesn't work, your other can't either. It needs a partner. You might think you could walk on the good one and drag the other, but you can't. Not at first, at least."

"I seen a man, where I grew up, only had one, but it was kind of in the middle, like he kind of balanced, and he could hop along. It was the queerest thing I ever seen."

They laughed, watching to see if Randall laughed, and it did seem to them that his lips extended in the direction of a smile, and there was a tiny contraction of his eyes. Mrs. Lincoln seized Ivy's arm.

"See that? He heard us."

"I agree," Ivy said. "I think he did," and Mrs. Lincoln was suddenly holding her in her arms and crying.

39

Perry Briggs and Mark Silver, the intern and resident on call, were summoned from a meeting in the x-ray reading room to witness Randall Lincoln's return to consciousness. They had to agree that he heard them, and responded to their directions by weakly squeezing their hands and blinking his eyes. Perry couldn't help but be happy, to see the joy in Mrs. Lincoln, the outcome, so like the outcome of a television drama, where faithful watching and belief pay off. Not to rule out miracles, either. Even in medical school, their professors had been careful to remind them that miracles did happen.

"Our job is to help miracles happen. Medicine is a kind of prayer," Professor Lathrop had always said. "As with praying, we never know the answer or the outcome, defeat or miracle, because the organism has a soul. There are too many mysteries yet, and always will be."

And, mysteriously, here was Randall Lincoln, weak but possibly sentient, with his mother and a throng of joyful staff peering over him, twittering, unbelieving, with Mrs. Lincoln sobbing and accepting congratulations and embraces.

"Hey, Randall, I'm Ivy Tarro, we were at Lowell?" Ivy said, when it seemed he looked at her.

"Could you get these people out now," Mark said to the nurse, "so we can find out what's going on?" and people went regretfully away. Mrs. Lincoln went to telephone her husband and Randall's brother at Fort Benning. Mark and Perry began the careful business of listening to Randall's heart and checking the dials on the machines. Somebody went to call Philip Watts.

The meeting in the x-ray reading room had been of the Journal Club. The interns and residents got together every week to report on articles and editorials from medical journals, things that would help them study for their board examinations. At one meeting a month, people gave reports on articles in the *Wall Street Journal* and investment magazines, so that when those of the housestaff who meant to go into practice actually did so, and the money began to roll in, they would know what to do with it. They needed to learn to keep records, and the difference between full-service and discount brokers, and what a limited partnership was.

"Doctors are notoriously stupid investors, that's what my brother-in-law told me. He's a bond salesman," Mark Silver said. "Doctors go for the high-risk-go-for-broke kind of thing, and apparently they always get taken."

This had weighed with a number of them, and they planned to take the warning and become informed before the day came. They felt a certain satisfaction, though, in being high-risk, impulsive types instead of parsimonious and watchful, like lawyers. At first, Perry had found the whole idea of the Wall Street Journal Club shocking and distasteful, though when his turn had come to make a report, and he had actually begun to read about drug stock R & D, he'd found it very interesting, especially in the new field of gene splicing, which you could imagine was going to have fantastic medical applications and equally fantastic commercial rewards.

In the morning, amid the general joy that spread with the news of Randall's waking up, Mimi felt ashamed to remain preoccupied with Philip and with her real estate problem. Other people had such serious, profound problems that it seemed wrong, when she was such a fortunate person, with her health and lovely children, to keep thinking about her house and someone else's husband.

What really to do about the house filled a larger and larger part of her days. Reading the paper in the morning now involved reading the Houses for Sale section of the want ads. Driving anywhere, her eyes would travel the faces of buildings, noticing the realtors' signs. Desire corrupted the former contentment with which she had focused on the really important things, her job and children. She felt ashamed of being an envious person, and tried not to look at the large, splendid houses that now seemed to multiply on every hand, the gaiety of their Victorian façades suggesting a party to which she wasn't invited.

The plainness of her life beset her. Mimi noticed that the advice of each of her most confidential friends depended on what their own problems were. Hannah was very maternal. Charlie, a librarian with whom she had once had a brief affair, thought she should remodel. To no one could she confide her troubled preoccupation with Philip Watts.

She didn't sleep very well, would get up and roam, and poor Warren would rise stiffly from his dog nest with slow wags of his tail and suppose it was time to go out. She'd like to marry and move somewhere different, a new place altogether, maybe Colorado. She daydreamed that Philip left Jennifer behind and took her instead to live down the peninsula. She thought of all the other people who must be staring awake at this hour, some of them with terrible pain or sorrow. How brave people were to get through life! She knew she was becoming depressed, but couldn't seem to snap out of it or find any prospect that cheered her. Maybe it was the approach of Christmas, she told herself. People often get depressed at Christmas; it was practically normal.

———

On the bulletin board at her Safeway, and on the telephone poles at several corners, where she saw them during Warren's walk, and even attached to parking meters right outside the hospital, were notices headed SAVE OUR NEIGHBORHOOD. BLOCK HOSPITAL EXPANSION, announcing a meeting that Mimi decided to attend. It was held at eight in a nice Victorian house on the better side of California Street. Mimi, walking over, found herself on the front porch at the same time that others were arriving. Two youngish couples—one male, one mixed—introduced themselves as they waited for someone to answer the door. Inside, two dozen people on chairs and the sofa smiled and shifted their bottoms, symbolically making room for the newcomers, though there were in fact no seats available. A woman called up the stairs in the hallway for someone to bring more chairs. Mimi's heart warmed, as if all these people had convened especially to support her, though she knew it was self-interest in their cases too. "They want to take my house for the parking lot," she explained to the person next to her.

A discussion was already underway. A woman in a green sweater suspended her words and watched with pointed graciousness while Mimi and the others were settled. Mimi was given a chair, the young man and woman sat on the lower step of the stairs, and the male couple remained standing in the hall.

"That's okay, we can hear," they said.

"The point is, low-level radiation is still a totally unknown hazard," the woman in the green sweater continued. "The more they find out, the more everything points to increased danger, and we know for a certainty the hospital uses radioactive materials. Are we the Love Canal or what? What kind of neighborhood is this, that they can pollute with radioactive waste? They have absolutely refused to give us any assurance that they won't use radioactive materials, and they won't talk about disposal plans. I have all the correspondence right here, and I'll pass it." She turned to place a fat sheaf of letters in the lap of the man nearest her. She sat down, then stood up and added, "Also some literature on radioactive isotopes, that's in with the letters."

"The parking problem is what I'm worried about," the next speaker said, compelling Mimi's attention. "They put in pay parking, and that just increases the street-parking crunch, as well as the traffic and circulation, because now you'll have people circling the neighborhood slowly in their cars, looking for free parking spaces. I wouldn't even object if they'd put in a free parking facility, but pay parking just means trouble for the neighbors."

"We have someone here from the hospital to speak to that," said a woman who was evidently the chairman.

Now Mimi saw the dreaded Mr. Tabor himself, appearing from among those who were standing in the doorway of the dining room. Smoothly he took the floor, unrolling a large chart and installing it on a kind of music stand, which he produced and expertly unfolded with a motion of his wrist. They saw a handsome sketch of a structure resembling an ocean liner, with sleek horizontal lines, in a smartly planted landscape of cypress and rounded privet shrubs. Nearly invisible circles representing taillights and headlights suggested the automobiles within, and a smiling man in a kiosk seemed to represent order and protection for all passersby.

"This is what we have in mind," he said. Mimi studied the drawing, bearing in mind that her own house presently stood, with all its shabby imperfections, on the exact site of this stylish rendering. She imagined it knocked down and paved over, to be excavated by some future generation, like the Roman baths she had heard of being discovered under the cathedral of Notre Dame. Small personal items of her own, Warren's leash, lodged in the debris, to be carted off by archaeologists and souvenir hunters.

"I would just like to hear about the plans for the radioactive waste," said the woman in the green sweater.

"Realistically," said Mr. Tabor, "the levels of laboratory radioactive materials are so low they pose no hazard whatsoever. There's absolutely no reason to fear . . ." Here he was opposed by a rising lamentation of questions and shouts. Mimi, though she was tremendously cheered by the combative mood of this crowd, couldn't help but know that Mr. Tabor was right on the matter of radioactivity. The hospital, she was almost sure, was very careful. She felt her palms begin to grow damp, and her throat began to tighten; she knew she wasn't going to be able to say anything. Luckily, at the moment it became her turn, the woman next to her obligingly said, "And they want to tear down this woman's house from over her head!"

Feeling the support of the neighbors like cement beneath her feet, Mimi nodded. The words were repeated by the chairwoman, who turned to the others and added, "Isn't that incredible!"

"It really is," others agreed, each repeating the statement to someone else, so that Mimi found herself the center of attention without having had to speak. She could feel, across the room, the enmity of Mr. Tabor, who was casting angry glances over the heads of the crowd, a tacit acknowledgment that she alone held the key to defeating the parking plan. Mimi blushed and smiled at her supporters.

The weight of all this collective interest was palpable. Mimi felt obliged to sit down, buoyed, but constrained by it too.

"Of course you'll resist," people said. "You won't let them get away with it. They can't do that to you," making her fear, if she were to give in, the anger of this active and irate group. She imagined Mr. Tabor handing her an enormous check, herself obliged to leave town in a hurry.

"Isn't it true that they just dump the radioactive stuff down the drain?" someone said, returning to the earlier subject.

"Not even enough to speak of," Mr. Tabor said. "For instance, it's of no concern to the city; it's never turned up in the sewer system. Trace amounts."

"I'd like to mention animal research," said one of the men who had come in with her, starting another outcry, in which the assembly enthusiastically joined. Mimi continued to feel a certain conflict, a stab of loyal indignation on behalf of the hospital where she spent so much time. She knew Alta Buena to be well-meaning, and not given to poisoning the public water or to the random slaughter of innocent puppies and kittens. But she said nothing out loud in its defense.

"Randall Lincoln woke up today," said Philip to Jennifer.

"Oh, but that's wonderful," said Jennifer.

"I'm not sure," Philip said. "Doesn't it just raise all their hopes, and make his death more painful, now, because he'll be aware of it?"

"Is he suffering?"

"Dialysis is a kind of misery. And he'll eventually have another episode of sickling. And we don't know yet if his brain was damaged when his heart stopped."

"Yet—a few more weeks of life? Isn't it worth it? Isn't his mother happy?"

"Ecstatic," said Philip. "And the cost is staggering."

"Well, I don't think you should think about that," Jennifer said. "You're just miffed because this refutes your predictions. It's a challenge to your omniscience."

"Don't be ridiculous," said Philip testily.

40

Preparations for Christmas, underway since before Thanksgiving in the world outside, were only begun in the hospital in mid-December, as if the staff wanted to avoid reminding too poignantly those who, for one reason or the other, could not be expected still to be around at the holidays.

Mr. Dolph Dobbs, in executive consultation with Mr. Tabor, MacGregor Bunting, and others, had chosen Randall Lincoln to represent the triumph of Alta Buena care at the gala fund-raising dinner, and on the posters and promotional material. Photographers came onto the ward to take his picture as he sat in a wheelchair in the day room, smiling, his parents beside him. It was the private mortification of the doctors that poor Randall could hardly speak or sit up in the chair, and it was still not clear how much his brain had been damaged by the episode of cardiac arrest, his prolonged coma, the kidney toxins remaining in his blood despite dialysis, and by his underlying disease.

"I'm afraid he's a gork," as Mark Silver put it.

Yet the pictures showed a handsome, strapping young man with his radiant parents. Behind them, a garland of holly had been strung to emphasize the heartwarming good luck of his emergence from irreversible coma in time for Christmas.

When he first came to America, Wei-chi had not realized the religious significance such images as the man, his arms outstretched on a wooden cross, wearing an uncomfortable-looking headdress of barbed wire. This ignorance, when revealed, greatly amused the nurses and other doctors, who now took pains to instruct him on the iconography of the approaching Christmas season: three bearded men riding large, lumpy camels, or a family with a newborn baby and gold moons behind their heads, or circles floating above them like a tracery of neon, a star in the sky, sprinkles of white powder or cotton to simulate snow.

"You see," he defended himself, "in China, these images were probably taken down during the Cultural Revolution, hence I never saw them." He felt embarrassed by his discourtesy in not having informed himself about their religion. Of course there had been many missionaries and Christians in China, although he personally did not know any, and when he came to think of it, certain aspects of the decorations were like decorations at the New Year in China. On every hand, people had begun to beautify the wards with strands of silver paper, and red bells of shining foil, and pictures of snow scenes. Though he himself felt that the climate in San Francisco was far superior to that of places with snow, snowflakes of paper were pinned to the curtains or pasted on glass partitions, much improving the ordinary ugliness of the gray-and-beige color scheme.

The holiday spirit of the others, though, made him feel gloomy and far away from his family, and made the hostility of his sister all the more wounding and inexplicable. The goodness of Dr. Watts and his wife amazed him, and the comfort of his room at the Wattses' hardened his heart a little, in retrospect, against certain things he had endured in China, and even against his privations at his sister's, where he had had to sleep on the sofa. The educated person deserved a little reward, and people here recognized that. Unlike in China, where the farmers were rewarded for the dirt and backache of their lives, while people like himself were penalized for having the luxury of an interesting job, and the chance to travel and study in America. He was ambivalent about which was the right principle. No one should have to suffer at all, of course, if it could be helped. He thought of the country people in China, shivering in their shabby padded jackets, and of their thin faces, and of the fatness of Americans, each one encircled in rolls of flesh. They would never even feel the cold in China.

At the Wattses', the thermometer was kept—he verified this often—at sixty-eight degrees, the best temperature for humans, as if it were a laboratory or hatchery. Sixty-eight degrees was perhaps even too warm. Organisms could sprout, possibly why Americans had these repulsive diseases, passed from person to person in the sperm.

There were many things Americans did not know. "Mrs. Tarro have very small feet," he had said, with a meaningful smile, one day in the doctors' dining room to Perry Briggs and Mark Silver. No one understood his meaning. "For a woman her size," he added.

"What is it with the Chinese and small feet, Wei-chi?" Perry asked. Wei-chi had been surprised that Western men did not have this information. Still, it wasn't something you could speak of.

"They are, ah, admired," Wei-chi conceded.

"But why?"

"It is a sign of—" he collapsed into a mortified silence. "It is well known that a woman have small feet have small somewhere else," he finally said. Perry was puzzled, but Mark soon gave a shout.

"Small feet, small snatch," he explained to Perry. "Snatch" was a term Wei-chi had not heard.

This was the morning Ivy saw that Mrs. Tate was going to die. Her eyes were closed but she was not asleep. Ivy gazed at her around the curtain. Her hands on the coverlet jumped with spasms, like a dreaming cat. Her mouth, slightly open, sucked air into her throat with a desperate rasp, and her skin was the color of a rimed window pane. Noting these signs, Ivy resigned herself to it, though a tear stung her eye. This is what happened in hospitals to cancer victims, to everyone eventually, and there was no point in looking away.

"Mrs. Tate, can you hear me?" she asked.

She could have told, anyway, by the increased activity of the hospital staff. Merci came in every few minutes and took the tiny wrist and looked at her watch. Mark Silver came in, without a word to Ivy, and listened to Mrs. Tate's chest.

"Maybe some Levophed," he said. "But I don't think it's gonna work. Maybe we should put her in 109."

Then Merci spent a while suspending new bottles on Mrs. Tate's IV rack. Mrs. Tate's eyes flew open once, containing a defiant expression of sentience, and she looked straight at Ivy. Ivy wondered if Mrs. Tate would like someone to hold her hand or say something to her.

"Mrs. Tate?" she whispered.

But Mrs. Tate did not reply. Soon afterward, Edgardo and an orderly came in and slowly wheeled her out, so her death would not upset the living.

"Dear Mrs. Tate," Ivy began to say, her throat lumpy, thinking that she should stay with Mrs. Tate, or that someone should. She put her robe on, intending to go along.

"The daughter's here," Mark Silver said. Ivy should not therefore intrude. Death just came, eventually, no way around it. Ivy brooded on the things she knew now that she had not confronted before. To be in the hospital was like having an open grave before you, when you had been thinking yourself immortal. Still, it was hard to accept that the last she would ever see of Mrs. Tate was her little crocheted cap, its ruffles standing out as they took her off to a quarantined place for dying in. At least Ivy supposed that's what it was. She said a prayer for Mrs. Tate, and though she felt the pain of tears behind her eyes, she didn't shed them.

Sitting in the day room, lonely, she spoke to the young man in the uniform of an army private.

"I've seen you; you've stayed with Randall a lot."

"I'm Franklin Lincoln. I'm Randall's brother. I just came in from Fort Benning."

"You must be happy now that he's better."

"I am. I got to feeling that if I wasn't here he might die. I know that wasn't true, but you get to feeling it, that just by being here you keep him alive. Not just me, but somebody in the family, and my mom and dad couldn't do it all by themselves. Especially my mother. If something happened to Randall, I think she'd die herself."

"But," Ivy began, "do you think Randall's going to get a lot better?"

"I hope so," Franklin said. "My sister died, you know. Marilyn. She was older than Randall, and she had it too. I don't have it. It's ironic, too, because Randall and Marilyn were both really good students, and they done real well at everything, and I—I know I was kind of a screw-up. It'd just kill my folks to lose Randall. Sometimes I think it should have been me. I mean, I think they could have spared me, if one of their, I don't know, better children could live."

"Oh! You shouldn't feel that way," Ivy cried. "I'm sure your folks don't!" She felt sorry she hadn't talked to Franklin before. No one ever talked to him, and now these feelings all came rushing out of him. "Of course they don't!"

"In their hearts I'm not so sure," he said. "I got arrested, and I dropped out of school."

"And you're in the army?"

"Yeah, but they let me be here while Randall's sick, a grave family emergency."

"It's a good thing you are," Ivy said. "For your folks' sake."

Philip, noticing Ivy in the day room, sat down next to her to spend a moment or two. He was always hoping, despite the brisk, professional pace of their meetings, that she would once again say something direct and personal, as she had when her pulse had raced. But it was usually just small talk. Now, though she had been looking sad, she brightened and smiled when she saw him. There was the usual pause during which they both tried to think of things to say.

"There's something touching about men's bathrobes," she said, finally, as Mr. Gibson came in, doing his lonely pacing as usual, carrying his catheter and bottle, wearing a mustard-colored bathrobe. "Their suits are all so alike, I guess their bathrobes are their self-expression."

"I suppose so," said Philip, thinking that his bathrobe, which he never wore, had been given him by Jennifer and was therefore an expression of Jennifer, and that that would be true of most men. But he made no mention of wives.

"I thought of men as sort of free," Ivy said. "Women encumbered with their purses, and fastenings for their hair, and jewelry—but now I see that men have bathrobes." Her bathrobe was a pale green, and in the sunlight of the day-lounge window, her hair looked like a curly copper thing Jennifer scoured pans with, and her face was beautiful. A moment passed while she tried to think of something more to add.

"Dr. Evans thinks I'll be out soon," she said. "Do you think so?"

"A couple days, maybe. We'd like to see you walking better. It shouldn't be too long."

"I'm getting better," she agreed.

"If you should—you know—need a ride home or anything," he said, "I'd be happy—just tell me."

"Thanks," she said. "Everybody is so incredibly kind." It seemed to him that her eyes had blinked with surprise, and he had surprised himself.

"I might," she added. "Thanks."

Ivy kept thinking about Dr. Watts's offer to take her home, and with more and more ornamental detail. He would be wearing his white coat, or, no, his street clothes. She had never seen him in them, but he would look handsome. His car would be—something not embarrassingly large and doctorlike but elegant or sporty, say, an Alfa. His grave, beautiful face concentrated on handing her carefully into the front seat.

In this version she could move her damned leg. Her cheeks fired with the horror of her stupid leg, her puffy arm, the numbness at the corner of her upper lip. Why would he want to take her home? No man would ever want her again.

He would have to come upstairs, helping her up the stairs, and carry her little case for her. She would have a little case, in this version, and Delia would still be at the babysitter's.

Here maternal emotions contending with a sort of generalized prurience blotted out the narrative. Delia ought to be there, and she ought to want her there, but then what would happen with Dr. Watts? Nothing could happen.

All at once she is crazed to get out of this terrible place, away from zombies like Perfecto and Randall, and poor Mrs. Tate dragged off to die. Desire is unauthorized here. And yet it is thickly here. She wants to get out in the world, where her body will be well, her own again, and she can sleep with a man when she wants to. Oh, she's getting better, must be almost well!

Delia at the babysitter's. Dr. Watts would insist that she get right into bed. Carries her case into the bedroom. She calls out that she's making him a cup of tea. "No tea," he says. "You get into bed. Remember that you're just out of the hospital." She comes into the bedroom. . . .

41

Philip thought he ought to go back to the hospital after dinner to look in on Dr. Kim, who was worse and might be developing pneumonia. At least this was the excuse he gave himself. He also wanted to be alone to putter in his office, where people were constantly bothering him during the day. He knew he could have been alone at home, since Jennifer was going to an art opening, and Wei-chi had not been there at dinner—was probably still at the hospital himself, or was on one of his slightly furtive disappearances into Chinatown, where he could speak Chinese and get Chinese food. Philip wished Wei-chi would have more social life, though of course social life for any intern had to be mainly at the hospital. Luckily he had now met Kim's pretty daughter, the one who was an anesthesiology resident at Stanford, who came in as often as she could.

He listened to Dr. Kim's chest and checked the lab work. Then, noticing Mrs. Kim and one of the brothers in the day room, he went in to see them.

"I just want to give you a progress report," he began, horrified when they jumped to their feet with joyful faces. He realized they had mistaken the English significance of "progress" to mean some beneficial progress or good news. "No, no," he apologized, "it's not good news." He must learn not to speak so loosely. They settled back with the same dispirited expressions they had worn before.

When he had explained Dr. Kim's worsening condition, and urged them to get some sleep, he went along to his office. The hospital, usually so familiar, with the lingering odors of dinner and the pine smell he liked, and smells of medicines and antiseptics, the collective murmur of televisions in the rooms, the low, fugitive conversations among the nurses and housestaff in the halls, tonight it all had a repellant, unfamiliar air that Philip recognized to be a reflex of his mood, some alien chemistry of gathering forces within himself.

The surly Brian Smeed, who had been resentful and distant with Philip since the discussion of the dress code, came into his office to discuss a detail of Mr. Holmes's continuing decline. He gave Philip a perfunctory greeting and launched into his recitation of the clinical status.

"We're going to have to pull the plug on Mr. Holmes," Philip interrupted. "We've tortured that poor devil long enough." He expected some argument from Smeed, but got a shrug of assent. By the time they were chief residents, they began to get the idea that death was sometimes inevitable.

"On the other hand," Smeed said, "the family of Mrs. Carson is *urging* us to pull the plug. She's been virtually unconscious for nine days, and if she comes out of it, she goes back to her expensive nursing home."

"I'll talk to them. Is their name Carson too? I have a hunch that Mrs. Carson is going to make it, in fact. They'd better recognize the possibility."

Brian Smeed, as chief resident, carried the Code Blue beeper, and as they were speaking the thing went off with a call from the OB-GYN service two floors above—an unusual quarter for cardiac emergencies, so unusual that Philip went along with Smeed, bolting up the stairs two at a time, faster than elevators. The OB intern, waiting at the elevator, heard them and led them to the room. A second or two later, Mark Silver arrived on the elevator with the resuscitation cart, and without waiting for the anesthesiologist, they converged on a young woman lying on the bed, apparently dead.

As they set into motion, almost automatically, their routine for resuscitation, the intern explained the situation. "A C-section yesterday, everything normal, she was up, and then began complaining of shortness of breath and chest pains, and then this morning she didn't want to get up, but the nurses insisted, and just now she collapsed, maybe a heart attack? Or what?" His voice quivered with panic and surprise. You went into OB-GYN to see happy new life and babies.

Above the mons pubis lay the tidy incision. Smeed began pressing on her chest. Mark was trying to get her mouth open, hollering at the anesthesiologist, who had just run in.

"Streptokinase," said Philip, after a few seconds, guessing it was pulmonary embolism. "Mark, get down to our place and get whatever was left over from Mrs. Tarro. I'll call Vita to find it. It's kind of a long chance." Philip grabbed the phone as Mark dashed off.

The anesthesia resident slipped a tube into her windpipe and began the process of inflating her lungs. Philip looked at his watch. His heart was beating with the strange sort of happiness that sometimes came of right guesses, long chances, the possibility of winning, and with the terror of each elongated second. He saw the darkening of the nipples of her dead breasts that would be brought back to life if he was right and Vita could lay her hands on the streptokinase without having to send down to the pharmacy—if by some luck there was still some on hand from Ivy Tarro's treatment. A series of blood clots generated by lower abdominal surgery, a real hazard of Caesarean sections, these brutes in OB-GYN doing them right and left, of course in the long run the fault of lawyers, acting as if every malformed baby sent by nature was the doctor's fault or mistake. What a society! He was looking at his watch, automatically tracking the intervals. She'd been getting air for a minute; her heart still wasn't starting. In another minute the intern came back with a syringe, and Philip took it, making Smeed step back, and injected her femoral vein.

"We'll get some of this into her, and if her heart can turn it over once or twice, it might get somewhere."

"Shit," said Brian Smeed, staring at the screen of the EKG, "she's still not starting."

"Keep trying," Philip said, pushing on her chest, thinking sometimes death can be pushed back.

"She just dropped before my eyes," a nurse said behind him. "She said she didn't want to get up, and I said she should, then she just dropped."

Philip looked again at his watch, imagining the emboli like viscous bubbles, like corks in narrow necks of bottles, like miners stuck in tunnels, the blood backing up behind them. The lungs without air, all the small arteries blocked by clots, and without oxygen the discouraged heart refuses to beat, and stops. This agent, so misused, in his view, might in this instance if they could propel it through her veins, assault and dissolve the clots and let blood trickle through, and if the electric current could shock the heart into contracting, if life enough remained in the tissue, the heartbeat and oxygen might bring her back. Only a minute or two more and they would have to give up; her brain would be irretrievably damaged. A young woman, looked to be in her twenties. He thought of Ivy. Streptokinase. Ivy having a baby. This could have been Ivy.

Something went thunk, with a crack, he hoped not her sternum as he pushed on it, but it was Mark Silver's watch as with a sudden gesture he bumped into the cart, crying "Aha" at something on the screen. Now they were all looking not at the patient but at the machine.

"Got a beat! Got a beat!" Smeed cried. The OB intern gasped.

"Come on, come on," they all cried. Philip looked now at her face, which seemed imperceptibly to bloom. On the screen another beat showed its silver trail, lethargic but moving, like a waking snake. Thump, thump. With that much activity the drug would make its way through the veins, could attack the emboli in her lungs. Now, on the assumption that she might live, people moved into other positions, bumping into the OB nurse, pushing the bed around. The anesthesiology resident fiddled with the respirator, and Mark turned off the electric stimulator.

Half an hour more and he was sure the heartbeat was reliable. Philip gave a few more instructions and tactfully effaced himself, leaving Brian Smeed in charge. He was thankful he happened to be there with Smeed, as it was unlikely that the residents would have thought in time of pulmonary embolus, or known what to do beyond the ordinary techniques of resuscitation.

His own heart, or whatever organ of emotion it was, expanded with relief and with the joy that always came with life-and-death narrow escapes. This particular joy was the best thing about medicine, and unlike other sorts of joy, tonight's was made more precious by the youth of the woman. She surely had not been meant to die just yet.

Walking down the stairs in this soaring mood, he was amazed to find Ivy Tarro, who had just been in his thoughts and ought at this hour to be in her room asleep, and instead was here on the darkened exit stairs. Her eyes were wide, as if she had witnessed the drama upstairs. At the door they had a little contretemps about who was going in, coming out, first, last, after you, each pause and step seeming to bring them an inch or two nearer each other so that it eventually seemed natural, given his mood of elation and power, to take, or receive, a congratulatory hug, as if she had seen what they had done, his reward a kiss on the lips, then another, serious, real kiss, there in the dark stairwell, before a rattle of the doors at the top and a step scared the hell out of him, and he dropped her, desperately wanting to keep on. He heard himself whisper, "Come down to my office," and her intake of breath before she disappeared back into the ward. Philip waited on the stair for Mark, for it was he, coming down to get some more streptokinase.

"God, that was scary. That was close," Mark said.

"Very," Philip agreed, knowing they were talking about the woman on OB-GYN. He held the door for Mark. As they stepped into the ward, Ivy was nowhere to be seen.

Mark went on down to the pharmacy. Philip walked slowly, and as naturally as possible, along the ward, agitated with tumultuous unnamed feelings. The patients were asleep, the slow wheezes of machines in ICU were audible in the passage, like snores. Vita Dawson, through the nurses' conference room window, was crying, or so it appeared, and was being comforted by two other nurses. This crying could not have been caused by anything on the ward, so he guessed some personal matter. His spirit, and his high, reckless mood pulled against the deliberation of his footsteps. Walking normally. His mind evaded frank examination of what he was doing—preparing to keep an assignation, a clandestine rendezvous in his office. Ivy! He was aware that he had time to change his mind. He walked, as slowly and naturally as he could, past Perfecto's corpselike form, nodding to Mrs. Lincoln, who was just leaving Randall for the night. It must be ten o'clock. He tried to keep from running. He opened his office door, went in, and left the door slightly ajar. He saw how ugly and messy the office was.

After a few minutes, during which he riffled papers on his desk and tried not to think about whether she would come, he heard a tap. She pushed the door open and stole inside.

"Can you lock it?" she asked. Apparently there was to be no false reluctance or delay about her visit. Despite his excitement, Philip felt a pang of conditioned dread. To be alone in an office with a woman patient had been the subject of cautionary lectures since medical school. Short of amputating the wrong limb, it was the riskiest thing a person could do, courting the most horrendous consequences—rape charges, lawsuits, hysterical illnesses. He reached around her and fit his key into the lock. He'd never tried to lock it from the inside. The key turned. Ivy was reading his diplomas and licenses with an entranced expression. In a beautiful gesture, as if she were tying it up, she pushed her hair off her neck.

"No one will come in?"

"No."

"Oh," she sighed. She crossed to sit against the edge of his desk, rosy in her green bathrobe and loose-necked gown. A painful pulse throbbed in Philip's temple, making him think of cerebral hemorrhage. She had a sort of wild-looking smile all right, and was extending her arms. He stood uncertainly, light-headed, blood rushing to his midsection in a familiar way. Her gesture was of welcome or encouragement. As he bent over her, her arms slid around his neck.

"We just have to do this," she whispered. "Otherwise I'd just die."

Philip kissed her, not feeling exactly responsible for this, his compunctions vanishing. The lips he had so wanted to taste, slightly salty with aspirin or tears, the little breasts, no longer green. He rooted awkwardly around at the neck and then at the sleeve of her gown. She shrugged out of her bathrobe. Philip helped her with the left sleeve when she couldn't manage the movement of her arm. A patient! Infirm, delicate. Yet she seemed reassuringly determined on this, breathing passionate sighs into his neck, accepting, returning feverish kisses. No, she wasn't feverish, actually; her forehead was cool. Her poor arm was weak but less distended than before. Frantically he kissed the conjunction of her poor arm and lovely breast, and pressed her nipples to his lips as it had crossed his mind on so many rounds to do, through the cotton of her nightie.

"Oooh, good, please, now," she was murmuring and gasping, and reaching for his belt. As he took off his trousers, Philip had the astonishing thought that this was the single most dangerously interdicted thing he had ever done.

However, how to do it was not so clear. Not on the cold, slablike floor. On the desk. He pushed her backward a little and into a more horizontal position, half lifting her in order to pull up the wretched nightgown. His fingers touched her opening, thickly juicy. He would have to climb onto the desk, he saw, and sort of kneel over her. She was laughing and saying into his shoulder, "Oh, please, help me with this damned leg!" He had to more or less lift the leg. It was heavier, cooler than her other leg. Then, in some fashion, he was inside her. Ivy, propped clumsily under him on her elbows, was gasping and groaning with pleasure and thrashing her head from side to side. This lasted some moments, which he did not want to end, but they ended, he could not have said in how long. He held her longer, shuddering with afterspasms, and kissed her fervently.

"I would have died without that, I mean it," Ivy sighed. "You have no idea."

A step in the hall chilled them, a rustle or sound that might almost have been in the room. They disentangled, Philip helping Ivy with her clumsy leg. He helped her with her clothing, showering kisses on her exquisite neck. Satisfaction and pleasure warmed him. He felt that he had entered a new plane of existence, liberated, happy, and well deserved.

She disentangled herself and moved toward the door. He unlocked it for her with formal courtesy and she drifted with apparent non-chalance down the hall. No one would see the flame-pink of her cheeks or know what it meant. She came by the nurses' station, heard sobs from the room behind it, went to her room. Philip followed her in his imagination, unaware that in the little file room off his office, where Wei-chi was accustomed to seek refuge, reading or nodding off in the comfortingly small, dark space, the horrified intern was frozen in shock and the fear that Philip would come in and find him.

Jennifer, coming home at about the same time Philip did, appeared to notice nothing changed or special about him, which puzzled and relieved him, and disappointed.

"Household objects glued to kites," she said of the art show she'd been at.

"Not meant to be flown, I guess," Philip said.

"Right, they'll never fly." She laughed, getting one of his T-shirts from his drawer. It was what she wore to bed.

"Why don't you just put them in your drawer to begin with," he said, peevishly. She looked surprised.

"My dear! Is it my wearing them or my getting things out of your drawer that you mind?"

"I don't know," Philip said, turning on his side away from her to end the conversation.

42

Philip woke at five, in a state of high anxiety. Sexual intercourse in his office with a patient! This was so unlike anything he would ever do he felt mad with eagerness to get to the hospital, to reassure himself that it, and he, were unchanged.

There was nothing changed or different about the hospital. The door to Ivy's room was closed. She would still be asleep. Soon the nurses would wake her—bath, breakfast, the making of the bed. He walked through the ward as quickly as possible, noting at a glance the state of things on ICU. In his office the only signs of what had happened were the objects rearranged on his desk, pushed to one side. Methodically, he repositioned them in their regular places.

He was surprised at a knock on his door this early, and at the strange leap of his heart with the hope it might be Ivy. Instead it was Rank Briscoe, the ebullient thoracic surgeon. It was early, Philip thought, even for a surgeon.

"Good, Phil, I was hoping to catch you," Briscoe said, stepping into Philip's office and half sitting on Philip's worktable, the picture of friendly insouciance.

"If I could talk to you a minute. As a friend. Several of us have been saying—I think you know what I mean. And I said I'd be the one to approach you, because you and I have always been good friends."

Philip was startled. Briscoe could not be talking about last night, could he? So Philip had no idea what he meant. Talk about what? He waited politely for Briscoe to expand. The redness of Briscoe's countenance was even more pronounced than usual against the white of his coat, shining, even, from his morning shave, or from emotion.

"Well, to come directly to the point, you've seemed on edge to a lot of people these days, Phil. A number of people have noticed this. People are concerned. About you, and, well, of course the patients, too."

Philip stared, unable to believe that this barely competent surgeon could be talking about him. "Has there been some particular incident?" he managed stiffly, still beset with horrible notions that Ivy had told someone about last night, between last night and now, and his colleagues had held some midnight convocation. And yet this couldn't be true.

"No, no," Briscoe said, "but patient care could get to be a concern, if you're having a personal problem. This is a preventive conversation we're having. There was the business in the OR. There've been a couple of incidents with the housestaff. And then the whole Randall Lincoln débacle. And the way you overreacted to that cocaine incident. I wondered about that. And your seemingly excessive vendetta against Wice Morris. But this is not a bill of complaints, buddy, these are just the things people have mentioned to show why people have been concerned, and I'm just here as a friend to ask if there's any way you might need help. Believe me, we can all imagine getting in over our heads. I know you're not much of a drinking man, or I never thought so, it sounds more like trouble at home to me. Or—are you feeling okay?"

Philip was too stupefied to think. What was he being accused of? Briscoe was here as a wise man! He, Philip Watts, junior AOA, first in his class, trained at Mass. General, was somehow being accused of, was the object of, the subject of . . . his head whirled.

"This incident in the OR sounds a little out of control, Phil. You apparently took a patient right off the table?" Briscoe went on. "And you said some very strange things to the chief medical resident— accused him of being dirty, something like that? Then there was a complaint from the nurses about ethnic slurs. It all sounds a bit out of control, Phil. Is everything all right is what I want to know? And we want you to know that if you need any kind of help, we're here for you. Most things can be handled, you know. You know you're not alone."

Philip, who thought of himself as a pacific person, resisted his impulse to knock Briscoe down. He was still capable of the elementary calculation that to hit him would aggravate these astonishing charges. Not that he cared! They were none of them true. Or rather, they were all true but they were not in the aggregate the actions of a—of a what? What were they thinking? Drink? Drugs? Mental illness? Brain tumor?

"Maybe talking to somebody, getting some help with, with whatever it is," Briscoe went on. Philip decided to hit him but did not.

"Thanks, Rank," he said instead, when he could speak. "Nothing wrong in particular. A few things on my mind. You know I'm taking the job at Stanford? It's a big decision. Sorry if I've been causing concern. . . ." This was so false that he couldn't continue. Himself, Philip Watts, a true blue arrow. The three wise men! This had to be the work of Mack Bunting or some such asshole. Fury contended with shame and dismay.

"I trust there's no concern about patients," he added.

Briscoe, apparently hearing menace in Philip's voice, backed away a step. "Nothing, no. But concern that there could be."

"Nothing happening on my watch that wouldn't happen ordinarily?" Philip pressed on.

"No, not really. Just the things I've mentioned, and this business about the recipes. That seemed strange to me, I'll admit it, out of bounds, really."

"Recipes?"

"Getting your wife to edit the surgical recipes out of the cookbook. That isn't something you'd ordinarily do, Phil. I've known you a long time and you're not a petty person. That was the signal for me."

This last allegation made so little sense that Philip thought it must be Rank who was going mad.

"Between you and me, Phil, Stanford may be just the thing. It's a terrific chance, and new challenges. Everyone is very glad for you. I think I can say that no one will stand in your way here."

"Right, Rank," said Philip, hoping only to get rid of Briscoe, to have a few minutes to deal with this stupefying development before he had to be sentient and collected on rounds. "I appreciate your concern. It's a help to know I can talk to you."

Briscoe, apparently as eager to go as Philip was to get rid of him, leaped up and clasped Philip's shoulder. "Phil, you sure can. Remember. And do me a favor, get things checked out, you know, before anything serious comes up. Hey!" and he tapped Philip's biceps.

"Excuse me, Rank, I've got rounds," Philip said, nearly trembling with the hypocrisy of his mild tone, and shook Briscoe's hand.

Ivy, too excited to sleep, had gotten a pill from Vita in the middle of the night, and now slept late in a Valium torpor. All night she had dreamed of making love to Philip Watts, but in her dream it had been dangerous and was interrupted by zoo screams and the image of the hand of an animal—a gorilla or a bear—reaching through a window screen, fumbling for the latch. Now, as she lay, half awake, trying to trap this image and understand it, someone knocked at the door and immediately opened it. Dr. Evans. She roused herself to smile and say good morning. He was brisk.

"Hello. I think we're going to get you out of here today. Thought that'd wake you up!"

"Really?" She did wake up, all the way, and sat up. "Good! Oh, good!" He pulled the pillow up behind her, like a nurse, and took her arm, sighting down it like a gun barrel and lifting it above her head. She waved it cooperatively above her head for him.

"See? Back to normal," he said. "And your speech is almost normal."

"I don't sound quite right to myself. Sometimes I can't think of words," she said.

"It'll take time. The use of your leg will gradually improve. Remember to do the home exercises the physiotherapist has given you, and come in for the physiotherapy appointments. That's very important. You'll soon be waltzing. Then I want to see you in the office next week."

"It's hard to realize." Ivy smiled, the happiness of being thought healthy again, and free to go, was beginning to raise her spirits from their druggy and voluptuous complacency.

"Hop out of bed for me here," Dr. Evans said, "and let me put you through your paces."

Obediently, Ivy climbed out of bed and showed him how well she could walk, and swing her arm, and smile. She smiled, too, at the doctors in the hall as they walked by on their rounds. Her glance connected for a fraction of a second with Philip Watts's. His beauty, in his white coat, leading the pack of doctors, made desire burn in her, under the very gaze of Dr. Evans. Philip's eyes seemed to communicate to hers messages of urgent rapport.

"I'm definitely well!" she cried to Dr. Evans.

This coincidence of glances, the second's impression Philip had had of Ivy in yellow standing in her room, tore Philip's heart in two directions, equipoised between longing to hold and talk to her and a craven dread of facing her at all, wondering what he would say, wondering what new footing they were on. Were they in love? Were they to laugh, shake hands, say goodbye? Obviously nothing would happen again here in the hospital. But later? What did he hope? These thoughts, unformed, started up as he was speaking to his residents, with no time to settle or develop them; they just rattled loose in his head like dice in a box. After rounds, in his office, he tried again to think what he ought to say to Ivy, what he wished he had said to Rank Briscoe. But now he was interrupted by the daughter-in-law of Mrs. Carson, the cardiac insufficiency with pulmonary edema.

"I'm Delphine Trask, Mrs. Carson's daughter?" An imposing woman in a red cardigan.

"Come in," said Philip, rising. "I guess it's your husband I've talked to?"

"Yes. Doctor, we're concerned. This is going on and on, and poor Mother has always said she doesn't want measures—you know, drastic measures. 'When the time comes, just let me go'—she's said this a hundred times if at all. We are behind her wishes. Doctor, she wants to go."

"Mrs. . . . Trask," said Philip. "Our position is that we must provide reasonable medical care. We aren't doing anything drastic to your mother. She's on life support because there's every chance she'll pull out of this. I know it seems long."

"Just looking into her eyes. She can't talk, of course, with that terrible tube, but the tortured expression—I know if she were herself, she would ask us to turn off the machines."

"People who think they would want the machines turned off quite often don't, when it comes to that point. Despite her age, your mother has a treatable illness, and there's nothing wrong with her mind or spirits. I talked to her when she came in, and I think she'll walk out of here. Well, in her walker."

"Just the torment of knowing she's bankrupting the family—she's always said she never would want to bankrupt the family," said Mrs. Trask.

"I understand," said Philip. "Nonetheless, there's nothing we can do." He always seemed one way or another to be saying that there was nothing they could do. Of course there were many things they did do. But at some point, always, there was a conflict of medical judgment with human wishes, and medicine was always on the unpleasant side of reality. Unpleasant from someone's point of view. Love, it crossed his mind, was the only arena where fact and desire sometimes cooperated.

"Dr. Mudd has studied these issues and I think can explain the general ethical position we operate from here," he said, stepping toward Mrs. Trask. "Let me call Dr. Mudd and see if she's in her office."

"Yes, let me talk to her," agreed Mrs. Trask. Philip made the phone call. "Her office is on 7F. I'm on my way to X-Ray, I'll show you the way," he said, leading her firmly out of his office.

43

When Dr. Evans had gone, Ivy waited for a while, expecting something more to happen, some ceremony of release, but no one came. She guessed that when the doctor said you could go, they put you out, in their minds, then and there, mentally taking the sheets off after you, whether you'd died or gone home. All the hospital part of yourself, your hospital emotional life, the laughs and the terrors, you had to leave behind you in a heap with the dirty sheets, in a pile outside the room. You could only take with you the array of unfamiliar objects you had brought in—glass beads, purse, scuffed-looking shoes.

She took a shower and got dressed. Her clothes looked faded and dusty, even dirty. Could she really have been walking around in, going to the doctor in, such clothes as these? The jeans were loose around the waist. Her breasts, formerly fat and full of milk, were now just ordinary small breasts. It seemed to her that they were smaller than ever, slightly flattened or something, the nipples darker. They had a memory of Dr. Watts's caresses. How was she now to allude to him in her thoughts? Philip? Dr. Watts? Dr. Philip Watts? Her bra had a sour-milk smell where little stains of leaked milk had dried. Now she had no more milk for her baby. She suddenly began to cry, but she made herself stop.

Altogether diminished. Dazed, almost, to think of walking out of here. Happy, she supposed, and yet she knew it would be flat to be home, as after any adventure when things go on being the same, and the sameness hurts like a glare in the eyes, like sun on a hot wall, and you have to look away.

No one came. She looked at the flowers, the plants. She wondered if she ought to wash out the pretty vase that Deirdre Jenkins's flowers had come in, and take it back to Deirdre; it was obviously a nice one.

All at once Rosemary Hunt came in, carrying a little paper sack with a string handle, and the words ALTA BUENA printed on it. She opened it and put in the awful bottle of hospital mouthwash and the lotion, from the nightstand. She waved it at Ivy to remind her to take it.

"Your medication's in here too, honey. Did you find your clothes okay?"

"Thanks, Rosemary, thanks for everything," Ivy said. Rosemary smiled.

"Girl, we're sure happy to see you goin' like this."

Perry Briggs, seeing Ivy in the hall, at first hardly knew her, people looked so different in their clothes, competent, renewed. In her jeans, Ivy was a girl you might take out. She looked beautiful and radiant, though she walked a little faultily, in a way that tugged at the emotions.

"I've been sprung!" she laughed.

"Way to go!" said Perry, pierced with the realization that he would never see her again. People just came and went. She flung her arms around him and hugged him.

"I'm in line for some of that!" Mark Silver, walking by, hugged her too. Rosemary Hunt brought the wheelchair out of Room 209.

"They make you go in that?" Ivy said, dismayed. "I don't need that!"

"We know, you're great," they all said. Ivy hugged Rosemary. They waited for the wheelchair volunteer. Ivy looked anxiously around, suddenly fearing that Dr. Watts, Philip, was not going to know that she was going.

"Good work," said Carmel Hodgkiss, coming by with charts in her hand. "Have they sent for your paperwork?"

"My walking papers?"

"Yes, you have to have your walking papers," they said, laughing. Mrs. Howell, the wheelchair volunteer, said she would take Ivy first to the Discharge Office.

"Goodbye, goodbye, goodbye," said her loved ones on the ward.

"Have you got someone coming for you?" asked Mrs. Howell, in the elevator.

"I'm going on the bus," Ivy said. "Dr. Evans brought me. Everyone I know would be at work this time of day."

The volunteer, accustomed to the ritual of discharge, which usually involved some relative in a car, stationed, motor running, at the curb outside the Emergency Room entrance, was worried by this, could imagine Ivy feeling faint on the bus. "I'm going to call down to the Volunteers Office, to see if there's someone who could drive you," she said.

"No, really, don't," Ivy said. "I'll be fine." She couldn't help but think of Philip Watts's offer to take her home, and of her fantasy of how it would be. But of course he was busy somewhere else, saving lives.

"It's a rule," Mrs. Howell insisted, leaving Ivy to sit in her wheelchair in the lobby, holding her paper sack, to wait for her paperwork.

This was the morning Mimi took magazines to OB-GYN. She never took them books, because the patients didn't stay long enough. She found the OB-GYN ward in a state of breezy cheer. The head OB nurse, Andrea Pfister, told Mimi about it as Mimi arranged the cart: the previous night, a C-section, the wife of an intern at Cedars, had nearly died of a massive pulmonary embolism, and when normal resuscitation techniques had been to no avail, Dr. Philip Watts had done something brilliant. She had been dead, but had been brought back to life and was going to be able to nurse her baby and be fine.

Mimi, who was always moved by such stories, found herself thinking about it all morning, in connection with her own life. How wonderful it would be actually to save someone's life. How modest Philip was; he was often seen at late, inconvenient hours making some decision of life or death, about whether to tap the lungs or draw blood off the heart or biopsy the liver. He made decisions, while she just dithered and couldn't make a decision, even when no one's life was at stake.

Today, all morning as she looked around, all the hospital scenes seemed intensified, charged with drama and significance. It had to do, she was sure, with her generally agitated mood, but as she walked through the surgery day room, she saw with ghastly clarity the dreaded purple blotch on the cheek of a young man waiting there, and felt the goodness of the little nurse Delores tottering as she tried to support an immense old man—she even felt the goodness of Carmel Hodgkiss, whom she saw talking in a kind way to someone's crying family, and of Mark Silver, scowling with preoccupation, reading a chart. With unusual acuity she could hear the hum of all the machines plugged into all the sick; it rose around her like the music of life itself. It came to her with perfect clearness that she couldn't obstruct with her own concerns the interests of life itself. Of course she would sell the hospital her house.

However unromantic it was to think of parking, parking in a larger sense was part of it all, of the hospital and its force for life and healing, for the poor young man walking out with his arm around his friend, so frail, thin, ill, and the dear old gentleman with tears in his eyes, with his wife, and the interns running around, tired-looking, their eyes red. How simple it was to decide! How plainly did a right action clear away the pain of indecision, and though it didn't promise that the future would be visible at the end of the tunnel, it seemed to say that the tunnel would be lit along the way. She would, definitely, sell her house. She felt a little shaky, and when she saw Mr. Tabor outside the Volunteers Office, she almost didn't say, as she'd intended, "I'd like to talk to you about my house." But then she did. A gratified, smooth expression slid smilingly across his villain's face.

"When?" he said.

"When I've found something suitable for myself," she said, in what she believed was a satisfactorily authoritative tone. "Then we'll discuss the price and the shares of parking corporation stock." How bold she sounded to herself, and perhaps to Mr. Tabor, too, for he seemed to be looking at her with respect. The satisfaction of this did something to mitigate the pain of what she had actually decided. She was now a homeless person.

In her office, tears came, awfully silly, she thought. She was glad to get a call from the Volunteers Office, asking if she could drive a patient home. She'd just as soon leave, she thought, and she had to pick up Narnia at the airport later anyway. She picked up a carton of books she was taking to give to the Goodwill, and set out for home to get her car. She hadn't asked who the patient was, but she would spot the wheelchair, the paper sack.

There was something frightening, Ivy thought, in the looks of the little party of people from the business office who got off the elevator and approached her as she sat like an invalid in the stupid wheelchair. They had a certain solemn, even reverent bearing she found worrying. A young woman in glasses held a large folder of papers, and there was a man she had often seen in the halls.

"Mrs. Tarro, here is your bill," said the woman briskly. "Here is the total and this is the sum we have agreed on with your insurance company. This is what you will be paying. Mr. Tabor here thought we should discuss the payment schedule today, but if you'd like to come back in a few days, you might have a better idea of your general situation."

The wheelchair volunteer fixed the two financial people with a look of distaste. "She shouldn't tire herself today."

"When you come back to see your doctor, then," the financial woman suggested.

Ivy felt new apprehensions. Of course she'd been here two weeks, nearly three. But she had insurance. Probably she had to sign or they wouldn't let her go. She took the pen the woman handed her, and signed where someone had written an X. Her eyes took in, but her mind could scarcely register, the figure, $48,206.

"This is the total," said the woman. "But you'll only be paying the $24,103. That's the arrangement we made with your insurance. Your private doctor will bill you separately."

"Do you own your own home?" Mr. Tabor was saying. She could scarcely hear him through the strange, dizzy hum in her ears. The room bobbled and wheeled.

She began to read the paper in her hand. "The hospital maintains personnel and facilities to assist your physicians and surgeon(s) in their performance of various surgical operations and other special diagnostic and therapeutic procedures. These operations and procedures may all involve risks of unsuccessful results, complications, injury, or even death, from both known and unforeseen causes, and no warranty or guarantee is made as to result or cure. You have the right to be informed of the risks. . . ." Quickly she stuffed the papers in her bag.

"Yes, of course, I'll come back," she said. "When I come back next week to see my doctor."

Philip hurried back after x-ray conference, without anything clear in his mind to say to Ivy, just wanting to see her, and found her room empty. He was shocked. Even though he had known that Evans would be discharging her soon, the sight of the empty bed brought back the moment that he had found her gone to surgery. A loss of light in the room, after the flare of her hair, reminded of death, and tore at him so sharply that he looked away. He recognized it was the end of an unexpected emotional episode. He had not expected it to end so simply, but that she was gone seemed a signal from her. He looked again in the room in case there was something there, an envelope addressed to him, or something that should be returned to her.

The disarray of his emotions—for him who wasn't used to feeling this particular sensation of sentimental loss, or the injured rage of the morning visit by Rank Briscoe—left him overwhelmed with a wish to get out of the hospital. He hung up his coat and went down to the parking lot. In his turbulent but nonspecific pain, he was disoriented and couldn't for a minute find his car. He felt like someone standing in a twilight zone of misery and excitement, with a positive pole of love and excitement and sexual tension contending with fury and chagrin and a sense of injustice. Model of rectitude as he knew himself to be, being perceived by his colleagues as irresponsible and troubled, even dangerous. It was not surprising that surgeons should be behind an attack on him, but it was stupefying that anyone else could be brought to see it, and think it necessary to approach him, and warn him to take the Stanford job—that had sounded like a threat.

Unless—unless they were somehow right and he had slipped or was cracking up. Were you yourself the first to know? Might not you be the last to know? No, people in trouble were the first to know, though they often denied the knowledge to themselves and went through the stages. Well, and here he had just been fucking a patient in his office! There was no denying it! But of course, she was Ivy. In the positive, or joyful, mode, Philip felt himself to be on the brink of first love.

Had he and Jennifer ever loved each other at all? He couldn't remember. Not like this! Had they? No, he didn't think so, couldn't remember, ever, this feeling of tenderness and longing, this curiosity, this happiness merely to fasten his thoughts on this lovely girl. He thought of all the questions he wanted to ask and answer, all the terrific sex ahead of them.

So what had that preposterous buffoon Briscoe been talking about? He could think of no untoward deaths, no glaring errors he had made. Yes, a harsh word or two to the residents. Jesus Christ, the tantrums his own old professors used to have! Even as he was opening his car door, he had no idea where he was going. He could go do his Christmas shopping. Perhaps this plan was prompted by his guilty feeling toward Jennifer, but anyhow he had to do it, it was nearly Christmas Eve.

44

Mimi ran into Philip Watts as she crossed the parking lot on the way home to get her car and bring it around to the Emergency Room entrance to pick up the patient. He was getting into his car, wearing a preoccupied, morose expression—the natural effect, she understood, of all the grave cares heaped on him during a hospital day. Her impulse was to tell him about her house decision, if only to put herself on record and make it harder to change her mind.

"Hello," she said. He smiled with his accustomed politeness, and, noticing her heavy box of books, took it from her. As he walked with her toward her house, she told him she'd decided to sell it. "I feel peculiar, but I know it's the right thing," she said. His nod was understanding and sympathetic.

As when they had gone out to dinner, his company had an agitating effect on her rather inappropriate to the ordinariness of the occasion, walking among fenders and bumpers in the late morning. She hardly ever saw Philip outside the ward or the doctors' dining room, and there, in his white coat, he was entirely a doctor, while here he was an attractive man, in a different category, and more accessible.

"You may find that you've liberated the future in some unexpected way," he was saying, of her house. "One thing has to happen before the next thing can." Mimi had not noticed before that Philip Watts was given to philosophizing like this.

"Yes, I guess I feel a little liberated already," she agreed, wondering if he had invested in the doctors' parking consortium. She noticed his slightly frayed cuffs, and, as he put the books in her trunk, a hole in his pants pocket where his wallet had worn through. She would take better care of him if he were hers, she thought.

"Anyway, I bet you won't be sorry," Philip said. His smile, she thought, was of particular radiance and sincerity. He was obviously happy to have seen her; only a minute before, when she had seen him from a distance, his expression had been troubled and preoccupied.

"Mimi, don't you think a person can be too timid and unreflective in their life?" he said. "You have to take some chances." He looked at her, direct and thoughtful.

"Of course, yes." She sighed, her already susceptible emotions churning hopefully. What did he mean? How charming, how good-looking, how compassionate he was! Doctors at their best were excellent human beings! It was a profession that either made or broke the character, and Philip's character was exemplary.

"Are you doing anything right now? Have you got time for coffee? You could show me your house," he said. "The famous house."

What was he suggesting? Philip was asking to come in, and here she had to go pick up this wretched patient! How could she get out of it? She could call and say her car wouldn't start. Not really. Poor patient waiting in wheelchair for an hour while they rounded up someone else. And also Philip would hear her telling this lie. But she consoled herself that what Philip had suggested this once he would suggest again.

"Oh, damn," she said, so he couldn't mistake her willingness to ask him in. "I'm just setting out to pick up a patient—even now waiting for me at the ER entrance."

"Oh, well, another time," he said, perfectly cheerfully.

There is something between us, she thought. Free of the burden of her house, her thoughts could rove down any avenue they pleased. She was in love with Philip Watts. Not just with his white coat, but with Philip the man, with whom she had had so many interesting chats in the doctors' dining room, never once being disappointed in his responses, sense, kindness, or medical judgment. She watched him walk back to his own car, admiring his attractive, athletic stride.

She drove around to the Emergency Room entrance, and was delighted to see that it was Ivy Tarro waiting in the wheelchair to go home, talking with Fran Howell, who had pushed her out here and waited with her, and opened the door on the passenger side for Ivy to get in. When Ivy was settled, Fran handed Ivy's purse and other things in.

It was wonderful to think of Ivy being cured, well again, going home for Christmas, reunited with her baby, everything restored to happiness. With her trendy food-world job, and her prettiness, she must have lovers, she must have an interesting life, Mimi thought. Ivy's face, in the sunlight, was paler than when she'd been admitted, and she was thinner, more ethereal, like a romantic TB victim in a Victorian novel. Mimi glanced anxiously at her as they drove, for fear she'd slump or sway. People were weak when they left the hospital, even if they were well. Mimi wondered why no friends or family had come to get her. But some people were funny and didn't like their loved ones to see them sick. Mimi was a little like that herself. Of course she was never sick.

Ivy didn't seem inclined to talk, so Mimi's thoughts drifted back to Philip, and this newest unmistakable indication that he was attracted to her too. Looking back, she could see any number of signs. He always made a point of sitting with her in the doctors' dining room, and over the years they had become rather intimate, in a way, and the frankness with which they confided in each other must mean something. This morning was a definite escalation!

"It was very, very expensive, getting sick," Ivy said eventually, in a stunned voice.

"Horrible," Mimi agreed. Then Ivy seemed lost in contemplation of this, and said nothing further. At intervals she sighed or drew in her breath in sharp gasps, as if overcome by the pain of some thought. It would have sounded like a sob, except that she was well, getting out of the hospital, being reunited with her baby, so of course she must be happy.

Mimi, at the stop signs, watched her from the corner of her eye and thought of Philip. Of course, be serious, she told herself, Philip is happily married. Staying away from married men was the most recurrent practical admonition shared among the single women she knew, and almost all the women she knew were single. Just as all the attractive men were married. The rule was that you can be in love, you just can't do anything about it. She did remember those long conversations with Bradford Evans when he was still married, but they hadn't gone out until he was separated. Or maybe just before. Anyhow, she hadn't been in love with Bradford Evans! Absolutely not! It was clear that she had always been in love with Philip Watts.

"Turn left on Lombard," Ivy said when they had turned up Grant. "Then I'm just on the right."

"What about your baby?" Mimi asked. "Will she be there? Should I take you somewhere to pick her up?"

"My babysitter's just around the corner on Stockton. She can bring her over when I call her. Here, this is it."

Mimi parked near a hydrant and got out to open Ivy's door for her, like a man or a nurse. Belatedly, Ivy stirred, smiled, made a gesture toward the door handle. Then she sprang out with normal vigor. "Thanks so much, Mimi," she said.

"I'll see you up. It's absolutely protocol," Mimi said.

"Come up and have a cup of tea," Ivy said. "You can leave the car here; they usually don't give tickets this time of day."

Ivy's apartment was the upper of two in a shabby Victorian duplex that had been covered with asphalt shingles. The stairwell was of dark, varnished wood, with a grim brown stair carpet on the steps. Her apartment, though, was a blaze of light and views looking out over the bay. Container ships steamed across the foreground, and sailboats spangled the blue water. North Beach rooftops with their little gardens spread below them.

"What a great place!" Mimi said, looking around. It was spare; there were a kilim and a plywood Eames chair, a sofa, some paintings, and a wooden crate in the corner filled with records and tapes. Several pieces of baby paraphernalia—a stroller, a car seat, a folded playpen—stood in the other corner. Beyond the living room, in the bedroom, Mimi could see a baby's crib.

"Thanks," Ivy said, going to the kitchen, sighing heavily. Mimi sat on the sofa. She thought of Philip Watts. The heart has no laws! He kept coming into her thoughts like a sea to fill a hole left by the absence of a house. It was as if, some little chink taken away, a great rush of feeling could come swooping through. Philip Watts, her almost daily companion for at least a moment or two in the doctors' dining room. From such little daily passages, strong feelings can build and grow, unbeknownst, and then suddenly declare themselves. Mimi felt almost physically dizzy with these thoughts.

"It's funny coming home," Ivy remarked from the kitchen, "when you hadn't expected to be away. Sort of Rip van Winkle, but in reverse. You've changed, but nothing else has. When I walked out of here three weeks ago, I just thought—I just thought that my life was my normal life."

Mimi came into the kitchen. "This is such a great place! Did you have trouble finding it?"

"Not really. I can walk to work from here, so I wanted this neighborhood. I don't know what I'll do when Delia goes to school. But that's years. Anyway, I suppose they have a school. I never noticed one, but there are things you never notice until you have a child."

"I know," Mimi agreed, staring, entranced, out the windows. I could live in an apartment in North Beach, she thought, or I could go to Italy, or whatever. All you need is an orange crate and some records.

"Do you want milk?" Ivy asked. "Only of course there's no milk."

Mimi thought of living in bare rooms glowing with shiny, creamy paint, blue water beyond. She remembered her first idea, of Tiburon or Sausalito. She thought of giving her furniture to Narnia, or to Ivy. She could imagine Narnia, dressed for success, renting her first apartment, dressed like the young women you saw downtown, with briefcases and a slightly awkward pitch to their stance in high heels. This in turn made her think of Jennifer Watts, with her expensive clothes and flat shoes.

This is ridiculous, forget it, her heart said. There has never been a word from Philip Watts, not a phrase, and not a hint to suggest that he is other than perfectly happy with the horrible, acerbic Jennifer. Mimi now realized that her mind had inventoried and stored each compliment and personal conversation she had ever had with Philip Watts. She reviewed them. Just this week he had said, "You look nice," and, more meaningfully, just now, "A person can be too timid and too unreflective." How true!

Ivy poured some thick curdled gobs of milk down the sink.

Seeing her, Mimi felt like a monster, her thoughts on herself, letting Ivy, just out of the hospital, fix tea and act the hostess. She could see that the girl was frail. What had seemed her healthy strength in the hospital, Mimi now understood, was only relative. In the light of the window, Ivy was shadowed with hospital hollows, and she had the usual slightly shrunken look and tentative gait of someone newly up after illness. "I'm sorry!" Mimi cried, jumping up. "What a brute I am! You sit down, Ivy. Let me go to the store and get some groceries for you. You should have somebody at home here with you. Do you have any help?"

"I feel fine—really," Ivy protested. "Dr. Evans said I can even go back to work a few hours every day. Honestly, I feel perfectly well, perfectly normal. Remember, I've been exercising like a stevedore."

But Mimi was struck by how subdued her manner was, compared with that of the burning and forceful stalker of the hospital corridors. There she had seemed to marshal her vigor and radiate it like a stove. Now she seemed reduced to an ashen core, only a tiny glow, which would, no doubt, ignite and fan back into flame once she was over the shock of coming home. "Make a list," said Mimi firmly, pulling herself together and getting ready to go to the store for Ivy.

45

To his other emotions, as Philip went shopping, were added the emotions of anxious resentment Christmas always brought him. It wasn't that he didn't like to give presents, but he hated to be wrong, and therefore feared and disliked the hints of wronged forbearance in the reactions of people he gave presents to when he hadn't bought them the unsuitable things they sometimes seemed to want. And, like everyone, he resented the commercialization, the tinsel hung before Thanksgiving and all the rest of it.

He parked in the Sutter-Stockton garage and came out on Stockton Street, threading his way through the throng of Chinese waiting for the 30 bus, and the homeless who had made their camps between the garage and the corner. From behind him, the resonance of cars in the cement bowels of the parking structure, the tinny caws of the Chinese, and the mellifluous wheedles of people squatted along the sidewalk gave him an impression of emerging from a cave into the world of somewhere else, Calcutta or Babel. He looked at the belligerent stares and hand-lettered signs of the sidewalk dwellers. Sooner or later, all of them would turn up at Alta Buena. He always forgot—so seldom was he out in the world in daylight hours—that it was now necessary, in California as in Calcutta, to carry small amounts of change to pass out among the homeless. There seemed to be more of them all the time, come West, he had heard, to escape the cold, though it was cold in San Francisco too. They had mistaken it for Los Angeles. MY PUPPIE AND ME OUT ON THE STREET'S NO WHERE TO GO. By the time he had fished a dollar out of his wallet, walking quickly to avoid actually encountering the eye of any one person—why was this?—he had walked by the last of them, OUT OF A JOB, and so stuffed the bill into the Salvation Army bucket at the corner of Post Street. Here he saw a long, jostling queue, which by some association of ideas he took at first for a breadline. This line of people extended from the corner to Gumps, the antiques shop where he'd been heading. But now he could see that the queue had nothing to do with the homeless; it was festive and well dressed.

Turning the corner, he could see, further, that these people were lined up to file past Gumps's windows. Of course, since it was Christmas, Gumps had probably done some especially charming windows, little trains or quaint Victorian puppets, and was, by the look of the crowd, having a brilliant success. Hundreds, maybe more than a thousand people, with happy, expectant faces, many of them leading little kids by the hand. He remembered taking his own children to such things, and half wished for a little kid this minute to take by the hand and show something charming to. He could imagine himself carrying Ivy Tarro's dusky baby, the child in his fantasy a little older than her present three or four months, looking around with her huge brown eyes and laughing that hysterical laugh of happiness little kids have. He began to feel more in a Christmas mood than he had.

Being tall, he could see over the heads of most of the crowd. In the windows the store had fashioned a series of little cozy rooms, with fireplaces in them, and hearth rugs, and paisley-covered three-foot sofas, and a tiny Christmas tree in one, surrounded by presents exquisitely wrapped in foil and gold ribbon. Philip studied the rooms for signs of their inhabitants, perhaps Tiny Tim's family, or the children of "The Night Before Christmas." Then a dozing puppy figurine sprang to life and trotted up to the window to watch the assembly of people watching him. When he wagged his tail, everyone laughed, as if by being real, he'd performed a trick of immense cleverness. People called, and made clucking noises to attract his attention.

Philip now saw that in each room a puppy or kitten crouched under a little table, or snoozed on the rug—uniformly cute baby animals to

whom the Christmas viewers waved and cooed. Near the main doorway to the store, a woman stood, wearing a badge that read SFSPCA,
and a straw hat of the kind that people wear at political conventions.
Behind her, a large sign read ADOPT.

In the next window, a family of orange tabbies nestled together on
a doll bed. Philip watched, bemused by the somewhat obvious irony
implicit in this scene of coddled animals living in luxury so near the
litter of homeless humans around the corner. Now and then, a person
among the admiring throng would step forward, wearing a resolute,
beaming face, and accost the adoption lady. She in turn pointed toward the interior of the store. "They will interview you inside," she
said. How charming the expressions of delight on the faces of the
toddlers held up by their parents to see a fuzzy kitten, perchance to
qualify to be taken home. Only the cute, the adoptable, no doubt,
had been brought in. Before the passage of a recent law forbidding
the animal-care societies to sell animals for research, they had done
so. These very creatures might have ended up at Alta Buena. Pushing
closer, he read the placard in the main window, which announced
that eighty-seven cats and twenty-three dogs had so far been adopted.
He was pleased to hear this, had a tangible swelling sensation in his
throat of emotion of some kind.

Next, to his considerable astonishment, his own wife, Jennifer,
came walking out of Gumps, wearing the straw hat, the letters
SFSPCA on a ribbon around the crown, and a red blazer, vaguely
military—the SPCA militant—and a green necktie. He was deeply
shocked. He hadn't known that Jennifer was a member of the SPCA.
His sensation of unpleasant surprise must come not from disapproval
but from the realization that he knew nothing about Jennifer, despite
knowing her so well for twenty years. Of course he knew she donated
money and time to charitable causes. Of course he knew she was an
animal lover, as who was not? But there did seem something a little
pointed about being involved so publicly with the fate of dumb animals
a stone's throw from the human misery her husband was pledged to
help alleviate, or as if it were a comment on the animal experiments
they all did—as humanely as possible, that went without saying. Or
on the futility of medicine. Or was he being touchy?

"Oh! Why, Philip!" said Jennifer.

"Doing my Christmas shopping," he said.

"Good!" said Jennifer. "Are you finished? You could give me a ride home."

"I guess so, yes," he said, since he could hardly go in and buy her Christmas present right now. "Sure. I'm parked around the corner in Sutter-Stockton."

46

When Mimi had left, Ivy went to the refrigerator and began to take things out. Acrid, spoiled smells rushed up from under the lids of dishes, leaked through plastic containers, and oozed through glass. The sliced lamb, three weeks old, had a crust of green and fuzzy white, veined with slime. The gravy, white-crusted like a scab, ran a trickle of thin fluid, leaving a sludge of horrible paste in the bottom of the bowl. The sour, serumlike milk splatted curds into the sink. The flesh of the tomatoes rotted across the bottom of the vegetable bin. The lettuce, withered into liquid black stalks, dissolved under her fingers. She felt a bitter taste in her mouth as her stomach turned. She felt weak, too, and light-headed. She could imagine that her own flesh was like that of the putrefying tomatoes, the desiccated oranges, the shriveled, dying, spoiled ingredients of her refrigerator. The connection to her rotten life was too clear. She thought with unspeakable panic of how the diaper pail would be, after three weeks. Was she quite ready to have Delia home?

Her bed was unmade and crumpled, a hair trailing across the pillow. In the bathroom, wads of green toothpaste stuck on the sink. Was she really like this? The laundry basket held musty clothes and disgusting underpants with yellowed crotches. It came to her that her periods would come back, now that she wasn't nursing. Teeth clenched, she lifted the lid of the diaper pail, and quickly replaced it. She went to get a plastic bag from the kitchen and dumped the whole contents of the pail into it, and tightly twisted it shut before the smell could fill the apartment.

Then she called Petra. "I'm here, home," she said. "Could you bring Delia?"

Petra remonstrated. "Oh, darling, why didn't you call me to come get you?"

When the doorbell rang, it was Mimi with a sack of oranges and milk and baby food. She helped Ivy put away her groceries. When she had left, Ivy put the hospital papers out before her on the table and read them over while she waited for Petra to bring Delia home.

Your signature below constitutes your acknowledgment that (1) you have read and agree to the foregoing; (2) that the operations or procedures set forth below have been adequately explained to you by your supervising physician or surgeon(s); and that you have received and understand all of the information you desire concerning such operations or procedures; and (3) that you authorize and consent to the performance of the operations or procedures, including but not limited to the administration and maintenance of anesthesia, and the performance of services including radiology and pathology.

She read this paragraph again and again, trying to remember any explanations, information, agreements, or anything remotely resembling the processes implied by this paragraph, and she could remember nothing of the kind. Everything had just happened. Arm, hospital, blood, stroke, one thing at a time like destiny's plan, culminating in this agreement. With her signature on it. There was her signature: Ivy Louise Tarro. When had she signed it? She must have, but when? Her stomach crawled with this new anxiety, eternal debt added to all other anxieties—vocation, motherhood—newly added to her life, like horrible, twisting, ugly, slimy creatures that had suddenly appeared at the bottom of her fridge. In the hall below she could hear Delia's high-pitched wail, her relentless screaming as Petra climbed the stairs.

47

Daniel, at school in the East, would spend Christmas with Walter, but Narnia was coming home this afternoon. Mimi had not seen her since June, because she had spent the summer doing an internship at a cereal company in Minnesota, and had gone from there straight to her college. Mimi was pleasantly excited and prepared to find her, in just these few months, changed and grown, and she was eager to tell her about the house.

Of course Narnia was entirely unchanged. Mimi waited anxiously at the airline gate, and here came the old Narnia, perhaps a few pounds heavier, the one thing that had worried Mimi about Narnia's adolescence, and that she had kept herself from ever mentioning to Narnia. Of course she looked lovely, too, and delighted to see Mimi, and happy to be home, just as she always was. Narnia always seemed to Mimi somehow too young to be in college, more like a high school girl. Mimi had never known how experienced Narnia was—had she tried drugs? sex? Though Mimi was perfectly aware of the conventional wisdom about the need to discuss these painful topics with your child, they had somehow not come up with Narnia, who always seemed perfectly informed, and communicative, and had had these very explicit classes in school. It had never been prudery that lay between them, but politeness.

They hugged, kissed, Mimi commented on Narnia's sweater, the heaviness of her satchel, the bright Christmas weather Narnia was in for. Narnia began her account of college doings. As they drove home, Mimi was conscious of the great pleasure of feeling that the worst was over with Narnia, and that they would always go on being friends. She didn't start right in with her news about the house, though.

Then, at dinner, she brought it up. Narnia was appalled. "You're just letting them fuck you over, Mom, pardon me, but that's really the word for it."

"I haven't agreed to any terms, I haven't signed anything," Mimi protested. "If it's unfair in any way, I can change my mind."

"But where would we live?" Narnia asked, her face that of a displaced little girl wondering what would happen to her room, and Mimi could see that although she thought of Narnia as an emancipated grownup Narnia did not. Wasn't it supposed to be the other way around?

Mimi remembered a conversation with Bradford Evans, his telling her about how when he had gone to the Korean War his mother had given away his street clothes, as if she didn't expect him to come back, and he had been crushed.

"I can understand that," Mimi had said. "I can understand a kind of gesture of superstitious fear."

"As if she didn't want me to come back," Bradford had said.

"She was afraid to tempt fate by planning on it," Mimi had said. And then she had remembered some other man telling her that his mother had also given away his clothes; it must have been in the Vietnam War. As if all mothers did that, and all sons were made to feel expendable or lost. Mothers resigning themselves to doing without their cherished boys, and it was this evidence of maternal autonomy that bothered sons, and bothered Narnia now.

"We'll find something much nicer. More residential," Mimi promised. "I've never liked living right in the shadow of the hospital. I hate the way it keeps encroaching. I've thought of Sausalito." This appeared to affect Narnia even more. She rolled her eyes as if Mimi were hopelessly demented.

"Besides," Mimi went on, "it's the right thing to do. They really do need the parking facility. A virtuous institution in need of space. It seems kind of inconsistent to be working there and obstructing them at the same time."

"They're taking advantage of you," Narnia said.

"It was just coincidental that it was my house. They had no idea I was the owner," Mimi said.

"I bet," said Narnia. "Anyway, you should get a bundle. Don't handle this yourself, Mom. Get a lawyer. What you need to say is, it doesn't matter what the fair market value is. What you have to insist on is replacement value. Do you understand the difference?"

Mimi was startled by the hard note of practicality that entered Narnia's voice, with its slightly patronizing undertone, as if she herself were elderly and out of touch. And Narnia only a sophomore—in business administration, it was true.

———

Philip dropped Jennifer at home, and drove back to the hospital for signout rounds before dinner. He was frustrated not to have bought anything, which meant another shopping trip. Ordinarily he would not make another trip downtown until January, when there was a sale at Brooks Brothers, and Jennifer made him buy three shirts, three T-shirts, and three pairs of boxer shorts. Then he would go again in May for Jennifer's and Daphne's birthdays, and that was pretty much it. The idea of another trip into the Christmas fracas filled him with an instant of panic over this, a reckless waste of time when he ought to be working.

On the ward, things seemed calm. The mobile dialysis unit was hooked into Randall, cleaning his blood. Mrs. Lincoln read a story to him as he nodded off. Little Dr. Kim was better. He was alert, despite the endotracheal tube in his windpipe, and smiled his eager smile, and waved his delicate hands in an effort to signal or reassure. Philip squeezed his hands and said, "I think we can get you off the ventilator soon, Dr. Kim," and one of the many daughters—not the one who spoke English—smiled broadly and dipped her head in a series of approving bows. A Mrs. Chasen, cardiac arrest, was doing better. He left the ICU patients and walked along the ward, feeling calmer himself, in charge. He could almost put Ivy and Rank Briscoe out of mind, as if nothing had happened, for minutes at a time.

In the doctors' dining room, Wei-chi was defending Chinese medicine. "There are many very backward things there. We need very much to catch up to Western medicine, and we acknowledge this, but some things are better."

"For instance?" the others wondered, quite willing to believe it. They all wanted to learn acupuncture and things about herbs. These, however, were not what Wei-chi wished to defend.

"For one thing, I think it is horrible how people are put out of hospital fast, before they get well. In China you go to hospital, you can stay till you get well, maybe a month. Longer if you need to. Here people go home, they still too sick to walk, have to be put in a chair and wheeled right out. It seems very cruel."

"It's a lot safer to be out of the hospital than in it," Mark Silver said, laughing.

"Also, for instance, in China the doctors would not be permitted to enjoy the women patients," Wei-chi went on. Seeing the alert, fascinated expressions come over the faces of his companions, he stopped. They leaned toward him.

"You mean, unlike here?" asked Brian Smeed.

"Perhaps it is only the head doctor? Or—forgive me, there are many things I do not understand," Wei-chi went on, realizing that he had been about to reveal something that must not be spoken of. Despite their cries of "what doctor? what patient?" he refused to say anything further. The young American doctors regaled him with guesses and threats and laughter, but not a word further would he say. Nonetheless, by morning they thought they'd worked it out, by elimination. There was only one head doctor, one plausible patient. Although Wei-chi miserably wondered if he should confess to Dr. Watts that he had spread scandal about him, he didn't. But he could not conceal from himself that he had spoken in anger and disappointment, to think that Dr. Watts, that Mrs. Tarro, would do—such things. He had even spoken, perhaps, in malice.

48

Philip could not remember passing a day like this, wrapped up in himself, distracted. He was fairly sure his mood was owing to the shock and insult of Rank Briscoe's visit, and its implications for a future of trouble, defense, discredit, disgrace—undeserved but nonetheless inevitable. A bitter chill formed in his spirit whenever he recalled this conversation, every stinging word of it. It kept coming back and back upon him—at his desk, rounds, reading, x-ray conferences, writing notes in the charts at the end of the day. But when he thought of Ivy Tarro, the chill would relent and be replaced by warming pangs of desire.

Thus he wavered between the prudent wish to defend his reputation and the strong impulse to fling it to hell with some wilder expression of his raging inner self, say, going off to Tahiti with Ivy. Why should you spend your whole life doing one thing anyhow? But through these yearnings, his wounded but reasonable self would reassert itself, and remind him of the need to clear up this nonsense with the surgeons, and buy something really nice for Jennifer for Christmas.

Yet he was plagued with a nagging sense of a meal left unfinished, something delectable and nourishing mislaid by the telephone, or taken back to the kitchen by the waiter before you were done. He saw that it would be cruel, or at least impolite, not to call Ivy up, the poor young woman whose vulnerability he had so exploited, misusing his status and his professional advantage over her. Some comment or gesture was obligatory.

He tried not to brood about this. Guilt was one thing you as a doctor learned to deal with. He could forgive himself for foolishly yielding to a sexual impulse, and even for taking a huge personal risk, but he was not going to go on doing it. He easily found Ivy's address and phone number in her records.

In the afternoon, skipping Morbidity and Mortality Conference, he drove to North Beach, with the idea of buying in Chinatown the jade bracelet he had planned to buy Jennifer at Gumps. Out of the hospital, he felt more cheerful, though a little strange, being loose in the afternoon world for the second time this week. Walking up Grant Avenue, he felt his heart soar, a description he had heard applied to this curious sensation of lightness and disembodied happiness in which serious contemplation of forthcoming hell-to-pay, or even of expected pleasures, was suspended, and all the immediate beauty of the actual world—drunks, dogshit, Longevity-brand mandarin orange sections in cans in a pyramid in a window—struck him like primary sensations on a tabula rasa. He must try to get out more. He didn't delude himself that he wasn't here to see Ivy. He was walking straight up Grant to where she must live.

To have called her in advance would have required too much calculation. He just let it occur to him to walk up the hill and see how she was doing, how it felt to be home. Of course, she might not be home, in which case—fate, karma, relief, disappointment. He was interested to find that it is possible to think up self-serving rationalizations for one's conduct, and not be deceived by them, but to operate by them nonetheless.

The world attracted him. It had a preoccupied, teeming hum. People emerged with packages from doorways. Brownish sprigs of mistletoe dangled from doorways. Everybody was carrying something. On ordinary days, he was hardly ever not at the hospital, and at night, when he and Jennifer went out to dinner, they usually drove, so that he never had the fun of just walking along like this, in broad daylight, on a weekday. How richly interesting. Past the window of the cleaners, plants festooned with red ribbons and Chinese writing in the window. Through the open door of a storefront, a dozen young Oriental women at sewing machines, sewing to the keening of Chinese Musak. An old man walked a dog and pushed a child in a stroller. In the window of a graphics studio, little rusted Victorian toys. China cats smiled out from the herb store, and in the Italian bakery, a Christmas tree was decorated with congealed-looking cookies, probably a health hazard. His feeling of excitement and vast happiness kept expanding. He felt a celebratory impulse of love toward the world in all its diversity. He had spent his life inside hospitals. Remembering his gloom of the morning, compared to his happiness now, it occurred to him to wonder if he could be a manic-depressive.

Hospitals, so full of sickness and pain, you have to harden your heart or it would break. Another lesson hospitals taught was never to take chances with people's lives, and so you got out of the habit of taking chances with your own. In the hospital, every action is too fraught with consequences. In the real world, some actions—delirious thought—may be without consequences. Here he thought, involuntarily, of the dusky color of Ivy's baby.

He rang her doorbell, without any hesitation, and waited, suspended, until in a minute, in a voice clouded with static, she spoke over the intercom.

"Philip Watts," he shouted. "I've come to see how you are." The thing buzzed in answer. He pulled, pushed, failed to open the door. Ring again, buzz, push, there. He rushed up the steep stairs. She was waiting, dressed in blue jeans, her baby at her hip, her frenzied bunch of Pre-Raphaelite hair backlit against the sun coming in through the window behind her, like a figure in a stained-glass window. Large horn-rimmed glasses! The moment when he might have seized her in a frenzied embrace evaporated, or did not materialize. He became aware that in contrast to her sunburst of hair, her face had a worrying pallor, and a frostiness of expression.

"Won't you come in?" she said, in a formal voice.

"I was in the neighborhood," he said. "How are you? How are you getting along?"

"Oh," she said, "all right. It's funny, coming home. It's hard, in a way. In the hospital, I thought all I wanted to do was get out. But it's like being thrown off a dock, really."

His mind took in the bare but meditated room, its elements arranged, and belonging to some particular style—Jennifer would know. The effect was Japanese or something, and there was nothing ugly, except the baby paraphernalia—a small crib pen thing on the floor in the corner, with plastic birds suspended over it, and the yellow kiddie seat propped on the couch. When you saw people in the hospital, he thought, it was more like meeting them newborn—naked, without possessions. Eventually, in the closet, you glimpsed their scuffed shoes, the sad jacket. Especially the wallet—something always got him about their wallets, especially if the owner had died and the wallet remained, creased with the contours of his body, softened and thinned by its companionable presence on his hip, and the creased cards and unexpected words jotted on ragged folded bits of paper, now meaningless.

Now here was Ivy in a material place with possessions, each one symbolic of some act of decision, prior considerations, an existence before she knew him. Her dusky baby. He felt a wave of longing to travel backward, to have already been in her other life, to have known her a long time, to have helped her get a better sofa, a different baby.

"You should have someone to help you, with the baby and all. It'll take some time for you to feel like yourself," he said.

"Ha," she said, ambiguously. "Can I offer you something? Coffee? Beer? I have dozens of cases of beer. I'd laid it in because everyone said it helped you make lots of milk plus having a tranquilizing effect on the baby. No doubt, or at least on one."

"Sure, I'll drink a beer," Philip said, following her to the kitchen, where six or eight cases of Miller Lite were stacked up in the corner.

"Needless to say, I haven't got my milk back. I guess it was too long without nursing. But if she was nursed for three months, that would be long enough to give her some advantages, don't you think? The immunity and so on?"

Philip had not at first realized she was talking about breast feeding. Some aspect of this turned a clinical tumbler in his mind, but when his fingers in taking the glass brushed her, he lost the thought.

"It's nice of you to look in on me," she said.

They walked into the living room. Ivy occupied herself with putting the baby in her playpen, arranging blankets over her, turning her head, pulling her snuggie cozily down over her feet. Philip gazed at this infant.

"House call," Philip said, apropos of nothing, thinking how beautiful Ivy was at home. He was unprepared for a stricken look of fear, which suddenly made her look paler, more fragile, more adorable, as she shrank from him.

"I'm sorry," she said in a second. "I know you're kidding."

She sat on the sofa, at a distance, and gestured toward a chair. "I know our relationship is personal, I guess we could say. I mean, I know you're not even my doctor. But my first thought was, Jesus, seventy-five dollars. Maybe a hundred. I bet you're a hundred-dollar doctor, at least, am I right?"

Philip, disconcerted by an unexpected edge of hostility—was it?—in her voice, laughed apologetically.

"I don't make house calls, actually."

"No, right," she said.

"I mean, I don't have a practice, or anything like that. I'd never take money from sick people." He had said this to people before, to reassure them, and usually they smiled, reassured, but Ivy just wore this same expression of somber intensity.

"I'm sorry, I'm just being . . ."

The clinical detail struck its insistent little chime in his mind again. Mother's milk, milk leg. Milk arm? "Did you tell Dr. Evans that you were breast-feeding?"

She stared, trying to remember. "No," she said. "Should I have? Wasn't it obvious?"

"No. I just wondered," he hurried to say, as the ghastly idea took a firmer hold in his mind: healthy young nursing mother, swollen arm, could have been something in the mammary glands clogging the

. . . but it never did any good to discuss this sort of afterthought with people, it only upset them. But how typical of Evans, so gung-ho, to have missed something like this and gone all out with the streptokinase.

"I expect he noticed," he said, and perhaps, of course, he had. Though he, Philip, hadn't. Though maybe her lactation had stopped by the time he had examined her breasts. And of course he himself had no idea about lactation, wasn't an obstetrician, after all. While his mind whirled, she was looking at him attentively.

"I should have told him, because maybe there was a way to keep my milk going, but I was sort of demoralized, I wasn't myself. I wasn't thinking right about anything."

"Well, you were sick." Philip smiled. "But now you look very well. You look beautiful," he added, as the power of this quality seemed to rearrange his blood cells, like a magnet passing over him.

"You think it had something to do with it, don't you?" she asked. "That I was nursing?" She leaned forward, now flushed like a peach blossom.

"Not really," he said. "No."

Ivy got up and walked back and forth in front of her window. Behind her, Philip could see a trio of battleships being towed by tiny tugs across the landscape.

"It's just that I keep going over it and over it in my mind. I mean, twenty-four thousand dollars. And it could happen again tomorrow, or something else could. I can't even sleep, thinking of how something could happen. And I'll never get it paid off, or have a house for Delia— my whole future is ruined, and so is my . . . I suppose my consciousness. Where I used to trust the future, and the nature of things. I can't explain it." He saw that her hands were in fists. "I used to just walk around, you know, two feet on the ground, or even skip along, or dance along—that's how I think back on my attitude, my way of going around in the world. I'm trying to explain—and now it's as if I'm on a tightrope, or some tiny balance beam, stretched across a black bottomless chasm, trying to get across safely, and the wind is blowing, and I'm trying to balance with just my puny arms."

He wanted to embrace and comfort her, but was somehow kept back by the frenzy of her pacing. "Would you like a prescription for something?" he asked, knowing this to be the response of a jerk. "Just to help you through the first couple of days at home?"

"For God's sake!" she cried, in a fury. "If I hadn't gone to the doctor in the first place, I'd be all right. That's what I know in my heart. It's true, isn't it?"

"Ivy," said Philip, "we don't know what caused your arm—we don't always—we seldom know, we . . ."

"Don't 'we' me, either," she screamed. "Please just go." Tears now erupted from her eyes. "Just go. I know it isn't your fault, I mean, it wasn't you—can't we just talk some other time?"

Philip rose, hovered, longed to take her in his arms. He backed politely toward the entry hall. She turned her back and gazed out to sea. Twenty-four thousand dollars was, he had to agree, a fucking big hospital bill. He wondered if she had any insurance. He would try to think of some way to help.

"Goodbye," he said, trying to see her face, but she resolutely kept it turned away. "I'll call you tomorrow to see how you are." The sound of her sobs rang in his ears as he drove back to the hospital. It was strange, because all the time she had been in the hospital she had been brave, she hadn't cried.

He went back for signout rounds. As he was getting his white coat on in his office, the phone rang. "You don't know me," said an unfamiliar voice. "I'm down here at Stanford."

"Hello," said Philip, tentatively, since the speaker had not identified himself, and he thought there was something unfriendly in his tone.

"I'm calling to tell you—some of us down here think you'd be better off staying at Alta Buena."

"Oh?" Philip said, still not understanding the exact tone here—friendly or unfriendly?

"If you take the job here, someone would be bound to tell your wife about your little red-headed friend," said the voice, in a strange rush, as if he were reading it off a paper. For an instant, Philip had no idea what he was talking about. Then he felt a chill of fear and surprise.

"Well, I'll think about that," he said hastily, and hung up the receiver, immediately regretting he hadn't kept the fellow on the line. His heart was hammering as if he had run for miles. He had expected retribution, but he had never realized that retribution could be as prompt as this. In two days word of his adventure had spread to Stanford, where someone was threatening to tell his wife unless he stayed away. Was this possible?

49

All evening, and all the next day, his thoughts kept rocketing back
to this phone call. What ought he to do? On the one hand, you don't
cave in to blackmailers—any American moviegoer or reader of mysteries knew that. On the other hand, when blackmail improbably
happened in your own life, your instinct is to do what the urgent and
menacing voice tells you. Jennifer must certainly not find out about
Ivy. It was an isolated incident, a lapse never to recur. It would hurt
her unreasonably, and of course he loved Jennifer, and the whole
stable basis of his life.

But was it worth giving up the Stanford job to protect her? She'd
get over it. Plenty, perhaps most, husbands had an episode, and the
wives got over it. Wives had a lot to lose—their standing, their support—this he gathered from the alimony sagas he heard in the doctors'
dining room. Jennifer, however, didn't need him for economic reasons,
which had always been one of the nicest things about their accord.

And then, he had to wonder if the voice had been serious. How
could anyone at Stanford have known? Was there some way Ivy herself
could have told anyone? Here he was plagued by unworthy, paranoid
thoughts of a setup. At least eleven people down there did not want
him to come as the new director, but Ivy herself was the only person
who could have known what happened between them—or some nurse,
maybe, lurking outside. New imaginings of a collection of nurses and
housestaff gathered attentively outside his office door, listening to the
cries and gasps, the unmistakable moans of pleasure from within. This
would mean that people at Alta Buena knew too. With horror he
thought of Rank Briscoe writing up this new addition to his bill of
complaints.

Scenario: he doesn't resign the Stanford job, the blackmailer tells
Jennifer, Jennifer doesn't want to move anyway, so she uses this Ivy
thing as an excuse to leave him. Second scenario: he does resign the
Stanford job and stays at Alta Buena, no one tells Jennifer, and—
and—he is still in San Francisco, near Ivy. He despised this wicked
mélange of self-interest and concupiscence, but it was the solution

that appealed to him. In its service he was able to revive, and newly believe in, all his old arguments against the Stanford job—the administrative headaches, the endless grant writing, falling out of touch with clinical medicine. The sole arguments in favor of the job had been the prestige, the space, and the research opportunities, but these might be found somewhere else, in time.

Since he was decisive by nature and by training—life and death cannot wait on an endless review of alternatives—it sufficed him to review them once or twice and decide. Headlong, he picked up the phone, dialed the dean at Stanford, and told him regretfully that for personal reasons he couldn't take the job as director of the Knowles Institute.

As soon as he had done it, he knew it was the wrong decision. If you held back from life and risk, the few times these dangerous opportunities presented themselves, life seals up its fate.

He had made a decision, but his heart remained troubled. Instead of progressing and changing, he would go on and on at Alta Buena, becoming older, becoming a curmudgeonly object of veneration, or contempt. Or, only now did he consider, if Rank Briscoe and the others knew about Ivy, the mysterious vendetta against him by his Alta Buena colleagues might also succeed and he'd have no job at all. He suddenly saw himself in the position of Wice Morris—failed, fallen, turpitudinous, broken, old, hands shaking, unemployed. He had become a doctor to help people! Was it all to be over because of one act of passion, one night?

For some reason he thought of his father, could just see him in his plaid ranch shirt, standing by the barn, holding a bridle and telling Philip of his hopes for him. "I think you should go East, Phil," he had said. "Just trust me on that point. Afterward you can come back." Philip had done as he was told, had succeeded, had pleased the old man at every point, and now would disappoint him. Philip's parents would be coming soon for their Christmas visit, and he would have to tell his father he wasn't going to Stanford, and his father would tell him he'd made a big mistake. And he knew he had.

———

Over the next few days, Philip talked countless times to Ivy, without developing a feeling for how she would receive his calls. "Hello, Ivy, this is Dr. Watts—Philip."

"Hello, Dr. Watts—Philip," they corrected themselves in a chorus.

"Maybe I could take you to lunch?"

"Well—all right, fine."

She wouldn't sound happy, in these exchanges, but she didn't say no, either, would go out with him, and would return his passionate kisses in the foyer of her apartment building. But that was all. The reckless gaiety of their hospital liaison was gone. In some moods, she was intimate, and said things over the phone that shocked and excited him; but it was just as likely that she would snap, and make accusations about doctors and hospitals that were not unlike those made by Jennifer. He sent her four dozen red roses. He bought a jade bracelet, like the one he had bought Jennifer, to give her for Christmas. He gazed at her across the table at the China Sea Restaurant, Delia parked in her portable seat in a chair next to him, telling himself he loved her. But her mind seemed not to be on love.

She told him that people—she would not say who—were telling her to sue the hospital and Bradford Evans. She had a case, Philip privately thought, but was glad she didn't ask his opinion of what she should do. It was clear that she believed him to be so solidly a part of the hospital establishment that she knew his response in advance. He would not have advised her to sue. Since no harm had come to her in the long run—she was going to be perfect—she didn't stand much of a chance of collecting a large sum. He knew too, that for every doctor who would say in court that Bradford Evans was wrong there would be one who would say he had been right, and, anyway, these things were not black and white, something he understood better this week than he had even last week, when he had been a different man.

He tried to understand Ivy. She was reluctant to talk much about herself. "Well, sure, I have a story," she would say, looking up at him in the way that so stirred him. "But I'm a little bored with it."

"Where were you born? What kind of little girl were you?"

"Thin, skinny," Ivy said. "I liked to swim, I got good grades. I had to sit in the front row to see the blackboard."

In his sentimental, vulnerable mood, it tortured Philip not to have known her all along. "Uh—were you married?"

"No," she said, "I'm the proverbial single mother. I just wanted a baby. I mean, when I found out I was pregnant, I thought, Well, why not—I mean, I'll be twenty-eight. I knew it would make my life harder but better. I don't plan to marry," she added, as if to cheer or warn him.

Philip was defeated by her teasing refusal to talk about the father of Delia. Was she wounded by some bitter event or was it a matter of indifference to her, something she truly thought was not interesting to him? Did it matter? Didn't he love her no matter what?

But he hardly knew her. The more he knew her, the more he liked her, luckily, but she made him anxious, too. When was she going to want to make love again? He had her taste in his mouth like some marvelous sweet. He had never before—it seemed to him—enjoyed such infatuation and desire. Yet all human wisdom taught that such powers, such emotions, and such novelties do not last, and that they ought to act on them soon.

It seemed like an infinitude of time but it was only Wednesday, when he had stolen an hour before x-ray conference, that her interest in sex seemed to revive, with a jolt. With a misty fixed expression, she took him on the living room floor—Delia was in her crib in the bedroom—shuddering and groaning in the distinctly involved way she had before, and wanting him to go on and on. The intensity of her pleasure made him feel extravagantly that he had been born to make love to Ivy.

"Philip," she said, when at last he had to get up to go. She stroked his arm, reaching along it to find his hand and lead it to her neck, "feel right here." She indicated a spot below her ear. Philip stroked the smooth skin, the pretty neck, tugged at the tiny lobe of her perfect ear. "What?"

"Do you feel anything?"

"No."

"Kind of a lump. Not a lump, but a thickening."

"I don't feel anything." He pulled himself closer and kissed this spot.

"What do they mean, 'thickening,' anyway?"

"Who?"

"It's one of the seven danger signals: 'A lump or thickening. Bloody discharges, a persistent cough, changes in digestion . . .' "

"Darling, you don't have a thickening."

"My neck feels funny, though. It feels like there's a pressure in it, as though my arteries were thinner at that point, making a kind of outward pressure."

"Does it hurt? Does your head ache?"

"No," said Ivy. "It's just that it feels different sitting up or lying down. It's just sort of an awareness. When I put my finger on this pulse spot, it seems like it pounds more than before, and it sort of goes up into my ears . . ."

Philip obediently slid his finger over Ivy's vein and counted her perfectly strong, normal, healthy, slow pulse—slower than his own, after their lovemaking. He felt his own.

"My darling, your pulse is perfect. You've made a wonderful recovery."

"I have this pain in my side," she said. "It kind of wraps around here."

"Ivy, nothing is the matter. You're just frightened after being in the hospital. You've got the medical student syndrome."

Ivy sat up. "What's that?"

"You know, you get all the diseases. Medical students do that. I did, everyone does. Each new thing you learn about you get the symptoms of. That's what's happening to you now."

"I could be a medical student. I could be a doctor! It's what I'd like to be, only here I am, almost thirty, how could I?"

"Ha ha," laughed Philip, only realizing later that she was perfectly serious. "Tell it to Bradford Evans. He's on the admissions committee. You could say very pointedly that if you don't go to medical school you're going to go to law school." He laughed with pleasure at the idea of the discomfited Evans, who must know in his heart that he'd mismanaged Ivy's case.

Philip dozed for a few minutes in the winter sun that struck them as they lay on the crib blanket they had spread on the floor. When he woke a few minutes later, she was still staring thoughtfully out at the bay.

I must be crazy, Ivy was thinking, falling into bed with Dr. Watts,

Philip, at the drop of a hat, like a welfare mother or whatever, a loser. I have to pull myself together.

But she couldn't find where together was. She was too tired. Delia was still taking six feedings, three of them at night, and she soon had to go back to work. She knew her life was at a turning point, a watershed; she couldn't go on working in restaurants at night, she had a child, she had a debt, she'd be thirty, your body can turn on you, nothing lasts.

50

The great occasion of the fund-raising dinner was Wednesday night. Mimi had hesitated about whether she could afford the $300 donation, which she wanted to make, both because it was a good cause and because it promised to be a splendid event, and to stay home from it in her present state of mind would have made her feel even more forlorn than she was feeling anyway, now that she was in effect homeless.

She settled on her one cocktail dress, of blue jersey with a design outlined with a discreet number of pretty sequins and net shoulders backed by beige silk. She thought of it as her Christmas-season dress, and knew she looked nice in it.

She decided to take a taxi to the Teniers' rather than to try to park. In all her years of single life, she had never come to feel comfortable with the logistics of getting to parties and home again by herself. She always felt relieved when some male friend offered to pick her up, but she knew it was such a nuisance to people she never permitted herself to ask them. If she had to drive herself, she dreaded the disagreeable parking on some dark street, and the idea of remembering not to become tipsy before driving home, these considerations casting a tiny shadow on her perfect, happy anticipation of a nice party.

When she got to the Teniers', she saw white-coated parking attendants standing in the street to take the cars and put them somewhere. She consoled herself that she would have had to tip them about as much as the taxi had cost. And someone would probably give her a ride home.

As she paid the taxi, she could see Rosemary and Edgardo, in charge of bringing Randall Lincoln, pulling up in a hospital van. His aunt the nurse climbed out, dressed like the others in white uniform. Here too were Mr. and Mrs. Lincoln, and the brother, in the uniform of an army private. This party stood on the curbing while Edgardo unfolded the wheelchair and lifted Randall out of the van into it. Rosemary put a blanket over his lap.

Mimi greeted them with a wave. As she hurried inside she felt slightly ashamed of her haste to avoid them, not wanting to be taken for someone sent by the hospital instead of a guest. Edgardo pushed Randall along behind Mimi. Randall's head bobbed slightly to one side, like the nodding head of a daisy, and more than one liked of the whites of his eyes showed, rolling like a movie darky's, or the eyes of someone who had just been struck on the head. He clung to the arms of his wheelchair. As Mimi handed the maid her coat and gloves, a butler stepped forward and discreetly directed Edgardo down another hall, where Randall could be positioned at a table before the other guests came in to dinner.

The maid asked Mimi's name and gave her a card bearing a little map that showed the way to the table where she was to sit. On the desk where these cards were laid out, a stack of cookbooks reminded each newcomer of the fund-raising purpose of the evening. Amy Jacobs, a volunteer, aided by another Tenier butler, stood by to make change from a serious-looking cash box for those who wanted to buy one— nearly everyone who crowded into the foyer.

The Teniers lived in a vast, square Palladian house, the size of a small hotel, which it resembled in the scale and decoration of the large public rooms, where cocktails were being served. The draperies were as stiff as if they had been carved, in fluted columns like tomb sculpture, and the furniture was imitation Boule, or perhaps real Boule made to look imitation by restorers and gilders. Screens and cushions picked up the dots of color provided by little paintings by Renoir and Degas. During champagne in the living room, Mimi was aware of the eyes of Bradford Evans on her. She moved hastily out of view, as if away from dangerous radiation, and went to talk to Sarah Miles in the anteroom.

The tables were laid in a vast solarium off the living room, among giant palms and potted groves of bamboo, and festive candelabra burning hundreds of candles. There were twenty tables covered in Christmas red-and-green cloths, with a small Christmas tree in the center of each one, sparkling with tinsel and miniature lights.

Mimi saw, as they went in to dinner, that the waiters looked familiar, each having come from the famous local restaurants that were donating the dinner. A printed menu at each place explained the courses. Following her map, she found her table, greeting others as they hunted their places, and exchanging Christmas wishes.

At first, she was slightly disappointed at the composition of her table, which consisted of a couple named Krielander, of whom she'd never heard. He was a lawyer, real estate. Then, a radiologist and his wife, the Franks, and Mark Silver. It surprised her that Mark could be here on a resident's salary. A black city councilwoman named Mary Jones, and a man whose name she didn't catch. Covert glances at other tables confirmed that while the principle of mixing hospital and town had been followed at each one, some tables were more prestigious than others. Dr. MacGregor Bunting sat at the right of Jane Tenier, Philip Watts had been placed at her left, and at another table Jennifer Watts sat with Fulton Tenier, the host, and some people familiar-looking from the society pages, which Mimi didn't exactly read but was somehow aware of.

The arrival of the Wattses had commanded a long moment of Mimi's attention, since rumors had begun of their having marital troubles arising from the projected Stanford move. As Mimi watched, they chatted together with perfect friendliness. Was there perhaps something a little formal in Philip's careful handling of her coat? But they did look firmly married. At the table, Jennifer Watts seemed merry and calm. Philip leaned gravely toward the ear of Mrs. Tenier, who smiled at him flirtatiously and lit her own cigarette after cigarette from the flame of the candles. Philip would not collaborate with someone's smoking a cigarette.

Mimi soon decided that, though not glamorous, her table was going to be agreeable. The Krielanders leaned across to smile and learn her name; the large and dignified Mary Jones was a compelling presence, whom many people stopped to greet. Mimi, sitting between Mark Silver and Dr. Frank, conscientiously tried to draw them out, and had no trouble. They were funny and voluble.

Before them lay beautiful Limoges plates, which white-gloved waiters suddenly began to snatch away. Mark, looking anxious, whispered to Mimi, "Hey, what are they doing?"

"Those are the service plates," Mimi reassured him.

"Boy, isn't it fancy?" Mark observed, contentedly.

New, even fancier plates arrived, each with a spoonful of salmon mousse, garnished with raw fish and little carved radishes and kiwifruit. They consulted their menus to learn which famous restaurant had sent it.

"Oh, how great," Mark sighed. "Mimi, you look fantastic tonight. You look about thirty years old."

"Thanks," she said, smiling, not as pleased as she might have been by the compliment, with its implication that she usually looked more. She had another glass of champagne, Veuve Clicquot Brut.

With the coffee, Fulton Tenier stood up and rapped with his spoon on his goblet, which gave off an expensive reverberation. The room little by little fell silent, as people finished what they were saying, with a laugh, a cough.

"I want to welcome you," he said. "It's a real pleasure for Jane and myself to have you here tonight in such a good cause. We've been supporters of Alta Buena for a long time. I've never personally been hospitalized there, knock wood—well, if you had to be hospitalized, that would be the place, and all the good it does in our community can hardly be expressed. So it's with a real feeling of commitment that we are behind the hospital drive, and I know we all share that here tonight, and I'll turn things over to Dr. Bunting, who's going to give you some specifics and introduce some of the doctors and nurses who make Alta Buena great, and also, I understand, a very special study in courage that will inspire the rest of us."

Now Dr. Bunting, at another table, rose, bent to say something to Jane Tenier, and then extended his arms as if blessing the gathering.

"This is a fabulously heart-warming response to Alta Buena. I want to thank the Teniers, first of all . . ."

Here Mimi accepted another glass of wine and tuned out a little.

She looked again around the room. Now she could see Bradford Evans, sitting at a table at the other side of the room. She couldn't see who he had brought. He looked dignified and somehow slender in his dinner jacket and bow tie of electric blue. At his table, Philip appeared not to be listening to Dr. Bunting but was gazing abstractedly into the candlelight. At his elbow, Mrs. Tenier twisted her hair with absentminded impatience as Dr. Bunting went on.

Dr. Bunting was now describing the ordeal of Randall Lincoln: "Some of you may remember Randall Lincoln when he was class president and first-string guard on the Lowell High School team. His tragic illness brought him to Alta Buena, and he lay weeks in a coma, resuscitated by the heroic resuscitation unit when he was clinically dead. He still receives dialysis from our modern, up-to-date dialysis unit." He went on to describe the weeks of coma, the expensive and sophisticated equipment that had helped Randall, the extraordinary costs, the caring staff, the faithful parents, the evils of the sickle cell, the responsible community attitude behind the sickle-cell clinic at Alta Buena that made its expertise available to all, and finally, the miracle that made it possible for Randall to be here tonight, a tribute to all the courage and faith and money lavished upon him.

Now Randall was wheeled in his chair by Rosemary Hunt to a position next to Dr. Bunting. He had been dressed in a tweed jacket and red tie, and he continued to list to one side. Rosemary was seen to lean on him slightly, correcting him upright in front of the microphone.

"Thank you all. Thanks, Alta Buena," he said. His speech was slurred and very slow, but intelligible, and his voice was unexpectedly loud in his thin body. "I—wooor," he said. "Raaahh." His mother and Rosemary Hunt looked anxiously at each other. Mrs. Lincoln after a moment leaned over Randall's shoulder and said, "He's hopin' to get back to his job real soon. He was just starting as a clinical psychologist with the San Francisco schools." Randall grinned and waved his weak hand, thumb up, at the audience, which cheered as if it were a football game.

The ceremonies were now over, and people got up to speak to people at other tables, or approached the head table to speak to Dr. Bunting or the Lincolns. Mimi saw Philip Watts move toward Mrs.

Lincoln, who, all smiles, thanked people and dabbed at tears. Musicians moved into position at one end of the room and announced the beginning of dancing.

In the center of the dance floor, Mimi could see the Wattses, dancing a few steps together, smiling, saying something; the familiarity of Philip's grasp of Jennifer's waist invoking the reality of their marriage, their existence as a couple, with all this implied of possessions and family discussions and Philip on vacation in old clothes doing something with a campfire or fishing, discussing matters to do with his or Jennifer's parents, and, of course, making love. She had never been under any illusions about Philip's having an outside life, but seeing them together, so smoothly, so monochromatically a couple, made Mimi feel as if the gate to a pleasant garden had shut on her, just as she had been about to go in. Herself with only a parking lot. All around the Wattses, other couples twirled and shuffled in a festival of married happiness, decked in satin. The red and gold lights of the little Christmas trees spangled the dancers.

The palatial house, to one who was now homeless, the couples on the dance floor, reminding her that all the world was a couple, the music and wine—emblems of amusement and pleasure . . . Mimi's head quite unexpectedly began to spin with dismay and a desperate sense of personal failure; for it was she herself, she saw, who was to blame for all her problems. She hadn't attended to her life properly, had believed in the wrong things. That she was someone without house, love, or money was entirely her own fault. This pang was as sharp as it had been the first time she had felt it, at the meeting of the fund-raising committee, but now it included this new element of self-reproach, and the fear that people who are lacking in the most elementary instincts of self-preservation end up being a burden to others, sour and disappointed.

As she sat chatting to Mrs. Krielander, she tried not to show her anguish. She reassured herself that all was well. They would make a lot of money for the hospital, the dinner companions had been nice, the food delicious, the turbulence of her mind with respect to her house, resolved. Nonetheless, a strange sensation, a sort of chilliness in the middle of her forehead, made her upper lip break out in a sweat. She looked at others to see if they could see that something was the matter with her.

No one seemed to notice anything wrong. Mrs. Krielander leaned over her husband to speak to Mimi of Kim Ridley, the actress, who was expected to sing, and she didn't say, "What's the matter?" so Mimi guessed the feeling was all within. And yet a little spin began at the top of her head, almost as if she were dancing.

She grasped the rim of the table, and heard her own voice saying that Kim Ridley had been very good in *Long Time Down*. She could hear that she sounded perfectly normal, and yet her head seemed oddly light. Over Mrs. Krielander's shoulder, on the patch of dance floor, Mimi could see Philip and Mrs. MacGregor Bunting doing a sort of stately two-step while the dancers around them bobbed their knees and flung their arms in the approved style of the moment. Maybe, thought Mimi, she'd had too much to drink. Despite her funny feeling, she rather wanted to dance. The room swung around.

She held on to the edge of the table with both hands, but now the chair seemed treacherously to slide from beneath her. She felt herself smile awkwardly, apologizing. "I'm terribly sorry," she began to say, as she slipped sideways off the chair and thumped to the floor.

Mark Silver and Dr. Frank leaped quickly to her side. In a moment she opened her eyes to see their anxious faces, with a sense of a crowd behind them, and heard people saying, "Stand back" and "Give her air."

"Mimi, what happened?" asked Mark, who was holding her wrist. An unexpected moan came out when she meant to say, "Nothing, I don't know."

"She fainted," said Dr. Frank. "She just fell off her chair in a faint."

"That can happen," someone said.

"Here," Mark said, helping her to sit up a little and pressing some water to her lips. Puzzlement, confusion, and shame rushed in on Mimi, as she helplessly leaned against Mark's arm and took the water. She was not the sort of person to faint, had never fainted, hated to be the center of things, and certainly did not want to spoil the occasion.

"I'll just go sit in the other room for a few minutes," she whispered to Mark. "I'm all right, really. It was the heat or something." Since the room was not in the least too warm, this last remark made Mark and Dr. Frank look meaningfully at each other.

"Just carry on," she heard Mary Jones saying, in her deep, authoritative voice to people on the perimeter of the circle who had crowded around. Mimi almost did not dare to look up, did not want to see the patronizing concern on familiar faces. Her head still felt strange, her ears rang.

Mark and Dr. Frank carefully helped Mimi up. She leaned woozily on Mark's arm, stunned by the strangeness of this, and by the slow stir of the room. Discreetly, the room, to avoid embarrassing her, went on with the party.

"Let's get you out of here," Mark said.

The perfect white-gloved functionaries, lurking in the hall, led them briskly into the ladies' cloakroom, where pipe racks had been rolled in to hold the coats, and a maid in white apron stood by with hand towels, as if in a good restaurant. Mimi sank to the flowered chintz sofa.

"I'll be fine," she said to Mark, and Mark, realizing himself to be in the ladies' room, assured her that he'd come back in a minute and left. Mimi put her head back and tried to remember each glass of champagne.

In a few minutes, Mark came back with Philip and Jennifer Watts. Philip laid his fingers along her wrist and gazed at her with a grave expression.

"Please, I'm really all right," Mimi pleaded. "Something just came over me. It's nothing, really." She especially hated Philip to see her ill.

"She might have hit her head, though," Mark said. "I tried to catch her but she hit the floor with an incredible splat."

"We should get you home, Mimi," Philip said. "I'll drive you."

"I have no intention of going home," Mimi protested. "My head is fine. I think I just guzzled too much champagne." When she persisted in this vein, they allowed her to stand up. She was feeling perfectly steady now, she told them. Relieved, Philip took her arm, and they began to leave the powder room. At the door, Mimi felt the room spin again, but Philip and Mark, on either side of her, caught her as she fell.

51

In Philip Watts's car, Mimi rallied, protesting that she was fine and chatting brightly about the evening, Randall, the food, and the dresses. In the absence of Jennifer, who had wanted to stay at the party, she felt her own animation increase.

Philip seemed preoccupied, even gloomy. "Randall told me he was glad we didn't let him die," he said presently. "He's glad to be alive. It's funny how some people value their lives, however pitiful and limited, and others destroy themselves. Like Perfecto Rainwater. And still others complain about their full, happy lives and would as soon be dead." Mimi hoped he didn't think of her as a complainer.

"Thank you so much, Philip," she said when they were at her house. "I can't tell you how idiotic I feel." She put her hand on the car door, prepared to get out. Philip leaped out on his side and came around.

"Nonsense. Mimi, it's not necessarily serious to faint, it happens, but it should be checked out." He took her hand.

"I'm completely healthy. It was drink, I'm sure." She laughed. "I'm so embarrassed." She still did not feel well, felt odd and weak. But she could not possibly mention this to Philip.

"It was hot in that room," he agreed. "Anyhow." He kissed her cheek and said, "See you tomorrow."

She came in quietly in order not to wake Narnia, and went to wash her face. Her house smelled old. As she was standing at the bathroom sink, she felt as if a band or red-hot hand had clamped itself down on her shoulder. She gasped with pain. This pain came shooting through from her back to her heart, as if she had been shot with a shower of sizzling arrows. Dizzy, she sat on the edge of the tub, afraid to move and exaggerate this unspeakable agony. Bent over, she crept to her room and lowered herself onto her bed.

"My God, Mother," Narnia said, peering from her bedroom door. "What's the matter? You cried out!"

"Oh—I have—oh—an agonizing pain," Mimi said apologetically. "I'll be all right. Ooh." She could not suppress these groans. Narnia came into the room, and took her arm, which made her cringe.

"Mother! Where does it hurt? What is it?"

"I don't know, Narnie. I think there's something the matter," Mimi admitted. Narnia helped her to roll into a better position.

"You're completely white!" Narnia touched her forehead, which Mimi could herself tell was damp and cold. She knew she was not having a heart attack—people didn't have heart attacks when they were forty; it must be food poisoning. How funny to get poisoned by the Teniers! She thought of tales of an exotic fish which when you ate it gave you dreams of death, and then, waking in a sweat of fear, you died.

"I'm going to call the doctor," Narnia said, and Mimi, racked with this attack, did not protest. It crossed her mind, to see Narnia's worried face gazing down on her, that their roles had reversed, a moment which must come to every parent and child.

Their doctor, Dr. Purvis, was not on call that night. Dr. Adams, his associate, would take the call. Narnia relayed this to the terrified Mimi. Dr. Adams would call them back when his answering service located him. Narnia paced anxiously between her mother and the telephone, asking at intervals, "Do you feel any better?"

"I'm afraid not," Mimi gasped. "I can't imagine what it can be. It feels like someone is standing on my back, crushing me."

When in twenty minutes the phone had not rung, Narnia called the doctor's answering service again. The operator said she had been trying to get Dr. Adams, but no one was answering at his house.

"Then call Dr. Purvis!"

"Dr. Purvis is not on call." Mimi could hear Narnia's irritated remonstrances. How forceful Narnia was! Nonetheless, they would have to wait for Dr. Adams. Another forty minutes passed.

"Maybe we could call Philip Watts, it was he who brought me home, he'd be home by now. I was a little ill at the party. I could just ask him what I should do. His home number's in the hospital directory, or look under Jennifer Watts in the regular book." She would never ever in the world be talking like this, she told herself, except that this was the worst pain she had ever experienced. Her breath began to come like a woman's in labor, with an undertone of moan. Now she could hear Narnia on the phone talking to Jennifer Watts.

"Mrs. Watts, this is Narnia Franklin; my mother just left you? The thing is, she seems to be really sick, and she thought if she could just speak to Dr. Watts? I'm kind of worried."

Narnia appeared to listen for some period, then thanked Jennifer and hung up.

"Mrs. Watts says he's not home yet, so he probably went to the hospital," Narnia said, "and she suggests we do that too, that is, go over to the Emergency Room. I think you should, Mom."

Mimi attended within herself to the pain—was it worse? Better? Neither. "All right," she agreed, "maybe I should."

"Can you walk over? I could get the car and sort of drive you through the parking lot."

"I think I can walk," Mimi said, not so sure.

"Is it, like, your back?"

"It's inside, it comes from the back to the front—I can't describe it."

Narnia, her face knotted with concern, got Mimi's coat, pulled it over Mimi's meek arms, and hefted it onto her shoulders. Mimi sat on the edge of her bed, trying to nerve herself up to walk, which seemed to make the pain disperse in jagged waves assaulting her whole chest cavity. She felt herself shaking. Narnia, with nurselike gentleness, helped Mimi to her feet, and they began the slow business of creeping through the doctors' parking lot toward the lighted entrance of the Emergency Room, where in the distance they could see a parked ambulance, its lights flashing, and an assembly of people, and a reassuring aura of midnight vigilance and expertise.

The nurse at the desk asked for her name and her insurance card. Mimi's name appeared to mean nothing to her—she was a night emergency nurse, removed from the busy daytime life of the hospital volunteers.

"Oh, I didn't bring it," Mimi apologized.

"She didn't bring her purse," Narnia said. "I'll go get it."

"Do you remember who the carrier is?" asked the nurse.

"Prudential major," Mimi said. "It is the insurance this hospital carries for its employees."

"Why don't you lie down?" the nurse said, and helped Mimi onto a gurney—a tumbril it seemed to Mimi. She was glad to be horizontal and safely where medical care was near.

The young admitting intern didn't recognize her either, but seemed to dislike her party clothes and the idea of richly dressed revelers coming in after hours. Mimi, feeling foolish, heard herself emphasize that she'd been at the hospital benefit. There she had fainted, then had developed these pains. She hoped she knew enough by now to give a coherent history. She did not insist upon her own theory, that her attack had somehow been caused by drink. Meantime, she yearned for them to give her something to help the pain. They did not.

"You were at a party, felt pains," he said, writing.

"No, no, I felt dizzy at the party. I'm afraid I fainted. Twice, actually. I've never fainted before. Then I felt better."

"Transient dizziness. Then what?"

"Then I went home, feeling better, and then when I was washing my face, I got these terrible pains."

"Mmmmmmmm," he said.

"Dr. Watts, Philip Watts, a family friend, drove me home. He thought I was fine at that point," Mimi added, anxiously hoping that to mention Philip's eminent name might somehow galvanize the young doctor. But he continued calmly to write. Then he listened to her heart.

"Maybe Dr. Watts is here in the hospital? Could you page him?" Narnia added.

"Did you have much to drink at the party?" he asked.

"Well—champagne. And some wine," Mimi said. "With the dinner."

"Do you have any food allergies?"

"No," Mimi said.

"Well, take off the dress and put on this gown. I'll try and find Dr. Watts," the intern said. "Meantime, let's get an IV started here. And an ECG," he added to the nurse. This new nurse was a stranger, too, but of course Mimi had never been here at night. Suddenly she really heard the words: IV, ECG—these people were concerned! There was something the matter with her.

The nurse, now at her side, wiped her arm with alcohol and inserted something into her skin, and laid a tube along her forearm, taping it down. Mimi stopped looking. The intern was beginning to stick little terminals to her chest.

"Are you still having the pains?" he asked presently.

"Yes, the pain, it just keeps on," Mimi murmured, beginning to feel quite worn down by it. Narnia held her hand reassuringly.

Then he went away and the nurse pushed Mimi on her gurney into a corner of the room. She left. Something dripping into Mimi's veins made her feel calmer. She was aware of someone muttering, out of the range of her vision, the intern with someone else, then with Narnia, who said "Sure," in her California schoolgirl voice. They approached Mimi's cart.

"Mrs. Franklin, we're going to admit you just for the night, for observation, but you should be feeling better now with the IV."

"What's in it?" she asked.

"Oh, it's an agent that relaxes the cardiovascular and nervous systems," he explained.

"May we have her insurance card?" another nurse came in to ask Narnia.

"She told them, she didn't bring it," Narnia said, a hint of exasperation in her tone.

"I mean, what's causing this?" Mimi asked.

"We're not sure. We'll be looking at a few more tests. Who is your regular doctor?"

"Jerry Purvis," Mimi said.

"We're going to ask a cardiologist to look at your ECG."

"A cardiologist?" Mimi was astonished. Of all the things she had worried about, her heart had never been one. Where was Philip? Had they paged him?

Somebody pushed her farther into the corner. From this spot she could see the police bring a disheveled man in through the double doors. He was holding a rag to his arm, and blood spurted when the nurse took his hand away. A plume of gory red struck across the breast of her white dress. Mimi closed her eyes.

"A dirtball," someone said.

It seemed a long time before a young black orderly came and seized the foot of her bed. He propelled it along a corridor, clanging and colliding with the elevator doors, and she heard herself calling, "Narnia, Narnia!" like a disappearing person, feebly and to no avail.

52

Franni and much of the staff were occupied at the gala, so Ivy pretty much had to go back to work on Thursday; there was no one else to oversee things at the restaurant. She got there about four. Nothing had changed, yet it seemed to her covered in gray, as if her eyes had lost their sense of color. A pall hung over the food. She felt she would rather be hanged than taste the lemon tart. Everyone fussed over her and made her sit down, but she smiled stoutly and hoped to appear as if nothing had ever been the matter with her, ever.

Almost immediately she felt unequal to the business of smiling and leading people to their tables and asking them if everything was all right. Gusts of food smells in delicious variety wafting from the open kitchen ought to have made her hungry but instead made her feel overwhelmed with disgust. The chaste pork roasts and prune custard of the hospital had the retrospective allure of nursery food, next to this foreign, fat, garlicky, affected stuff. Even the smells were revolting. To think of eating the oily, cheesy, vegetable topping of the chic pizzas being marched by made her stomach turn. She thought of people filling their stomachs with it, piling it up on the other stuff already in their stomachs, the look of things in there being rendered by the hydrochloric acids, soon to be excreted as sausages. . . .

On a platter in the kitchen, three uncooked trout goggled up at her with staring eyes like Mrs. Tate's. She hurried out of the kitchen and sat at the bar counter on a tall stool, feeling ill. Maybe she'd come back to work too soon. Dr. Evans had said it would be all right. Her ankle and calf ached with a numb, slow, bruised ache.

She put a party of three in one of the booths at the back and a couple of couples nearby so nobody would feel he was dining alone. Nobody wanted to eat this early, six, but it was later than you ate at the hospital, where they sensibly wanted to get dinner over so they could get on with giving out the medicine and helping with sleep. Here people would eat and eat and gorge themselves on into the night, what a nuisance. She understood that the feeling of disgust she was going through was just reentry shock.

She could not help but think that if she'd met T. J. tonight instead of fourteen months ago, he would have meant nothing to her, all would have passed safely, and there would be no Delia. Instead, she had gone to a film festival in Mexico City and had gotten knocked up, all because he was sitting there, at table twelve, so attractive, so exotic—"Brazilian," she had exclaimed, relieved, as there had been something Hispanic about him, but also something black, which could have been quite domestic, Oakland, say—but Brazil! Those Latin rhythms! Had she really been someone who would dance off to a film festival in Mexico City with someone whose heritage included people who wore bananas on their heads? Delia's heritage! She would never tell her. What were the trivial gratifications of the cha-cha and black beans compared to the antiseptic northern brilliance of doctors with their test tubes! She thought of people in spangled clothes and tail-coats, doing the tango. Then she thought of the quiet beauty of men in white coats.

There was no way she could now explain to herself how she had happened to pick up a diner. Incredible! With no Delia then, they had spent all day Sunday at her apartment, and then Mexico City, why not? This led her to remember a few more things she had done, with no more thought than that they were fun, and she a person in her twenties, not a kid by any means, still going on like that, in spite of censorious letters from her brother, well deserved, too.

And for that matter, the episode with Dr. Watts had been kind of flaky, she could see that now, though this was a matter of love, was it not? But not long term, not commitment, she couldn't get into that and let herself fall really in love, all that drama with the wife, heartbreak.

On the counter, ostensibly to tantalize and tempt, a berry pie, horrible clots of berries leaking bloodstains onto a white napkin. The lemon tart, urine-colored and macerated-looking, with a thin sticky fluid oozing over the top. Unutterable sausages going by on a plate, with black beans and cilantro. Her stomach knotted.

"Ivy, what do you want to eat?" someone asked her from the kitchen. "Don't you want to eat now, before the rush at seven?"

"Oh, no, I'll eat later," she said. "Things are too busy already."

Madge Bruce, the restaurant critic of the *Chronicle*, and Dave Apter, came in for dinner and hugged her. This was her home, to say nothing of her livelihood, yet the sense of dismayed alienation, even revulsion, persisted. She knew it was transient, she knew it would pass, yet she couldn't seem to shake it off, and would rather have died than eat.

Philip had been mildly concerned about Mimi, but tended to believe her own diagnosis—drink. One was usually right to believe the patient's own diagnosis; people had a better sense than doctors of what went on in their bodies. Too much champagne, a not uncommon affliction, and possibly fatigue, the strain over her house, the problems with rushing the cookbook in time for sale at the gala, a thousand details of her job—he had gleaned all this from their talks in the doctors' dining room. Philip understood how much work the volunteers did, and how the hospital couldn't run without them, and how good Mimi was.

Now, the evening's festivities, the champagne he'd drunk himself, the charm of being alone in his car at midnight in the decorated streets, made him cheerful and wakeful, not oppressed with the hopelessness of his recent cares but buoyant and expansive. He thought of Ivy.

He wondered if she'd have gone home yet. If she was at home, she'd be asleep, unless she was up feeding her baby. If she was still at Franni's restaurant, it might just be worthwhile looking in, though he had seen her for a half hour at five. He headed toward North Beach. He found a parking place on Columbus, easier at this time of night, and went into Franni's. A tempting smell of garlic and grill. People looked at him in his evening clothes. He supposed he looked out of place. The headwaiter said, "I'm sorry, sir, we close at eleven-thirty." Philip looked around for Ivy.

"I thought Ivy Tarro might be here," he said. The waiter looked around. Together they saw Ivy sitting at a side table talking to a man. Feeling their eyes on her, she looked around and, seeing Philip, got up and walked toward them.

She was wearing a pretty dress of bright green, pearls, and high-heeled shoes that made her limp more pronounced. She walked slowly, but she was smiling. Philip's heart pounded with protective love. She wore bright lipstick and eye makeup, so that her face was like the beautiful face of an actress, distant and masklike, her real face none-theless under it.

"Hello," she said.

"Are you nearly finished here? Would you like me to take you home? Should you be here at all, so soon . . . ?"

"Thanks," she said. "I'm more tired than I thought I'd be. I'm going to go now, Harry," she said to the waiter. "I'll get my coat."

In the car, Philip kissed her, just so the purpose of his visit would be clearly seen to be more than medical, and she trembled receptively in his arms. Then he started his car, and made a U-turn to go up Grant. Ivy said nothing, maybe trying to think of what to say. He parked illegally in front of the hydrant by her house and followed her up the stairs.

"Where's Delia?" he asked.

"She's here," Ivy said. "Petra's daughter Cindy is babysitting." She struggled to turn her key. A fat girl of fifteen or so opened the door before Ivy succeeded in opening it herself.

"Never open the door before you know who it is," Ivy told Cindy. Philip hung back while the girl put on her coat.

"Would you possibly mind walking her home?" Ivy asked. "It's just down the block at Stockton."

"Of course," Philip said, setting out in the night with this dour teenager, thinking of the times, years ago, when he had had to drive Daphne's babysitters home.

When he got back, Delia was up and Ivy was rocking her—a wide-awake, daytime-looking baby.

"It's nice to see you," Ivy said politely. Philip followed her to the bedroom, where she up-ended Delia on a pad on top of the bedroom bureau to change her diaper. Philip hovered like an unhelpful father. He went back to sit in the living room.

Presently Ivy came into the room, came directly to him, sat on his lap, and kissed him.

"Thank God I came through all this with my nature intact." She laughed. "I feel like a terrible sex maniac. I think about you all the time." They kissed again, amid fretful cries from the other room.

"She'll settle down," Ivy breathed heavily into his shoulder. "Undo my zipper." She turned her back to him. He unzipped her dress and kissed her pale freckled shoulders, and unhooked the clasp of her brassiere. They went into the bedroom.

"Oh, God, we can't in front of—what do we do?" Ivy said, looking at Delia. Philip hung a blanket over the side of the crib, blocking Delia's view of the bed. Ivy slid out of her clothes and waited for him to undress.

"How come you're out so late in those clothes?" she asked. "No, tell me later."

Philip gathered her into his arms, filled with desire and intention. He would make love to her leisurely. He would make certain that she was pleased. He would make her feel his passion, his emotion, his love. He began with tender kisses on her eyes, the lobes of her ears, the little hollows of her collarbones.

Philip lay in Ivy's arms, knowing he should get up and go home. He would have considerable explaining to do as it was. He'd say he had gone back to the hospital. Ivy was asleep. He spent some time looking at the smooth curve of her shoulder, the glitter of her hair in the light on the night table. They could make love again—he felt the inclination returning. She was so passionate! How he loved her! When he kissed her, her eyes flew open. She looked past him to the nightstand, closed them again and groaned.

"Oh, it's almost two," she sighed. Philip pressed kisses on her lips, her throat. She parted her legs, she seemed to shudder with pleasure, but she seemed, also, obstinately asleep. In a few moments, at the climax, they heard hiccuping little cries from Delia's crib.

"Two o'clock," Ivy said, definitively opening her eyes. "She gets fed at two." She rolled from under Philip and sat up. "Oh," she said, "oh, Philip, I'm so tired." He thought of her recent illness, her fragility, her stroke, her passionate kisses. She drooped against his chest.

"Why don't you let me give her her bottle?" he said. "I'll be getting up anyway."

"Oh," she said, her eyes for some reason filling with tears. "Would you really?"

"Yes, my darling, yes." He wanted to say something to her as he picked Delia up, but she had collapsed into her pillow and was asleep already. He supposed he ought to change the child's diaper.

53

The next thing Mimi knew, she was in a bed, in a room. It was the middle of the night and Merci Yezema was standing over her with a hypodermic. It seemed strange that Merci could be here when she had just now been at the gala, in aqua tulle. The way Merci gave shots, they hurt incredibly.

Then it was morning. The pains were gone. Mimi lay, chagrined, embarrassed, but peaceful, in the hospital bed, listening in the unfamiliar role of patient to the familiar bustle in the corridor. How strangely reassuring the bang of pans, the aroma of toast suppressing the smell of disinfectant. From the window she could see a chilly morning fog rising outside, signifying the presence of the winter sun somewhere beyond. It came to her that it was Christmas Eve.

It was a luxury to be rid of the dreadful pains. She could remember having had them, but not how they had felt, as in childbirth. She wondered where Narnia was, and thought over Narnia's kindness and resourcefulness with a feeling of maternal satisfaction. But what on earth had happened? Some ghastly food poisoning? A healthy person doesn't fall suddenly into illness. Thinking back on how real those racking pangs had been made her almost afraid to get out of bed.

Edgardo came in with a breakfast tray. "How do you feel this morning, Mrs. Franklin? All you get is a mouthful of toast—the tests—hope you aren't too hungry."

"I think I'm fine. I'm terribly ashamed of myself. It all seems like a dream," Mimi said.

"Your doctor's coming in to see you pretty soon. And they called a cardiology consult. Meantime, we'll be taking you down for tests."

"Absolutely not," she said. "I'm fine. Whatever it was is gone." When Edgardo had left, she went to the bathroom, peed, combed her hair with her fingers, and planned to go home. She looked in the closet for her purse, but there was only her blue dress, looking oddly like a theatrical costume, spangly and disposable. She would have to put it on to go home in, and walk across the doctors' parking lot in the sheepish overdress of a reveler in the morning.

There was a knock on the door, and in answer to her reply, to her astonishment, Bradford Evans came into the room. He too seemed surprised, aghast, stepped into the room, and upon seeing her shrank backward. "Mimi!" he cried.

"Oh!" she said at the same time.

"I—I beg your pardon. I mean, I had no idea Grace M. Franklin was you. That the patient was you." He seemed even more discomfited than Mimi felt herself to be, but continued to stand there, seemingly frozen with shock.

"Yes," she said.

"I had a call from the ER resident. I suspected—but of course I didn't realize it was you he was talking about. Good God, what happened?" His expression seemed very concerned, but the whole humiliation of the situation, the inequity of the doctor and patient relationship was borne upon her—she stricken, hospitalized, without makeup, while this man was fully in charge of what would now happen.

"I'm fine this morning," Mimi assured him. "I have no idea what it was. I was just attacked by excruciating pains after the party last night," she said.

"We must get to the bottom of that. That's horrible. My dear Mimi . . ." he said, stammering oddly. "I'll call someone else. I'm obviously not the person to get involved in this." With that he abruptly rushed from the room.

At this, Mimi felt the dreaded pain begin behind her shoulder blade. She found it hard to breathe. Shocked, she got back into bed, and lay as still as she could, in the hope of driving off the pain, and tried to put this odd encounter out of her mind. But really she was furious. Bradford Evans had refused to treat her! Violating what must be the first ethic of doctors, to treat anyone sick! Her indignation fed on his discomfited expression, his desperate, hasty exit, but she was unable to understand it.

In a few moments the new pangs seemed to subside, leaving a little hole for breakfast. She ate, although the toast was cold. A label on the tray informed her that the coffee was Sanka. She sipped the strong brew and nibbled on the toast, attending to the response of her body and brooding on the odd behavior of Bradford Evans. Why had he come in? Why had he rushed out? Would her body send new pains or not? Why had it just done so? What was making her feel these pains? She suddenly understood why people took up the anxious detective work, so boring to friends, by which they tried to track some miscreant symptoms of their bodies on a trail leading them from doctor to doctor, along with obsessively reading the labels on food, adding bottle after bottle of vitamins and tonic to their morning regime. She resolved she was not going to become one of those detectives.

Narnia came in and kissed Mimi, with a rather deathbed respect, it seemed to Mimi, and sat down in the bedside chair. Rosemary Hunt came in right after Narnia and put some mouthwash and a bottle of skin lotion on the nightstand. "I'm going to bring the ECG in now," she said.

"Mother, I called Daniel," Narnia said anxiously. "He's not coming for the moment, is that okay? But he will if we say."

Rosemary Hunt said to Narnia, "We're going to take your mother for some tests now," exactly as if Mimi were not in the room. Mimi lay back, fighting a swell of panic. Was she sicker than she felt?

Now she was swept by the imperatives of hospital tests. Various members of the staff, people she knew perfectly well, people normally her friends, after perfunctory greetings acknowledging this, wheeled her hither and thither like an anonymous log, as if she were no longer Mimi, or they no longer knew her. A new, impersonal, professional note even came into Rosemary's voice as she said, "You got to swallow this for me now," and in Edgardo's when he said, "This isn't going to hurt."

She found herself, with anxiety increasing, lying outside X-Ray, in the hall, waiting for someone to come. Dr. Field, head of the hospital Gourmet Wine and Food Society, as she very well knew, without even greeting her, made her drink a nasty concoction that seemed like calamine lotion, and then waited, watching her as if his x-ray eyes could tell when it had reached a certain point in her body. Then she found herself shoved into a large, drumlike object as if into an oven. It made terrifying, grinding noises above her. An attack of claustrophobia made her want to scream, made her sweat. They shoved frightening wires into her body, turned dials, saying, "Mmmmmm."

"We want to look at that esophagus," the x-ray nurse said.

"There's *nothing* the matter with my digestion," Mimi protested.

But none of her protests were attended to. People were firm, kind, and paid no attention. Mimi wished that nurses and doctors would have to go through something like this themselves.

She was rendered virtually immobile all day, strapped, led, wheeled, carted. She tried not to think about the radiation she was getting, probably hundreds of rads, the rays probably sowing the seeds of some future cancer right now as they penetrated to her liver, and scattered into her pancreas, wherever that was, or her colon, or esophagus, that was a bad one, you got it years after exposure.

For the first time she began to fear and mistrust the hospital. How would they assemble all this information? Who would carry all these little pieces of paper, tracings, lead markers, to her doctor? Who was her doctor? How would they keep her fluids in their little cups apart from those of others, how know whose results were whose? Would her body miss the blood they carried off in dark vials? Was the needle clean?

After the drafty corridors, Mimi was actually glad to get back to her hospital room. The unsympathetic stares of strangers, the feeling of being a stranger herself. If the tests were all right, she could go home at dinnertime, Rosemary Hunt said the doctors said. Mimi was sure the tests would be all right. She was fine.

In the late afternoon, Philip Watts knocked and came in, in his white coat, his stethoscope in his pocket.

"Mimi, what is this?" he asked, taking her hands. He sat by the bedside and peered at her. "Tell me about it. What happened after I left you?" She told him as carefully as she could all that she had experienced since.

"Good God, I thought you seemed very much better, you seemed okay when I left you—I thought it had just been the hot room, something like that. This is terrible! How would you describe the pain?"

Mimi laid her hand across her chest. "Something pressing here, and then also on my back, like being clapped on the back by a hot fiery hand." Her face flushed with humiliation. "It's gone now," she said.

Philip shrugged, his expression puzzled. "I've just looked at all your tests. We could get another ECG, then ultrasound, and check some enzymes in your blood. It might be your lungs. Maybe ECG more chest films too. I'll see if I can schedule an angiogram for tomorrow, but let me look at the chest films first. In fact . . ."

"Philip, I'm fine," Mimi began to protest.

"Are you feeling anything now?" he asked.

"Nothing," she said. "I had a few twinges before breakfast, but they quickly went away. Do you have a—a theory? Of what it could be?" Why did one feel so diffident, so intrusive, asking a doctor his opinion about oneself?

"In fact, actually, I can't find that there's much going on," Philip said. "Frankly, all the tests were normal."

"Well, good, though that makes me feel even more like a fraud," Mimi said.

Philip smiled. "I think your coronary arteries are the arteries of a fifteen-year-old. I've been over all your tests and over them, and there's nothing at all wrong, as I said. But of course I know you felt these pains, and I've been asking myself what all the causes might be of functional pains . . ."

"Functional pains are like imaginary pains? Hysterical pains?"

"Your pains weren't imaginary, I know that," Philip said. "I know you felt them. I think you've got—around here we call it nurses' syndrome." He smiled.

"Good grief, what's that?" Mimi asked, imagining terrible crippling conditions of the back or feet, or something arising from sleeplessness.

"Nurses seem to get it. They seem to get it quite often. I think it must come from being a well person who's around sick people all the time. Perhaps it's a sympathetic response of some kind." He was choosing his words, Mimi could see, with care, trying to avoid calling her a crazy hypochondriac. She felt rather cross with him.

"Do doctors get it?" she asked.

"Well, no, they don't seem to, not that I know of," Philip said. "Their problems seem to take them in other ways," he added. "But it seemed to me you are kind of a candidate, if that doesn't offend you."

"I see," she said, very offended. Nurses' syndrome. Thinking about imaginary maladies, Mimi could see there were explanations Philip hadn't stressed. He might also have said: The nurse wants some attention for herself. Working long hours, underpaid, having to deal with the ailments and crotchets of countless others, while no one attended to hers—it seemed quite natural to Mimi that a nurse would get heart pains or stomach pains. But what did that have to do with her?

To ask the question was to see the answer. Poor Mimi, she's wrapped up in it. Too wrapped up in the hospital, no life of her own. Her moment of emotion at the gala, which she had until this moment not remembered, came back to her in all its significance. No house, or husband. Poor Mimi.

"Philip, my dear, I must think about this. But I'm glad to hear there's nothing really wrong. Did you know they had actually called Bradford Evans about my heart? Imagine!" Of course she realized he would not know why she should find this astonishing.

"Yes, it was Buck who asked me to see you. He disqualified himself—said he was too involved, he couldn't be objective. I didn't realize that you two were involved with each other, though I guess I should have, from the way he's always defending you in the parking committee meetings. You can understand you were coming in for a little vilification."

Mimi took this in silence, puzzled. Too involved? What on earth did that mean, when they barely spoke to each other? She was surprised not to feel the anger and revulsion she would have expected to feel. Quite the contrary.

"He's obviously very stuck on you," Philip said.

"You must have misunderstood," she said.

"Well, the tests tomorrow will be just to rule out something extremely rare and weird." Philip rose and put his stethoscope in his ears. "Let me have a listen."

Mimi's heart had started so oddly at the idea of Philip listening to her heart that she was afraid he was bound to hear some very peculiar beats. But in fact, so tactfully impersonal and detached was Philip's poking between her breasts and under her hospital gown that her anxiety diminished at once. Her heart continued in its normal, stately way. Placing the cold little wafer against her breast, his chin quite near, he listened to the mysteries of her interior. She could smell his pleasant, soapy, masculine smell, and inspect the way his hair was cut, and his superb ears. She felt admiration, but that was all. She felt nothing more. She studied his expression for anything revealing, but it was blank, studious, concentrated. Now she began to worry. Was he hearing something awful?

"What is it?" she asked presently. He shook his head and signaled for her to turn over. As he pressed the metal thing here and there on her back, her worry intensified. It was as if he were plotting each inch of her back on some map in his memory. Now he thumped her quite hard between the shoulder blades, listened again, and thumped again. Mimi let out a cry of pain. He took his instrument out of his ears.

"Does that hurt, right there?" he asked, quite unnecessarily.

"Yes! That's it! Horrible," she cried.

"Well, you have a terrible bruise on your back. It probably hadn't come out last night when you were admitted. You must have smacked yourself some way when you fainted and hurt your spine and ribs."

"I suppose I might have. I don't remember. It didn't seem so."

"A fracture would have shown up on the films, I think. I'll have another look. I think it's just a major bruise."

"Oh, Philip," Mimi said. "I feel like a fool. Can I go home?"

"Yes, you can go if you want," Philip agreed. "I think this is solved. I'll call downstairs." He raged silently at the stupidity of the ER resident and all those who must have looked at her back today as they pushed her to and fro.

When Philip had left, Narnia came in. Mimi said, "They say there's nothing the matter." Narnia, having convinced herself that Mimi had cancer, looked both relieved and let down to think that her Christmas vacation was not going to contain stress and tragedy.

"It doesn't seem like Christmas Eve, does it?" Narnia said. The preoccupied Mimi tried to turn her thoughts to it. There was so much to be done! She hadn't even bought a turkey. Almost too late in the day to make their Christmas Eve calls back East, too late to make the pudding for tomorrow. She put her blue dress on.

"Oh, Narnie, I'm so embarrassed," she said.

Mimi pulled rank absolutely, and refused to sit in a wheelchair to be released, though she knew she should herself obey the rules she had so often insisted that others obey. Done with obedience! A hospital experience was a little like an emotional lavage, leaving one ready for new insights. She was done with railroading perfectly fit people with bandaged fingers into the hated chair. She herself felt wonderfully fit, and refused Narnia's concerned offer of an arm, as if she were an old, old lady trying to cross the street. She accepted the paper bag containing, she knew, mouthwash, skin lotion, and some medicine. She stepped briskly down the steps at the back entrance and set off across the doctors' parking lot, her mind spinning with new realizations. She had felt nothing for Philip but friendship. Bradford Evans had called himself "too involved."

"We'll have to try to find a turkey somewhere," she said. Bradford Evans! Too involved! How badly I have behaved to Bradford, she thought, avoiding him the way she had.

"Well, Mother, I did the shopping today, of course. The stores will be closed tomorrow," Narnia was saying in an injured voice, to think that Mimi hadn't imagined her capable of doing the most elementary things. To Mimi, it was an unexpected Christmas present that her daughter had somehow absorbed the importance of the Christmas things, and done them, and had wanted to do them, or had felt the normal female promptings of need to do them.

"Actually, I don't know how you're going to feel about this, but I couldn't see how the two of us were going to eat a whole turkey, so I bought one of those turkey roasts," Narnia added. This seemed to Mimi a rather repulsive idea, but she offered no reproach.

"That sounds just fine, Narnie," she said, thinking of Bradford Evans.

"Mimi Franklin was admitted to the hospital last night," Philip told Jennifer at dinner—tart of ratatouille, a salad of *frisée*.

"Yes, I know," Jennifer said. "Her daughter called here last night looking for you. They couldn't find their regular doctor. I said you had probably dropped by the hospital."

"Yes," Philip said.

"Then the daughter called back to say she couldn't find you at the hospital," Jennifer said. "Evidently you weren't there." Her voice was innocent of innuendo, it was uninflected, and she was not looking at him. Or had there been a slight hardening of emphasis on "weren't"?

Philip, not a practiced liar, nonetheless felt several false but plausible explanations rise to his command. But he said nothing. People got trapped in their lies. He pretended to think she had not said anything of significance.

"It looked like her heart," Philip went on. "Some arrhythmia, or some carotid body thing. But then I looked at her back—black-and-blue. She'd injured herself. Nobody had noticed it all day."

"I hope nothing serious," Jennifer said. "Where were you, actually?"

"Oh, at the hospital," Philip said. "Since I was so near, after I took Mimi home, I went up to my office."

After a silence, Jennifer said, "Philip, I really hope you haven't started to fool around. That would be so tiresome, it would really make me mad." Now she did look directly at him, so that his truthful nature quailed. He couldn't bring himself to say, "Of course not," as the occasion required.

"When I think of how I've played the good-doctor's-wife game—these committees, public service, these recipes—ye gods."

"Of course you've been a good wife, Jennifer. It's something that happened to me, it has nothing to do with you," he miserably blurted. This statement sank in on both of them.

"Well, it must, mustn't it? It's always the wife's fault when the husband begins to stray."

Philip could hear the anger and pain in her voice, but felt himself reacting angrily in his turn. He disliked her characterization of his behavior as fooling around and straying, the assignment of him to some category out of Boccaccio or Chaucer, wayward husband. He was different. He was not a wayward husband, something had happened to him, arising out of himself, his life, his—he felt—heretofore slow emotional development. Of course it had nothing to do with Jennifer, how could it?

Were they now having the fabled, archetypal accusations-of-adultery final fight? It seemed rather low-key for that. Jennifer had gone to the kitchen to bring in the cheese. Luckily Wei-chi was on duty tonight. Their voices were barely raised, and yet the words were like wire cutters crunching through strong links.

"Some nurse, I suppose? Or Mimi herself perhaps?"

"Jennifer, nothing has happened," Philip said, meaning nothing to change his view of his satisfactory marital arrangements.

"Philip, please feel you can talk to me," she said finally. "We have always been candid with each other. We've been best friends, I always thought."

"Uh, I know, Jennifer, nothing has changed," he said. It didn't seem like the moment to tell her he had turned down the Stanford job, though it would please her.

54

Mimi, preoccupied by an inner drama of chagrin and remorse, went through the rituals of Christmas only inattentively. They cooked their turkey roast, and Narnia made a stuffing they were obliged to bake in a separate dish. They talked to Daniel and called their relatives in Virginia and New Hampshire. They opened their presents as slowly as possible, to extend the festivity, and put the presents back on display under the tree—candied fruit, nightgowns and scarves, address books, and coasters. It was a Christmas like other Christmases, except for Daniel's not being there, and except for a narrow escape from the hospital, which with its sinister implications of mortality shadowed the future, and hence the present, by warning against complacency.

Jennifer had ordered a platter of oysters, opened, from Swann's for Christmas lunch, as was their custom, and Philip picked it up on his way home from making morning rounds. The day was sunny, so they opened the doors to the garden and set the table on the deck.

They had invited the doctor daughter of Dr. Kim, in the hope of encouraging Wei-chi's acquaintance, and this was a success, they thought. Wei-chi appeared fascinated with her red, red lipstick and long dragon-lady fingernails. Wei-chi gave them, from a supply he had brought to give as gifts to Westerners, the nicest and most intricate paper cutouts, a filigree lady under a tree of blossoms, and a mountain with clouds and birds. He explained how aged craftsmen did this clever cutting with the sharpest of scissors, and how the images conferred happiness and long life. Jennifer's mother and Philip's parents asked affably for information about China and Vietnam and were entranced by Wei-chi's stories.

Jennifer had bought Wei-chi a shirt from Brooks Brothers and a leather toilet case, which she had marked as being from Philip. Miss Kim and Wei-chi admired Jennifer's jade bracelet. Philip opened the champagne, and let the corks fly as far as they could across the garden, beyond the pyrocanthus, so far no one could see where they landed. He felt something like one of those corks.

Ivy and Delia were invited to the Christmas dinner Franni always gave for the people who worked in the restaurant and their families, but all at once she didn't want to go. She knew that when they got to Franni's they would have a happy time, but she didn't want a happy time, she would rather sleep. Festivity would just be confusing, would soften her sense that her life was in crisis when she needed to focus on it, think about it, decide things.

She changed Delia and put on her little shoes and bonnet, marveling as usual at the pinkness of her palms and the soles of her feet. She had almost stopped seeing Delia's brownness, but the beauty of her tiny hands always caught at Ivy and made her wonder if Delia would mind being different from her mother. She would never meet her father, Ivy had resolved.

It was certain she was going to stop doing stuff like that. The new fragility of her body had altered in some way her sense of time. Where life had seemed leisurely, with long mornings before work, and plenty of time to lie around reading or watering her plants and laughing on the telephone to her friends, and lots of conversations at the restaurant, so at the end of the day she would have the sensation of having lived three days, each crammed with chat and laughter, and nine meals of delicious food—this impression coming from the assortment of clams and calzone and carrot cake she'd pick at, at work—now she was oppressed with a sense of life's brevity, the urgency of making something of it. It was like being stranded on a bleak shore, watching the ship leave without her, mocked by the cawing of gulls.

She struggled down the steps with the stroller and Delia and put Delia in it at the bottom, and arranged the little canopy and tucked the blanket in. The day was cold but bright. They walked toward

Fisherman's Wharf. Nobody out but a few Chinese, and a few tourists. The barbershop was open; that seemed funny. The barber was small, and sat forlornly by the window. Why had he come to his shop on Christmas? Had he no family or expectation of turkey, no television set, at least? She felt a new sense of kinship with the frail, with small or lonely people she saw, and thought of a Sunday-school phrase, about extending the hand of fellowship. She didn't extend the hand of fellowship to anyone, wouldn't have known how, but she gave the barber a smile. Probably people felt sorry for her, too, walking her baby alone on Christmas past empty store windows with decorations of spray-on snow and wreaths that seemed anachronistic already. She told herself this was the last day she could be aimless. Tomorrow she would think seriously of computer programming or graduate school. Or medical school. Could that be seriously thought of?

Though the day was bright, the wind was stiff. She wrapped Delia more closely in her blanket and tilted the bonnet of the stroller protectively. She found a bench at Fisherman's Wharf, and sat there, liking the sound of seals baying and the gulls, and the calls of T-shirt hawkers, business as usual. A few tourists wandered by, looking dislocated. She must look the same, she supposed. Why is that young woman alone?

She wanted to think seriously about her life. It is changed. It's serious and hard, debt and solitude, motherhood and hard work, endeavor, chastity. . . . Icons of these grim virtues, like frowning ancestors, appeared to her imagination as stern ghosts of Christmas Future revealing herself—now about forty, limping, dyed hair, and hard expression, working in a now much seedier restaurant, leaning on the oilcloth-covered table to rest her sore leg. Branches of mistletoe waving over her head, ignored by handsome young male customers, no one desiring her. Her mouth had the thin, hard smile of a waitress. For she was a waitress.

This is what would become of her if she didn't pull herself together. Now she sees herself outside the hospital. Philip Watts comes out, handsome, distinguished, white hair. He doesn't see her. No, he sees her and abruptly turns his face away. His wife is waiting for him in her Mercedes 250SL.

What's his wife like, anyway? He hasn't mentioned her. He doesn't hate her—he probably loves her, just likes to get a little on the side, probably gets a lot, everyone wants to make the doctor.

Now Christmas Future assumes the guise of a smart, white-coated technocrat, suavely showing her herself wearing a white coat, with a stethoscope in her pocket. A door opens. Beyond, a roomful of doctors are waiting. They wait for her to tell them something.

She tries to think clearly and seriously, but she is always so tired. What's the difference if she makes love to Philip Watts or not? It has nothing to do with the future—will not per se bring her down; she might as well. She just has to think of these things separately: love, and what she's going to do about her life. In whatever direction her thoughts whirled up, like a dust storm, they settled again on a bare landscape: her lack of money. You couldn't feel the same way about things when you had a child and a twenty-four-thousand-dollar hospital bill. She just needed one thing at a time in her life, and now she needed to think about medical school and money. Maybe you could get loans. Maybe the hospital would wait for the money she owed it. Maybe they could see what was for sure the handwriting on the wall, that she'd be a lot more likely to be able to pay them if she was a doctor than if she was a waitress. Or maybe she should sue them? But then she would never get into medical school. What she would do with her life was the important thing. On Thursday she went to State and asked to see a transcript of her grades and what science courses she'd taken. And she resolved to have a very frank talk with Dr. Evans.

The more she thought about medicine, the more plausible, the more inevitable it seemed, and the stranger it was that she had never thought of it before. It had seemed too hard, too distant, was for men, was for grinds. She had never thought of it, to tell the truth. But that was before she had been to doctors, been in the hospital, seen the sick, been sick. An emotion like religious conversion, like spiritual re-dedication, burned across her forehead like the wimple of a nun. She wanted to be a doctor.

55

The week between Christmas and New Year's was flat, mild, and foggy. The Christmas decorations took on their customary anachronistic tarnish. Each morning in the gutters, as he drove to the hospital, Philip could see another Christmas tree, snail's-trailed with tinsel, thrown out by the peremptory and resolute and forward-facing as the world turned toward the new year. Philip could never understand what the hurry was. He never liked to see these abandoned trees, used and broken and flung in the gutter for the trash pickup people, too much like life itself. The rule in their house was that the tree stayed up until after New Year's, but Jennifer, he suspected, left to herself, would dismantle it sooner.

A smaller staff at holidays made the hospital seem emptier even than it was, as if by agreement death had been suspended. In some way, people kept from getting sick at this time of year, and waited till after New Year's to have elective things done to themselves, so the beds were only filled with the long-term, the hopeless, and the terminal. Little Dr. Kim was dying at last.

Mimi went to work as usual on the day after Christmas. She felt well, even especially well, as if her body, when she for once listened respectfully and attentively to it, produced extra sensations of well-being and health to reassure her. There was nothing wrong with her! Nonetheless she moved carefully for a few days, for if she moved the wrong way, the terrible pain would reappear. When it was really gone, she went to her Sunday morning aerobics class as usual, and as usual it made her feel even more vigorous. Looking at the other women in the room, she was reassured that much younger women than she had breasts that drooped, or big fannies. She had made an appointment for Monday morning at Sybil, the expensive hair place on Maiden Lane, and told them to put some blond streaks in her hair, just enough to make it appear that she'd been out in the sun.

She kept thinking that she ought to call Bradford Evans. Hearing that he continued to speak well of her and felt involved made her feel she owed him an apology for her behavior—her rudeness and the hard thoughts she had had of him, and, probably, for making him feel insecure about his sexual performance as well. But now that several days had passed, her excuse—to assure him she was all right—no longer served, since he would have heard by now that she was no longer hospitalized, or would have noticed for himself as he came along the ward. She hoped to run into him at just the right moment, somewhere private enough so that she could say what was on her mind.

On Monday afternoon Mimi did some work in the hospital library, pasting new checkout slips in the fronts of books, renewing magazine subscriptions, freshening up the plastic jackets, and other tasks associated with the coming of a new year. She was surprised to see Jennifer Watts come into the Volunteers Office next to the library—normally the volunteers didn't come in between Christmas and New Year's. She was even more surprised when Jennifer came on into the library.

"Mimi, how are you feeling? I heard you were in the hospital," she said with an unusually concerned note in her voice.

"Oh, I'm fine. I'd hurt my back," Mimi said. "It was a ghastly experience."

"Philip was so concerned. He thinks so highly of you," Jennifer said. She was looking thoughtfully at Mimi's hair.

"He was wonderful. I'd still be in there submitting to tests if he hadn't noticed the bruise on my back," Mimi said. Jennifer's eyes betrayed a flicker of something; her brows knit for a second.

"You see so much of Philip—more than I, in a way."

"The office wife," Mimi said, laughing. She could see now that the poised Jennifer was actually distraught about something, and her unspoken wish to confide or communicate hung in the air. Mimi's reference to office wives deepened Jennifer's frown.

"They always say the real wife is the last to know what her husband is up to," Jennifer began. She stopped.

"So they always say," Mimi agreed. The peculiar silence deepened. Jennifer gave a heavy sigh. Then she tossed her hair, and pushed her sunglasses up to hold it back.

"It would be hopeless to be the wronged wife. I'd so much rather be the bad person, wouldn't you? It's an untenable, humiliating position, being wronged. And being the last to know."

It seemed to Mimi a non sequitur, but she agreed, even as she realized that she herself was always finding herself—or putting herself—in the position of being wronged. But what was Jennifer talking about here, anyway? Could it be that she was talking about Philip, and had mistaken Philip's attentions to her the night of the gala?

"Philip has always seemed to be the personification of a perfect husband," Mimi said carefully. Jennifer seemed to inspect the sincerity of this remark.

"Dear Mimi." She suddenly smiled. "I'm happy you're better. Doesn't your hair look nice! I'm sure I should have mine done. I just wish I could bring myself to go to a beauty shop. Is there anything you want me to do downstairs?"

"No, we've wrapped everything up pretty much until after New Year's," Mimi said.

"How was it, being in our hospital, from a patient's point of view?"

"Quite appalling," Mimi admitted.

She puzzled over this odd conversation. Jennifer had had the air of a woman who was worried about her husband. Mimi felt complimented, in a way, that Jennifer might think she was the rival. Alas, she was not. But in fact she had not heard a word of gossip about the blameless Philip. Maybe Jennifer was just an anxious, jealous wife? When Mark Silver came in, to return *Moby-Dick*, Mimi asked him circumspectly to fill her in on any rumors she might have missed over Christmas.

"Well, you've heard about Philip Watts and Ivy Tarro, haven't you? That one's all over the place." But he had few details. It was only a rumor. Mimi could not explain her emotion, exactly. Not exactly shock. But it was another confrontation with reality, these coming thick and fast, it seemed.

When Mark had left, Mimi closed the library door and devoted herself to some hard thinking. While knowing she had no reason to feel personally involved, she did. The words of Jennifer Watts kept coming back to her: it is an untenable, humiliating thing to be the wronged person. She had allowed herself to be the wronged person in her relationship with Bradford—when it was really he who was wronged, by her hard thoughts of him. She had allowed herself to be paralyzed by her feeling of being wronged in the matter of her house. For an instant she had even felt wronged by Philip, deceiving her, in a way, by never mentioning his secret life, and letting her think—it wouldn't do. She opened the library door and hurried along to find Jennifer, with a certain unexamined hardness of heart.

Then she came back to her office. Without completely understanding her conflicting emotions, she felt perfectly certain she was doing the right thing in telephoning Mr. Krielander, the prominent real estate lawyer who had been at her table the night of the gala. She explained the situation of her house.

"The thing is, you can see, I think I should have not the market but the replacement value for my house." She spoke firmly, knowledgeably.

"You're absolutely right, it's a greatly different thing," he agreed with enthusiasm. "I think we can do very well out of this, Mrs. Franklin. I don't like to use the word 'a killing.' " Mimi made an appointment to see him the following day. She wasn't so sure she had done right in mentioning to Jennifer the rumor about Ivy, but she had taken Jennifer at her word, and she knew that in the same position she herself would want to know. She did not allow herself to consider that she might have felt a trace of malice, for she was not a malicious person. And Jennifer had seemed appreciative, even relieved, to think of an anonymous, casual hospital-patient rival. She had laughed.

Dr. Kim died on Monday evening. Philip had expected it on Christmas Eve, but when the moment had come to withhold further treatment, when his heart had finally failed for good and all, and his frail chest with its battered lungs could scarcely respond to the direction of the respirator, his family had inexplicably opposed taking away the respirator, even with the odious endotracheal tube. Philip was surprised. The daughter, who was a doctor herself, must have known that further effort was futile, even painful and horrible, and that a time came when people had to die. He had often noticed that even doctors were unreasonably hopeful when it came to their own families, and then their judgments became as irrational as anyone's. But this situation was so clear, and the Kims had seemed so wise and loving, that he was surprised at their attitude.

Wei-chi cleared up the mystery by telling him that in many Asian cultures you could not withhold air or water from the dying. "We could withhold the antibiotic, of course," he had suggested. Then, when Philip mentioned to the daughter that the antibiotic did not appear any longer to be helpful, she brightened and took his hand in thanks. Philip marveled, as he often did, at the mysteries of culture, and at how ignorant people were, or rather, how you were always needing to add new cultures to the ones you already knew the customs of. In medical school they had observed gypsies, Hispanics, and the differences between Catholics, Protestants, and Jews, and eventually Japanese. In San Francisco you met Chinese as well; and now here were Vietnamese. At the M. & M. Conference, he made the residents listen to a little disquisition on being aware of the way in which people with different cultural traditions choose to die.

For once the residents seemed to accept that the physician had to cooperate and sometimes to decide on death. "No one likes to play God," he reminded them, "but someone has to do it, and very often it's going to be you." Eventually, he thought but did not add, you get so you don't mind it, and would rather it were you than someone less competent. He would have to write very specific orders for the benefit of Henry Statler, the next attending man. It would be a great mistake, for example, to bronchoscope Mr. Hewitt, though Statler, or anyone, would naturally think of doing so. And there were one or two more things that might be done for Mrs. Ames.

Coming home with Wei-chi at nine that night, Philip found a suitcase of his belongings in the front hall, and Wei-chi's blue nylon bag-on-wheels beside it. He instantly understood the significance of this, but read the note anyway.

It simply said that although she had hoped they could coexist in a civilized way, it was just too difficult, unnatural, living together in these strained circumstances—and he'd better move out for a while, till things were straightened out. She'd booked him into the El Driscoll. And he should take his Chinese intern, for whom she hadn't made a reservation at the El Driscoll. "Probably Dr. Lum would not be comfortable here with just me," said the note.

Wei-chi, veteran of these rejections, understood that they were being put out. He could go back to the hospital, he said. Philip was touched by his stricken, truly devastated expression, which he sensed was for his sake and not Wei-chi's own. He was unwilling, and actually unable, to explain to Wei-chi what had happened, so he stoically apologized that his wife did unexpected things, and Wei-chi agreed that women were indeed like that. "Oh, I am so sorry," he kept saying, almost as if he thought himself to blame.

Philip drove him back to the hospital and then went to the El Driscoll and had a drink in the bar. He thought about calling Ivy, but she'd be at work, and anyway might not be delighted to hear this. He wouldn't want to make her feel responsible for his situation. It would be like getting a slightly unwelcome and uninvited relative as a houseguest, some unwieldy uncle or reprobate cousin.

As he thought about it, he got angrier at Jennifer than he had been at first. But in the hierarchy of the evils that had recently befallen him, being thrown out of his house seemed only medium bad, had a certain classical suitability, was almost a rite of passage from the uninspected life he had been leading to this new one, whatever it was. When the time came, he would make decisions, agonize, take steps, but for the moment—he supposed he was a little stunned by everything—he was inclined to wait to see what the drift was before he began to battle against the current, or else decided to bail out and swim.

When he went to his room, he went to bed at once, but lay awake thinking of all the men that had been thrown out of their houses, throughout human history and known to him personally, and he found the idea of these impenitent manly forebears supportive. In this mood he rather liked the spectacle of the ruin of his life—a man brought to ruin by passion, which was a hell of a lot better than incompetence or addiction, if you had to be ruined.

Yet ruin was so unlike what he had expected of his own destiny. He turned the idea of his destiny around and around in his mind, like a woman in a new dress, almost admiring it. He had always expected his life to change, but in the direction of fame and influence and scientific achievement. He had never expected it to change for the worse. In any case, he wasn't able to dwell on the condition of his life because he lacked the practice and the habit of introspection, and the set of psychological terms to do it in. Eventually, he just went to sleep and would see what happened tomorrow.

56

Where Mimi had constantly been running into Bradford Evans when she had dreaded it, now she couldn't seem to find him anywhere. It became clear to her that he had found a new relationship and was off with her for the holidays, and she stung with self-reproach at her own obtuseness—her own unforgivable egotism, wasn't that it really?— by which she had been rendered blind to his persistent, affectionate attentions. Where had she gotten the whimsical notion that he had been bored by their afternoon? Probably he really had to go into the hospital. She thought about him all the time. Why had she been so self-involved and insecure?

She lingered in the lobby and dawdled along the medical wards with the book cart. The medical patients had never received such detailed and personalized library service. She remembered doing just this as a teenaged girl, walking very, very slowly in certain hallways, hoping to glimpse Rodney Clark. The more thwarted she was in her hopes of seeing Bradford Evans, the more desperately adolescent her wish to see him, if only to straighten out that old misunderstanding. Wednesday was her only peaceful day because she knew it was his day off. On Thursday, at last, she saw him pulling into the doctors' parking lot as she was walking over to the hospital.

"Oh, Bradford," she began, feeling her face begin to develop its detested peony color. "I should thank you for coming in to see me, even if—even if . . ." Here she faltered, realizing it would sound reproachful to mention what had actually happened. Even if you refused to treat me. Even if you couldn't get out of the room fast enough.

"I'm glad it turned out to be nothing in particular. Philip said a back injury?" he said politely, and, it seemed, without particular warmth. Though not coldly either. Polite. How could she go on without seeming to be wanting to restart, resurrect, rekindle what was clearly over? How could he want to resume their friendship after she had behaved so badly! Her voice froze in her throat. Then she noticed that he too seemed stricken. His words came out in a rush.

"Mimi," he said, "I'm sorry I acted kind of strange in the hospital. But it was a shock seeing you there. I'd just seen you at the gala, you were looking so lovely, and I couldn't imagine . . . So now I've been saying to myself, Buck, why don't you just bulldoze in and ask her, What did I do?"

"You looked like you'd seen a ghost and rushed from the room," Mimi said.

"No, I mean the time we tried to go sailing."

"Oh." There was a silence, while he, presumably, was remembering the afternoon as clearly as she did. "Nothing. It was just a notion I got," Mimi said, "that you didn't want to go on, I mean. I guess I thought . . ." She couldn't explain. "It was a lovely afternoon, really," she added. She felt herself becoming calmer. "I'm sorry for the way I acted. It was nothing you did, it was me."

"Yikes. I'll never understand women. I've done everything but stand on my head," said Bradford Evans. A relieved, surprised grin had begun to extend along his face. "We need to iron this out." They had a long talk in the doctors' dining room.

Philip had to keep reminding himself that his life was shattered: thrown out of the house by his wife, impulsively giving up a desired job, accused and disgraced in the eyes of some, at least, of his colleagues. But he was so unaccustomed to thinking of himself as a person who has difficulties in his life that these thoughts accumulating were like drops on the outside of a windowpane, unable quite to reach his warm, secure, inner self. This bemused state lasted through signout rounds the next day, but gave way during his solitary dinner in the doctors' dining room to a more active and acute sense of misery. He longed for Jennifer's asperities and the comforts of his handsome house. And the issue of the Stanford job, so neatly foreclosed by the blackmailing voice on the phone, was now before him again. If Jennifer was not going to be surprised by any revelations, and his marriage was breaking up, he could have gone to Stanford after all. Probably he would just call them now. But did he want to? How had his career decisions got mixed up this way with his erotic life? Upon thinking about it, he saw that it was often so. He could think of a number of examples among his friends where life disruptions had occurred in pairs; people got divorced and then changed jobs, or changed jobs and shortly after got divorced. And people usually survived.

On the other hand, though he was not going to Stanford, he still had to face the accusations of his Alta Buena colleagues. He thought objectively about the idea of leaving—running away, it would be said. This alternative no longer seemed attractive either. However ridiculous he might find the absurd vendetta with the surgeons, he could hardly leave until he had faced down his hospital accusers, not in so many words or by a confrontation, but by his undisputed and unequaled excellence. It wasn't too much to say that; he knew he was a good doctor. His honor required him to stay at Alta Buena. Yet to think of his ruined chances cost him a bitter pang.

Also thinking of his domestic arrangements: it looked like those were going to change, and yet he felt his marriage had not changed— his feelings for Jennifer were the same. It was more that by loving Ivy—did he love her?—he had added to his life. But by what forgotten clause in what ancient treaty now invoked unexpectedly by Jennifer had he to give up something in order to get something? None of this would surprise his puritan ancestors, and it didn't surprise him, but he regretted the treaty had gone into effect the first time he had stepped over the line. Why was this happening to him?

Jennifer would talk to him on the phone but only to denounce him. Each time he telephoned, trying to say something soothing, she became more angry. Her accusations tumbled out with a force that must have been building up for years, or else she had suddenly begun to mind—was it the menopause?—things that hadn't bothered her before: his long hours, or his failure to have been much help bringing up Daphne. Often it was his character itself she attacked—a character she had previously seemed to like and admire—and also the medical profession itself, a profession the whole of which she held him responsible for.

He rather hoped for some sympathy from Ivy, but it was not forthcoming. Ivy had never asked about his personal life. He didn't feel aggrieved about this, but he noticed it. Here he had been put out of his house, his marriage and his career were in disarray, if not ruins, disgrace impended, he was beset with blackmailers and enemies—if he let his thoughts run on in this way about his situation, they could come to resemble the mad ruminations of someone out of Dostoevsky, say, or on the psychiatric ward. He tried to keep his mind on his work, but his troubles intruded, along with his tormenting desire for Ivy.

Rumors, sponsored by the indefatigable Mark and the vengeful Brian Smeed, now continued to waft through the hospital corridors. The Wattses were having trouble; the lofty Philip Watts had fallen for some chick. This happened with some regularity—one or another of the senior men, it could be predicted, would fall for some young woman each year, and the event was even welcomed, like a law of nature, whose seasonal occurrence confirmed that all phenomena are predictable. That the chick had been a patient added to the amusement.

The whole episode was received with a little more glee than usual. Certain critics of Jennifer Watts were not surprised. Others claimed to have noticed that Philip had long had a wandering eye. What would happen to the Watts marriage was the variable and the focus of interest—that and what would happen afterward, since it often turned out that the chick fell by the wayside, and an opportunity presented itself for a nice nurse or female intern. Vita Dawson thought that Carmel Hodgkiss seemed particularly invigorated by this new development, Dr. Watts up for grabs. In the mind of others, Vita herself might be a candidate, now that she had lost her custody fight and had more time to fix her hair and was a good-looking girl, in her big Australian way.

"Just think, Mother," Narnia said, "if you were to marry Dr. Evans, and also exercise your stock option, the two of you would hold the controlling interest in the parking structure. That could be a sensational investment."

Narnia went with Mimi to the lawyer, Mr. Krielander's office, and was so full of suggestions and conditions about what the hospital should pay for the house that Mimi let her do the talking. Narnia and

Mr. Krielander were on exactly the same wavelength and mentioned astounding sums. Mimi felt that she was rapidly gaining a form of self-respect she had never had—that which comes from having a large sum of money.

"Philip, Dr. Watts," Ivy said definitively when he called on Friday, "I—look, it's been wonderful. You've been lovely to me. But I'm not going to see you anymore. It's just messing me up," and nothing the frantic and stupefied Philip could say would make Ivy change her mind.

57

The day of New Year's Eve was also Philip's last day of attending until April, and the last day of the administrative year, bringing extra tasks—final reports to be written, accounting, year-end résumés. He went into the hospital before six in the morning, the sight of lights just going on in houses, and the wintry quiet of the streets reinforcing his sense of melancholy isolation. Neither Jennifer nor Ivy would talk to him. He longed for them both.

He had invited Sir Lawrence Browne, the great English cardiologist, to give grand rounds in midmorning. The rounds were well attended, by the faculty from Moffitt and the VA hospitals, as well as by the staff of Alta Buena, all crowding into the amphitheater for the discussion. Much of the popularity of this event could have been owing to curiosity about Sir Lawrence's legendary use of the monocle, which was attached to his lapel by a cord, and would fall from his eye at dramatic moments in his presentation, and Sir Lawrence would catch it in midair without looking, with the dexterity of a juggler.

At the end of rounds, the housestaff thanked Dr. Browne, and then, to Philip's surprise, continued with a year-end presentation, thanking Philip himself for his excellence as an attending man, and saying that they had voted him the Osler Award as the most valuable faculty member for the year. Perry Briggs, with a big smile, gave him a plaque of wood and brass with his name engraved on it. Philip was touched and astonished, and warmed with the feeling of self-justification peculiar to the misunderstood.

He had lunch in the doctors' dining room with Mimi Franklin. Mimi looked nice—looked as if she'd done something to her hair. He was glad to see her—the one woman of his acquaintance who seemed not to have changed lately, except for the hair. Her quality of sympathy and cheerfulness had always remained the same, and she'd been a good sport about her house, saying now, with a serene expression, that she was sure her arrangements were going to be satisfactory.

"Happy New Year, Philip," she said.

"May the next one be better than this one," he said. "How are you feeling, Mimi? Any recurrence of the pains?"

"No," she said. "It helped me, though, what you said about nurses' syndrome—not that I can suddenly get a glamorous job and a sense of purpose. But it helped me to realize—I don't know. Whatever I realized."

"Is it better to realize, or just to soldier on? It's a really good question," Philip said.

"I'm sorry to hear about you and Jennifer," Mimi said, truthfully enough, and she would also have liked terribly to know the secret of Philip's rumored affair with Ivy Tarro. Hard to imagine Philip with a secret life of sexual liaisons with young women and all that implied, in her view, of inner disappointment, anxiety, incipient baldness—whatever it was that impelled men into these unseemly antics.

He shrugged. "Did you know that doctors have one of the highest divorce rates of any professional group? I just happened to read that."

Did he mean, Mimi wondered, that things were not really his own fault, that he was a victim of some actuarial inevitability? "Does that mean you're getting a divorce?" she asked.

"I don't know," Philip said. His air of passive mystification, as if he had nothing to do with what would happen, irritated her.

"Sometimes there are misunderstandings," she couldn't help but observe. She was thinking of Bradford. "Sometimes perfectly good relationships are lost because—just because, without real reasons. I mean, you ought to have a feeling about your life, Philip. Don't just let things happen."

"Oh, I know," said Philip earnestly. "I have to make up my mind.

I have to do something. But I don't seem to be ready, and I don't know what to do."

"Actually, I suppose," Mimi thoughtfully said, "it doesn't matter. Doctors in general, and you in particular, Philip, I suspect, will always come out all right."

"Do you think so?" Philip asked. It was not so unlike what he had always trustfully believed, though his confidence had been shaken this week.

"Yes," said Mimi, controlling the note of irony that had crept into her voice. "All will be forgiven, if forgiveness is what you want. Nothing bad happens to doctors."

Philip hoped she was right. He imagined Stanford forgiving him, and giving him the job after all. And Jennifer, of course. As he lingered in the doctors' dining room with a second cup of coffee, various members of the faculty and housestaff greeted him or congratulated him on the Osler Award, or sat down a moment to gulp their coffee and ask his advice, and it did seem to him that they were treating him in a slightly new, even friendlier way. What had been in their voices a note of respectful pity was perhaps now just respect. It was the tone often taken with people whose presence here at odd or long hours signified that they were having problems at home. It was a brotherly tone.

And respect was definitely part of it too. He suddenly understood that though you went on for years and years, a paragon of hard work and calm judgment, like a medical robot, it was when it was suddenly seen that you had rage, passion, a harrowing outside life, a sexy young mistress, a shattering lawsuit, an addiction, bone cancer—there seemed to him, in some moods, not much to choose among these conditions—people welcomed and respected you. Especially if you looked like a man who was getting laid a lot.

"Philip, listen, buddy, I'd like to come in next week and talk to you about our idea of transplanting Randall Lincoln's kidney," said Jeffrey Fowler, stopping at his table in an extremely friendly manner. Seeing Philip's expression of shocked disapproval, he quickly added, "Heard this one? How do you tell if a lawyer is lying? Look to see if his lips are moving."

"We, ah, as you know, celebrate the New Year at another time," Wei-chi was telling him that afternoon. "Next year will be the Year of the Rat."

"New Year's Eve must be one of the few times it's safer to be in the hospital than out of it," Philip said. "With drunk driving, revelry, and fights, the ER is a zoo on New Year's Eve." He hoped that Jennifer and Ivy were not going to be out driving or being driven. He thought of Jennifer first, then Ivy. This demonstrated to him how falling in love with someone new just increased one's state of emotional peril. Without giving up your old fears, you got another hostage to fortune, extended your gallery of worries. He had a horrible image of Ivy being hurled against a windshield. Would she be the type to wear seat belts or to disdain them? Jennifer, he knew, wore her seat belt, and anyway, Jennifer wouldn't be going out tonight. They were still married; she would be at home.

"In China, it is very gay at New Year, with many fireworks and dragon parade, and the restaurants are closed because this is the only night the waiter gets off in the whole year," Wei-chi went on, making Philip think of Ivy working late in her restaurant, the obstreperous drunks, her dangerous walk home. He couldn't allow it. He decided to disregard her most recent refusal to see him and turn up at the restaurant after midnight. His mind turned briefly on the sex scene that would follow.

In the early evening, Bradford Evans came through the ward in evening dress. He greeted Philip warmly. "Heard about your using streptokinase on that cardiac arrest on OB," he said. "It's a good drug. I'm using it a lot in my patients."

"Well, it worked like magic in *that* situation," Philip agreed, not supposing, however, that his ironic tone would be understood. "In the case of Mrs. Tarro . . ." He could not resist adding this taunt, but it was partly for the pleasure of mentioning Ivy's name.

Evans beamed. He seemed in an unusually good mood. "She's doing beautifully," Evans said. "Saw her this afternoon. I don't think she's going to have any residual effects of her stroke. Nice young woman. Intelligent. Ambitious. She talked about going to medical school, and I think she could do it. That's the kind of deserving person we can help out. I'm getting behind her candidacy, and I hear you've taken an interest too."

Philip was startled, but only for an instant. Then he sighed. He thought of Ivy cutting up a cadaver. He thought of Keats, the poet, cutting up a cadaver. He thought of his medical school cadaver, Anita. He thought of long, boring nights helping Ivy memorize the cranial nerves and the bones of the hand. "On Old Olympus' Towering Top . . ."

"Anyway, Happy New Year, Philip," Evans said, with a wink. Philip could not but reflect that it was true, that for reasons he could not understand, so far from being an object of pity, unfairly vilified, he had become once again the object of everyone's approval. Can it be that there are those who can have their cake and eat it? He was invigorated by a sense of the fullness of life, and of trouble as a kind of happiness. He telephoned Jennifer to say Happy New Year.

Later, his attention was attracted by a stir of activity at the nurses' station. He had been expecting the party of Indians—Native Americans, you had to call them—whom he had given permission to try reviving Perfecto, defending his decision by pointing out that hospital policy allotted the same courtesy to anyone's family doctor or minister to perform whatever rites.

But the stir at the nurses' station was because Ivy had arrived, carrying a stack of huge, oily boxes, and was unpacking hors d'oeuvres—melted cheese on bits of flaky crust, asparagus tips wrapped in bacon, a loaf of her restaurant's special bread, pears, mincemeat tarts. She included Philip impersonally in her smiles, in her profusion of thanks and affection and expressions of gratitude to all these people who had so helped in her recovery. Of course she didn't realize they all seemed to have heard the gossip.

Her red hair was drawn back, her face was flushed. As usual, upon seeing her, Philip's heart became a tumult of anxious desire, proprietary love, and new, as yet unlabeled emotions. As he accepted a chicken liver, the light touch of her hand, a second's intersection of their glances confirmed that despite her words on the telephone— never want to see you again—she was still . . . his.

Indeed, the benign smiles of the housestaff confirmed that it was somehow accepted, that it was spoken of, that he was officially the lover of this undeniably lovely but unfamiliar woman, a former patient on 3F. Philip felt a little embarrassed, but not exactly reluctant. He wondered if he was now expected to form a relationship with the exigent Delia and feel fatherly feelings toward her. Did Ivy belong to him in a way that required moral support, financial help, and some accountability for his whereabouts?

Bemused, he greeted her as warmly, but as professionally, as the others did, suppressing his impulse to put his arm around her in a proprietary way, to take possession. Ivy's expression was radiant, happy, charged with excitement. She continued playing the role of the grateful patient who happens to work in a restaurant, bringing a New Year's feast for the dedicated staff, with Vita and Edgardo, Merci and the other Filipinas from the ICU, Perry, Mark, Brian Smeed, even Carmel Hodgkiss, all crowding round, cheerfully eating. Philip noticed that Carmel was wearing half glasses on a string around her neck. How old was Carmel anyway? She'd been here a long time, come to think of it. When had she started to wear those glasses?

After everyone had eaten, with a feeling of involvement and proprietary love for Ward 3F, Ivy followed the doctors at a polite distance as they made evening rounds. She knew this would be the last night on the medical service for Perry and Wei-chi. Perry was going on to a month on orthopedics, and Wei-chi would go to OB-GYN. A new attending man would take Philip's ward duties. The doctors did not seem to share her sentimental feeling of regret: they were just getting on with rewriting orders and listening to chests and pulses. "Happy New Year," they were saying cheerfully to patients and each other. She could imagine one day doing this same thing, newly brisk and competent, yet full of compassion, and perhaps by then with some of the admired brusqueness of manner they seemed to work to acquire. She tried to remember what Perry had been like at the beginning of the month, for now he seemed scarcely to see the gruesome bloodstains oozing through the neat white bandages, and the entrail-like pink tubes, like guts sticking out, and the strangling sounds on every hand.

They had entered the intensive care area. Here these sounds, these sights, were particularly unsettling. There were the weird and horrible electronic music of the monitors, the stoplights of red or flashing green. Ivy tried to remember being one of these recumbent, moribund bodies, but she could not. Life, excitement surged in her.

Before them lay a little figure trussed in blankets from which her bare feet emerged, with things stuck to them, and tubes dripping blood and fluid from seven bottles suspended above her, and a breathing machine that made a sound like someone sighing in a tunnel, or in hell, as if you suddenly got to listen in on the damned, or to victims of a mine accident somewhere far below. Ivy knew it wasn't the patient who made these terrifying sounds, only the machines, and yet she wanted to hold the woman's hand, to quiet her. Only when she drew a little nearer could she see, shocked, that this was Mrs. Tate! Her own gasp was inaudible amid the general sounds.

"It's Mrs. Tate!" she cried to Perry, who was standing nearest her.

"That's right, you were her roommate for a while," Perry said.

"But I thought—I thought she was dead!"

"Well, she wasn't doing too well, but then her daughter talked to a new oncologist who said he wanted to give her a course of dysthrothropamine-B, they've been having promising results with that, if we could just treat her pneumonia, so we decided to treat her."

"You mean she might pull through?" Ivy was suddenly hopeful.

"No, she's not doing too well," Perry said.

"Then it's horrible!" Ivy protested. "Look at her!" She peered again at the bloody wounds on Mrs. Tate's bare feet, and the little sores on the fragile skin where bits had been scraped off, and the blue bruises on her ankles and on the arm that lay outside the covers, bound in tubes.

"But her numbers were a little better yesterday; she had a PO_2 of 60 and a creatinine of 4.5," Perry said, looking for encouragement to Philip.

"Poor Mrs. Tate," said Philip. Ivy could see he had not agreed with the private oncologist. Would she be an oncologist? No, too horrible. Intensive care was exciting, dynamic giving of life right here and now. It was inexcusable that poor Mrs. Tate should be tortured like this, yet, it was true, Mrs. Tate had been a person to try things. She noticed the plug of the apparatus, visible in its socket, within arm's reach, and saw how the expression had arisen, "Pull the plug," and also the temptation to do it. If the daughter should come, she would tell her the things Mrs. Tate had told her. She tried to think—had Mrs. Tate ever said anything about going in dignity when her time came? Ivy couldn't remember. She'd been too concerned with herself. She was stricken to think that she hadn't listened carefully to Mrs. Tate, who was now being tortured.

"Isn't there something you could do?" she asked Philip.

"No, not against the wishes of her family," Philip said.

"Mrs. Tate, it's Ivy, can you hear me?" Ivy called to her, but Mrs. Tate could not hear.

At nine, Mimi, wearing her blue dress, and Bradford Evans were shown to their table at Fontainebleu, the elegant restaurant, which had been especially tented for New Year's Eve with golden tulle. A pianist in a tailcoat played songs of Duchin and Porter.

Talking of their weekend again, they found themselves laughing. She couldn't at all explain those months of anger and coldness, but her smile apologized. The realistic mind, when it discovers the truth of things, finds its emotions falling harmoniously into step. She could love Bradford. In a mood of mellow gladness, warmed with champagne and their new mood of accord, secure in affection proven through misunderstanding, Bradford and Mimi raised their glasses to the New Year, and Mimi continued to feel an odd sensation of reprieve, as if she had found something prized that she feared she had lost—something valuable, a grandmother's ring, long gone and finally turned up at the bottom of a sewing box. A feeling of unexpected gladness at being given something she had deserved to lose, happiness that fate had not held her carelessness against her and was now offering it back.

Bradford Evans, thinking of Mimi's loveliness, and of the real affinity of their natures, considered himself lucky too. More than lucky, he found himself daring for the first time to indulge the hope—but now it was more than a hope, it was a certainty—that he had found the woman of his dreams, the ideal companion, tall, strong, beautiful, resolute, cheerful, with whom to realize his lifelong ambition to sail around the world. He almost could not bear having to wait for the perfect moment to broach this. He knew it would be sometime in the future, and that for now they had much to do to catch up, but that this would be wonderful too.

As the quail were served, Mimi also basked in the silence of their respective reflections. She was thinking for some reason of Ivy and Delia, and of how adorable Delia was. I'm not too old to have a baby myself, she thought. How charming it would be. She could just see the splendid house they would live in, the nursery, a frilly bassinet, herself with the leisure and resolve to do everything perfectly, not rushed, herself not as immature as she had been with Narnia and Daniel, though thank heavens they had turned out wonderfully. But she would be a better mother now, and a better wife.

"To the future, dear Mimi," said Bradford, his voice betraying his emotion, slightly gruff.

"Oh, Brad," said Mimi happily, wondering how she had happened to deserve this great good fortune. They raised their glasses again.

"The Indians are here," Mark Silver came to announce. Philip walked to the end of the ward to greet four men, two in jeans, two in business suits, one wearing a feathered headdress.

"I'm Jerry Blackfeather," the man in the business suit said. "I'm also a practitioner, but in fact Lame Thunder will be doing the treatment." Lame Thunder, in the headdress, shook Philip's hand. Perfecto's wife and girlfriend trailed at a distance, with disapproving looks.

Philip, thinking of the effect of a wild Indian powwow in the corridor, said they would move Perfecto's roommate somewhere else. When all was arranged, and the other patient, Mr. Larome, had been put in a different room, Philip went to watch, with Ivy and Perry and Wei-chi. Lame Thunder had taken from his briefcase two arrows decorated with feathers, and dangling with cords and leather strips. He had girded his loins with the skin of a little pig, so that its head and furious eyes stared out from his groin, and now when he moved, he seemed to jingle from bells concealed somewhere.

With the extreme solemnity, even anger of his expression, and the fantastic beauty of his headdress, he was an impressive sight. All these artifacts of sacrifice from the animal world lent to his endeavor an impression of a cooperative universe. There was certainly something awe-inspiring about them, Philip could readily see, and if Perfecto had been awake, he might easily have been shocked into wellness.

Probably, thought Philip, our white coats have the same function; he would remember to make this point to Smeed. The white coat has intrinsic healing power.

A little crowd of residents and nurses was now collecting in the hall and pushing at the doorway, hoping to see. Philip stood farther inside the room. He drew Ivy around in front of him, with a proprietary touch, so she could see better. The Indians did not seem to mind the gallery. Now Lame Thunder was sweeping Perfecto's body with a sort of feather broom, which he waved over every inch of the large, inert, and rubbery form. Philip became aware of Tabor, the hospital administrator, and a newspaper photographer, jostling for better places. Tabor gave Philip a grin and a thumbs-up gesture. "Great publicity," he whispered, "showing hospital cooperation with persons of all religions and races."

Jerry Blackfeather, looking in Lame Thunder's briefcase, took out a plastic sack, and from it a piece of raw meat, which he laid on the windowsill next to a vase of shriveled rosebuds. Lame Thunder turned and shook his broom over the meat, as if dropping onto it whatever he was collecting from the air over Perfecto's body, perhaps transferring the evil.

"Look!" cried Ivy. Everyone looked at her. "I'm sorry, I thought I saw him move," she said. Looking back at Perfecto, they saw that his form appeared as inert as ever. Perhaps their collective strong hopes, directed at Perfecto, like table turning, could make him move. Philip could feel a certain tension form within himself, which he could not identify as a wish that Lame Thunder would, or wouldn't, succeed. He wanted him to succeed, and he knew it was impossible, and he thought it might succeed. What was medicine but tricks and ritual, anyway? He looked aside at Ivy, who was staring, entranced.

"Are we part of the treatment?" Philip asked Blackfeather. "Is an audience necessary?"

"Yes. My companions are from Perfecto's mother's tribe. That is an important part of it, one's family watching. To be sick in the first place is a sign of personal disorder, but also disorder in the society. Before we can make him well, the young man must want to be in order again. What the medicine does, exactly, is to kill the anger of his spirit, the anger that made the kid take the drug."

"Psychiatry, in effect."

"Well, living in harmony with the Great Spirit. But look, it's not my intention to play the part of the intuitive primitive—for one thing, I went to Johns Hopkins Medical School. I know our art is far from perfect. At the moment on our reservation, people are dying right and left of diabetes and cirrhosis, and we seem not to be able to prevent it. The spirits of my people are angry. Look at this, now he is asking the young man why he wants to get well."

The medicine man had begun exhorting Perfecto in loud monosyllables and was pressing something to his forehead. Nonetheless, the brain-dead Perfecto did not answer.

Philip found himself thinking not so much about Perfecto as about Randall. Randall's life, which as far as Philip could see was so dreadfully limited as to be no life, was yet more life than Perfecto had. Would Perfecto change places with Randall, or would he prefer the oblivion of his present state? Which state would the wife and the girlfriend choose to have him in, really? Would they choose to have Perfecto a sort of waking vegetable, capable of making demands and needing things but not capable of doing anything—not working, walking, thinking, making love? By the feat of consciousness alone he would be transformed into a tyrant who would dominate their lives the way Randall dominated the lives of his mother and father and the poor brother—and all without being able to give them anything back except the gift of his being.

Yet, for the first time, Philip could understand their choice. He remembered Ivy lying there, and he remembered thinking of what he would give just to have her eyes open, and with no conditions put on it. Just to see the light of life in the eyes was enough, and that was all Mrs. Rainwater wanted, all Mrs. Lincoln wanted. What about Perfecto and Randall? Well—Randall had told him. Thank you not to have let me die. Not dying was all anybody wanted. Not to die. Yet sometimes people begged to die. You should be able to let them decide for themselves, but they could not. Someone, Lame Thunder or himself, had to decide.

He was willing to do that. He was trained to do it. His own spirit felt strangely serene, as it usually did on the ward, one place where there was no time for thinking about personal problems and where he usually knew what he was doing. Maybe this feeling of peace was the product of some karma left over by the Indians, who were now packing up their equipment. It was not clear what Lame Thunder was going to do with the large piece of sirloin steak. He was leaving it on the windowsill. It seemed to Philip that it should be sacrificed somehow to the Great Spirit, and certainly you couldn't leave it there in Perfecto's room to draw flies.

Perfecto himself lay as before, unmoving, a slight bulge of tongue visible from between his bluish lips. It seemed, however, to the startled Philip that the rosebuds in the vase had plumped up and might open.

"That's the best we can do," Jerry Blackfeather was saying. "He may wake up, he may not, you just have to wait and see."

"Uh, well, that's pretty much what we've been doing," Philip said. Jerry Blackfeather nodded and looked for another moment deeply into Perfecto's face.

"There's a lot we don't understand," he said, frowning.

It was after nine. Ivy had to go back to the restaurant. She began to say her goodbyes and repeat her thanks to her friends on Ward 3F. Philip Watts, so handsome, so formal, so distinguished in his white coat, said goodbye with the rest, exciting her desire, her thoughts of what they would do later. She directed a meaningful glance into his eyes. How could she bear to give up the intoxicating caresses of this famous physician? They were all so beautiful, she thought, even Mark wasn't so bad, kind of cute in fact. She felt toward them all a wave of genial, unselective desire and love. She wondered if Philip could ever be persuaded to keep his white coat on while they made love.

Then she went to say her own mental goodbyes to Mrs. Tate again. Despite her sorrow, she could not help but admire the intricacies of vein and artery that lay below Mrs. Tate's skin, the dumbly beating heart, the suave needles insinuating life-bringing or painkilling substances in heady powerful doses into the elaborate system. You had to admire it, even if it was rather lost on poor Mrs. Tate. The idea of the pulse. Think of the pulse! Ivy could almost feel the pulses in her own throat and temple and wrist. So alive was she. She thought of making love all night with Philip Watts. She thought of dexterous fingers tying knots in arteries and veins. With a knife cutting away macerated tissue, and diseased tonsils, and wombs, and repairing torn muscles and flaccid hearts. She had so much to learn; it would be long, hard—it would all be up to her, her life was up to her. What choice did she have? Otherwise she was just a poor girl in a restaurant with a lifetime of debt, destined to get her heart broken by a doctor. Surgery, she thought. Oh, definitely, surgery is the thing.